Ireland on Stage: Beckett and After

Ireland on Stage: Beckett and After

Edited by

Hiroko Mikami

Minako Okamuro

Naoko Yagi

Carysfort Press

A Carysfort Press Book

Ireland on Stage: Beckett and After
Edited by
Hiroko Mikami
Minako Okamuro
Naoko Yagi

First published in Ireland in 2007 as a paperback original by
Carysfort Press, 58 Woodfield, Scholarstown Road
Dublin 16, Ireland

© Copyright remains with the authors

Typeset by Carysfort Press

Printed and bound by eprint limited
35 Coolmine Industrial Estate, Dublin 15

Caution: All rights reserved. No part of this book may be
printed or reproduced or utilized in any form or by any
electronic, mechanical, or other means, now known or
hereafter invented including photocopying and recording,
or in any information storage or retrieval system without
permission in writing from the publishers.

This paperback is sold subject to the conditions that it
shall not, by way of trade or otherwise, be lent, resold,
hired out, or otherwise circulated in any form of binding,
or cover other than that in which it is published and
without a similar condition, including this condition, being
imposed on the subsequent purchaser.

Contents

Introduction   1

Part One: Performing Ireland Now

1   'Close to Home but Distant':
     Irish Drama in the 1990s
          Anthony Roche   5
2   desperate optimists' Time-Bomb:
     Hard Wired/Tender Bodies
          Cathy Leeney   29
3   Staging Bankruptcy of Male Sexual Fantasy:
     Lolita at the National Theatre
          Futoshi Sakauchi   39

Part Two: Excavating Recondite Inter-Textuality

4   Taking a Position:
     Beckett, Mary Manning, and *Eleutheria* (1947)
          Christopher Murray   55
5   Beyond the Mask:
     Frank McGuinness and Oscar Wilde
          Noreen Doody   69
6   Turning a Square Wheel:
     Yeats, Joyce and Beckett's *Quad*
          Minako Okamuro   87

viii   Ireland on Stage: Beckett and After

Part Three: New Aesthetics in Irish Theatre

7   Multiple Monologues as a Narrative:
From Beckett to McPherson
      Naoko Yagi   107

8   Frank McGuinness:
Plays of Survival and Identity
      Joseph Long   121

Part Four:
Re-Staging Irish Past/Present and Inbetween

9   'The Saga will Go on':
Story as History in *Bailegangaire*
      Hiroko Mikami   135

10   Dancing at Lughnasa:
Between First and Third World
      Declan Kiberd   153

Contributors   177
Index   181

Introduction

Ireland on Stage: Beckett and After, a collection of ten essays on contemporary Irish theatre, focuses primarily on Irish playwrights and their works, both in text and on stage, in the latter half of the twentieth century. It is symbolic that most of the editorial work for this book was carried out in 2006, the centenary year of the birth of Samuel Beckett. The central figure for the book is certainly Beckett, a colossus of a writer whose *Waiting for Godot* should be familiar even to non-academics with little prior knowledge of Irish drama. While the editors consider Beckett to be the most important of all playwrights in post-1950 Irish theatre, it should be noted that the contributors to the book are not bound in any sense by Beckettian criticism of any kind. The contributors freely draw on Beckett and his work: some examine Beckett's plays in detail, while others, for whom Beckett remains an indispensable springboard to their discussions, pay closer attention to his or their own contemporaries, ranging from Brian Friel and Frank McGuinness to Marina Carr and Conor McPherson.

Our editorial policy is also flexible enough to allow contributors to go as far back as a hundred years in their attempt to contextualise post-1950 Irish theatre. The works of Oscar Wilde, W.B. Yeats, J.M. Synge, Bernard Shaw, Seán O'Casey, and James Joyce are frequently mentioned throughout the book; this no doubt adds to the dynamics as well as the rigour which the editors believe will be apparent in the collection as a whole. It was intended that all essays in the collection should be written in such a manner that they would attract a wide range of readership. While some contributors may turn to contemporary literary theory, including, for example, post-colonialism or trauma theory, in presenting their thoughts and ideas, the editors have attempted to ensure that none of the essays is dominated by theoretical jargon.

Three essays that constitute Part One, entitled 'Performing Ireland Now,' are an introduction to the 'performing' aspect of contemporary

Irish theatre. Anthony Roche's essay looks at the works of arguably four of the most talented playwrights in the English-speaking world today, namely, Sebastian Barry, Marina Carr, Conor McPherson, and Martin McDonagh. Essays by Cathy Leeney and Futoshi Sakauchi address the problem of theatre companies putting adapted modern classics on the stage; Cathy Leeney focuses on a 'desperate optimists' production of Synge's *The Playboy of the Western World*, while Futoshi Sakauchi discusses the Michael West adaptation of Vladimir Nabokov's *Lolita*, performed by the Corn Exchange.

In Part Two, 'Excavating Recondite Inter-Textuality', three contributors explore opportunities for a synchronic exchange between texts in question. First, Christopher Murray proposes that *Eleutheria*, Beckett's first play, is in fact a version of the tragicomedy *Youth's the Season ...?*, which was written by Mary Manning, a friend of Beckett's. Noreen Doody in her essay discusses the mask, which she sees as a key to her juxtaposing the works of McGuinness with those of Wilde. Finally, Minako Okamuro demonstrates that Beckett's *Quad* is an attempt to combine Joyce's 'cyclewheeling' cosmology and Yeats's 'gyres'. Two essays in 'New Aesthetics in Irish Theatre', Part Three of the book, discuss the problems of monologue, memory, and space from a practical-analytical point of view. Naoko Yagi turns to multiple monologues in the works of Beckett, Friel, and McPherson, while Joseph Long concentrates on two of McGuinness's plays, *Carthaginians* and *Observe the Sons of Ulster Marching Towards the Somme*, analysing them according to a critical method proposed by dramatist Armand Gatti. Part Four, 'Re-Staging Irish Past/Present and Inbetween,' has two essays, in which the contributors take up two of the leading playwrights in late-twentieth-century Ireland, namely, Tom Murphy and Brian Friel, focusing on their epoch-making plays. Hiroko Mikami's essay focuses on Murphy's *Bailegangaire* and examines the mechanism of memory in the context of family history, while Declan Kiberd reassesses rural Ireland past and present, drawing the reader's attention to the chronological aspect of Friel's *Dancing at Lughnasa*.

Contributors to the book are categorized into two groups by their origins: some from Waseda University, Japan, and others from University College Dublin, Ireland. Waseda and UCD have enjoyed a good, longstanding relationship, especially in the field of Irish writing in English. Each contributor from Waseda has received remarkable benefits through the exchange in one way or another: some spent sabbatical leave at UCD and enjoyed a fruitful year there; some studied at the Belfield Campus and received a PhD; another PhD thesis written by a Waseda contributor was externally examined by a UCD contributor; one, who had started her career as a scholar of Pinter, has been dragged into the field of Irish theatre; and all of them fully enjoyed the academic stimuli given at the lectures by the UCD contributors whenever they visited Japan. (The ones who have not yet visited Waseda will certainly follow the lead of their colleagues in the very near future.) This book is, in a way, an interim report of over twenty years of this happy, fruitful exchange, which will certainly continue in the future.

We would like to express our thanks to Japan Society for the Promotion of Science for awarding us Grant-in-Aid for Scientific Research in 2003 (No. 15320040, Grant-in-Aid for Scientific Research B), which enabled us to conduct the research and hold seminars in Dublin in 2005, which eventually resulted in the book itself. For their support of Carysfort Press, our thanks are due to the 21st Century Centre of Excellence Programme "Development of Research and Study Methodologies in Theatre" at Institute for Theatre Research. The institute is based at Tubouchi Memorial Theatre Museum, Waseda University.

Hiroko Mikami
Minako Okamuro
Naoko Yagi
November 2006, Tokyo

1 | 'Close to Home but Distant': Irish Drama in the 1990s

Anthony Roche

In 1994 I published a book-length study entitled *Contemporary Irish Drama: From Beckett to McGuinness*. During the five years I was working on the book, and in the five years following its publication, a number of exciting new names came to the fore whose work in that decade I wish to consider in this article: Sebastian Barry, Marina Carr, Conor McPherson and Martin McDonagh. If there is one concern that these four very different playwrights share, I think it would be that their people are damaged or hurt in some kind of profound way, whether this condition is presented with the lyrical tenderness of Sebastian Barry or the bleak comedy of Martin McDonagh. Further, the source of this internal wounding is not directly given in the play, nor is it dealt with in terms of a conventional conflict. Rather their characters are given the space in which to tell their story, to articulate their sense of pain, injury, betrayal or loneliness, even if the plays themselves offer no conventional resolution or panacea; the drama, however varied, is in the articulation. The 1990s is also the decade which brought to a century and hence to a centenary the experimental Irish theatre first set in motion by Yeats, Lady Gregory, and others; and so I would like at least to keep in mind what continuing relevance these early works might have in and for the Irish present, what (if anything) a playwright like Synge might offer to the young tigers of the 1990s.

The most important of living Irish playwrights is Brian Friel and that claim was further consolidated in this decade by the success of *Dancing at Lughnasa*. More than one critic dates the foundation of contemporary Irish drama from 28 September, 1964, the premiere of Friel's first significant play, *Philadelphia, Here I Come!* Another important date would be 1980, where Friel's play *Translations* seized

Irish public imagination and inaugurated the Field Day Theatre Company; it influenced the Company's decision to premiere a play annually at Derry's Guild Hall and then tour it throughout both Irelands. But in the shadow of that public achievement was Friel's 1979 *Faith Healer*, a stark existential drama whose influence is subsequently to be found in the work of younger Irish playwrights like Frank McGuinness and Conor McPherson. A third key date in Friel's career and in assessing his contribution was 1990, when *Dancing at Lughnasa* premiered at the Abbey. The play went on to lengthy runs in London and New York, and was awarded the Tony Award for Best New Play in 1992. Friel continued to be active throughout the decade, producing three original plays as well as several adaptations. The disappointment expressed towards *Wonderful Tennessee* (1993), in particular, created a critical ebb after the high tide of *Lughnasa*. But Friel as a playwright has never been afraid to risk failure, and the continuing theatrical quest of plays like *Molly Sweeney* (1994) and *Give Me Your Answer, Do* (1997) are the best evidence of the restlessness, originality and tenacity of his theatrical imagination.

Friel is unusual among senior Irish playwrights in his continued level of theatrical productivity. Tom Murphy, the other major figure of the senior generation of living playwrights, largely fell silent in the 1990s. Murphy's works had been central to dramatizing the turbulence of the three previous decades in the Republic of Ireland, in particular the challenge to various social and religious certainties posed by individual questioning. What had become evident to me while writing *Contemporary Irish Drama* was that the revolution initiated by those playwrights who first came to prominence in the late 1950s was coming to an end. Those who were most adept at dramatizing the conflict between the traditional and the modern in Irish society turned increasingly from the stage to the writing of novels. In 1994, Tom Murphy published his first novel, *The Seduction of Morality*, a story of a New York prostitute returning to her home town in the west of Ireland for a settling of accounts with her gold-digging family; Murphy subsequently mined this material for his 1997 play, *The Wake*. John B. Keane lived long enough to see early dramatic successes like *Sive* (1959) and *The Field* (1965) staged in the 1980s by the Abbey Theatre which once rejected them. This did not inspire him to write a new play; instead, he penned a number of novels. Hugh Leonard has announced his retirement from the Irish stage more than once; but the occasional play like *Chamber Music* (1994) could not match the succession of satiric commentaries on the developing Ireland which he wrote for the stage during the 1960s and the 1970s. The exception, as I noted above, has been Brian Friel; but one other figure should be mentioned. Thomas Kilroy has only managed a couple of plays a decade, but each of them has been a theatrically challenging

Irish Drama in the 1990s

exploration of various forms of social prejudice and inhibition; and the 1997 staging of his play, *The Secret Fall of Constance Wilde*, at the Abbey was an important occasion. I would direct the interested reader to the chapter on Kilroy's plays in my book.[1]

The other major playwright is Frank McGuinness, who had produced the single most important Irish play of the previous decade, *Observe the Sons of Ulster Marching Towards the Somme* (1985). This judgement was confirmed when the play was staged again by Patrick Mason at the Abbey Theatre in 1995 during the first Northern Ireland ceasefire. McGuinness's play proved even more timely in 1995 in urging its audience to look closely at and take seriously the multiple and conflicting allegiances of eight Northern Protestants of the 6,000 men of the 36th Ulster Division slaughtered at the Battle of Somme on 1 July 1916. In so doing, McGuinness not only confronted what he termed his own 'bigotry'[2] but raised unsettling questions about the extent to which Catholic Nationalism has appropriated the concept of 'Irishness' in this century. But McGuinness's continuing achievement, in plays like *Carthaginians* (1987) and *Someone Who'll Watch Over Me* (1992), was sufficiently apparent as I planned and worked on the book for him to share its subtitle with Samuel Beckett. It's on the four most significant playwrights who have emerged since that I now wish to concentrate.

The Irish playwright of the 1990s who has most foregrounded figures whose lives do not fit into the accepted grand narrative of Irish history is Sebastian Barry. He first came to critical notice with the staging at Dublin's Peacock Theatre of his first two plays, *Boss Grady's Boys* (1988) and *Prayers of Sherkin* (1990). But it was with *The Steward of Christendom* (1995) that Barry broke out of his loyal cult following and attracted a worldwide audience. It is on that play I would like to concentrate as a means of analysing the distinctiveness of his contribution.

In Sebastian Barry's play areas of Irish history that had been passed over and in some way denied articulation are brought to light. The plays confer dramatic life on members of his own family about whom little was said because they had in some way transgressed the taboos of Catholic Nationalist Ireland and so were consigned to oblivion. Fanny Hawke ends *Prayers of Sherkin* by leaving the island community of Quakers forever, sailing to the mainland and entering into a mixed marriage. *The Only True History of Lizzie Finn* (1995) displays Lizzie as a dancer on an English music-hall stage. In *The Steward of Christendom* Irishman Thomas Dunne sees himself as a loyal servant of Queen Victoria while his dead son has served as a British soldier at the Front in the First World War. Frank McGuinness's *Observe the Sons of Ulster* made the historical point that, in the narrative structuring of Irish history, 1916 belongs to those who occupied Dublin's General Post Office rather than those who fought at the Somme. McGuinness's play presents the latter as another blood sacrifice to set beside the Easter Rising. But what his play leaves untouched is the fact that not only Northern Irish Protestants but Southern Irish Catholics were to be found at the Front, following the constitutional nationalist John Redmond's political counsel, and in greater numbers than occupied the GPO. Sean O'Casey tried to represent this historical reality in his 1929 play, *The Silver Tassie*, and got himself rejected by the Abbey Theatre for his pains. And this is the point at which I would like to enter Sebastian Barry's *Steward of Christendom*. For Thomas Dunne has lost his beloved son, Willie, in the trenches and has only two mementoes, the uniform and his son's letter home. As he tells another character when he shyly opens and reads it to him, 'it's an historical document.'[3]

Thomas Dunne, powerfully played by the late Donal McCann in his last stage appearance, emerges in the play as Chief Superintendent of the Dublin Metropolitan Police during the 1913 Lock Out, the Easter Rising and the Civil War. At one point, he testifies to his sense of pride in the job:

> I had three hundred men in B Division, and kept all the great streets and squares of Dublin orderly and safe, and was proud, proud to do it well (245).

But he is now speaking in the past tense. For the Thomas Dunne we see in the play is no longer the proud head of Dublin's B Division of the DMP in the early years of the twentieth century. *The Steward of Christendom* is set in 1930s Ireland, the decade in which Fianna Fail and de Valera came to power, and Dunne is incarcerated in a mental home, a forlorn figure in a pair of dirty longjohns. He has been fighting a battle with his personal demons. The play also strongly suggests that he is part of a vanished world and that there is increasingly nowhere in the Free State Ireland which has come into being where Southern Unionists may find a home or refuge:

> A man that loves his King might still have gone to live in Crosshaven or Cobh, and called himself loyal and true. But soon there'll be nowhere in Ireland where such hearts may rest (262).

Although he never ruled this kingdom, but kept it in trust for king or queen and God, Thomas Dunne bears many resemblances to a Hibernian King Lear. He does so not least because he has three daughters who feature in the play, Maud, Annie and Dolly. Although Dolly the youngest is Dunne's favourite, neither he nor the playwright suffer any separation of the women into 'good' and 'bad' daughters, even where Maud, the moodiest and most difficult, is concerned. Nor do they all three inherit the kingdom when their father ceremonially hands over Dublin Castle to Michael Collins and his Irish army of rebels. Annie recalls how she was spat at when she saw off the British soldiers from the Dublin quays, members of the same army in which her brother served and lost his life:

> this woman, a middle-aged woman, quite well-to-do, she rises up and stands beside us like a long streak of misery, staring at us ... And she said we were Jezebels and should have our heads shaved and be whipped, for following the Tommies. And the conductor looked at her, and hadn't he served in France himself, as one of the Volunteers, oh, it was painful, the way she looked back at him, as if he were a viper, or a traitor.... A man that had risked himself, like Willie, but that had reached home at last (265).

We come in on this King Lear relatively late in his tragic trajectory, at the point where he has been shut out in the storm and has run mad. The opening gesture of *The Steward of Christendom*, with the cowering Dunne forced to strip naked by the asylum's attendants, evokes the Shakespearean scene in which Lear strips off his clothes to present himself as 'the poor, naked, shivering, forked animal, the thing itself'. The requirement for the actor playing Thomas Dunne to be stripped full frontally naked before a live audience is only one of the part's demands. (Another is that he remain continuously onstage for the entire two and a half hour's duration.) Barry writes with a keen theatrical awareness of the actors who will flesh out his imagined ancestors and a recognition that a great deal of their lives is invested in stripping, putting on (and off) one set of clothes or another. He creates a profound link, one central to all of his plays, between the theatrical necessity of wearing costume and the different historical roles filled by his ancestors. Much of the onstage activity of Act One of *Steward* involves Mrs O'Dea the seamstress trying to take the measure of the recalcitrant Dunne and make up an outfit for him in regulation black. Dunne's stubborn insistence that it contain gold braid bears on his official uniform in the days of the DMP, as he explains to her:

> I have a hankering now for a suit with a touch of gold. There was never enough gold in that uniform. If I had made commissioner, I might have had gold, but that wasn't a task for a Catholic, you understand, in the way of things, in those days (245).

The costume made up for Thomas Dunne in the asylum is a version, a travesty one might almost say, of the uniform he wore as chief superintendent, playfully augmented with gold in the theatrical space of the asylum to compensate for his lack of promotion in the real world of historical necessity.

But *The Steward of Christendom* does not stay in a fixed present of the 1930s: to do so would be to give that decade too much of a determining role in the characters' dramatic lives. Rather scenes flash back repeatedly to earlier periods in Dunne's life and career, vivid memories of a historicized time and place in Ireland as much of an individual's personal autobiography. At the beginning of Act Two, Dunne is being arrayed in his smart dress uniform by his daughters, topped off with a white rose for his buttonhole. The occasion is the transfer of power at Dublin Castle in 1922, the last public occasion on which the outgoing superintendent will wear his uniform.[4] But the play's conscious theatrics make it difficult to view the past from a fixed, detached position in the present. What we witness onstage in the play are two acts of theatrical investiture — one in which Dunne is fitted for a suit in an asylum, the other in which he is consciously dressing up for a public role, but one which will end by relegating him to permanent anonymity. As Fintan O'Toole has noted,[5] Sebastian Barry's plays lay great emphasis on the imagery of clothing; but I would add that they do so in ways that do not pin or confine the individual character to the social role (and fate) prescribed by such an outfit. His people not only take on and off the costumes they wear in public; they make alterations to them as their whim, size and personal circumstances dictate.

And yet Barry's plays reveal the extent to which in Ireland clothes are read historically as fixed signs proclaiming the permanent allegiances, even the core identity, of a man or woman. This is best illustrated in *Steward* by the discussion between Dunne and his tormentor, the nationalist Smith, over his son Willie and the latter's death in the First World War. In Act One, Smith taunts Dunne in terms of the historic role the latter has occupied, identifying him as a 'Castle Catholic'; he dubs the outfit Dunne has so much admired a badge of shame and source of recrimination. In Act Two, Smith trades in his own suit of customary black, worn in his public capacity at the asylum, and reappears onstage in an outlandish and historically unlikely costume, '*dressed like a cowboy complete with sixshooters*' (290); he does so, it turns out, not because he has suddenly decided to emigrate to the United States and thinks that this will pass for acceptable dress there but because he is on his way to a fancy dress party. Smith's change of costume, and the shift from historical to theatrical reality, allows for an expansion if not a change of heart, leading him to inquire into Dunne's relations with his son and asking to hear Dunne read the letter from the trenches.

In this play which has as much to do with fathers and sons as with fathers and daughters, the national dimension of such a relationship is represented in the figure of Michael Collins. He is something of a hate figure for the Dunne family, memorably anathematized in a speech by

Annie when she predicts that the 'like of Collins and his murdering men won't hold this place together' (278). Thomas Dunne's own instincts are to repudiate the new political order that is going to take over the country in 1922. But the shock of his direct personal encounter with Michel Collins during the exchange at Dublin Castle intimates a possible relationship between Dunne's Ireland and what is replacing it, some measure of continuity between Irish people of strikingly divergent political affiliations:

> I could scarce get over the sight of him. He was a black-haired handsome man, but with the big face and body of a boxer. He would have made a tremendous policeman in other days.... I felt rough near him, that cold morning, rough, secretly. There never was enough gold in that uniform, never. I thought too as I looked at him of my father, as if Collins could have been my son and could have been my father ... (285-6).

But those possibilities are denied in the emerging Irish State by the shooting of Michael Collins and the subsequent reign of 'King De Valera' (262), as Mrs O'Dea refers to him. That possibility, of an enlargement and transfer of traditional allegiances, emerges and vanishes just as briefly inside Thomas Dunne: 'I felt a shadow of that loyalty pass across my heart. But I closed my heart instantly against it.' (286)

The play's final image is of a no less impossible reconciliation between father and son. Although Willie would have been in his late teens when he died, he appears to his father on several occasions in the play, always at the age of thirteen or so, his voice not yet broken. In the closing moments, the dead son reappears, a child dressed in the costume of the First World War, and climbs into bed beside his father. Thomas Dunne tells Willie of a childhood incident in which he, Dunne, ran away from home with a dog that had killed sheep and was to be put down; when the two strays were rounded up and brought home, he thought they were both 'for slaughter' (301). Instead, he is swept up and embraced by his father: 'And I would call that the mercy of fathers, when the love that lies in them deeply ... is betrayed by an emergency, and the child sees at last that he is loved.' (301) Sebastian Barry's plays are remarkable for their intimate fusion of private and public event, for the love they bring to bear on relationships which have traditionally been fuelled by ignorance and misunderstanding.

When I came to write the conclusion of my book in 1993, I chose to highlight Marina Carr's work for three reasons: because I wanted to close by considering Irish women as the creators rather than merely the objects of representation; because I wanted a playwright who would be exemplary of the radical experimentation of the younger generation; and because Carr's 1989 play, *Low in the Dark*, bore out the persistence of Beckett's influence on contemporary Irish drama. Ironically, where the generation of Friel and Murphy fought shy of any reference to Beckett, his was a presence and example explicitly acknowledged by younger contemporary Irish playwrights like Frank McGuinness and Marina Carr. As a biographical note on Carr records, in 1988 'she enrolled at UCD to do a master's degree on Samuel Beckett — a thesis which has been left aside for a while.'[6] Instead, Marina Carr went on to write plays and in so doing managed a more creative play with Beckettian drama than academic procedures would have allowed. Carr's play, *Low in the Dark*, uses a variety of absurdist techniques to question whether 'it is the most natural thing in the world to have a baby.' (116) Her mother and daughter are named Bender and Binder and sound like characters from a late Beckett play, the Bam, Bem, Bim and Bom of 1983's *What Where*. In their dramatic interplay they also resemble female versions of *Waiting for Godot*'s Vladimir and Estragon. Carr writes with an increased emphasis on gender issues, however, as her version of Beckett's taking on and off of bowler hats indicates in its switching between male and female personae and voices: 'Listen. I have my work. (*Take off the hat.*) What about me? (*Hat back on.*) Don't I spend all the time I can with you? (*Hat off.*) It's not enough. I miss you.' (114)

Where *Low in the Dark* and *Ullaloo* (1991) displayed a radical experimentalism, in the vein of a Beckettian absurdist drama, it has been widely recognized that with *The Mai* (1994) and *Portia Coughlan* (1996) Marina Carr found her own voice and created a distinctive dramatic world. These two plays have also met with a high degree of critical and popular acclaim. Where it has been said that with *The Mai* Carr exorcized Beckett's influence, I would prefer to say that she had absorbed it. Beckett's influence remains subtly present in her work, for example in the way Act Three of *Portia Coughlan* repeats Act One, but it is no longer dominant. Carr's plays are centred on women's experience and, while adopting no Manichaean feminist line with regard to gender stereotypes (some of the women can be just as destructive of the heroine's desire as the men), provide a challenge and alternative to the male-dominated world of Irish playwriting.

In *The Mai*, its most traditional dramatic element is the troubled relationship between a married couple. The greater equality that now exists between men and women is signalled by the relative equality of their ages, where in earlier plays (as in Irish society earlier in the century) the husband tended to be much older than the wife. Here, the Mai is forty, Robert in his early forties. They have been married for seventeen years and have four children, though the only one we get to see in the play is the eldest, their sixteen-year-old daughter, Millie. The first act of the play signals the Mai's joyous expectation of her errant husband's return home after five years' absence. Two of the characters, speculating as to where he has been, suggest America, like his father before him. In defending the male family line, Robert asserts that his father went away to the United States to earn a living for his wife and family back in Ireland. The Mai's grandmother retorts that he should either have stayed at home or brought his family with him. Despite the Mai's delight at his return, Robert's presence turns out to be as provisional and qualified as before he left. He declares at one point that he needs more time on his own, that he would prefer his own company or that of other people to the at-home demands of the woman he has married.

What is less conventionally dramatic than the man's grandiose entrances and exits every few months or years is the woman's pattern of internal withdrawal while she remains physically confined within the house. In *The Mai*, to offset the title character's isolation, Marina Carr has filled the dramatic space with an ensemble support system of female energy: two sisters, two aunts, a daughter and a hundred-year-old grandmother. Grandma Fraochlain bears in her first name an archetypal female status and in her second the name of the island on which she reared the Mai when the natural mother, her daughter Ellen, died young. Grandma Fraochlain enlarges the scope of the play's environment with her exotic presence and her fund of stories drawn from her 'ancient and fantastical memory,'[7] her connection to the world of myth and legend. She offers a matrilineal line of support and continuity rather than a substitute patriarchy, acting as a living conduit to the dead. But Grandma Fraochlain can only do so much; and her surviving daughters argue that she may not have been the best of mothers, since her husband had all her love.

The play's crucial figure is the Mai's daughter, Millie, who bears the brunt of the tensions between her mother and father. But as Millie talks, we realize that she is not merely responding to what is occurring onstage but narrating to the audience an entire drama that has occurred many years in the past. To this extent, she resembles Michael in Friel's *Dancing at Lughnasa*, and reveals in the course of her narrative that her mother has died. Nowadays, when she meets her father, 'we shout and roar till we're exhausted or in tears or both, and then crawl away to lick our wounds already gathering venom for the next bout.' (27) This speech not only establishes Millie as the play's storyteller but shows that, far from being aligned with the words and deeds of her father, the Mai's husband, she is battling him verbally for control of the Mai's narrative, her legacy for the future. Carr's play remains open to that future, not only in Millie's survival and determination to tell her story, but in the references to Joseph, her five-year-old son.

At first glance, Marina Carr's *Portia Coughlan* bears certain striking resemblances to *The Mai* in its casting requirements and stage situations; but the sound and feel of it are very different, in ways that I wish briefly to examine, and mark yet another advance for Carr as a dramatist. Once again, there is a troubled young woman at its centre and in its title, and a drama that draws in an extraordinary cast of family and friends. Once again, that woman is trapped in an unsatisfactory marriage, though the reasons here are harder to find, since Raphael (unlike Robert) is in most respects a model husband to Portia. In *The Mai* Millie was a crucial presence, but the other sons and daughters were never seen. Here, all three children remain offstage, relegated to the sidelines and their minder, Portia's friend Stacia. The compelling onstage child is fifteen-year-old Gabriel Scully, Portia's twin brother, who was drowned at that age and continues to haunt her. There is once again a wonderfully diverse lineup of female relatives, including a mother of fifty and a grandmother of eighty whose power of audacious speech goes beyond even Grandma Fraochlain's. Although the Mai and Portia Coughlan are to a degree unreachable and living in a world of their own, the former did receive and acknowledge a consistent degree of support from the women in her life. But Portia's mother and grandmother are either indifferent or hostile to her; instead they are locked in an internecine feud over family secrets and over which family line caused the queerness of the twins, Portia and Gabriel. The sole unlikely source of support for Portia from among her female relatives is from her aunt, Maggie May, whose first entrance is described as follows: '*Enter Maggie May Doorley, an old prostitute, black mini skirt, black tights, sexy blouse, loads of costume jewellery, high heels, fag in her mouth.*'[8] Even more unlikely, perhaps, is the man who comes in her wake, fussy, nervous, skinny, endlessly asking for cups of tea with which he can wash down his supply of digestive biscuits. This is Senchil Doorley, Maggie May's husband, and their affectionate, loving relationship is as credible as it is initially surprising. As Maggie May remarks, in one of the play's best lines, Senchil wasn't born, he was knitted on a wet Sunday afternoon. Their relationship extends the range of Marina Carr's characterization and shows that marriage *per se* is not what bedevils Portia Coughlan.

With their physical mutilations and their verbally fuelled encounters the characters in *Portia Coughlan* are in many ways grotesque: Raphael walks with a limp, Stacia has lost an eye and is referred to as the Cyclops of Coolinarney. And yet they remain rooted in a detailed and recognizable social world, in which children have to be collected, meals prepared, in which old school rivalries and attractions persist into adulthood, in which there is a definite class structure separating the owner of the local factory from the young man working in the local bar. This is a world in which the central character is present more in body than in spirit, a world from which she threatens to float free and to which most of the other characters seek to recall her, mostly by insisting on her duties as daughter, wife and mother. Like the plays of Synge, though rooted in the real, Carr and her central characters hanker after the mythic. Portia says at one point that she married her husband Raphael because he was named after an angel. So, too, was her dead brother Gabriel. And it is in the direct staging of the dead brother's presence, established from the start, that the play most breaks with a conventional or narrow realism. As the light comes up on Portia Coughlan at home with a drink in her hand, the '*other light comes up simultaneously on Gabriel Scully, her dead twin. He stands at the bank of the Belmont river singing. They mirror one another's movement in an odd way, unconsciously.*' (239) Gabriel is never far away throughout the play and is evoked in three ways: by his physical presence onstage while a more realistic scene is in progress, troubling Portia's concentration; as an acoustic presence, through the high-pitched beautiful singing, a music which sometimes drowns or tunes out the dialogue in which Portia is involved; and through Gabriel's association with the Belmont river, the site which draws Portia repeatedly throughout the play and to which she is inevitably destined. There is a striking similarity between this ghostly boy in the Marina Carr play and the ghost of young Willie Dunne in Sebastian Barry's *The Steward of Christendom*, a coincidence underlined by the plays' being simultaneously staged in Dublin's Peacock and Gate Theatres in 1996. The simultaneity underscores the extent to which onstage ghosts have been a feature of recent Irish drama. In one sense, they are a way of dramatizing the persistence of the past in the present, a particularly if not exclusively Irish obsession; but they also figure in these plays as troubling reminders that economic prosperity leaves a good many atavisms unslaked, that the decline in the power of the Catholic church leaves the way open for a return of the irrational which the surface of Irish life no longer acknowledges.

Portia Coughlan, then, is caught midway between the worlds of the living and the dead, with the combined weight of nine living family and friends on the one hand and the singular and uncanny presence of her dead alter ego on the other. What complicates the equation, and the play's time sequence, is the short second act. It is clear from the start that the appeal of the Belmont river is going to prove fatally irresistible to her; and that what we are witnessing are the last hours or (at most) days of her life. Indeed, as I indicated earlier, the third act is a Beckettian repetition of the first, taking us through the encounters of two successive days, with variations. But the play disrupts chronology in its startling second act, which shows the dead body of Portia Coughlan being winched up from the Belmont river before the silent assembled cast of characters. In so disrupting linear time, as well as by bringing the ghost of Gabriel onstage, Carr makes apparent

16   Ireland on Stage: Beckett and After

that she is writing a drama of ritual rather than of realism. She achieves this by dramatizing death, not considered as an end in itself or as a single self-contained incident but as a process extending over (and disrupting) time and involving a wide group of family and friends as mourners.

My critical account of death as process here draws on terms from a valuable study by Fiona Macintosh,[9] which makes a series of sustained parallels in the treatment of death between the tragedies of Classical Greece and the plays of Yeats, Synge and O'Casey. Although Macintosh does not deal with contemporary Irish plays, a work like *Portia Coughlan* benefits from her analysis in showing how, while the precise moment of the heroine's suicide is elided, its implications inform her every living gesture in the world of the play. For in Macintosh's account of such a drama the dying character meets his or her death not once but many times; often, as the intensity of their suffering escalates, they are seen to occupy a liminal zone in which it is difficult to determine whether they are living or dead. As Portia says to her aunt in Act Three: 'Ah'm dead Maggie May, dead an' whah ya seen this long time gone be a ghost who chan't fin' her restin' place, is all.' (293) In the 'big speeches' which the title characters of Greek tragedy deliver, their auditors are as likely to be the ghosts they are going to encounter as the living they are leaving behind; here the ghost of Gabriel is increasingly addressed directly by Portia in an exchange which allows for a greater range of levels and registers of language. What we have in *Portia Coughlan* is a modern-day tragedy where the death of the individual character spirals out to implicate the fate of a family line and the spiritual well-being of the entire community.

What is finally so striking about the play is its language, what Frank McGuinness rightly calls its 'physical attack on the conventions of syntax, spelling and sounds of Standard English' (ix). In first attending the play, one had to tune in to what immediately strikes the listener as the heavy accent of the Irish Midlands and a dialect which either strikes out the final 't' in words or turns them into an 'h'. The following is a representative exchange:

> **Portia:** Busy ah tha factory?
> **Raphael:** Aye.
> **Portia:** Ud's me birtha taday.
> **Raphael:** Thah a fac'?
> **Portia:** Imagine, ah'm thirty…Jay, half me life's over.
> **Raphael:** Me heart goes ouh ta ya.
> **Portia:** Have wan wud me an me birtha.
> **Raphael:** Ah this hour, ya mus' be ouha yar mine (240).

The language also contains recognizable features of Hiberno-English pronunciation and usage, 'me' for 'my', 'seen' and 'done' for 'saw' and 'did.' But it is one thing to hear it spoken onstage; another to try and read the script from the printed page, where some of it borders on the incomprehensible. The only solution, I found, is actually to say the lines, following the phonetic spelling (in ways reminiscent of a very different Irish playwright, George Bernard Shaw, and his lifelong fascination with phonetics and the varieties of English). As you mouth the lines, they become clear—a true oral literature and an utterly distinct idiom. No more than Synge stopped at transcribing Hiberno-English, Marina Carr is doing more than merely replicating Midlands speech. Frank McGuinness describes her language as 'a haunting' (ix) and she herself describes the Midlands as 'a metaphor for the crossroads between the worlds' (310-11). She is fashioning a dramatic speech all her own, bending and shaping the forms of Standard English in ways that allow for the disruption of the linguistic present by the Irish past and evolving a flexible linguistic medium to address the living and the dead, the real and the mythic.

In such a survey of the plays of Sebastian Barry and Marina Carr, what alterations in the dramatic landscape from the earlier works of Brian Friel, Tom Murphy, et al. can be noted? When writing in *Contemporary Irish Drama* about such plays as Friel's *Philadelphia, Here I Come!* and Murphy's *The Gigli Concert*, I detected what I have termed the male double act as a central recurring phenomenon. As Beckett had done before them in *Waiting for Godot*, a striking number of Irish playwrights from the 1960s through the 1980s placed at the centre of their dramas two male characters whom the audience came to recognize as being psychologically interdependent on one another and paired in terms of likeness and difference. The two Gar O'Donnells in Friel's *Philadelphia* represented the public and private facets of the protagonist's character. Sometimes, the split was across time and divided into younger and older versions of the same character, as Hugh Leonard does in *Da* (1973) and Frank McGuinness in *Observe the Sons of Ulster*. Sometimes, two separate individuals are shown to be intimately bonded or interconnected, as if one fills out some missing part of the other or perversely mirrors them. This is true of Beckett's tramps and of his Hamm and Clov in *Endgame*. But it is no less true of Thomas Kilroy's two Irishmen in *Double Cross* (1986), the Brendan Bracken who becomes an Englishman and the William Joyce who broadcasts as Lord Haw Haw for the Nazis. And in Tom Murphy's *Gigli Concert* (1983) the Irish Man's obsession to sing like the Italian tenor Gigli is transferred to his English psychiatrist.

The dramatic phenomenon of the male double act was used in these plays primarily to address questions of Irish identity — of language and role playing, of relations between the Irish and the English or Ireland and the US, above all to dramatize the conflict between the claims of a narrow, traditional, supportive past and the alluring but uncertain and possibly anonymous prospect of a more open future. That phase has, I believe, come to an end; and as one consequence there are virtually no male double acts in the more recent plays. Interestingly, Sebastian Barry's first play in 1988, *Boss Grady's Boys*, was just such a piece, with its two old brothers on a Kerry farm enacting a surreal version of the Irish past, and can be seen as much a valediction as a beginning. In his subsequent plays, and those of Marina Carr, it could be argued that the dramatic focus has once more come to centre on a single character, a Thomas Dunne holding centrestage for the entire play, or Carr's eponymous women, the Mai and Portia Coughlan. And one can see why this might be the case. In plays centring on conflicts in Irish identity, certain governing assumptions were still being adhered to. One was that such conflicts were essentially masculine. And so, on the rare occasions up to, say, 1988, when women did feature in the male double acts of contemporary Irish drama, they were invariably relegated to the sidelines, the margins, since the dramatic emphasis was so squarely centered on the two male leads. The women were assigned a series of subordinate and dependent roles, socially as well as dramatically: the girlfriend or fiancée, the other woman, the woman as other. Marina Carr is naturally going to promote her women characters from the sidelines to the centre.

But what is so striking about Carr's plays, *The Mai* in particular, is how the title characters share the stage space with a theatrical ensemble. The Mai's experience cannot be represented without tracking back and forth through time, into the future to show her grownup daughter Millie's experience and back to her Grandma Fraochlain as an improbably feisty hundred-year-old. And room must also be found for her two sisters and her two aunts. As a play *The Mai* uses its central character as a prism to refract the range of women's experience historically across the past hundred years. And Sebastian Barry is also writing a new kind of history play. His drama confers life on his characters not only as members of his own family but as Irish people who were written out of the historical record, among them a goodly number of women: Fanny Hawke in *Prayers of Sherkin*; Lizzie Finn in her *Only True History*; an alcoholic grandmother in *Our Lady of Sligo* (1998). None of his people's stories, not even Thomas Dunne's, can be told in isolation, as an exercise in individuality. Rather, these shadowy, damaged figures have to re-enter their historical situations and the intimate interrelations that shaped them. The current Irish stage reveals more ensemble playing than ever before, one with greater space for women as well as men, for older as well as younger actors, for all to be equal players rather than merely character or bit parts. The plays are informed by the dramatic and democratic principle that each person on the stage has his or her own story to tell.

Sebastian Barry and Marina Carr first came to theatrical prominence in the 1980s. In the final section of this article, I want more briefly to consider two names that emerged in the 1990s, Conor McPherson and Martin McDonagh. I want to take the opportunity to examine their work, because I have found it theatrically exciting and because they are the most acclaimed of the younger Irish playwrights. But that is also the reason why I will devote less space to them and wish, in a sense, to consider them together. Both are young men, in their early thirties, writing in a pared down verbal style about characters who frequently harbour murderous impulses. Their scenarios are as likely to show the influence of television or movies as of theatre. And yet, for all of their youthful iconoclasm, both have found acclaim by writing plays set in remote, and familiar, Irish country settings with incidents and characters that evoke earlier Irish playwrights, notably Synge. The cynical in Ireland have pointed to the fact that both McDonagh and McPherson have broken through in London and gone on to suggest that they have done so by calculatedly appealing to the English notion of what constitutes an Irish play. The case, it may be said, is not so simple.

Although Conor McPherson broke through with the London staging of his play *This Lime Tree Bower* in 1996, he only achieved this on the back of many years of adventurously writing and staging his own plays. While an undergraduate and graduate student (of English and Philosophy) at University College Dublin, McPherson became proficient in the language of theatre both through his formal study of drama in the BA English degree and his immersion in UCD's dramatic society where he not only put on his own plays but acted in others by dramatists like Brian Friel and Harold Pinter. And in the four years following college Conor McPherson and some friends founded Fly by Night Theatre Company and staged their own productions, with a great deal of imagination and very little funding, at various venues around Dublin. One of these was seen by a London agent and soon McPherson was writer-in-residence at London's Bush Theatre, where his work attracted critical and commercial notice. A commission by the Royal Court Theatre resulted in *The Weir* (1997), which transferred from the small theatre upstairs to the larger venue downstairs at the Royal Court and was revived even more successfully in 1998; after three months at Dublin's Gate Theatre, it travelled to the United States, where it had an extended run. And yet with all this success, McPherson continues to rely on his own strength of character and determination to create a drama that relies very little on external effect and which generates itself by the verbal and histrionic ability of

20   Ireland on Stage: Beckett and After

the actor onstage to hold an audience with the power of his (or the playwright's) words.

Conor McPherson regards himself as a storyteller. This self-perception has resulted in plays which are frequently monologues, where the primary engagement is between the actor and the audience. As the playwright himself puts it: 'These plays are set "in a theatre". Why mess about? The character is *on stage*, perfectly aware that he is talking to a group of people.'[10] McPherson's plays are a reminder that Irish drama arguably had its origins as much in the communal art of oral storytelling in the home or in the pub as in a fourth wall drama performed on a proscenium stage. A play like Friel's *Dancing at Lughnasa* foregrounds the two theatrical modes with the more conventional drama of the five sisters in the kitchen complicated in its development and relation to the audience by the presence and activities of the storyteller-narrator, Michael. Friel fused the storytelling with the drama in his most radical play, 1979's *Faith Healer*, where three characters — the faith healer of the title, his wife Grace, and manager Teddy — appear in turn before the audience to tell their story and to deliver their faith-healing act. McPherson has clearly been influenced by *Faith Healer*, drawing on its structure of four interlocking monologues for *This Lime Tree Bower*. But there are formal storytellers in the plays of Beckett and Pinter also, who frequently face their audience with little more than their story to tell, and these playwrights constitute a resource for contemporary Irish playwrights like McPherson and McDonagh.

With *The Weir* McPherson has decided (or agreed) to write a play with five characters rather than one and for them to gather in a familiar locale (a pub in the Irish countryside) and engage in dialogue. But McPherson's distinctive handling of monologue remains central to *The Weir's* dramatic being, as four of the play's characters in turn tell a story which engages issues of life and death and which plays and preys on fear of the irrational in human behaviour. Since the newcomer is a woman, Valerie, the three men gathered in Brendan's pub are at some level trying to impress, if not scare her, especially in this desolate, windswept area, with its dark nights and isolation. But the play recognizes the extent to which traditional Irish storytelling has always drawn on the cluster of beliefs surrounding the fairy folk, the 'others,' those who enjoy a continued existence after death. It is a theme which fascinates McPherson — in his 1997 play, *St. Nicholas*, the seedy drama critic who tells us his story moves from the world of the theatre to a twilight existence with a group of vampires — and in *The Weir* McPherson plugs in to Irish folklore. Although Yeats and Lady Gregory recorded and commented on such beliefs as orally transmitted by old country people, it was Synge who made the greatest dramatic capital of such stories, drawing on what he witnessed of the impact of such beliefs on the lives of the Aran Islanders. Repeatedly, Synge steered the islanders' conversation to stories of the fairies and filled *The Aran Islands* with their accounts. His plays are, among other things, a complex exploration of truth and fiction in storytelling, from Maurya's account of the vision of her dead son at the well in *Riders to the Sea* to Christy Mahon's many versions of his father-slaying in *The Playboy of the Western World*.

The beginning of *The Weir* is deceptively low key. Brendan, a man in his thirties who runs the pub, greets two of the regulars in turn, Jack, a fiftysomething bachelor who runs a garage, and Jim, a fortysomething gentle man who lives with his mother. They are joined by Finbar, the local man made good, who now runs the big hotel, and is showing a young woman Valerie around the neighbourhood — showing her 'the natives', as Jack sardonically remarks.[11] McPherson has Jack begin the play's storytelling process with what might best be described as a 'pure story': an account he once heard by an old woman Mrs. Neylon of how, when she was a girl, she and her mother had been terrified while alone in the house one night by a repeated knocking at front and back. The fictive rationale supplied by the people at the time is that the Neylon house had been built on a fairy road, a traditional pathway whose access was generally left clear and unblocked. The rationale in the present of the play would appear to be to frighten Valerie, since it turns out that the house she has just moved into on her own is the same one the Neylons lived in. Finbar, whose married status does not seem to be preventing him from making a play for Valerie, has been the one to suggest that Jack tell the fairy fort story, and he is accused by the others of deliberately trying to frighten Valerie when the identity of her house is made known to them. We are never given definitive verification of whether Finbar has done this deliberately or unwittingly. But Valerie has herself asked to hear the story when Jack initially demurs.

Finbar, who continually decries such stories, is hoist with his own petard when the others make him tell of his own supernatural haunting which caused him to move house and quit smoking. Like the apocryphal story of the old Irish woman who was once asked if she believed in the fairies and replied 'I do not, but they're there anyway,' Finbar denies that the ghost is there on the stairs but describes how he was unable to move all the same. Jim's story is introduced as a realistic memory, of a story associated with a neighbour who died, and how he and the neighbour were once asked by the priest of the next parish to dig a grave. Left on his own at the digging, Jim encountered a man who directs him to dig in another area, in the grave of a young girl. From a later description, he finds that the dead man resembles the man he encountered and that the dead man was known to be a child molester. The folk value being endorsed here is that a ghost will continue to enact his or her crime even after death, while in social terms the fairy story is a means, as the researches of Angela Bourke and others have increasingly shown, of finding a narrative form to cope with social aberration in a traditional community.

The three men vow the stories have gone too far and, when Brendan brings Valerie back from the house (the Pub's 'Ladies' being out of order), say there will be no more fairy stories. But Valerie has her own story to tell and insists on doing so, one about the recent death by drowning of her young daughter and a communication from beyond the grave. The story is the most urban and 'realistic' of the four in its setting and details; and yet it builds and draws on elements from all of the stories so far told. More than that it turns the tables on the men and, in so doing, recalls Harold Pinter's *The Homecoming* where the men subject Ruth to their verbal attentions until she actively seizes control by turning their ploys against them. Valerie, and the play, seem more benign that that, doing no more than exposing and sending off Finbar and leaving Jack to promote a relationship between Brendan and Valerie. He does so with a final story, that isn't 'a ghostly story. Anyway' (47). It answers the question of why he never married by telling of his irrational fear of leaving his own place and following the woman he was courting to Dublin. Like all of the stories told in the play, Jack's story enacts the trauma of displacement, of the psychic disturbance caused by the inroads of social progress on traditional ways of life. Jack's story is a 'true' personal account, to balance the 'fairy' story he told earlier, but in ways his is the most uncanny and haunting of all. And the question remains: is Valerie's story true? Not so much her claim that she had a communication from her dead daughter, but its overall narrative emphasis on the death by drowning. Or is it a narrative calculated to achieve its effect on the men, as she feels theirs have been on her? There is nothing, finally, but the words as spoken on the stage, not even the degrees of verification allowed by Synge and Friel.

In a documentary broadcast by Radio Telefís Éireann early in 1998, Martin McDonagh also described himself as a storyteller. The documentary narrated the Broadway opening of McDonagh's acclaimed *The Beauty Queen of Leenane* and its nomination for six Tony Awards, four of which it went on to win. This twenty-six-year-old Londoner, son of Irish parents, was asked why he chose to set his plays in the West of Ireland and replied that he had tried writing plays set in London and America, but without success. It was when he recalled the setting and conversations from his summer visits as a child to relatives in the West of Ireland that he found his dramatic idiom: 'close to home but distant', as he put it. The process has reminded many of the similar cultural placement of John Millington Synge at the turn of the previous century (not least because Synge was

Irish Drama in the 1990s

taught Gaelic on Inishmaan by a Martin McDonagh!), and the parallel is instructive. Both playwrights have evoked a mixed response — acclaim (largely) from abroad for the theatrical *éclat*, dark humour and unconventionality of their plays, verbal protest in Ireland from some at any rate who feel that the playwrights are exploiting rather than expressing the people and conditions of which they treat. The crucial issue, it seems to me, is that of 'distance' and it is that of which I wish to raise some considerations by way of conclusion.

A striking feature of the claims being made about Martin McDonagh is that they are made on behalf of someone repeatedly described as an 'Irish playwright' who yet speaks with a distinctively London accent. McDonagh is one of the first, certainly the most high profile, playwright of the Irish diaspora — the son of Irish parents who emigrated to England, where he was born and raised. In the past, such emigrants — whatever they achieved in the countries to which they emigrated — were generally lost to Ireland. Even as transportation improved, and return visits became possible, they remained invisible in terms of a cultural contribution, at least a contribution that would be recognized as such. Perhaps it was the Irish soccer team of the late 1980s, where second- and third-generation exiles with Irish grannies and English accents were encouraged to play for Ireland, that redrew the boundaries. And a singer-songwriter like Shane McGowan, who managed to infuse Irish traditional music with a punk sensibility and so recover some of its anarchic energies, emerged at the head of a London-Irish artistic community. But these were from the popular arenas of football and rock music. Theatre is traditionally more highbrow, especially when dubbed 'national', and the introduction of McDonagh into that scene has predictably made waves.

In what has come to be known as the Leenane trilogy — comprising *The Beauty Queen of Leenane*, *A Skull in Connemara* and *The Lonesome West* — there are only a couple of scenes which draw directly on the Irish emigrant experience in London. In scene 5 of *The Beauty Queen of Leenane* the emigrant Pato Dooley sits beside a table in his London bedsit and recites a letter home:

> Well, Maureen, there is no major news here, except a Wexford man on the site a day ago, a rake of bricks fell on him from the scaffold and forty stitches he did have in his head and was lucky to be alive at all ... I do go out for a pint of a Saturday or a Friday but I don't know nobody and don't speak to anyone.[12]

The letter limns a recognizable picture of work on London building sites, bedsitting rooms and a drink in the local pub. But for the most part McDonagh's plays are set in locales that bear place names from the West of Ireland, such as Leenane and Inishmaan. And most of his characters purport to live there, even if one of them (the forty-year-old

Maureen in *Beauty Queen*) makes an abortive attempt to emigrate to the US with Pato Dooley. The characters McDonagh represents exist in suffocatingly close intimacy — Maureen and her mother, Mag; brothers Coleman and Valene in *The Lonesome West* — and are strikingly prone to violent outbursts. Mag protests that her only daughter is torturing her, a claim which we interpret as badmindedness until we actually see her do it; a shotgun is fired off murderously in *The Lonesome West* and, when all else fails, there is always the Hitchcockian resource of the kitchen knife. The charge of Stage Irishry, and in particular of racial stereotyping and misrepresentation of the Irish peasant as prone to violence, has been levelled at McDonagh, as it was before him at Synge. These writers, it is claimed, do not know these people and substitute for their lack of understanding a willful and calculated stage effect. The question, whether negatively or positively put, has to do with distance.

In an important article,[13] Thomas Kilroy writes of Anglo-Irish playwrights from Farquhar to Beckett in terms of 'a characteristic distancing effect, a cool remove of the playwright from his subject matter,' whatever the ostensible setting, and a concomitant concern with form. Hence the restlessness, whether of Synge's vagrants or of Beckett's immobiles who cannot stop the buzzing; there is a movement in their plays towards 'abstraction and the perfection of the idea, the radical reshaping of human action for particular effects.' But that distancing which Kilroy sees as inhering in the socially hyphenated category of the Anglo-Irish and as culminating in Beckett may have started up again and become relevant with dramatists of the Irish diaspora like Martin McDonagh. *The Beauty Queen of Leenane* operates so successfully in the theatre because its most direct engagement is between the playwright and the audience, because of the superb calibration of its formal dramatic effects. Pato is writing to Maureen to say that what they enjoyed on his few days home has meant more to him than a one night stand (despite appearances) and to ask her to join him in America. The fate of that letter is the pivot of the next scene, where Pato's dimwitted brother Ray leaves it in the unsafe keeping of Maureen's mother. Ray reluctantly departs, with repeated imprecations to Mag to be sure to deliver the letter, making a brief return to make sure she hasn't tampered with it. Finally, the scene remorselessly confirms our worst fears when the following stage action is indicated:

> Ray exits again, closing the door behind him fully this time. Mag listens to his footsteps fading away, then gets up, picks up the envelope and opens it, goes back to the range and lifts off the lid so that the flames are visible, and stands there reading the letter. She

> drops the first short page into the flames as she finishes it, then
> starts reading the second. Slow fade-out (42).

This is, to some, a device out of melodrama. But it is shorn of almost all surrounding plot complications that would have accompanied its nineteenth-century manifestation, and explored in almost purely formal terms. The challenge, as Kilroy writes, 'is to maintain the full expression of human feeling within this artifice,' and that is the nub of the question, I think, in connection with McDonagh. The fate of the letter, from its initial recitation through its misplaced reception to its incineration, is followed through with formal precision. But Maureen's hopes for a more fulfilling and meaningful life are located at the centre of the artifice and infuse the device with feeling. In a less successful McDonagh play, such as *A Skull in Connemara*, the question of whether Mick Dowd murdered his wife is never fully felt and proves a mere pretext for much onstage obliterating of skulls.

A final way of putting this is to look at the generally accepted humour in McDonagh's plays and their infliction of pain. Much of the humour is of the cartoon variety, the violence likewise, and our laughter springs from the exposed hollowness of the violent threat or its failure to cause the requisite damage. The most painful moment in *Beauty Queen* is when Maureen realizes that Pato has sent a letter and tortures her mother by pouring boiling oil over her hands to force her to confess; the reluctant confession only intensifies the torture. Does the scene go too far? McDonagh's art is so excessive, the question may seem unanswerable, but an aesthetic work can still be gauged. I think it does, that there is relish of the sadism and punishment for its own sake, and that we are closer here to the grand guignol of a movie like *Whatever Happened to Baby Jane?*

Thomas Kilroy's article implies that a native Catholic playwright could achieve an almost unmediated intimacy with his or her audience. I question whether that could ever have been the case. Perhaps an exception might have been John B. Keane, whose plays were disseminated by the countrywide amateur drama circuit and not by the urban metropolis; they could be said to have received their support from the communities from which they derived. But if that was so, it applied in and to the late 1950s and early 1960s, and has long since ceased to be the case—perhaps a reason why Keane gave up writing stage plays. And were not Keane's plays as equally derived from dramatic conventions, albeit a set of different ones, as those of Synge or Beckett?[14]

In the decades since, there have been certain key moments when a play like Friel's *Translations* or *Lughnasa* appeared to evoke a unified national response. But Friel's plays of the 1990s have all sought to address Ireland in the present and have met with a far more divided

26 Ireland on Stage: Beckett and After

response. My own feeling is that the smash-and-grab theatrics of Martin McDonagh have, in their impact, changed the Irish theatrical landscape irrevocably. A terrible beauty, indeed...

This paper was originally published in Colby Quarterly 34.4 (1998): 265-89.

---

[1]Anthony Roche, 'Kilroy's Doubles', *Contemporary Irish Drama: From Beckett to McGuinness* (Dublin: Gill & MacMillan, 1994; New York: St. Martin's Press, 1995): 189-215.

[2]'Speaking for the Dead: Playwright Frank McGuinness talks to Kevin Jackson', *The Independent* 27 September 1989.

[3]Sebastian Barry, *Plays 1* (London: Methuen, 1997): 292. The volume contains: *Boss Grady's Boys*; *Prayers of Sherkin*; *White Woman Street*; *The Only True History of Lizzie Finn*; *The Steward of Christendom*. All future references to *The Steward of Christendom* are to this edition and will be incorporated in the text.

[4]For a discussion of the historic resonances of this scene, see Roy Foster's Introduction to Barry's play, *Our Lady of Sligo* (London: Methuen, 1998).

[5]See Fintan O'Toole's Introduction to an earlier volume comprising three of Barry's plays: *The Only True History of Lizzie Finn*; *The Steward of Christendom*; *White Woman Street* (London: Methuen, 1995): ix. O'Toole also makes the King Lear comparison.

[6]Biographical note in a collection of plays containing *Low in the Dark*, *The Crack in the Emerald*: *New Irish Plays*, ed. David Grant (London: Nick Hern Books, 1990). Future references to the play are to this edition and will be incorporated in the text.

[7]Marina Carr, *The Mai* (Oldcastle, County Meath: Gallery Press, 1995): 22. All future references are to this edition and will be incorporated in the text.

[8]Marina Carr, *Portia Coughlan*, *The Dazzling Dark: New Irish Plays*, selected and introduced by Frank McGuinness (London and Boston: Faber and Faber, 1996): 241-42. All future references are to this edition and will be incorporated in the text.

[9]See Fiona Macintosh, Dying Acts: Death in Ancient Greek and Modern Irish Tragic Drama (Cork: Cork University Press, 1994).

[10]Conor McPherson, Author's note, *This Lime Tree Bower: Three Plays* (Dublin: New Island Books; London: Nick Hern Books, 1996).

[11]Conor McPherson, *The Weir* (London: Nick Hern Books, 1997; rev. ed., 1998): 5. All future references are to this edition and will be incorporated in the text.

[12]Martin McDonagh, *The Beauty Queen of Leenane* (London: Methuen, 1996): 34. All future references are to this edition and will be incorporated in the text.

[13]Thomas Kilroy, 'The Anglo-Irish Theatrical Imagination', *Bullán: An Irish*

Studies Journal 3. 2 (Winter 1997/Spring 1998): 5-12.

[14]The veteran actor Eamon Kelly, who has acted in most of the Keane revivals, says: 'I couldn't help thinking that in many ways John B. Keane was heir to Boucicault.' *The Journeyman* (Dublin: Marino; Boulder, Colorado: Irish American Book Co., 1998): 236.

2 | desperate optimists' *Time-Bomb*: Hard Wired/Tender Bodies

Cathy Leeney

In Beckett's *Ohio Impromptu*, the Reader describes the state of being 'alone together'.[1] Often now we are alone together with machines, in spaces that could be any place. Perhaps, by bringing the machines on stage, the theatre begins to explore how they change us, and how we might change them. We need to redefine loneliness in a time when we are never alone, but often on our own, often lonely. Electronic machinery as a stage setting is more than a reflection in contemporary theatre of our ordinary lives. The presence of electronic media equipment before an audience opens up the question of the relationship between theatre and its fellow media. This question reflects on the presence of performers, as different modes of representation are placed side by side. It reflects, too, on ideas of character in performance. It frames the relationship between performers, and with the audience, and the experience we share. If stages represent psychological and emotional states, as well as places, then technology on stage may represent the business of representation, and how it reflects, but also impacts on the state we are in.

Desperate optimists is a performance group formed in 1992 by Christine Molloy and Joe Lawlor. They have worked throughout the U.K. and in Ireland, exploring ideas of national identity, power, and performance. They exploit video, audio, and computing technologies on stage as part of their performance practice, and invite audiences to examine realities mediated by technology, and the power of live performance. Desperate optimists make work for sites, galleries, new media, and theatre. More recently, their work has moved out of the theatre and onto the web. Here, I will look at their 1998 production

Play-boy, but will concentrate mostly on their 2000 collaboration with Dublin Youth Theatre, entitled *Time-bomb*.

In one way, technology on the stage functions in realist terms, directly reflecting experience of contemporary life in Europe and North America. André Antoine, in his Théâtre Libre in 1888, made audiences sit up and regret their dinners, by setting Fernand Incres' one-act play *Les Bouchers* ('The Butchers') among sides of mutton. Perhaps the sight of masses of flex, plug boards, turntables, speakers, screens and digital control panels gives to a present day audience a parallel sense of immediacy, a confrontation with the messy, if bloodless, impact that electronics, and digital technologies have on us, our bodies, our sense of where we are, of who we are, of how we feel about each other, and of what we can do.

Technology on stage not only reflects contemporary reality, it poses questions of reality in our relation to it. The machinery of electronic media in performance proposes different parameters which define the experience of the bodies in performance. To speak in the old style, the machinery may be understood expressionistically, as a way of materializing issues of cultural and individual formation, physical power and danger, communality and isolation. Claude Schumacher argued that Antoine's use of animal carcasses in *Les Bouchers* is diminished by a purely realist interpretation.[2] Antoine filled the stage with offal, even on the floor, turning the setting of the butcher's shop into a parallel world that spoke expressionistically. When desperate optimists fill the stage with digital and electronic machines, I will argue, they turn the setting into a context for the exploration of identity, power, violence, and vulnerability in a highly technologized culture. Specifically, I will argue that desperate optimists pose questions about the connection between place and identity, and between place and technology in a supermodern world. I wish to make a connection with ideas about identity and place which are borrowed from anthropology. Marc Augé theorizes the idea of the 'non-place', that is, space which does not affirm sociological or cultural identities as they have been defined by social and psychological sciences.[3] Augé makes a convincing argument that non-places are proliferating and that we spend more and more time in them. He suggests some of the implications of this for the individual. It seems to me that desperate optimists confront some of these issues.

The role of place in defining self has been an important concern of psychologists as well as being a core part of anthropological studies. Rom Harré writes: 'the self is a location, not a substance or an attribute. The sense of self is the sense of being located at a point in space'; according to E.S. Casey 'where we are – the place we occupy, however briefly – has everything to do with what and who we are (and finally, *that* we are).'[4] In *Non-Places* Augé proposes that, increasingly, we spend our lives in spaces which do not function as places in the anthropological, sociological, or indeed ethnological sense: shopping centres, car parks, supermarkets, airports, hotel chains, motorways, in front of computers, or televisions, text-messaging in trains, watching films on planes. 'If a place can be defined as relational, historical and concerned with identity, then a space which cannot be defined as relational, or historical or concerned with identity will be a non-place.'[5] It is the non-place that the desperate optimists represent on stage in *Time-bomb*, and a way of living dominated by non-places is the over-arching concern of the performance.

As a French anthropologist turning his attention, not to far-away continents, but to 'the near', Augé is conscious of the crisis in applying the paradigms of his discipline to contemporary European existence. How are concepts central to anthropological analysis, such as tribe, genealogy, kinship structure, marriage, witchcraft, or bequest and exchange, to reveal and express the lives and habits of twenty-first-century Europeans? Augé chooses the example of Breton farmers who are more worried about EU farm policy and their loans from the Crédit Agricole than they are about their genealogies.[6] His analysis applies to contemporary life dominated by globalized economies and a high level of technological development; a 'supermodern' world which is the successor to the post-modern condition.

Augé proposes that this supermodern world is characterized by excess; this is its essential quality. He suggests three kinds of excess: time, space, and ego. It is chiefly excess of space that concerns me here, although time and ego are connected. Excess of space is, paradoxically, correlative with the shrinking of the planet. Travel into outer space and the view thus gained of our planet reduce our space to an infinitesimal point. But the world is also available to us as never before. Rapid means of transport have brought any destination within range of a few hours. Conversely, domestic media can bring the world into our living spaces, offering images of 'an instant, sometimes simultaneous vision of an event taking place on the other side of the planet.'[7] New kinds of spaces are created in which identities and impressions of reality are formed. While spaces proliferate, the relational function of place is destabilized. If ethnology seeks to delineate signifying spaces in the world, theatre practice seeks to create signifying stages. In the supermodern world, proliferating spaces contribute to redefine our sense of self, the quality of our experience, and our relations with one another. So, the theatrical representation of non-place impacts on notions of character, narrative and group behaviour, and on modes of representing them in performance.

The experience of the non-place, Augé suggests, is a turning back on the self.[8] The user of the non-place is defined by their contractual relationship with it. The contract relates to the individual identity of the contracting party. There is a sense of anonymity in the non-place, but it is dependent on an identity check: the pass-word, the credit card number, the photo ID. As Augé puts it, 'the user of the non-place is always required to prove their innocence.'[9] In the non-place, you become no more than what you do or experience in your role as user, passenger, client or audience. The non-place creates neither singular identity nor relatedness; it creates only solitude and similitude. It inflicts the individual consciousness 'to entirely new experiences and ordeals of solitude.'[10]

Such a sense of loneliness, together with questions of power and identity, are some of the concerns of desperate optimists, familiarly known as the desperates. Between 1992 and 1999 they created six live performances, the last of which was called *Play-boy*, which was performed in Dublin at the Project Arts Centre in 1999. *Play-boy* used J.M. Synge's *The Playboy of the Western World* as a way into loneliness, violence and heroism. In collaboration with photographer Chris Dorley-Brown, the desperates made video footage of people talking about Synge's *Playboy*, about being lonely, and about the big 'if' – what would our lives be like if we had made a different set of decisions. These talking heads interrupt and disrupt the live performance of Molloy and Lawlor, who narrate a fantasy account of an encounter between Synge and Trotsky, against a soundtrack of Latin dance music. Each person on video, in turn, unnerves the audience by taking a loaded gun, and firing it at us. We see the individual reactions to the weapon in their hands, the weight of it, their scrunched up faces, and their shock and surprise at the noise and impact of the explosion when they pull the trigger. All of these reactions mirror those of the audience who are placed on the receiving end of the act. The explosion is a useful image in relation to the desperates' work in *Play-boy*, and in *Time-bomb*; not only in the anarchic sense of violent eruption, but also in the idiomatic sense of exponential and uncontrolled growth, of excessive fragmentation, of the disappearance of familiar structures, and of the debris of current experience.

Desperate optimists' live work bears the marks of Philip Auslander's argument for the resistant political potential of postmodern performance. The desperates are suspicious of the power of presence in live performance. They resist what Auslander calls the 'apparent collusion between political structures of authority and the persuasive power of presence'.[11] Presence or 'charisma' in the performer resides in the relationship between actor and character through the text, whether that text is verbal or otherwise. The authority of the text is conferred upon the actor; as an authorizing power the text disappears behind the actor. The desperates deconstruct this relationship between performer, character, and text, by flattening and bleaching out performance style, refusing the illusion of character, and favouring the performance of role instead. By making the text 'visible' through fragmentation of narrative structure, by playing the 'not/but' of performative inverted commas, or by having the text as object on the stage, the desperates reveal the battle for control of the means of representation and persuasion.

In *Play-boy* the stage space is performative, not referential. It does not 'represent' another reality. It is an energy field in which stories are told. Also, the time-scale of the performance is not referential but performative. No other event is represented, and performance time becomes playful and musical as rhythms are repeated, actions mimicked, stories added to in the re-telling. In the mix of familiar facts with surreality, our gullibility as an audience is suggested as the performance hits its recurring themes: the disturbing thrill of violence, colonization as an image of loneliness, and history and heroism as stories, lies and revolution.

Auslander points out that in postmodern performance there is always a danger of confirming what one wishes to deconstruct. This is a central issue in *Time-bomb*, the production that is my main focus here. In 2000, the desperates were invited by Dublin Youth Theatre[12] to collaborate with young performers to create a piece that would detonate the complacencies surrounding the phenomenon which has become known as the 'Celtic Tiger', Ireland's miraculously thriving economy. In *Time-bomb*, nine young Dubliners examine the shrapnel of twenty-four hours of life in the boomtown capital.

Time-bomb was developed over the summer of 2000; the performers learned to use video and audio equipment to create video and sound loops for the performance. They wrote much of the text, based on their own stories and experiences. The script also included a number of passages from the United States film *Kids*.[13] The screenplay for *Kids* was written by twenty year-old Harmony Korine, and the film was directed by middle-aged photographer and seedy *bon viveur* Larry Clarke. As in his autobiographical photographic essay of his hometown, *Tulsa* (1971), Clarke used a documentary style to chart the fictional day of two young men in New York City. *Kids* has a very classical form; it takes place over twenty-four hours in the lives of

Telly and Casper, both about sixteen years old. Telly figures that the safest sex is with virgins, so he chalks up unprotected sexual encounters with thirteen year-old-girls, and brags about them to his friend Casper, who is more interested in drinking. Unknown to himself, Telly is HIV positive. Both boys are into drugs, theft, and casually beating people up. The narrative drive of the story is provided by Jenny, who has had sex just once, with Telly. Now she discovers he has infected her with HIV. She searches for him to confront him with this. She tracks him down to a party, but arrives too late to save yet another innocent from being infected by Telly.

The film caused some considerable controversy. In the United States it was released in cinemas with a warning 'No one under 18 admitted without a guardian'; its video release was banned in Ireland. The *New York Times* called it 'a wake up call to the world', while the *New Yorker* said it was 'nihilistic pornography'.[14] Whether *Kids* is seen as potentially corrupting or as a lesson in safe sexual practice, it presents a young audience with powerful images of themselves in their contemporary world. In *Time-bomb*, excerpts from the screenplay, including stage directions and camera angles, are read by the performers. Chief among the scenes chosen are the misogynistic exchanges between Telly and Casper, the vapid chat between Jennie and her friends as they attempt to express their feelings about relationships with boys, the hospital scene where Jennie and friend are HIV tested, and Jennie is coldly informed she is HIV positive. Lastly, is the final scene of the film at the party, when Jennie arrives too late.

The mode of performance of these scenes from *Kids* characterizes the style of *Time-bomb* in general. In no sense do the performers assume characters and give colour or feeling to what they say. Rather, they invite one another to read various parts, in matter-of-fact tones, and proceed to present the dialogue and the stage directions in a deadpan, unexpressive fashion. Paradoxically, the ironed-out delivery emphasizes the shocking nature of the exchanges, and does not normalize them. The readings from *Kids* are juxtaposed with the accounts of experiences of the performers themselves, and their views on love and sexuality. A powerful sense emerges of the challenges posed by images of behaviour as they appear in the mass media, in mainstream cinema. How are individuals, struggling to find their own values and ways of living, to negotiate the barrage of messages, images and information presented to them daily in late capitalist societies?

The documentary style of the film *Kids* is reflected in *Time-bomb*, but the performers eschew any charismatic sense of presence. This was very difficult for the young participants to achieve. The General

Manager of DYT in 2000, Maeve Coogan, described the challenges posed by the desperates in demanding the bleaching out of charisma in performance. Finally, the group of nine succeeded brilliantly, and as a result the production strongly affected audiences. Expectations of youthful ebullience and charm were undercut, and audiences were confronted instead with a darkly funny and startlingly direct vision.

Time-bomb features a number of fractured narratives and themes. Already outlined is the confrontation between film images of youthful New York lives and the realities of young people in Dublin, growing up in a post-Catholic, postnationalist, capitalist period of unexpected, and unprecedented expansion. Significantly, none of the concerns explored have very much to do with cultural specificity. In a supermodern world, culture becomes consumerism, and is globally uniform within the borders of economic privilege. Other narratives include Shane's account of his falling in love by closed-circuit television, and his inability to face his beloved in the flesh. He uses another performer as spokesperson for his feelings, and foregrounds the role of technology in trapping us in isolation, while also ventriloquizing our individual responses to experience.

Aoife tells us about the increase in the number of violent attacks in her neighbourhood and of the rape of a young woman near where she lives. The video footage she has made shows us the shadowy passages and alleyways she faces every day. Her sense of powerlessness intersects with the vulnerability of Jennie in *Kids*. High levels of surveillance by CCTV do nothing to create a sense of safety, or to counteract isolation; 'security' so-called, is predicated on fear. Another performer shows us her video account of a trip around the perimeter of the city on the DART[15] train which takes commuters along the coast from north and south of the city centre. The insulated carriages pass building sites, historic spots, housing estates, industrial wastelands, office high-rises, and the uniform stations at which passengers alight from and board the train; the city becomes a series of images blurred by the transience of the observer.

Like *Kids*, *Time-bomb* takes place over twenty-four hours. This, of course, has a special resonance in Dublin, echoing James Joyce's 16 June 1904 in *Ulysses*. The modernist masterpiece of the twentieth century is shattered into the shards of postmodern and post-postmodern mediated experience, dematerialized in the flickering images on the stage monitors. Yet, in the physicality of the performers, their eye contact with the audience, their refusal of protective illusion, we are never allowed to forget their gravely-borne, bodily, vulnerable existence.

The performance area for *Time-bomb* is an open space on one level, dominated by a shallow arch of metal tables behind which the performers sit. On the tables are microphones, and pages of text from which they read dialogue and narratives. Behind them is a bank of turntables, control panels, a computer and a video monitor. Another larger monitor sits down stage left of the tables. Before addressing us, the performers routinely adjust the microphones and make no secret of consulting the sheaves of papers before them. Their tone is routinely serious. They look down, then look us in the eye. They address one another by their real names with business-like politeness. The audience soon understands the one-day time-frame as individual performers punctuate the action by getting up and revealing various parts of their bodies: stomachs, backs, chests, on which are inscribed locations, times and states experienced. At only one point in the performance, which lasts about eighty minutes in total, do they all move down stage and dance. Each performer stands alone, facing the audience. The dance is choreographed but not at all showy. It is a parodic, bleached out, cool version of the boy/girl band dance routines seen on music videos, which set impossible standards of bodily beauty and sexiness. Each of the performers seem to dance a kind of unemotional reaching out, a bodily definition of the space around them as it separates them one from another. There are moments of absurdity, of hilarity, as Patrick describes his misadventures on a sofa; and when the DJ Glen pumps up the rhythms that make Kevin and Fiona want to lose themselves in music.

Time-bomb interrogates the place, Dublin, as it is experienced today. Is Dublin (or any city) experienced as a sociological place, as a culture localized in space and time, as an architectural, social and cultural arrangement that expresses a group identity? Or has Dublin been exploded into what Augé calls a non-place? In *Time-bomb* there is a sense of solitariness to each performer, despite the presence on stage of all nine performers all the time. The performance presents individual expression, offered as personally authentic, and shows how it becomes mediated by technology. These personal voices are juxtaposed with ventriloquized renderings of text from mass media sources. This dramatizes the issue of resistance to our merely contractual relationships within non-spaces. The value of individual response is tested. In the non-place, there is 'no room for history, unless it has been transformed into an element of spectacle'.[16] The heaviness of history, guilt, failure, redemption, forgiveness or justice are unbearable in the lightness of the non-place. In the non-place there is no history besides the last twenty-four hours of news, the unending histories of the present.

Hard Wired/Tender Bodies

Time-bomb explores the challenges of conferring the non-place with identity and relatedness, and the person's fear of being consigned to isolation and powerlessness. It illustrates how non-places impact on ideas of character, and the relationship in performance between role and presence, creating destabilizing truths within a layered narrative structure. The angular, hard surfaces of the electronic equipment and metal furniture contrast with the softness of the performers' bodies. The twenty-four hour ever-presentness of supermodern experience is inscribed on their mortally bare flesh. *Time-bomb* shows the feeling of solitude when we seem to be less and less alone. The vulnerable bodies of the performers bear the impact of this space that is no place; it is a theatre of being, as we all are, alone together.

In the staging of *Play-boy* and *Time-bomb* desperate optimists reflect the ubiquitous presence of technology in everyday life, and also confront the power of mediated experience as it effects subjectivity, the feeling of being, and the person's sense of self. Both productions are concerned with our appropriation of, or appropriation by media technologies, and with the relationship of audiences to media and live performers. Performance is deconstructed and demystified. The audience is not coerced into an impression of coherence; contests for power are exposed. In the supermodern world, places proliferate into spaces, and human groups become collections of individuals, facing new ordeals of solitude.

Time-bomb credits:

Makers: Glen Barry, Paul Butler, Patrick Bridgemen, Shane Carr, Mick Carroll, Fiona Carruthers, Fionnuala McBreen, Aoife Moriarty, Kevin Sherwin.

Collaborators: Joe Lawlor, Christine Molloy – desperate optimists; John Delaney – Assistant Director; desperate optimists – Lighting Design; Marie Tierney – Production Design; Joe St. Leger – Photography; Martin Murphy – DYT Artistic Director.

> *This article was first published in Australasian Drama Studies: Special Issue:* Performing Ireland, *eds Brian Singleton and Anna McMullan, 43 (2003): 76-88*

---

[1] Samuel Beckett, *Ohio Impromptu, The Complete Dramatic Works* (London: Faber and Faber, 1986): 446.

[2] Claude Schumacher, Introduction, *Naturalism and Symbolism in European Theatre, 1850-1918*, ed. Claude Schumacher (Cambridge: Cambridge

University Press, 1996): 7.

[3]Marc Augé, *Non-Places: Introduction to an Anthropology of Supermodernity*, trans. John Howe (London: Verso, 1995).

[4]Rom Harré, *Social Being*, 2nd ed. (Oxford: Blackwell, 1993): 4; and E.S. Casey, *Getting Back Into Place: Toward A Renewed Understanding of the Place-World* (Bloomington: Indiana University Press, 1993): xiii. Both are quoted by Ciarán Benson, *The Cultural Psychology of Self: Place, Morality and Art in Human Worlds* (London: Routledge, 2001): ix and 3 respectively.

[5]Augé, 77-78.

[6]Augé, 17.

[7]Augé, 31.

[8]Augé, 92.

[9]Augé, 102.

[10]Augé, 93.

[11]Philip Auslander, *From Acting to Performance: Essays in Modernism and Postmodernism* (London: Routledge, 1997): 62.

[12]Since its foundation in 1977, Dublin Youth Theatre (DYT) has forged a unique contribution to theatre and youth work in the city. It provides opportunities for young people in the 14 to 22 age group to gain experience in drama, theatre, and related arts. DYT aims to provide for the personal and social development of its members through participation in drama workshops and productions, and to attain high standards in the public performance of plays relevant to the lives of young people.

[13]*Kids*, dir., Larry Clarke, screenplay by Harmony Koirne, Miramax, 1995.

[14]Quoted by Elizabeth Snead, 'Is *Kids* Morally Corrupt or a Cautionary Tale?', *USA Today* 12 January 1998.

[15]Dublin Area Rapid Transit.

[16]Augé, 103.

3 | Staging Bankruptcy of Male Sexual Fantasy: *Lolita* at the Irish National Theatre

Futoshi Sakauchi

Introduction:

The audience at the Peacock Theatre, one of the National Theatres of Ireland, in 2002 observed that three productions incidentally created graphical harmony by placing a huge bed at the centre of the stage: in Aidan Mathews's *Communion* in April,[1] Tom Murphy's *Bailegangaire* in June,[2] and Michael West's dramatized adaptation of Vladimir Nabokov's *Lolita* in September.[3] This visual unity was enhanced by serious ambitions of those three male playwrights to empathize with women in their gross plight.

In Aidan Mathews's *Communion,* the playwright investigates how a mother and widow tragically devotes herself to her son, a victim of a terminal disease and an occupant of a huge bed at stage centre. Here the huge bed serves as a zone of human dignity where a young man fights against a progressive brain tumor for a meaning to his life and where his mother, who has to face the gradual and certain death of her son, searches for a meaning to being the mother of such a son and struggles for her dignity.

In Tom Murphy's *Bailegangaire*, Mommo struggles against senile dementia for reconciliation with her traumatic past and searches for a spiritual harmony with her future. In the play, Mommo finds her grandson perished in flames during her absence after she makes a troublesome journey home with her husband, and she loses her husband soon after the journey. The cursed memory haunts the old widow and hinders her from completing her nightly storytelling of the particular journey, articulating her past as the past, and from starting her new life. With the help of her two granddaughters, she eventually finishes her storytelling and makes inner peace with her past. At length, the long-lost sense of family and love is reestablished when three women share the huge bed, which Tom Murphy felt himself 'getting into' as the fourth woman.[4] Here her bed at the centre stage is a symbol of a field of battle for a female dignity, where the playwright secures Mommo and her granddaughters the space for their hard-earned subjectivity and he sympathetically shares it with the three women. Likewise, in Michael West's dramatized adaptation of Vladimir Nabokov's *Lolita*, a bed at centre stage works as an area where Charlotte, a middle-aged woman and widow, and her daughter Lolita pursue love, mental equilibrium and confidence.

Thus the three main productions of the year at the National Theatre visualized in succession the investigation into female dignity and subjectivity through the installation of a huge bed on the stage. Yet the last of the three, *Lolita*, seems to have deliberately exploited the repeated visualization of female subjectivity as subtle disguise in the previous two productions and to have made the theatre performance richly complex, which was unfortunately only to generate furious sparks from the audience. The conceptual association between a bed and a self-motivated girl/child like Lolita can easily produce the image of a seductive child and, therefore, be risky and misleading. Michael West altered the original text by heavily charging his Lolita with amorousness and sexual enchantment. Fintan O'Toole's denouncement of West's play as 'a version of reality that is morally obnoxious' is, as we shall see, an arguable and understandable reaction.[5] West should have expected such criticism before he put his risky enterprise on the stage. Then why did the playwright dare to introduce such alteration, choosing to provocatively combine female initiative and sexuality between a girl/child and a middle-aged man? Why should such a coattrailing play be staged now in Ireland? This paper is to frame the answer to these questions.

I. Alterations by Michael West of the Nabokov's Original:

Michael West's aesthetic decision to exploit the plays disturbing repercussions ranges not only over theatre performances of *Communion* and *Bailegangaire*, but also over the original text of *Lolita*. The playwright charged his play with Lolita's crudely erotic suggestion, which does not exist in the same implication in the original screenplay by Vladimir Nabokov or in Stanley Kubrick's influential film version.[6] A marked contrast between Nabokov's *Lolita* or Kubrick's film and West's theatre version appears in the sequence where Humbert and Lolita pass a night in a hotel. In Nabokov's screenplay, they sleep separately in the hotel room. When Humbert sees Lolita sleep soundly, 'the moon reaches her face', and her 'innocent helpless fragile infantine beauty arrests him', and then Humbert 'slinks back to his cot'.[7] Early the following morning, Lolita suggests 'playing a game',[8] and she and Humbert amuse themselves. Lolita's childlike laughing voice carries well and arouses a guest in a neighboring room, who 'looks at his watch and smiles' at the contagious laughter of the lively child.[9]

To film this sequence, Kubrick underlines Lolita's childlike mischievousness and helplessness in an ironic twist of circumstances. Lolita occupies a huge double bed by herself at the centre of the room while Humbert sleeps in a small collapsed 'collapsible' child cot. Through this comical role-exchange, where the adult is situated as a child and the child as an adult, Lolita is aware of her power over the man. Thus Lolita demonstrates her individual initiative in innocent games within the room, such as her false alarm of the burning of the hotel to the ground and her showing off a small eye-catching feat in the flexibility of her knuckle joints. In this sequence, the audience hears Lolita saying to Humbert, 'I learned some real good games in camp ... One in particularly [sic] was fun' and, in response to Humbert's complaint that he is 'not a very good guesser', she whispers, 'you have to be ... '[10] Although the rest of the line is lost to the audience in her low whisper, it is clear that her childish 'dare' game is indecent enough to perplex the educated grown-up, but nevertheless, her suggestion of playing a game does not directly imply the sexual act. Immediately after the sequence, they hit the road and continue their casual trip, followed by the news breaking of the death of Lolita's mother, which decisively shifts the initiative from the helpless child/girl to the adult patron.

But in Michael West's version, the audience witnesses Humbert slipping awkwardly into Lolita's bed. The audience also sees Lolita insist on playing a game that she and a boy 'played in the woods' when they 'should have been picking berries', and explain that it is 'a game lots of kids play nowadays'.[11] Here Lolita's lines are heavily charged with erotic emotions and accompanied by seductive body movements. Michael West underscores that her 'play' is a serious deviation from what children are allowed to do, and he makes it openly conflict with accepted morals. As West's Lolita apparently aims, her remarks about kids' play directly induce Humbert into sexual intercourse. In this context, it is clearly the girl/child who seduces the grown-up man into sexual relations. Lolita is keenly aware of her power over the adult, just as Lolita in the hotel sequence in Kubrick's film, but this power is, unlike that of Lolita in the film, exclusively a sexual and seductive one.

By charging Lolita's lines with lascivious eroticism, Michael West deliberately changed Nabokov's and Kubrick's well-reserved and meticulous investigation of emotional nuances into a sexually provocative sequence. The playwright also generalized Lolita's seduction as a powerful mode of sexuality among today's children by letting her assert that 'lots of kids' do the game today. That seems to be virtually equal to the generalization of the sexual seduction by 'kids' of elder men. No wonder one of the first reviewers accused the production at the Peacock Theatre of creating misleading imagery 'in a country torn apart by child sexual abuse.'[12] The concept of childhood as well as woman/manhood is, in its core, a socio-cultural construct. Thus the authority of literary or graphic representations of those concepts are often questioned in socio-cultural contexts, and much more the representation of them on the stage at a national theatre, where the audience, more or less, expects plays to investigate the national identity as much as the audience expects itself to quest for its own individual identity through the theatrical imagination. If Michael West's *Lolita* is nothing but a full-dramatization of the concepts of a juvenile temptress and a girl/child enchantress, the play will expose itself to criticism due to its promulgation of those images in Ireland, where a variety of child sexual abuse scandals in recent years has caused a crisis of confidence in figures of institutional authority, particularly in the Catholic church and its clergy.[13] Fintan O'Toole accused *Lolita* at the Peacock Theatre of being an irresponsibly staged 'paedophile's charter'.[14] But O'Toole's criticism inevitably raises a question: did Michael West and the director Annie Ryan put the play on the stage for such immoral normalization of sexual abuse? It is highly unlikely that any theatre company in Ireland would stage a play in order to shuffle the responsibility for child abuse onto the victimized children.

In the dramatized version of *Lolita* by Michael West, the playwright depicted plainly how Humbert, in contradiction to his ostensible position as a virtuous private tutor, deflowers the twelve-year-old girl/child and devastates her life, so that she becomes an aimless wanderer through countries. The play's allusion to child sexual abuse, a topic that has given rise to fierce public censure in Ireland, was tangible, and the theatre performances of the play have a more direct connection with Irish culture than might be expected from a description of West's play as the story, based on Nabokov's original, of 'the nymphet, now with a dash of Irish blood'.[15]

Lolita at the Irish National Theatre

The play's possible impact on the audience as a normalizer or as a justifier of paedophiliac activities is already inherent in the original, Nabokov's *Lolita*. Although Vladimir Nabokov claimed that *Lolita* was free from any ethical judgment and had 'no moral in tow', and that the only justification of literature for existence was 'aesthetic bliss'[16], we cannot deny the enormous impact of literature on any society or the significance of literature as a prime factor in our socialization and conditioning. The images of women disseminated by literature and books have worked as a mover of conditioning and socializing of both sexes. The reception and the promulgation of those images form an important part of our daily practices of gender issues. Arbitrary ideas of woman/motherhood, role models, and culturally accepted characteristics of women are promulgated through the representation of women in the drama, the poetry, the novel, and any other form of literature, as well as in the press. The text of Nabokov's *Lolita* involves the process of literary dissemination of women's images in its constant references to other literary works. *Lolita* is, as Linda Kauffman put it, 'an exercise in intertextuality' and 'a compendium of definitions of woman' in literary texts.[17] Thus the novel and the impact of its 'aesthetic bliss', and much less the dramatization of that, cannot evade its commitment to moral moulding, in which it is determined how women should be and behave, and what they are regarded as in a given society. Once aesthetic artifacts are put in a socio-gender context, as they should be, Michael West's *Lolita* as well as the original can no longer be evaluated solely on the basis of their 'aesthetic bliss', ignoring the plight of sexually abused children. West was apparently conscious of the impasse of Nabokovian aesthetic aloofness to the reality. If that was the case, then how could he be?

In order to guard against the accusation of the play being the dramatization of the idea of the girl/child as a temptress and promulgating the image of the juvenile as an enchantress, West's and Ryan's production placed the play within careful stylistic limits. The main body of Humbert's confession is placed in the style of commedia dell'arte, an Old Italian comedy form that is famous for its deliberately ludicrous buffoonery and exorbitant farce. This stylistic mode serves as a sign of Humbert's extravagantly biased perception. However, the opening and ending sequences of West's play are performed in a more reserved and more naturalistic fashion, giving the audience the psychological distance necessary for them to observe Humbert's conduct. The very first sequence of the play lets the audience witness a murder, in which Humbert intrudes into a manor house and shoots dead a talented and popular writer, Quilty. No conversation between them, no comments from Humbert to the victim, no hints of their feelings accompany the brief sequence. The event is reported to the audience in such an impersonal and objective way that this prologue exhibits a striking contrast to the following sequence, where the actors' movements are comically stylized with puppet-like physicality, with their painted faces underscoring a sense of grotesquery. Likewise, the epilogue is given to the audience in much less slapstick fashion. Humbert meets Lolita for the first time in years and finds her making only a bare living, and now pregnant by a poor laborer after her affections were trifled with by Quilty. His painful disappointment at seeing the devastated Lolita is expressed in a reserved atmosphere and more natural style that, through its similarity in mode and mood to the prologue, allows the audience to remember the prologue and to realize that Humbert's motive for the murder lies in Quilty's infringement on the territory of Humbert's arbitrary and sexual imagination of a girl/child as a seducer. The point of the introduction of two different styles is to draw the audience's attention to the play's deliberate framing of Humber's imagination by critical distance and to reveal to the audience the fact that they have been confined within Humbert's prolonged self-deceptive illusion and his male-centred sexual dystopia.

The real voice of Lolita is wiped out within Humbert's illusion and is inaccessible to the audience. Peter Crawley argues that 'louche Lolita' in West's play is an enchanter stylized with a comic stock character.[18] But he fails to ask why Lolita is described as a stereotypically shady and obscene seducer. Likewise, Nick McGinley denounces the seductive Lolita as 'a jailbait brat'.[19] Both of them eventually miss Humbert's louche prism, through which the audience witnesses the whole events on the stage. The audience is forced to listen to a one-sided story by an untrustworthy narrator about his imagined love story, which amounts to the sexual abuse of a girl/child in disguise. Humbert believes that he is seduced by Lolita, but it is he who induces her to have sexual relations with him. As a professor of English and French literature, he develops his imaginative literary creation of his 'nymphet' day by day, and, intoxicated with his own aesthetic beautification of the girl, he eventually creates his own sexual Pygmalion, a sex slave. Lolita is an object of his literary glorification and his lust, and her subjectivity is always trampled upon by Humbert's master narrative on femininity, which muffles her real voice. The images of a young enchantress, a luring siren, and a seductive vamp on the stage are not the direct embodiment of Lolita's personality but the reflections of the lust of the middle-aged man of literature. Thus the meaning of the huge bed on the stage is turned from a seeming symbol of the love act between the girl-siren and the middle-aged enchanted man within the main body of the play (namely, Humbert's self-indulgently protracted illusion) into a close reflection of Humbert's enormous lust for the girl, an abuse which only becomes visible from the critical distance of the outer frame of the play. Likewise, Lolita's remarks about kids' play, the implication being that seduction by children of adults is developing a prevailing mode of the sexuality among children, betrays its real character as a paedophile's convenient excuse.

II. Intent Engagement of Aesthetic Constructs to Child Abuse in Ireland:

Then what is the validity of such a play as a sophisticated description of sexuality now in Ireland, especially staged in one of the National Theatres of Ireland? A most probable answer to it can be elicited from the serious engagement of the aesthetic construct by the playwright with the reality in Ireland. It is gradually becoming more common in the country to revise the Catholic community's sense of prestige and the public confidence it enjoys as to its spiritual authority and high virtues through acts of pungent satire with a hint of child sexual abuse. Aidan Mathews grasped the bitterness of the mood in the burgeoning subversive attitude in his *Communion*, which was first performed at the Peacock Theatre five months before *Lolita* was put on the same stage. In the play, a woman's observations are described as candid and relentless in evaluating and cultivating closer relations with a person of the opposite sex, especially when his associations with the clergy can be detected:

Has he been in religious life? Is he going to go to prison for that?[20]

Roddy Doyle blazed a trail for the exploration of child sex abuse from the viewpoint of the victims in cultural media. He uses more outspoken words when he exercised his sarcasm about child abuse among the priests in his novel *The Commitments,* where Jimmy Rabbitte, the protagonist, talks about a 'singin' priest' for whom Jimmy served as a choirboy:

— Did he [the priest] brown yeh, Jimmy? Outspan asked.
— No. He just ran his fingers through me curly fellas.
— Aah! Stop tha'! said Natalie.[21]

When Alan Parker inserted into the film version of *The Commitments* religious scenes, in which one boy visits a priest for mental equilibrium, Doyle was 'annoyed' and 'uncomfortable' in that he felt the bond between kids and the clergy in the film was utterly

46 Ireland on Stage: Beckett and After

misleading and that does not reflect the reality in Ireland.[22] Likewise, in his *The Woman Who Walked Into Doors,* Doyle elaborately investigated the theme of abuse, this time, physical and sexual abuse of an adult woman by her husband. The novel, which originated Doyle's TV series in 1994, *Family,* and was first published as a novel in 1996, was later adapted for the stage as a play and an opera, and since its first appearance as a teleplay, it has drawn substantial attention of the public to the fact that not a few Irish women have been physically and sexually abused even within a domestic domain.[23] In *The Woman Who Walked Into Doors,* the woman suffers from seventeen years of physical and sexual abuse, which includes miscarriage by husband's force. She names her unborn baby Sally and gives the fetus some individuality, and by so doing, she articulately chooses to start a mother and child relationship, which is smashed when the baby is 'born by a fist'.[24] Doyle meticulously describes how the male sexual abuser and practical infanticide, whose behaviour is connived at in the society, is never accused, religiously or legally. A local priest tells her that all she needs to solve problems is to say the rosary, yet, as she asserts emphatically in retrospect, she practiced what the priest preached but found that useless ('I tried it; it didn't [work]' (138)). Even when she did 'sit in the church at mass' (186) or 'go up for communion' (187) with telltale evidences of abuse all over her body, such as 'broken nose, loose teeth, cracked ribs' (187), 'broken finger', 'black eyes' (175), 'burn' on her hand and 'missing hair' (164), the clergy never see her as she is. This clerical blindness forms grotesque complicity in the abuse and in the total devastation of her life, where 'the future stopped rolling in front of me [her]' (168). In the novel, a social function of religious orders are, as Dermot McCarthy argues, reduced 'to a literally empty symbol', namely, a completely dried-up holy water font that is knocked down and smashed into pieces in the midst of Paula's determined struggle against her abuser for her independence and freedom.[25] Moreover, a parish priest regularly visits her in her husband's absence and, greedy after a chance to sexually exploit her, casts lascivious glances at her ('the looks he [the priest] gave me when he was talking about faith and the Blessed Virgin, it wasn't my tea he was after, or my biscuits' (90)). Thus not only concrete evidence of violence and rape are perfectly overlooked, but also her dire predicament is painfully prolonged and deteriorated by the spiritual authority in a society.

The social and religious connivance in physical and sexual abuse was aggressively challenged by a theatre version of *The Woman Who Walked Into Doors* in 2003, for which Roddy Doyle wrote the script jointly with Joe O'Byrne, the director for the play. The challenge was most openly displayed when the abused woman, Paula Spencer, who was persuasively embodied by Hilda Fay, was suspended in mid-air on the stage of the big hall of the Helix. Here the audience sees Paula, punch-drunk and nearly brain dead, being raped again and again while her body is hanging from the flies of the theatre as if she were a fluttering flag to be put up. This deliberately provocative spectacle is a graphic representation of her vertigo after years of abuse and, at the same time, it can be read as the director's negation of unfamiliarity of abuse in Ireland. The sequence strongly suggests that sexual and physical abuse cannot be an as-yet-unrecognized factor in the state but has always been there just like an eye-catching flag hoisted high in the air, and that the Irish audience must have already known or witnessed the presence of sexual and physical abuse in their everyday life. This was the moment when the play displayed its direct confrontation with the Irish society. Through its gesture to intervene into the reality by advancing a warning, the sequence charges that the audience at the theatre, which consists of Irish citizens just as the clergy in the play, may have connived at and, therefore, practically formed complicity in sexual and physical abuse of women in Ireland.

Just as Roddy Doyle, Peter Mullan bluntly and unflinchingly depicted in his film *The Magdalene Sisters* the clergy's direct and/or complicit involvement in sexual and physical abuse.[26] Most of the film, which is in the director's phrase, 'a fictional film that unfortunately happens to be true',[27] has been regarded by ex-inmates as 'accurate' while some admitted that 'the reality was even worse',[28] and the film served as a breaker of the 'shamed silence' into which the victims of abuse in church-run institutions were forced from the fear that their local communities would accuse them, not their abusers, of being shameful sinners.[29] One of the film's blistering sequences involving a girl inmate describes how a locally acclaimed priest secretly forced the girl who is under the protective custody of a church-run institution into sexual relations with him. She is forced by the priest to give him oral sex immediately before she receives a piece of consecrated wafer at a Mass from the same priest on the tongue that must have just received his spermatic fluid as well. The sequence makes the abuser's assumption explicit to the audience by underscoring that the sexual contact is, from the viewpoint of the priest, divine favour secretly and intimately given from the religious order to the girl. Yet, there is a more blistering sequence to come at the end of the film when Mullan's camera sweeps, turning the audience's attention from a doctor and a visitor to a hospital isolation ward, and focuses on the abused girl, now an isolated patient. The audience clearly hears gross gaggling sounds from her when she, apparently insane, sticks her finger down her throat, then sees a caption stating that 'Crispina, real name Harriet, died of anorexia in 1971' and that 'she was 24 years old.' The implication of her anorexia nervosa is quite clear: after years of physical, psychological, and sexual abuse by the clergy and now trapped in mental trauma and seized with delirium, she still tries to cancel what she had to receive from the priest. Here her delirium can be seen as her struggle for a different way of being from that which she was forced to take within the church-run institution. Her abused mind makes a desperate homeward journey from the clergy-imposed false identity, Crispina, to her real self, Harriet, who is ironically confined within the walls as a lunatic. Here she is a psychological deviant from a socially accepted normality, just as in a Magdalene asylum as a sinner she was an ethical and religious deviant from socially accepted morals. The Roman Curia attacked the film and exercised pressure upon the potential audience, but eventually the Vatican's criticisms of the film created, as the director put it, 'some wonderful publicity' for the film.[30] It is possible that the potential audience sensed in the propaganda against the film the church's evasion of responsibility for child abuse within church-run institutions.

In reality, allegations and legal actions by the victims of abuse in Ireland are by degrees revealing that the clergy in its churches and in church-run institutions in Ireland, contradictory to their public principles as spiritual guides to traditional values, have sexually, physically, and emotionally abused children, girls and boys, younger and elder. The RTÉ documentary series, *States of Fear*, first broadcast in 1999, uncovered the hidden history of child abuse in institutions in Ireland and absorbed public attention. In the aftermath of the immense nationwide sensation it generated, An Taoiseach Bertie Ahern expressed an official apology to the victims of child abuse. The Laffoy Commission on Child Abuse has been established in order to hold a formal inquiry into the matter, and it has paved the way for official financial compensation to those who suffered abuse as children.[31] Humanitarian aid has been offered by official institutions or nonprofit corporations such as the Rape Crisis Centre and the National Counseling Service. It causes probably no wonder to the Irish audience that this grotesque issue is reflected in today's drama at the National Theatre in productions like *Communion* and *Lolita*. The spiritual crisis in the clergy means a spiritual crisis in the state. The close bond between the state and the clergy, which have long served as dominant regulators of social discourse and activities of the Irish people, and which have been, as Tom Inglis tersely put it, 'major power blocs', is now severely undermined.[32]

In Michael West's theatre version of *Lolita,* just as in the performance of *Communion* and *Bailegangaire,* the huge bed at the stage centre served as a symbol of investigation into female subjectivity. Yet in West's play, the investigation was given a serious twist in that it was not attended by the recovery of female dignity, but rather accompanied by a loss of that dignity. A 'nymphet' is deprived of her virginity by a college literature professor 'Humbert Humbert', who enjoys public confidence and a high cachet in society as a learned authority, although the process of the sexual abuse is disguised as a result of the female initiative. In this respect, the colossal bed on the stage is an area on which an image of a female initiative and another image of gross violation, that is act of sex between the middle-aged man and the girl/child, are superimposed. In *Lolita,* West gave a subtle treatment of the issue of spiritual damage done to a child by sexual abuse, which forms a close reflection of the reality in Ireland. The play essentially implies that a large number of Irish children have suffered similar experiences of abuse and misrepresentation of their sexuality as Lolita. What makes the issue of male empathetic participation in female experiences more complicated in Michael West's *Lolita* than in the other cultural productions discussed so far is the fact that the playwright heavily invested his play with incredibly erotic suggestion of a girl/child from a biased viewpoint of a paedophile, and then he urged the audience to question the validation of the male sexual fantasy.

Cast in the Irish context of child sexual abuse and caricatured in the style of commedia dell'arte, the theatre performance of *Lolita,* which emphasizes the literary glorification of Lolita by the expert of English and French literature, can be read as a general criticism of delusional literary beautification of women. Through its deliberate theatricality, the play underscores the fact that what the audience witnesses on the stage are dramatically constructed images, deliberately constructed within the framework of Humbert's self-deceptive imagination, not a reproduction of a natural reality in Ireland. By so doing, the play alludes to the possibility of our deceitful daily performances of such beautification of women, and questions the authority of conveniently glorified female images that can smother real female voices. As a mode of theatricality, the style adopted for *Lolita* germinated in 1988, when an American play *Alakazam! After the Dog Wars* was put on the stage in Los Angeles in a modernized fashion of commedia dell'arte.[33] The vast potential of the style for today's theatre which Annie Ryan keenly grasped was materialized by the playwright Michael West in *Lolita,* which was put on the stage in the Peacock Theatre by the team of Ryan and West. The most significant reason for the existence of commedia dell'arte consists, according to Ryan, in its nature as an 'improvisational theatre which brutally exposes the human condition using stock characters and cheap gags'.[34] Worthy of her own definition, her *Lolita* unflinchingly exposed some of women's conditions, their forfeiture of real voice and loss of subjectivity. Just as the Perpetually Pregnant Lady in *Alakazam! After the Dog Wars*, who finally is delivered of a television set and caricatures the cruel conditioning and socialization of woman/motherhood by the media, the *Lolita* in the style of commedia dell'arte brings to the public eye the gross images of a seductive nymphet created by Humbert's literary imaginations, and attacks them, using absurd gags and extravagant caricature, often accompanied by grotesquely stylized expressions of Lolita's spleen and discontent on the stage.

The commedia dell'arte in the past and in its counterparts today, in essence, 'represent[s] a recoil from our society's dominant respectable values, and attack[s] them' in their nonserious attitudes, which are 'defiantly frivolous or sullenly crude.'[35] In this sense, the commedia dell'arte is potentially subversive of social, religious, and cultural mores. The defiant frivolousness of the style in the theatre performance of *Lolita*, with its nonchalant attitudes, destroys the validity of what evolves in Humbert's mind as his excuse for his seduction of the girl/child by underscoring the speciousness of that excuse and the distortions of what the audience is forced to see through the distorted prism of Humbert's desire. The sense of distance that the style consequently created is based upon a seriousness disguised as nonseriousness and a feigned flinch from reality, which unflinchingly attacks the delusively aesthetic fantasy of the male seducer. The dramatization of Nabokov's *Lolita* still remains within the field of aesthetic constructs, and therefore, West's play is directly subversive and forms a literary counterblast to an aesthetic imagination that could easily be exploited by men of public confidence as an excuse for a concept of children as potential seducers.

Conclusion:

Theatre productions in Ireland have significant potential to provide the audience with unflinching comments and criticisms on particular issues of power abuse. They often demonstrate their keen sense of engagement with the situation of the state, and, just as this paper has tried to display, it is not rare for them to commit themselves, among other themes, to the revision of the status of woman/motherhood in Ireland. Michael West's *Lolita* urges the audience to challenge constructed images of a girl/child as a seducer and to face child abuse in the country.

The theatrical world in Ireland often intervenes in social, religious, cultural mores that have worked as repressive powers upon the audience and repeatedly provides the audience with suggestive mapping of a future, into which the theatre performances guide the audience. It is not rare for the theatre to create a new container of the future and to induce the audience to fill it. In that sense, theatre productions in contemporary Irish society have metaphorical functions as portraits of the society in the future. This is because, as Declan Kiberd puts it, 'in a culture where expression often precedes conceptualization, form will determine eventual content.'[36] Social, religious, and cultural mores are characterized by our everyday practices, and by those constant practices, they are continuously maintained, daily reinforced, and brought up to date in the community unless a new form of seeing things negates it. In this paper, I investigated how contemporary Irish theatre challenges these mores in the context of sexual abuse, smothered female voice, and the patriarchal culture and structure of the society that sanction these, which, as we have seen, have serious connections with the issues of abortion, illegitimacy, adoption, domestic violence, and the emotional, psychological, and physical plight of women and their lost female dignity that result. My focus has been upon how theatre performances have submitted anticipatory visions of achievement in the empowerment of women and of all the victims of patriarchy yet to be accomplished.

Dramatic productions are not so much the produced as the producer, that is, constant producers of new visions of Irish society. With those new visions, staged plays induce the audience to revise social, religious, cultural mores and long established values in new contexts. In that sense, we may say that the theatre's function is to anticipate self-portraits of the future society, whose visions are disseminated through performances and are expected to be accomplished in the everyday life of the audience.

---

[1]*Communion* opened at the Peacock Theatre on 25 April 2002.

[2]*Bailegangaire*, directed by Tom Murphy, was staged at the Peacock Theatre from 26 September to 8 October 2001. The production was brought back to the theatre by 'popular demand' and staged from 12 June to 20 July 2002.

[3]*Lolita*, adapted by Michael West and directed by Annie Ryan, opened at the Peacock Theatre on 3 September 2002. The production eventually enabled Clara Simpson, who played the role of Charlotte, to win an Irish Theatre Award 2002 as Best Supporting Actress.

[4]Anthony Roche, *Contemporary Irish Drama: from Beckett to McGuinness* (Dublin: Gill & Macmillan, 1994): 161.

[5]*The Irish Times* 6 September 2002.

[6]Stanley Kublick's film *Lolita* in 1962 was nominated for the Academy Award for the best adapted screenplay, and won the Golden Globe Award for the best promising newcomer (Sue Lyon). The film also grossed about 3.7 million dollars only in America. See John Baxter, *Stanley Kubrick: A Biography* (London: Harper Collins Publishers, 1998): 169.

[7]Vladimir Nabokov, *Lolita: a Screenplay* (New York: Vintage International, 1997): 108.

[8]Ibid., 110.

[9]Ibid., 111.

[10]*Lolita*, dir., Stanley Kubrick, MGM, 1962.

[11]Michael West, *Lolita*, 23. All the quotations are from an unpublished script of *Lolita* by Michael West. Page numbers may be different when it is published.

[12]See note 5.

[13]For example, sexual abuse scandals by members of the clergy recently caused its members to be described by the victims as 'a paedophile ring' in the Archdiocese of Dublin. Their administration is reported to face 450 legal actions as a significant result of clerical child sex abuse allegations. See *Cardinal Secrets: Prime Time*, RTÉ 1, 17 October 2002. See also *The Irish Times* 19 October 2002.

[14]See Notes 5 and 12.

[15]Vladimir Nabokov, *Lolita* (London: Penguin Books, Ltd., 2000): 312.

[16]Nabokov, 314.

[17]Linda Kauffman, 'Framing Lolita: Is There a Woman in the Text?' *Refiguring the Father: New Feminist Readings of Patriarchy*, eds Patricia Yaeger and Beth Kowaleski-Wallace (Carbondale and Edwardsville: Southern Illinois University Press, 1989): 138.

[18]Peter Crawley. '*Lolita* adapted from Vladimir Nabokov's screenplay by Michael West', *Irish Theatre Magazine* 2.13 (2002): 107.

[19]Nick McGinley, '*Lolita*', RTÉ Entertainment, 5 September 2002. <http://www.rte.ie/arts/2002/0905/lolita.html>

[20]Aidan Mathews, *Communion* (London: Nick Hern Books, 2002): 12.

[21]Roddy Doyle, *The Commitments* (London: Vintage, 1998): 79. *The Commitments* was first published by William Heinemann, Ltd., in 1988 and filmed in 1991 (Dir. Alan Parker. Beacon Communication Corporation).

[22]Caramine White, *Reading Roddy Doyle* (New York: Syracuse, 2001): 34.

[23]*The Woman Who Walked into Doors* was first published in 1996 (London: Jonathan Cape). The novel was adapted for the stage by Roddy Doyle and Joe O'Byrne and directed by Joe O'Byrne, and the play opened at the Helix on 1 May 2003. The original novel was also adapted for an opera, directed by Guy Cassiers and composed by Kris Defoort, and the opera was staged at the Gaiety Theatre on 9 October 2003. The novel has a close affinity to and grew out of BBC TV series, *Family*, for which Roddy Doyle wrote the

script in 1994. Doyle has recently published *Paula Spencer*, the sequel to *The Woman Who Walked into Doors* (London: Jonathan Cape, 2006).

[24]Roddy Doyle, *The Woman Who Walked Into Doors* (Middlesex: Penguin, 1997): 203. Future references to this edition will be incorporated in the text.

[25]Dermot McCarthy, *Roddy Doyle: Raining on the Parade* (Dublin: The Liffey Press, 2003): 181-82.

[26]*The Magdalene Sisters*, dir., Peter Mullan, Scottish Screen, The Film Council, and The Irish Film Board, 2002.

[27]*The Irish Times* 31 August 2002.

[28]*The Irish Times* 5 October 2002.

[29]The term is Mary Gordon's. See *New York Times* 3 August 2003.

[30]*The Irish Times* 7 October 2002.

[31]The Laffoy Commission was set up by the Government in 1999 for the purpose of comprehensive investigations of allegations of child abuse. Since the commission started to invite ex-residents of religious-run institutions, who 'consider that their experience of life in the institution was positive', the commission had been criticized by the victims of abuse for making 'appeasement to the religious' threats to stifle and stagnate the commission. In a disarray of delays, uncertainties, legal challenge by the Christian Brothers, and 'an adversarial, defensive and legalistic approach' of the religious orders, Ms Justice Mary Laffoy eventually resigned in September 2003, and the commission got stuck. Her position was taken over by Mr Seán Ryan SC and it is expected that the commission will complete its investigation into nearly 5,000 compensation claims for sexual abuse in religious and State-run institutions. The process of the investigation by the commission has displayed that it is extremely difficult to get hold of the reality of such a complicated and sensitive issue in Ireland. See *The Irish Times* 5 February 2000; 18 and 25 February 2003; 10 March 2003; 3, 4, 5, 6, 8, 27 September 2003; 4 October 2004.

[32]Tom Inglis, *Moral Monopoly: the Rise and Fall of the Catholic Church in Modern Ireland*, 2nd ed. (Dublin: University College Dublin Press, 1998): 77-82.

[33]For the influence of this play, co-written by Tim Robbins, on Annie Ryan's and Michael West's theatre company, see their official web-site of the Corn Exchange Theatre Co.: <www.cornexchange.ie>

[34]Annie Ryan, the director's note in the theatre programme for *Lolita* (Dublin: the Peacock Theatre, 2002).

[35]Martin Green and John Swan, *The Triumph of Pierrot: The commedia dell'arte and the Modern Imagination* (New York: Macmillan, 1986): xv-xvi.

[36]Declan Kiberd, *Inventing Ireland* (London: Vintage, 1996): 301.

4 | Taking a Position: Beckett, Mary Manning, and *Eleutheria* (1947)

Christopher Murray

I

In any survey of twentieth-century Irish drama Beckett has his place whether central or peripheral. To situate Beckett within this history is not easy. Strictly speaking, because of his indifference to the Abbey and its nationalist project, Beckett has little to do with mainstream Irish drama. He chose not to write of Irish subjects or for Irish theatres, although the radio play *All That Fall* (1957) must always be regarded as something of an exception, even though it was written for the British Broadcasting Company. Arguments that Beckett was crypto-Irish in his stage plays remain unconvincing.[1] The notion of an 'Irish Beckett' is destined to remain 'a borderline instance'.[2] On the other hand Beckett has had much to do with the history of Irish theatre, notably of alternative or avant-garde Irish theatre in the mid-century, notably the Pike Theatre, founded by Alan Simpson and Carolyn Swift, which premiered *Waiting for Godot* in Dublin in 1955.[3] After that date the history of Beckett production in the Irish theatre is a reasonably full one.[4] There was even an English-language premiere at the Abbey, admittedly of a short piece, the 'dramaticule' *Come and Go*, and admittedly in the Abbey's annex, the Peacock, in 1968. Further, Beckett's influence on later twentieth-century drama is considerable, from Brian Friel's *Faith Healer* (1979), through Tom Murphy's *Bailegangaire* (1985) and Frank McGuinness's *Baglady* (1985), to the early work of Marina Carr and the plentiful use of the monologue form in the 1990s by Conor McPherson and Mark O'Rowe.[5]

56 Ireland on Stage: Beckett and After

In this essay I shall leave aside the essentialist issue of Beckett's Irishness in order to explore the unstaged play published after his death, *Eleutheria*.[6] As is well known, this was one of two plays Beckett's partner Suzanne hawked all around Paris in 1952 in search of an enterprising theatre director. Had she encountered someone other than Roger Blin, who can say how different the history of the second half of the twentieth-century drama might have been? We can comfortably accept that the right choice was made and that the world was enriched by the lucky chance of Blin's having a slot into which to insert *Waiting for Godot* at the Théâtre de Babylone in 1953. Nevertheless, its companion, its poor relation, deserves attention now that we have the text, for its concerns are quite different from its famous 'other'. Moreover, the argument of this article is that in *Eleutheria* one finds Beckett taking up an aesthetic position which paves the way for the proper reception of Beckett's plays from *Godot*. The publication of *Eleutheria* allows us to understand more clearly that in turning from fiction to drama after World War II Beckett was returning for his subject matter to crises in his early life as an artist.

In order to do so Beckett had to face certain ghosts from the past, if it is not too melodramatic to put the matter thus. This backward glance took him back also to the fragmented Dublin world he had attempted, with no great success, to chart in the volume of short stories *More Pricks Than Kicks* (1934) and in the impossible *Dream of Fair to middling Women*, another text also to remain unpublished until after his death. But the play was to put the juvenile Beckett into perspective. For *Eleutheria* wrestles with the father-son relationship and the necessity for the son as artist to shake off the pressures and the guilt induced by middle-class society, and spares us the Bohemian low-jinks of the early fiction. In returning to the details of his own traumatic life in Dublin in the early 1930s, it will be argued, Beckett confronted images of himself in a play by long-time friend Mary Manning to which he had himself contributed a key character. This was *Youth's the Season ... ?* (1931), an all but forgotten tragicomedy which in part deals with the problems of a despairing writer. In a sense rewriting Manning's play in *Eleutheria*, Beckett not only came to terms with his earlier self and his nihilism but also was enabled to assume a new position for the post-war dramatist and, as the saying goes, move on.

Although *Eleutheria* belongs to the post-war period its roots go back to Beckett's early visits to Paris in 1928-30 and his subsequent life in Dublin. The play portrays the artist-as-hero, or more accurately as anti-hero, Victor Krap, in his attempts to break away from a domineering bourgeois family. The parallel with Beckett's own family situation *c.* 1930 is inescapable. Back from Paris to take up a lectureship at Trinity College, Dublin, Beckett was already a published writer, and his short study on Marcel Proust would be published in March 1931. But he brought back to Dublin also such a collection of neuroses and such a 'scrofulous' appearance[7] that he wrote to a friend: 'This life is terrible and I don't understand how it can be endured.'[8] After a fierce row with his mother Beckett left the family home in Foxrock and settled into a depressive lifestyle in rooms in Trinity. He grew withdrawn, dishevelled, and spoke of suicide.[9] The neglect of his appearance, at least, did not go unnoticed:

> When Beckett did venture forth the state of his clothes and general appearance caused comment—in college, in Cooldrinagh [the family home] and among his acquaintance generally. His usual garb was a grey shirt, grey Aran sweater and a pair of grey flannel pants. Both the sweater and trousers showed plentiful traces of food, drink and other matter. On top of these he wore a belted trenchcoat which was also in need of cleaning and sometimes his black beret. His shoes too were permanently dirty and in need of repair. It was all a far cry from the bowler-hatted young man his mother would like to have seen.[10]

In *Eleutheria*, by comparison, one finds this passage:

> **Mlle Skunk:** Yes. The critics said he would make a name for himself.
> **Glazier:** Someone must have played a dirty trick on him.
> **Dr Piouk:** Right. He used to write. He doesn't write any more. He used to associate with his family normally. He has left them and doesn't want to see them any more ... (*E* 104).

The central experience in *Eleutheria* is the death of Victor's father, which briefly coaxes Victor out of his bunker but leaves him with an overwhelming sense of failure. This event has reference to the death of Beckett's own father in June 1933. It was a momentous experience, which complicated Beckett's already complex psychological situation. In Act III of *Eleutheria*, Victor, having returned from seeing his father's corpse, has a disturbed dream in which his father tries to persuade him to venture from a diving board into the sea. The fact that Beckett was still drawing on this actual experience when he wrote his autobiographical novella *Company* in 1980 indicates what an important memory it was; its prior appearance in *Eleutheria* shows how closely that play probed his personal history. Six months after his father's death Beckett left Dublin for London, where he underwent extended psychotherapy and where his first fictional work, *More Pricks Than Kicks*, which is a thinly disguised record of Beckett's bohemian life in Dublin, was published in 1934. Under the influence of Joyce, Beckett transformed personal experience into fiction, although in his case the exercise was considerably less controlled at this juncture and was likely to include characters and confidences too close to actuality not to be either embarrassing or simply insufficiently transmuted into the stuff of art. *Eleutheria* dates from a later period, after Beckett had completed the trilogy (*Molloy, Malone Dies*, and *The Unnamable*), when Beckett had learned a far greater degree of control over his material. It provides a confrontation with extremely difficult psychic experience, and an exorcism of much pain which had its basis in family discord. It is a Janus text: it bids farewell to a traumatic period in Beckett's life while it heralds a whole new artistic stance which was to lead, in fact, to the sort of creative confessionalism which distinguishes Beckett's later prose style, and to the cool experimentalism which distinguishes his dramatic form.

If it can be accepted, then, that *Eleutheria* is a condensed, abstracted, and indeed surrealistic version of Beckett's own early history as artist, the events of his Dublin life after 1930 take on special significance for the Beckett scholar. The play explores artistic choice, ennui, the role of the hero, the possibility of suicide, and, circumscribing all these issues, the theme of freedom (=*eleutheria*). In exploring a text of this kind, rooted in specifics yet formally abstract, it is useful to look to the cultural ethos of the period of its psychic origins. Often another text reveals itself as the key one, genetic of the creative pattern which is recreated by the subsequent text. Often, again, the primary, inspirational text is received as an irritant, something to be mocked or satirized, but is simultaneously recharged and reshaped into an entirely different form, infused by a radically different spirit, style, and feeling. Indeed, one might go further and claim that the birth of style derives from such a simultaneous irritation and revision. But Beckett's case is rather more complex. One sees him in the 1930s reworking Dante, to be sure, imitating Joyce, and paying homage to Proust, but he is slow to cast off, slow to anger in the way that many original writers (Marlowe, Cervantes, Fielding, Austen, Emily Dickinson) turn upon their predecessors and strike out on their own, the 'anxiety of influence' fruitfully assuaged. Avant-garde though his literary interests were, Beckett was actually a conservative writer. Thus it is worth looking about for the occasion when one might spot him as it were collaborating with another talent which he would in time make use of to define his own, individual dramatic style. In his book on Shakespeare, Ted Hughes argued that in a writer's oeuvre there are 'inexplicable yet apparently necessary regressions'. He explains in some detail, and as the idea is important here I quote at length:

Almost every *developing artist* (as distinct from those artists whose work shows no marked development) occasionally produces a work that they recognize as being 'out of phase'—an outrider from some future stage of the inner development. The problem then is to bring the whole level of production up to that point... . Some artists release nothing but works that express these stages of newness. But most artists produce for a while within a mode, then move more or less suddenly to a new mode which is the next stage of a development: and so on. It is among this second group that 'out of phase' works are most recognizable. But even among the other group artists sometimes produce a work, or some part of a work, from so far ahead that it sticks out plainly in any survey of their whole oeuvre. In other words, in all artists there are two parallel sequences... . The outer chronological sequence is the one in which the artist actually finishes the works, while the other goes on at a psychic depth beyond any significant interference from the artist's will or conscious craftsmanship, and could be called the organically alive, as-if-biological development of the Muse's creative process [italics in original].[11]

In this regard, the transitional, out-of-phase work in Beckett's oeuvre would appear to be *Eleutheria*, which has no fellow and yet looks forward to the perfectly balanced works which were to follow upon its awkwardness.

It may well be that the key to *Eleutheria* is a forgotten play teasingly entitled *Youth's the Season ...?*, which had its premiere performance at the Gate Theatre in Dublin on 8 December 1931, was revived and revised one year later and was published in 1936.[12] Feminist critics might well complain that Mary Manning's play has been neglected simply because the author was a woman. But from the first it created unease. At the time of the premiere the reviewer for the *Irish Times* was shocked by the blatant exposure of Dublin's middle-class disillusioned youth. Describing this set of 'selfish neurotics', the reviewer maintained that 'a more unpleasant collection of people has rarely been gathered within the three acts of a single play'. Yet the reviewer had to admit that the play was very amusing and entertaining. It was the shock of this new generation which proved dismaying: 'Noel Coward has done it all for London ... but Miss Manning can be congratulated for having the courage to be a Coward in Dublin.' Indeed, rather inconsistently the reviewer then concludes with high praise: 'the play is finely written, with many telling lines. It has a light wit that should make it acceptable elsewhere, but probably nowhere else but in Dublin will its loving cruelty be fully appreciated.'[13] The phrase 'loving cruelty' is the key one in the whole review. It sums up Mary Manning's dramatic style. It explains why Samuel Beckett was sufficiently interested to help her with the play.

The matter of Beckett's involvement with Manning's play has been strangely handled. James Knowlson, Beckett's definitive biographer, ignores the text completely. Deirdre Bair, by wrongly dating the production in 1936, gives a wholly misleading context to Beckett's involvement and offers a distorted account of both play and production.[14] In his biography published in 1996 Anthony Cronin follows Bair and further distorts the context.[15] Curtis Canfield, when including *Youth's the Season ... ?* in his representative anthology of Irish plays, significantly described Manning's play as 'unique in being the only Irish play concerned with Dublin high life'.[16] Yet Canfield wrongly dates the revival of *Youth's the Season ... ?*, on which his text is based, as December 1933, for 1932.[17] It is time to put these matters right and to give Mary Manning her due place in orientating Beckett as dramatist.

II

Just three months younger than Beckett, Mary Manning was born in Sandymount, Dublin, on 30 June 1906. She was descended 'of an Anglo-Irish family with remarkable people on both sides'.[18] In the close-knit community of middle-class Dublin Protestants at this time, her mother Susan Manning and Beckett's mother May became friends, and the two families seem to have been quite close. In one of her plays Manning introduced young 'Sam' into Act I, set in the drawing room of a piano teacher in suburban Dublin. In reality, as Knowlson documents, the young Beckett attended a small kindergarten run by two German-born sisters, the Misses Elsner, who also taught music.[19] Whether Manning attended the same kindergarten is not clear, but she did attend the same girls' school as Beckett's cousins who lived with him, Molly and Sheila Roe: Miss Wade's, which is referred to in Beckett's 'dramaticule' *Come and Go*, written in 1965. In any case, in *Outlook Unsettled* Sam appears for his piano lesson in the company of two girls, one of whom (Tina) is based on Manning herself. She depicts Sam as an obnoxious, precocious child and manoeuvres the scene (set against the war of independence in 1920) towards the punch line where the piano teacher, Miss Beatrice Hepworth, unperturbed by a nationalist explosion offstage, issues the parodic command: 'play it again, Sam'. In Act Two, set five years later on the stage of the Abbey Theatre, the young girls are training to be actresses under Sara Allgood, as Manning briefly did. In one of the many intervals when

Allgood absents herself from the class the following exchange takes place among the pupils:

> **Tina:** [the Manning character] You play the piano awfully well Michael. I am hopeless. Fingers like sausages. Do you remember the Miss Hepworths, Maisie, in Seapoint?
> **Maisie:** I'm trying to concentrate. (*She lays out the* [playing] *cards*) Yes, one of them had a cavalry moustache. The kind you twirl.
> **Tina:** Two of them died since. There's one left—Miss Beatrice. She lives alone—Mummy brings her down little treats sometimes, so does Sam's Mother. Do you remember Sam?
> **Maisie:** A dreadful boy. So good at everything. Is he still winning?
> **Tina:** I don't know; he's at boarding school.
> **Michael:** Good at everything? I know the type; he'll be found hanging, someday![20]

The reference here to potential suicide is highly instructive, as will appear below.

Whether or not Anthony Cronin is correct when he claims that Beckett and Manning 'had a relationship ... which was all but an affair',[21] they were sufficiently friendly in 1931 for Beckett to be, in Manning's own term, 'script advisor' to *Youth's the Season ... ?*.[22] Subsequently, after Beckett left Dublin for good, she became one of his most important correspondents, even after her move to Boston in 1936 where she married and settled. Manning returned to Dublin about 1970, when she gained a reputation as a theatre reviewer of sometimes libellous impatience. But she had never been other than wittily outspoken. As drama critic for the *Irish Independent* in 1930 she roused the anger of Hilton Edwards who called her to the Gate Theatre and told her he would 'like to take a whip and lash you across the shoulders!' Though duly terrified (for here was a naked image of the patriarchy at the time), Manning yet managed to get Edwards to agree to accept her play, direct it, and have his partner Micheál Mac Liammóir star in it as the patently homosexual son Desmond Millington.[23] Manning became a prominent member of the Gate establishment in the early 1930s, and edited the house magazine *Motley*, for which she herself wrote startlingly modern film reviews.[24]

Youth's the Season ... ?, set in a rather upper-middle-class Dublin household (which has, besides servants before whom one must speak French if confidences are to be preserved, a library *and* a studio), is a sophisticated exploration of the social life of bright, bored young people in revolt against the standards and ambitions of their parents. It is very much the milieu of *Dream of Fair to middling Women*. There are two themes, at least, which Beckett was later to combine in *Eleutheria*. One was the conflict between son and father over the question whether Desmond Millington will join the family business (the 'firm') and settle into respectability or leave for London and the life of an artist. In the end Desmond loses, and resigns himself to the trappings of life as his father's successor, 'a bowler hat, and an umbrella' (*Y* 404). The twenty-first birthday party Desmond holds in the family home in Act II is the catalyst for the whole play: it not only infuriates his father because of its riotous nature but also has a major influence on the two love affairs which give the play its main interest. This son-father theme, so important in *Eleutheria*, is combined with another: the *poète maudit*. One of the romantic affairs in Manning's play is between Desmond's sister Connie and a decadent poet (whom she eventually rejects in favour of Harry, a hearty colonial type, or 'Empire Builder' as he is called, home on leave from Kenya). The poet, Terence Killigrew, is described as 'that incorrigible waster ... who's never done anything in his life but scribble a few imitative bits of poetry and consume an inordinate quantity of alcohol' (*Y* 327). Desmond calls him 'one of the many minor poets, whose names are writ in whiskey' (*Y* 383). This witticism, typical of Manning's epigrammatic style, inverts the famous epitaph on the grave of John Keats in Rome: 'Here lies one whose name is writ in water.' But Terence Killigrew, like Beckett, is not just a minor poet. On his first entrance he describes himself as writing a novel and 'playing with the thought of suicide', but confesses: 'I've no faith, no capacity for work, no purpose, and to be born without continuity of purpose is to be born under a sentence of death. I am foredoomed to failure.' (*Youth the Season ... ?*, 331-32) In short, Killigrew is a serious psychological case. Played by the dramatist Denis Johnston (who also directed the play), the character gave expression to a contemporary, Anglo-Irish ennui then part of Johnston's own dramaturgy, exemplified by the world-weary Dobelle in his *The Moon in the Yellow River* at the Abbey earlier that year (1931). Beckett clearly took an interest in this world-weary type in Manning's version of it and suggested a companion for Killigrew in the text.

Killigrew is accompanied everywhere by Horace Egosmith, a silent, rather menacing figure who is described as his *Doppelgänger*: 'Egosmith is Terence [Killigrew]. Terence is Egosmith; the two in one, Dr. Jekyll and Mr. Hyde; and it's war to the death between them.' (*Youth the Season ... ?*, 395) An expressionist device, Egosmith serves as an emblem of Killigrew's self-absorption. Further, since Egosmith, especially at the wonderfully observed birthday party in Act II, acts as a sounding board for all of the young people's confidences, he has the effect of a classical confidant, rather like the butler Jacques in *Eleutheria* (who cannot remember a word the hero Victor apparently

Taking a Position 63

uttered in the offstage revelation after the death of Victor's father). This parodic device may have been the sum total of Beckett's contribution to Manning's play. She was not exactly the type to seek out a collaborator, and Mac Liammóir, whose acting in *Youth's the Season ... ?* was praised as 'the best thing he has yet done',[25] makes no mention of Beckett or any collaborator when he refers to the play in his autobiography.[26] On the contrary, Manning may well have been providing something of a parody of Beckett himself in the character of Killigrew. She and Beckett were obviously able to satirize each other without offence. The corollary is the rather vicious sketch of Manning in Beckett's story 'A Wet Night' written shortly after the play and possibly included as a kind of revenge. In the story, a suburban party is held in the Frica's house. The Frica, according to Knowlson, is Mary Manning.[27] In the story Belacqua arrives at the Frica's house drenched to the skin. 'There was no nonsense about the Frica. When she meant skin she said skin. "Every stitch" she gloated "must come off at once, this very instant."'[28] She is described as having bursting eyes, protruding teeth, and a bristling lip 'writhing up and away in a kind of a duck or a cobra sneer to the quivering snout.'[29] Knowlson says Manning did not for long take offence at this portrait.[30] (Beckett has a very similar scene in *Dream of Fair to middling Women*, where Frica is also called Mary.[31]) This can only be because in the next breath Beckett had the good taste to mock himself by echoing Manning's portrait of him as Killigrew. In *Youth's the Season ... ?* Killigrew causes a major row at the party and is disgraced. The next afternoon he reappears, '*soaked to the skin, almost unrecognisable, haggard and wild-eyed*' (*Y* 400). Belacqua's appearance at and expulsion from the party at the Frica's house is thus a compression of two distinct scenes in Manning's play.

But there is more. When he reappears in Act Three, as aforesaid, soaking wet 'to the skin', Killigrew has got rid of Egosmith. In triumph he describes his liberation. The night before, after his expulsion from the party, he went down to the sea at Sandycove, the famous Forty-Foot recalled in Victor Krap's dream of his father in *Eleutheria*, and experienced something resembling what that other Krapp describes in *Krapp's Last Tape*, 'the vision at last'.[32] Killigrew says:

> You think I'm mad. I can see you both think I'm mad. I have moments of insanity that are the very breath of life to me. Last night I was mad—down there alone with those melancholy waves, those eternal rocks, eternal pain—something did snap in my brain. Suddenly I felt light as air... . I realized it was finished. Egosmith had left me—I was free. Oh, how could I ever explain to you the boundless depths of my freedom! (*Y* 402)

So there it is: *eleutheria*, freedom. The Beckett scholar might even be tempted to add: eureka!

However, Manning's scene is not over. Once having declared himself free Killigrew spectacularly kills himself in the drawing room of this upper-middle-class and ultra respectable Dublin house. But before he shoots himself Killigrew announces his fixed opposition to any form of hope: 'I can no longer endure the habit of hoping. It's only a habit, you know.' (*Y* 402) The phrase is Beckettian. In *Proust* (1931) Beckett defines habit as 'a compromise effected between the individual and his environment ... the ballast that chains the dog to his vomit. Breathing is habit. Life is habit.'[33] In *Youth's the Season* ... ? Killigrew earlier accused himself of being 'mentally constipated' from 'too much Proust. Too much Joyce'. (*Y* 366) This was Manning poking fun at Beckett, whom she had doubtless heard expounding his TCD thesis on Proust. But in the later, deadly serious passage in Act Three just quoted Killigrew has awoken to life's futility. He goes on: 'I am a void. There is no desire in me, no desire for anything but death.' (*Y* 403) Freedom for him is breaking the habit and illusion of living.

What, then, did Beckett make of the 'cracked looking glass'[34]—in an expensive gilded frame in this instance—which was Manning's well-made play? I would propose that Beckett resolutely opposed Killigrew's philosophy when he came to write *Eleutheria*; indeed, that the portrait of Victor Krap is something of a riposte. It is fair to say that, having supplied the *Doppelgänger* in *Youth's the Season* ... ?, Beckett accepted Killigrew as a self-portrait and then got his revenge in 'A Wet Night'. He and Manning remained friends. They had a good deal in common, including caustic wit and a detestation of sentimentality, but Manning was more buoyant and had none of Beckett's depressive tendencies. He had, perhaps, to struggle hard to make *Eleutheria* come out as positively as it does. In spite of Ted Hughes's theory (above), the working through of this transitional play looks more like a willed exercise than a subconscious reaching after future skills, a determined effort to confront an older version of the artist himself, be that in his memory or in the hard-hitting portrait by a friend who wished him well. When he came to write his first full-length play, then, Beckett returned to the picture of revolt and hopelessness raised within Manning's *Youth's the Season* ... ? (querying the words of the song 'Youth's the Season Made for Joy' and subtitled, as *Waiting for Godot* would be subtitled, a tragicomedy). In *Eleutheria*, Beckett kept to the conventional three-act form, spread in time over three days: both features of Manning's play, where they are not just aspects of bourgeois culture but mockeries of these. The three-day paradigm indicates the parodic Passion-Play pattern Manning had in the first instance: hers is a drama of a scapegoat's non-redemption. Beckett's play is the drama of a victim's self-redemption. Like Manning, Beckett mimicked a set of drawing-room conventions in his play (to a far greater degree in the first act), and delighted in parodying the conventions of classical drama (of both Molière and Racine) at the same time. Specifically, the Racinian hero is parodied in Victor Krap, the hopeless, passive recipient of advice from confidant (Glazier) and Chorus (Spectator) alike. As Katharine Worth has pointed out, such touches look forward to the kind of ironic self-consciousness in the major plays, when Beckett deliberately breaks the stage illusion to invite the audience into his theatricalism: '"Nothing bores like boredom", quips the Glazier in *Eleutheria*, and the Audience member amusingly climbs out of a stage box to demand on our behalf more action and at least *some* meaning.'[35]

The basic question put to Victor as anti-hero when he is cornered by the spokesmen for 'normality' in Act Three of *Eleutheria* is, 'what kind of life is it that you've been leading?' (*E* 143) The only reply Victor can at first formulate is, 'It's the life of someone who doesn't want to lead your kind of life.' (*E* 146) Pushed further, however, he says: 'It's a life consumed by its own liberty.' (*E* 147) Beckett wants a freedom which transcends suicide: he rules out Killigrew's option. This was not always the case. At around the time he was advising Manning on *Youth's the Season ... ?* in 1931 he spoke, according to fellow writer Mervyn Wall, most of the time of suicide. 'One left [Beckett's rooms at Trinity College] filled with thoughts of dissolution and gloom.'[36] A different Beckett wrote *Eleutheria* in 1947, one for whom suicide was not a serious option. (In *Waiting for Godot*, of course, it is an out-and-out joke. But then jokes can mask genuine fears also.) In *Eleutheria* Dr Piouk [no doubt pronounced 'puke'] offers Victor a pill which will end it all: he calls his pill 'Liberty!' (*E* 162) Victor's response is characteristically ambiguous: 'I don't need it. I shall keep it, though.' (*E* 163) This shilly-shallying is simply amusing.[37]

Unlike Manning's Killigrew also, Victor Krap refuses the love of the woman who dotes on him, Mlle. Skunk. No doubt, the very name is enough to dispel all thoughts of romantic developments. Yet Victor's rejection of Mlle. Skunk, while reversing Connie Middleton's rejection of Terence Killigrew, is not what one would call comic. The anti-hero asserts his freedom not to be free: 'I shall never be free. (*pause*) But I shall always feel that I am becoming free.' He will spend his life in a kind of 'limbo' of 'peace and quiet' (*E* 164). Here, of course, we have defined the true, the real Beckettian hero, first glimpsed in Murphy before he is literally and not at all in the Wildean sense (referring to

66 Ireland on Stage: Beckett and After

Bunbury) quite exploded. For all that, the Beckettian anti-hero is always a double act.

III

Mary Manning faded from the Dublin literary scene after 1980 like some late Beckettian heroine, so that even her intellectual footfalls are scarcely heard nowadays along that thin strip which is the Dublin literary scene. She died in Boston in 1999. She was a far better writer than she has yet been given credit for. In 1936 Crutis Canfield was quick to recognize the originality of *Youth's the Season ... ?* and called it 'an unspoken and daring play, and symptomatic of the modern feeling that the boundaries of theatrical subject matter are being extended in every direction'. He saw the play, in fact, as decidedly experimental: 'because of its sophisticated treatment of metropolitan life, [it] stands further away than any other realistic play in this book from traditional Irish drama'.[38] This is a description which neatly paves the way for Beckett's *Eleutheria*. For Manning was not only a significant (though neglected) writer and critic but, as this essay has argued, a significant influence on Beckett as dramatist. Manning greatly helped Beckett towards the definition of the anti-hero found in *Eleutheria*, the passive but willing sufferer, the opponent of all bourgeois commitments, the enemy of freedom. What he did with this material, while unspectacular, nevertheless points towards the transcendence of tragedy in the outrageous subversive qualities of the plays to come.

As *Eleutheria* comes to an end Victor rids his room of all human presence and moves his bed downstage, parallel to the footlights. *'Then he lies down, turning his emaciated back on humanity.'* (*E* 170) The gesture, turning his back on the audience, is defiant in many ways (an 'emaciated' back is perhaps another matter, an image out of World War II it may be). The gesture defies old-fashioned dramatic convention and it symbolizes defiance of common notions of responsibility. In one striking movement it parts company with Manning's modernism and ushers in a wholly new postmodernist dramatic form. It thus marks a literal taking up of a position within the modern theatre, soon to be given startling justification in *Waiting for Godot*. For *Eleutheria* is no more, really, than a promissory note, a declaration of intent, the assumption of a position from which to make a stylistic revolution. Yet Manning's forgotten play helps to clarify what went into that taking up of a position. For 'every cripple', as the Dublin expression goes, 'has his own way of walking'. Perhaps also *her* own way of walking, if the Frica's distinctive locomotion be given its due regard.

---

[1] I have in mind in particular Mary Junker, *Beckett: The Irish Dimension* (Dublin: Wolfhound, 1995).

[2] J.C.C. Mays, 'Irish Beckett: A Borderline Instance', *Beckett in Dublin*, ed. S.E. Wilmer (Dublin: Lilliput, 1992): 133-46.

[3] Alan Simpson, *Beckett and Behan and a Theatre in Dublin* (London: Routledge and Kegan Paul, 1962).

[4] Alec Reid, *All I Can Manage, More Than I Could* (Dublin: Dolmen, 1968), and Christopher Murray, 'Beckett Productions in Ireland: A Survey', *The Irish University Review* 14.1 (1984): 103-25.

[5] See Anthony Roche, *Contemporary Irish Drama from Beckett to McGuinness* (Dublin: Gill & Macmillan, 1994).

[6] Samuel Beckett, *Eleuthéria*, trans. Michael Brodsky (New York: Foxrock, 1995). Also, Samuel Beckett, *Eleuthéria: A Play in Three Acts*, trans. Barbara Wright (London and Boston: Faber and Faber, 1996). For the purposes of this article the text cited is the latter, Faber edition and subsequent references are cited in the text parenthetically as (*E* page).

[7] James Knowlson, *Damned to Fame: The Life of Samuel Beckett* (London: Bloomsbury, 1996): 119.

[8] Knowlson, 121.

[9] Anthony Cronin, *Samuel Beckett: The Last Modernist* (London: Harper Collins, 1996): 139.

[10] Cronin, 139.

[11] Ted Hughes, *Shakespeare and the Goddess of Complete Being* (London: Faber and Faber, 1992): 97.

[12] Mary Manning, *Youth's the Season ... ?*, in *Plays of Changing Ireland*, ed. Curtis Canfield (New York: Macmillan, 1936): 321-404. Subsequent references are cited in the text parenthetically as (*Y* page)

[13] '"Youth's the Season—?": Gate Theatre New Play', *The Irish Times* 9 December 1931: 6. Coward's *The Vortex* (1924), *Fallen Angels* (1925), and *Private Lives* (1930) are among the plays which set the tone for Manning's bitter-sweet comedy of manners.

[14] Deirdre Bair, *Samuel Beckett: A Biography* (London: Pan, 1980): 203.

[15] Cronin, 256.

[16] Canfield, ed., Plays of Changing Ireland, 198.

[17] See the review in *The Irish Times* 7 December 1932: 6.

[18] 'The Saturday Interview: Maeve Kennedy Talked to Mary Manning the Playwright and Novelist', *The Irish Times* 9 October 1982. For further information, see Robert Hogan, 'Mary Manning', *Dictionary of Irish Literature, M-Z*, rev. and expanded ed. (Westport: Greenwood, 1996): 822.

[19] Knowlson, 24-25.

[20] Mary Manning, 'Drama Class 1925', Act Two of *Outlook Unsettled*, staged at the Project Arts Centre, Dublin, 7-26 April 1976. The full text of *Outlook Unsettled*, a play in three acts, remains unpublished and does not seem to

have survived. Typescript of Act Two, from which the above quotation is derived (p. 21), courtesy of Agnes Bernelle, who played Sara Allgood in the 1976 production. The present writer saw this production. See Kane Archer, '"Outlook Unsettled" at the Project', *The Irish Times* 8 April 1976: 11.

[21]Cronin, 23.

[22]'Kennedy, The Saturday Interview'.

[23]Christopher Fitz-Simon, *The Boys: A Double Biography* (London: Nick Hern, 1994): 63.

[24]*Motley* ran for nineteen issues between 1932 and 1934. A full set, annotated by Denis Johnston, who played in the revival of *Youth's the Season ... ?* in 1932, is in the Irish Theatre Archive, Dublin.

[25]'"Youth's the Season—?": Gate Theatre New Play', 6.

[26]Micheál Mac Liammóir, *All for Hecuba: An Irish Theatrical Autobiography* (Dublin: Progress, 1961): 138-40.

[27]Knowlson, 154. Knowlson is here discussing *Dream of Fair to middling Women*, but 'A Wet Day', published in *More Pricks Than Kicks* in 1934, derives from that novel, written in 1932 though remaining unpublished until 1992.

[28]Samuel Beckett, *More Pricks Than Kicks* (London: Calder, 1993): 79.

[29]Beckett, *More Pricks Than Kicks*, 79-80.

[30]Knowlson, 184.

[31]Samuel Beckett, *Dream of Fair to middling Women*, eds Eoin O'Brien and Edith Fournier (Dublin: Black Cat, 1992): 180.

[32]' ... that memorable night in March, at the end of the jetty, in the howling wind, never to be forgotten ... The vision at last.' See Samuel Beckett, *The Complete Dramatic Works* (London and Boston: Faber and Faber, 1986): 220.

[33]Samuel Beckett, *Proust; [and] Three Dialogues: Samuel Beckett & Georges Duthuit* (London: John Calder, 1987): 18-19.

[34]A version of the present article was first published in *The Cracked Lookingglass: Contributions to the Study of Irish Literature*, ed. Carla de Petris, et al. (Rome: Bulzoni, 1999): 159-71. Republished by kind permission of Bulzoni Editore.

[35]Katharine Worth, *Samuel Beckett's Theatre: Life Journeys* (Oxford: Clarendon, 1999): 67.

[36]Cronin, 139.

[37]In *Dream of Fair to middling Women*, Beckett refers to the bridge from which suicides jump as 'the hyphen of passion between Shilly and Shally' (*Dream of Fair to middling Women*, 27).

[38]Canfield, 198.

5 | Beyond the Mask:
Frank McGuinness and Oscar Wilde

Noreen Doody

The characters in Frank McGuinness's plays conceal and reveal themselves by means of the mask; artist figures fabricate reality from imagination; women become something like their fathers and men are indebted to their mothers; wit and magic inform language as protagonists confront each other through humour. Many creative concerns of Oscar Wilde resonate within these dramatic themes. Beyond these themes, McGuinness seeks some form of ultimate truth about what it is to be human; he situates his characters within circumstances stripped of convention and uncovers in the human condition a savage strength and a quiet beauty. This ultimate concern of McGuinness's with the nature of being recalls Oscar Wilde's writings, perhaps, most dramatically, *De Profundis* – the work in which Wilde depicts his extreme isolation and spiritual survival in Reading Gaol. Whether it is at this profound level of enquiry or at the more accidental level of similarity, Wilde's texts have major implications for McGuinness's work. This chapter will explore these implications and the creative relations that exist between these two dramatists.

Frank McGuinness has a deep and scholarly knowledge of Wilde's texts and their influence proceeds in several ways throughout his work. It is important to see influence as not merely imitative but as an active component of the creative imagination working in alliance with the critical faculty. The process of influence involves attraction, selection and assimilation of the precursor's ideas and images and their re-configuration in a new way within the later writer's work. Literary influence works in various ways: it may be a conscious or unconscious process and may express itself in an agonistic or benign manner. Harold Bloom, in his theory of the anxiety of influence sees the process of influence as always agonistic, as a struggle in which the later writer attempts to usurp the position of the precursor. Bloom directs his theory primarily at male writers; he maintains that the later artist seeks to purloin that which he most admires in the precursor's work so that its merit accrues to his own text.

A more benign form of influence is that which takes the shape of a critique of a previous text, and becomes something like a palimpsest in which the energy of the new text emanates from an underlying precursor text. Such work may come about through the admiration or sense of affinity of the later writer for the precursor and be carried out in the spirit of 'this is what they really meant to say'.

Wilde proposes in his essay 'The Critic as Artist' an alternative theory of influence, he suggests that a text represents the 'jumping off' point, or inspiration, for a new literary creation.[1] It may also happen that a writer becomes so familiar with the work of another writer that their awareness of the boundaries between their own and the precursor's ideas become indistinct and blurred. Conversely, there are those creative writers who quite consciously take a ludic delight in the imaginative re-arrangement of precursor texts.

The similarity that exists between McGuinness's and Oscar Wilde's work has been discussed by Hiroko Mikami in her book, *Frank McGuinness and his Theatre of Paradox*. She finds many resemblances between McGuinness's wit and Wilde's, particularly, in relation to Wilde's master comedy, *The Importance of Being Earnest,* and suggests that McGuinness's character, Rima, in *Dolly West's Kitchen* represents, 'Lady Bracknell's avatar in present day Donegal'.[2] Mikami illustrates a close relationship between various lines in McGuinness's drama and those of Wilde in *The Importance of Being Earnest*: she finds, for instance, in Rima's humorous reference to being lost an echo of the 'lost' parents in Wilde's play[3] while the File's comment in McGuinness's *Mutabilitie*, 'I didn't think it polite to listen to a Protestant prayer'[4] recalls for her the remark of Wilde's butler, Lane, 'I didn't think it polite to listen.'

There are a number of witticisms scattered throughout McGuinness's work which bear a certain resemblance to Wilde's work but then both dramatists are witty men, nurtured by a common tradition whose artistic sensibility is in tune with each other. It is, perhaps, this very creative empathy that forms the basis for McGuinness's initial reception of Wilde's influence. McGuinness often seems to be at play with Wilde's words, consciously reassembling them in sheer creative fun: Wilde defines fiction as that in which 'the good end happily and the bad unhappily' (*W* 376) while McGuinness's character, Rosemary in *The Factory Girls* declares: 'It will end happily. It always does in *Bunty*'. *Bunty* is, of course, a weekly comic of fictitious adventures for young girls.[5] In *The Bird Sanctuary* Eleanor speaks to her nephew, Stephen, explaining how she hates most of her family but has some liking for him: 'I hate your mother – I detest my sister. I ignore your father. But I like you, a little. Until you turn against me. As you will, I hope'.[6] Eleanor's words strike one as McGuinness's playful response to the received wisdom of his precursor that 'Children begin by loving their parents. After a time they judge them. Rarely, if ever, do they forgive them.' (*W* 490) McGuinness again seems to be playing with Wildean lines in the play, *Dolly West's Kitchen* in Rima's statement, 'One thing about the English – when they keep their mouths shut they're grand.' (*P2* 211) This line parodies Wilde's witticism: 'If one could only teach the English how to talk, and the Irish how to listen, society here would be quite civilized.' (*W* 564) However, if we were to listen to Lady Bracknell we would know that 'the line is immaterial' (*W* 369) which may well be so, as similarity often indicates a mere superficial influence when, more importantly, there is present in McGuinness's work a deeper sub-conscious vein of influence that resonates with the aesthetic and philosophical views of Oscar Wilde.

When asked if Wilde had influenced his drama, McGuinness replied that *The Importance of Being Earnest* is such a complete and narcissistic achievement that all he could do was admire it, but allowed that 'the prime influence of Wilde in [his] theatre' related to the tradition of wit in Irish theatre.[7] McGuinness's response is almost prescriptive in its Bloomian correctness; he sidesteps the issue of direct precursorship and disperses any major indebtedness into a more general, homogenous literary heritage. Bloom maintains that a creative writer must never admit to influence because such an admission would endanger the writer's creativity. The denial of influence, on the other hand, according to Bloom, is a proof of influence – a measure of the deep anxiety experienced by the later writer in relation to the precursor's presence in his work. Although McGuinness is correct to include himself and Wilde within a comic tradition that Vivien Mercier suggests might well be considered the central tradition of Irish literature,[8] this does not except him from a particular creative indebtedness to Wilde. Indeed there is a striking correspondence in the ways in which McGuinness and Wilde make use of humour in their plays: characters confront each other through humour and wit is deployed as a weapon. In Wilde's *The Importance of Being Earnest* Cecily and Gwendolen claim proprietorship of Earnest by crossing swords in a lethal exchange of wit:

72   Ireland on Stage: Beckett and After

> **Cecily:** Do you suggest, Miss Fairfax, that I entrapped Earnest into an engagement? How dare you? This is no time for wearing the shallow mask of manners. When I see a spade I call it a spade.
> **Gwendolen:** (*satirically*) I am glad to say that I have never seen a spade. It is obvious that our social spheres have been widely different (*W* 399).

Verbal daggers are drawn in *Observe the Sons of Ulster Marching Towards the Somme* where the following exchange occurs between McGuinness's protagonists, Pyper and Roulston:

> **Roulston:** Pyper?
> **Pyper:** I hoped you'd never forget my face
> **Craig:** You two know each other?
> **Roulston:** We schooled together
> **Pyper:** But we never shared together. Roulston's best friends were always much younger.
> **Roulston:** You've kept your tongue
> **Pyper:** Are you asking to see it?
> **Roulston:** I've heard little of you
> **Pyper:** Impossible. You've heard everything
> **Roulston:** I try to avoid scandal (*P1* 119).

Declamatory funny one liners proliferate throughout the work of each writer: humour is expressed by nonsequitors and by the back and forth of quick, pithy insults while inversion, insolence and the unexpected characterize the work of both dramatists. Lines such as Wilde's 'The only possible society is oneself' (*W* 554) or 'Her hair has turned quite gold from grief' (*W* 364) are reflected in the off hand hauteur of McGuinness's characters: 'You poor boy, geography will be the death of you' (*P2* 240) or 'You can pick up anything on Booterstown strand.'(*P2* 275)

Both writers use the unexpected to undermine complacency. The listener is startled to attention through laughter instigated by the shock of the unusual as social assumptions are exploded and the audience is put in the wrong, being placed in an unexpected vantage point from which to view what had hitherto been taken for granted. McGuinness illustrates this particular use of humour in *Dolly West's Kitchen*:

> **Marco:** My name's Mary – Mary O'Shaughnessy.
> **Ned:** That's very unusual
> **Marco:** Yes, isn't it? But all the men in my family are called O'Shaughnessy (*P2* 210).

Of course Ned is referring to the female first name but McGuinness's subtext is questioning the societal notion that 'men' is a generic grouping in which each man is alike, leaving no room for individual or gender difference. Wilde uses a similar strategy in *Lady Windermere's Fan* to interrogate the social dogma of the 'good woman'.

> **Lord Darlington:** Oh! She doesn't love me. She is a good woman. She is the only good woman I have ever met in my life.
> **Cecil Graham:** The only good woman you have ever met in your life.
> **Lord Darlington:** Yes!
> **Cecil Graham:** (*lighting a cigarette*) Well, you are a lucky fellow! Why I have met hundreds of good women. I never seem to meet any but good women. The world is perfectly packed with good women. To know them is a middle-class education (*W* 451-52).

Cecil Graham turns Lord Darlington's idealization of woman on its head and alerts the audience to the hollow, mediocre ideology that has been responsible for the manufacture of what society views as the 'good woman'. Indeed, far from the ideal of pure nature, the 'good woman' image is shown up as a mask of middle class respectability.

This use of inversion is one of the finest traits Wilde and McGuinness hold in common in their artistic use of humour. Another stylistic technique that both writers put to good effect is the double reaction, a device in which a second burst of laughter is elicited from the audience after the joke seems to have been already delivered. Wilde uses this device in the Duches of Berwick's speech in *Lady Windermere's Fan*:

> Ah, we know your value, Mr. Hopper. We wish there were more like you. It would make life so much easier. Do you know, Mr. Hopper, dear Agatha and I are so much interested in Australia. It must be so pretty with all the dear little kangaroos flying about. Agatha has found it on the map. What a curious shape it is! Just like a large packing case. However, it is a very young country, isn't it? (*W* 433)

The first part of the Duchess of Berwick's speech shows her eagerness to fulfil her duty as a Victorian mother and marry off her daughter to an eligible and wealthy man and the audience laugh at the chasm between Mr. Hopper's and the Duchess's understanding of language. The Duchess's appalling imperialist and inadequate understanding of the continent of Australia gives rise to the second peal of laughter.

In *Observe the Sons of Ulster* Pyper tells the gullible Moore a story of how he once married a Catholic woman who was a prostitute in Paris, only to discover that she had three legs.

> **Pyper:** She asked me if I'd ever been alone with a woman like this before. A standard question for one of her profession, so I lied and

74   Ireland on Stage: Beckett and After

said, yes, but never with a Papist. When she heard this she told me I
had a surprise coming. She took off her petticoat and there they
were.
Moore: What?
Pyper: Three legs.
Moore: What?
Pyper: She had three legs. The middle one shorter than the normal
two.
(*Craig starts to laugh.*)
Moore: Don't laugh. That's the truth.
Millen: You believe that?
Moore: I've heard that three-legged rumour before, but only in
relation to nuns. There's the big convent in Portstewart ...
Pyper: She could've started out as a nun. I don't know (*P1* 126-27).

The joke builds becoming funnier and more preposterous at every
step. The notion of a three legged woman and its inherent sexual
ambiguity is funny but the laughter is doubly aroused by Moore's
gullibility which rests on his ignorance of the 'other', in this case
Catholics. As in Wilde's play where humour acts as a mask to expose
the colonized situation, religious bias and ignorance is similarly
exposed by McGuinness.

Both Wilde's and McGuinness's characters employ humorous but
conventionally unacceptable behaviour or language as a mask through
which they project versions of their inner self and behind which they
conceal another. In Wilde's *The Importance of Being Earnest* Algy
adopts the guise of preposterous characters paying imaginary visits to
a fictitious ailing friend, Bunbury, that he might put into practice a
fantasy life of fun and adventure. Behind a profane and irreverent wit,
Lord Goring in *An Ideal Husband* pursues a righteous and honourable
path.

In McGuinness's play, *Someone Who'll Watch Over Me*, the terror
and fear felt by his characters is masked by diverse expressions of
humour. The play tells the story of three hostages, an Irishman,
Englishman and American, held by terrorists in a Beiruit cell and the
very terms of the play recall the old joke format: 'Paddy Irishman,
Englishman and Scotchman' in its blackest mode. McGuinness plays
with all sorts of imaginings and inventions as his characters adopt
many voices and personae in an effort to create an alternative reality
to the world in which they exist. Eamonn Jordan refers to role-playing
in McGuinness's work as confronting rigidity and promoting
possibility and tolerance while providing access to a different, if
temporary, reality.[9] The hostages succeed sporadically in accessing an
alternative world and the masks that they adopt illuminate their
individual selves. McGuinness appears to be playing with Wilde's

dictum: 'Man is least himself when he talks in his own person. Give him a mask, and he will tell you the truth.' (*W* 1142)

McGuinness continues this strategy in *Dolly West's Kitchen* in which Rima constructs a mask of eccentricity from behind which she articulates what cannot be said in conventional social terms. Rima is a widowed mother, the central figure of an Irish household, to whom traditional pieties attach iconic status. The role she assumes is at loggerheads with the notion of sainted Irish motherhood; the persona whom she projects is outrageous and ribald and this expansive mask allows her put into action an incisive plan that will advance the happiness of her children. In a flamboyant and wilfully capricious manner she invites two American soldiers, the gay Marco and the straight Jamie, to dinner in her home - in some respects they are the dinner being offered as nourishment by Rima to her sexually famished son and daughter. Rima's gregarious mask of bonhomie allows her to express her 'real' self. While the mask distracts and disarms its viewers it reveals the generous colourful spirit of its wearer – as Wilde has cautioned – the mask speaks the truth. Indeed, Rima says as much. In answer to Dolly's request to have done with obfustication and say what she means, Rima replies: 'I say what I mean.'

Rima's son, Justin, also projects a mask: his self-deception wears a mask of extreme nationalism. He makes an impassioned speech at the dinner table in which he vilifies the English, directing his remarks at the English officer, Alec: 'Alec, do you know how deeply you are hated? How deservedly you are hated?' (*P2* 215) he asks. Believing Alec to have called him a coward, Justin exits the room in fury followed by Marco and a conversation ensues in which Marco deciphers Justin's mask and reveals him to himself:

> *On the shore Marco takes Justin's cigarette from his lips. He lights his own with it.*
> **Marco:** I like your hatred. Don't lose your hatred.
> **Justin:** What would you know about it?
> **Marco:** Everything.
> **Justin:** What would you know about me?
> **Marco:** What you've told me.
> **Justin:** What have I told you?
> **Marco:** Everything
> *Marco touches Justin's face. Justin kisses Marco's hands* (*P2* 217).

Marco has correctly read Justin's austere and hyper patriotic mask into which he had displaced his frustrated sexuality.

McGuinness's exploration of the mask takes many forms, often gaining impetus from a Wildean directive. The various characters in his play, *The Bird Sanctuary*, project opposing masks. McGuinness seems to be experimenting here with Wilde's proposal: 'what is interesting about people in good society ... is the mask that each one of them wears, not the reality that lies behind it' (*W* 1075) and arrives, as Yeats had done in his contemplation of the Wildean mask, at a point of play between self and anti-self. Behind the arrogant mask of artist, Eleanor, is a fragile, anxious person who depends on the safety of her sanctuary to survive while her sister-in-law, Tina, who appears to be a weak, accommodating housewife is a strong woman, a nurturer who saves the life of Eleanor. Tina's son, Stephen, casts aside his conservative mask and uncovers an opposing self that seeks sanctuary with Eleanor. Eleanor's sister, Marianne, divulges her self-conscious attempts to construct, in opposition to her Irish identity, a mask of Englishness.

McGuinness's interest in the imaginative fabrication of masks is but a part of his more general concern with the place of the imaginative within the total experience of reality. Wilde's concept of the imaginary composition of reality is considered in McGuinness's work and often finds expression along similar lines or in a reconfiguration of the original theory. In his essay 'The Decay of Lying', Wilde proposes that reality is dependent on perception, and that perception is always informed by the arts and culture to which the individual has been exposed. More particularly, he suggests that it is the artist who creates reality, putting forward in illustration of this thesis the fact that the public perception of London fogs and sunrises changed in accordance with the images people were exposed to in the pictures of the Impressionist painters. Indeed, Wilde suggests that the nineteenth-century idea of Japan was dependent upon the graceful, delicate paintings of that country which artists had presented to the public, so that there is no such thing as a real country called Japan – all that exists is merely the impression of the artist.

Wilde's masterpiece, *The Importance of Being Earnest,* is a play about the creative power of the imagination. Things exist, Wilde writes, because the artist has observed it should be so. In *The Importance of Being Earnest* Wilde proves his thesis: Jack Worthing plays the part of Earnest and becomes Earnest; he imagines a younger brother and a younger brother comes into being. Cecily dreams up a fiancé and an engagement and writes of it in her diary and all of this comes to pass. Miss Prism's three volume novel metamorphoses into a baby. Bunbury, the product of Algy's imagination, cannot just fade away but has gained such life that he must be killed. Jack's brother, Earnest, also imaginary, requires a funeral and mourning. All of the 'artists' within the play – Cecily whose journal is a book of fiction, Miss Prism who writes a three-volume novel, Jack and Algy who imagine themselves fictitious characters – create the reality of life from their imaginings.

There are times when McGuinness comes close to fully accepting Wilde's position that reality is wholly reliant on the imagination and always that the imagination plays a decisive part in what we term reality. In McGuinness's play, *The Bird Sanctuary*, the imagination works to create reality. Marianne proposes that Eleanor should work her magic to kill her husband's lover. There is no question among the women that such a thing cannot be achieved. Eleanor is the artist, she creates a charm from bones and threads and through the power of her imagination the death is accomplished. Eleanor not only imagines the act into reality but her ability to do this is enabled by – as Oscar Wilde puts it – 'the arts and culture to which she has been exposed'. Eleanor's powerful act of imagination has a compelling source in the ancient Irish belief in the power of words, of satire, to inflict harm on its subject and the source of that satire in magic. McGuinness also plays with this ancient belief in *Mutabilitie*. Indeed, in this play the poet, File, says: 'You are yourself what you imagined, as I am what I imagined.' (*M* 93)

Eleanor creates the reality in which she lives; she secures her house, the environment necessary to her survival and again, through her art she secures the bird sanctuary in translating it on to her canvas. We are told that the immense painting of the bird sanctuary is scattered throughout the house, Eleanor has extended her artwork to encompass her entire environment. She finishes work on the painting by the end of the play and when the backdrop rises to reveal the actual bird sanctuary, the stage directions indicate that the colours should reflect the colours of the interior of the house, intimating that the house and sanctuary have become one through the power of art. All becomes, one place wherein endangered species, such as Eleanor and Stephen, might live. McGuinness's play acknowledges the imagination as a major contributing force in what is accepted as reality.

There is a difference, however, in how McGuinness's characters are aware of how imagination works and the level on which Wilde's characters accept it as the air they breathe. Stephen's imaginative projection of himself and Marianne's husband as lovers, for example, relieves Marianne's hurt but the projection works only as story – 'say if' – rather than having the agency which similar imaginative concoctions have in Wilde's play. The power of the imagination in McGuinness's play is under control, nothing happens without the will of the character imagining. All are already in the know – no one is taken by surprise and left to wonder - unlike Jack who finds out that all his lies had actually been truths.

McGuinness does not accept fully Wilde's concept of reality as the construct of the artist but as we see in *Observe the Sons of Ulster* he considers the role of the artistic imagination in conjunction with the artist's duty to reveal truth. In his considerations McGuinness works with a theory akin to Wilde's belief that 'a truth in art is that whose contradictory is also true'(*W* 1173). This theory of Wilde's far from being spurious or facetious expresses succinctly the complexity and wonder of any search for truth and points towards the coincidence of polarities as a way towards the realization of a truth. Towards the end of McGuinness's *Observe the Sons of Ulster* the artist figure, Pyper, becomes preoccupied with a familiar smell that he finds emanates from the river Somme. Suddenly it occurs to him that the reason for its familiarity is that it smells like all the rivers of Ulster: the Bann, the Foyle, the Lagan. In that moment he imagines the fight in Flanders as a continuance of the fight of Protestant Ulster; they have always been in a war situation; King Billy and the Battle at the River Boyne is a founding myth. Pyper, like some Celtic River god who inhabits the Boyne or one of 'the Protestant gods' (*P1* 189) on Lough Erne, tries to convey his imaginative view of reality to the others and addresses them with all his eloquence: 'You weren't dreaming about Lough Erne, David. You're on it. It surrounds you. Moore, the Bann is flowing outside. The Somme, it's not what we think it is. It's the Lagan, the Foyle, the Bann ...' (*P1* 188). Pyper is brought up abruptly by Craig: 'you won't save us, you won't save yourself, imagining things. There's nothing imaginary about this, Kenneth. This is the last battle. We're going out to die' (*P1* 188). The magical, imaginative weavings and fabrications of art are drawn up short as Craig invokes the absolute, death, the only certainty of life. One is reminded of the breadth of difference Synge discerns between the 'gallous act' and the 'dirty deed' in his *The Playboy of the Western World* – the unbridgeable gap between the story and its factual enactment.

Pyper spins the story, fabricates the reasons, finds the symbols and the metaphors to make sense and give substance to life and Craig calls his bluff; he discounts any imaginary account of what is about to happen and sees the impending act of dying as graphic and actual, as not needing a gloss or any imaginative embellishment or interpretation. Pyper alone survives – it may be that he is condemned by his own imagination to live and recount the story – it is Pyper after all who in the mock battle topples King Billy and imaginatively disrupts and confounds the course of history as though the artist were in some unfathomable way, empowered to offer alternative realities and thwart the inevitable.

Craig tells Pyper: 'Damn you after listening to that bit of rabble rousing, I saw then. You're not of us, man. You're wasted here with us, man. You're a leader.' (*P1* 192) Pyper is a Pied Piper, who can cast a spell with words and compel others to follow his imaginative creation of life. He, like Wilde's artist figure, is capable of presenting reality to the world and the world lives it. Craig, on the other hand, who has alerted Pyper to the futility of his position, is also connected to the artist in the flip-side of the imaginative role of the artist, in the artistic duty to truth and accuracy. Craig is a blacksmith, not only a practical craftsman, but in Irish folk tradition, akin to the artist. Pyper and Craig, like the other characters in this play are two halves of a whole. One of the other characters, Moore, describing how Craig saved Pyper's life during battle, says: 'Together for eternity now. ... Did Pyper come back from the dead that time he fell? I saw it. I saw Craig, what he did. He blew his own breath into Pyper's mouth. It was a kiss.'(*P1* 159) In the case of these two characters, when placed together as one, they reveal the seemingly irreconcilable, contradictory nature not alone of art but also of reality, in their fusion of the imaginative and the material, life and death. 'A truth in art is that whose contradictory is also true.'

The kiss with which Craig reanimates his friend is the kiss of actual life and also that of love – the soul takes succour from the senses – as Wilde would have it. There is a great tenderness and care between these individuals poised on the borders of death and this aspect and capacity for human love is often explored by McGuinness in his work. As in Wilde's work, gender stereotypes are eschewed, and a more comprehensive focus on human love is struck. *Dolly West's Kitchen* is a play that fully embraces and encourages diversity. The title and concern of the play is with meals and with cooking; the central metaphor of the play suggests that a good meal depends on the many and varied ingredients of which it is composed just as the richness of life is provided by the variety of ideas and types of which it is composed. McGuinness subscribes to Wilde's emphasis on the individual nature of the human: 'There is no one type for man – there are as many perfections as there are imperfect men. And while to the claims of charity a man may yield and yet be free, to the claims of conformity no man may yield and remain free at all.' (*W* 1181) Rima is concerned for each one of her children: her son, Justin is a closet homosexual and her daughter, Esther, is in a sterile heterosexual marriage. The two young men whom Rima invites to dinner are cousins, a gay and a straight man – kinship emphasizing the close relationship and normality of all sexual expression. Gayness is not privileged among the other ingredients of the play, like everything else – it is merely a part of life's fabric.

Rima is an artist and the daughter of a blacksmith; she combines within her character imagination and a keen and accurate sense of life. At times it is as though she speaks in riddles – through anecdote, exaggeration and wit. Although Rima often seems to be talking tangentially or in unrelated anecdotes, she is actually using analogy and metaphor, the tools of the artist, to say exactly what she means as in the story she tells of the fisherman at Urris who caught a mermaid only to discover that it was really she who caught him. Rima challenges the silences of the orthodox. At dinner with her guests and family she poses fundamental questions and answers them in story:

> What's it like with two men in the bed? (*Silence. They all look at her.*) I'm only asking. There was a man like that here. Nice chap. A baker. That was years ago. The word was he had the biggest micky ever seen on any man in this town. Thirteen inches. It gave a whole new meaning to the baker's dozen. (*Silence.*) Can I say nothing this night? (*P2* 212)

Rima's seemingly naïve but Rabbelesian remarks are insinuated cunningly by her into the dinner table talk to suggest both the supposed oddness and normality of homosexuality. The subject is being addressed during a family meal and in a conversational way and this together with the fact that the baker is a commonplace figure in their very town 'years ago' – suggests that same sex attraction is not some strange phenomenon of modern times but a human activity which has been going on for many years. The oddness consists in ignorance: 'What's it like with two men in bed?' and myth – 'The baker's dozen' indicating a public perception of homosexuality as strange and unnatural.

Wilde often questions the inequality of rules of behaviour set down by society for the sexes and poses the rhetorical question in *The Importance of Being Earnest* and elsewhere: 'Why should there be one law for men and another for women?' (*W* 415) In McGuinness's drama all genders abide by the same law; difference is acknowledged and seen as desirable. McGuinness often ascribes societal aversion to gayness to unfamiliarity and dullness rather than any outright homophobic intention. He does not, however, underestimate the difficulties attached to the public expression of homosexuality in a mainly heterosexual society. The shock of the West family at hearing their mother's, Rima's, ponderings on two men in bed together suggests a social difficulty in the expression of same sex love rather than any moral judgement. In *The Bird Sanctuary* Stephen's mother, Tina, explains her difficulty in accepting her son's homosexuality as deriving in part from her previous shock in seeing a naked Cork man in his bed. (*P2* 334) There is no great difference between the problems attached to male and female sexuality in McGuinness's plays; all who deviate from the narrow socially approved model of gender relations suffer the opprobrium of society. Anna Owens, the young maid in *Dolly West's Kitchen* is scorned by Ned Horgan because her mother gave birth to her in the Home for unmarried mothers. The main distinction between society's disapproval of heterosexual and homosexual behaviour is the public's wider familiarity with one form of sexual relationships than another.

Rima's purpose in asking the two American boys to dinner is to bring choice and possibility to her family. It is Rima who invites her son to dance, to take his place in the dance of life: 'Son dear, would you get off your knees praying and dance?' (*P2* 189) Generosity marks Rima's character; she is someone who knows her own mind and acts accordingly. Wilde writes of this type of generosity in his essay, 'The Soul of Man under Socialism': 'Unselfishness recognizes infinite variety of type as a delightful thing, accepts it, acquiesces in it, enjoys it ... A red rose is not selfish because it wants to be a red rose. It would be horribly selfish if it called all the other flowers in the garden to be both red and roses.' (*W* 1195)

At the heart of McGuinness's discourse on gender lies Wilde's lament: 'All women become like their mothers. That is their tragedy. No man does. That's his.' Wilde sets out to confound the false polarity attributed by society to the sexes and the strict Victorian view of the binary nature of being. In *Earnest* Wilde disrupts the expectation that a man must be the emotionally bankrupt, hewer of wood and drawer of water while the female must involve herself with the incidental frivolities of life. The women are strong protagonists in *The Importance of Being Earnest*; Lady Bracknell takes on the paternal task of interviewing her daughter's would be suitor; young Cecily directs and controls Algernon in making him her fiancée while both Cecily and Gwendolyn, like so many of Wilde's females characters, perform through the mask of the dandy. Wilde's male characters, on the other hand, often display characteristics traditionally attributed to the female: they are concerned with trivialities, hairstyles, gossip and amusement. Male and female roles are also purposefully reversed in McGuinness's drama. The three women are the main protagonists of *The Bird Sanctuary*: Eleanor is a dandy figure and Marianne is said to have inherited the characteristics of her father. In *Dolly West's Kitchen* Esther is morose and considered a 'possible strayer' like her father. *The Factory Girls* undermines the stereotypical notion of the male as strong protector and leader of men: the women display the integrity and grit which tradition accords the male while the male authority figures show themselves to be commonplace and weak in intellect. A male Eve tempts Craig in *Observe the Sons of Ulster* as Pyper proffers him an apple, 'I can't tempt you?' (*P1* 104) he says. In *Someone Who'll Watch over Me* Edward speaks of his executed companion, Adam: 'He was beautiful to look at. I watched him as he slept one night ...He was innocent. Kind, gentle.' (*P2* 145) In the Old Testament Eve was made from the rib of Adam as he slept and in McGuinness's play something of that chemistry survives as Edward watches Adam sleep. It is as though some deep unsolicited desire, or even love, takes shape in Edward as he watches over his sleeping companion but once it is openly interrogated it must be denied. He answers Michael's query as to whether he had ever slept or desired to sleep with Adam with an unconvincing 'No'. There is a perception that the Biblical act of creating Adam's helpmate from his rib renders woman an imperfect male, however, while this may be so, the image of Adam separated from his rib, whether it has metamorphosed into imperfect female or imperfect male, may also illustrate the basic human need for completion by another and indifferent to any particular social construction of sexual identity.

The traditional social roles of man and woman are complicated and often reversed in the work of Wilde and McGuinness and genetic inheritance is equitably distributed from father to daughter and from mother to son. Freedom of emotional expression follows on the escape from gender stereotype: McGuinness's characters express sexual desire and all gender relationships develop and evolve into need and love between individuals. In McGuinness's work it is familiarity and ignorance that create the greatest divide between the expression of same sex love and heterosexual love. In *Dolly West's Kitchen* Esther says to Marco, 'You've crossed the border' to which he replies, 'Hasn't everyone?' (*P2* 206) In *Someone Who'll Watch over Me* and *Observe the Sons of Ulster* McGuinness clears a space from which the societal gaze is eliminated – a hostage cell and a battle-front – and the male protagonists have the freedom to be. This clearing allows these men exhibit a tenderness that far from betraying masculinity belongs with what is profound and fundamental to human behaviour. As the hostages in *Someone Who'll Watch over Me* await their uncertain fate they speak about the ancient warriors of Sparta who combed each other's hair before battle commenced. As Edward is about to regain his freedom and leave Michael alone in the cell, he solemnly and tenderly combs his hair. 'The bravest men sometimes behave like women.' (*P2* 158/168)

The liminal space that McGuinness creates in *Observe the Sons of Ulster* allows him to subvert social and traditional perceptions of manliness. This is an exclusively male world in which the characters invoke the old gods and patterns before going in to battle. The extreme horror and isolation of the situation gives them licence to doubt and to talk of their inner selves, expressing fear and care and examining the whole reality of their lives. In normal times such liberties would be impossible for these 'tough' men but now, in these conditions of isolation, they discover that they have 'soft skin'. Only Pyper had been aware from the outset that he had 'soft skin', but by the end of the play each man has comes to a personal realization of the complexity of his nature and through that realization a brotherhood of man is established. It is a brotherhood inclusive of male and female characteristics and betokens an equally vulnerable humanity shared by all.

Frank McGuinness's work is characterized by an ability to sensitively negotiate human relations at their most profound level. Often these relations are played out against the backdrop of some great crises – in *Observe the Sons* it is the war; in *The Factory Girls* it is loss of livelihood and sexist oppression - in these situations the individuals bond together against an oppressive, often faceless power. These circumstances allow the characters – far from ordinary life in which masks of convention must be worn and society's expectations fulfilled - the space to be them selves. The dictum, 'Be Thyself' (*W* 1180), is put forward by Wilde in his essay 'The Soul of Man under Socialism', as being the very purpose of life. In his last great prose work, *De Profundis*, Wilde describes how his condition of extreme isolation in a prison cell provided him with a space outside of the ordinary and brought him to a moment of radical self-awareness and realization. Moments like this occur for McGuinness's characters: the hostages in *Someone Who'll Watch Over Me* incarcerated in their cell come to such knowledge, the men facing death in *Observe the Sons of Ulster* and the eponymous factory girls abandoned by social and religious authority in their cell-like office come to realize their own power and integrity in their isolated conditions.

Wilde's essay 'The Soul of Man' proposes the primary importance of the individual personality and the necessity of cultivating and fulfilling the individual potential of each person. 'What a man really has, is what is in him. What is outside of him should be a matter of no importance' (*W* 1178). McGuinness brings his protagonists to a situation stripped of convention where all they have is the self – a place where individual nature can be perceived in the raw. This is the type of space similar to Wilde's in Reading Gaol. In his drama

McGuinness explores the shedding of the many masks of an individual until finally, confronted by extreme circumstances of life, the individual stands beyond the mask in the bare human condition. How the individual acts at this point is of great interest to McGuinness: he finds there a quiet acceptance of the situation, a reliance on innate resources and a savage courage to take on impossible odds. In his drama McGuinness realizes not the transcendent but an awful beauty in the full realization of what it is to be human.

The story which Pyper recounts after the death of his fellows pays tribute to the fundamental courage of humanity in all its frailty by employing the imagination to render an artistically accurate and true account of these men – as he observes them in their march towards death. The sons of Ulster are flawed individuals but each one is on his own legs marching. Wilde writes: 'In one divine moment, and by selecting its own mode of expression, a personality might make itself perfect.'(*W* 1181) Dolly West describes the frescoes she has seen in Ravenna in their superb artistic beauty, declaring that her life had meaning if its only duty was the preservation of the memory of the pictures for posterity. It is the vulnerability of these works of wonder that render them sublime for McGuinness; the frailty and endurance which characterize his protagonists finds expression in the perfect depiction of humanity at the heart of these frescoes: 'The walking was their glory for that made them human.' (*P2* 218)

It is the marching like the 'walking' in Ravenna that declares the men of Ulster human; the frailty of man is set against the immensity of circumstance. The artist 'observes' and with the critical distance that this implies preserves the act of human courage in every particular. Pyper disproves McIlwaine's accusation of artistic disinterest: 'To Hell with the truth so long as it rhymes.' (*P1* 176) He bears witness.

Compassion for humanity lies at the heart of McGuinness's work; Dolly says of Rima: 'She believed in this world, not the next.' (*P2* 242) Rima's wisdom and knowledge of the world is expressed in her recognition of the fundamental human need for companionship and love. In his thesis on *De Profundis* McGuinness suggests that Wilde wrote this painful epistle, a letter of complaint and desire, as a love letter to Lord Alfred Douglas and he perceives it as a cry of human loneliness, a desperate appeal for the love of one other.[10] McGuinness extends this notion in his plays: his characters pair for life: Rima does not leave or reject her wandering husband who wanders back to her; the Factory women fight with their husbands but remain loyal to them; Marianne kills her husband's lover but never thinks of leaving him; the young people in *Dolly West's Kitchen* pair up and join life's dance in twos; the boys in *Observe the Sons of Ulster* support each other in couples. It is always a *pas-de-deux* that McGuinness's characters dance.

McGuinness understands the need of the individual to fabricate masks, his characters sport and play with various disguises, but their deception is undone and one by one they leave aside their cover until they stand, as Wilde did in *De Profundis*, naked beyond the mask. At this point, what is revealed is the fragility and strength of the individual and the basic human need for 'someone to watch over you'.

---

[1] Oscar Wilde, *Complete Works of Oscar Wilde* (Glasgow: Harper Collins, 2004): 1127. Hereafter quotes from Wilde's works are from this edition and are indicated in the text in parentheses as (*W* 1127).

[2] Hiroko Mikami, *Frank McGuinness and his Theatre of Paradox* (Gerrards Cross: Colin Smythe, 2002): 155.

[3] Mikami, 155.

[4] Frank McGuinness, *Mutabilitie* (London: Faber and Faber, 1997): 23. Hereafter, quotes from this play are indicated in the text in parentheses as (*M* 23)

[5] Frank McGuinness, *Frank McGuinness: Plays One* (London: Faber and Faber, 1996): 43. This collection ontains *The Factory Girls; Observe the Sons of Ulster Marching Towards the Somme; Innocence; Carthaginians; and Baglady*. Hereafter, quotes from McGuinness's plays in this collection are indicated in the text in parentheses as (*P1* 43).

[6] Frank McGuinness, *Frank McGuinness: Plays 2* (London: Faber and Faber, 2002): 276. This collection contains *Mary and Lizzie; Someone Who'll Watch Over Me; Dolly West's Kitchen; and The Bird Sanctuary*. Hereafter, quotes from McGuinness's plays in this collection are indicated in the text in parentheses as (*P2* 276).

[7] Mikami, 148.

[8] Vivian Mercier, *The Irish Comic Tradition* (Oxford: Clarendon Press): 1962.

[9] Eamonn Jordan, 'From Playground to Background: metatheatricality in the plays of Frank McGuinness', *Theatre Stuff: Critical Essays on Contemporary Irish Theatre*, ed. Eamonn Jordan (Dublin: Carysfort Press, 2000): 197.

[10] Frank McGuinness, 'The spirit of play in Oscar Wilde's *De Profundis*', *Creativity and its Contexts*, ed. Chris Morash (Dublin: Lilliput Press, 1995): 49-59.

6 | Turning a Square Wheel: Yeats, Joyce, and Beckett's *Quad*

Minako Okamuro

Introduction:

A wheel-like image assumes great significance in Samuel Beckett's plays. For instance, *Waiting for Godot* and *Play* bear cyclic structures. In *Waiting for Godot*, the second act repeats what occurred (or what did not occur) in the first act, although the two acts are not identical. In both acts, two tramps await their saviour in vain. *Play* repeats the whole play more strictly. Three characters enclosed in urns are compelled to tell their individual variations of a triangular relationship. When it is about to end, the play returns to the very beginning, which suggests that their narration will continue endlessly. On the other hand, in *Quad*, a non-verbal short piece for television written in 1981, the wheel-like image is not used as structure but clearly visualized. The gyratory movement of four players on the square presents a concrete iconographical image of a turning wheel or, more strictly speaking, a turning square wheel. Here a simple question arises: how did Beckett conceive this strange image?

Once placed in an Irish context, this question immediately evokes the significance of cycles or spirals in the works of two literary masters, William Butler Yeats and James Joyce. This study aims to demonstrate that *Quad* is Beckett's attempt to combine Joyce's 'cyclewheeling' cosmology, developed in *Finnegans Wake*, and Yeats's gyres, represented in *A Vision*, especially in terms of alchemy.

No documentation has yet been found to indicate that Beckett was interested in alchemy. He rarely referred to it in his writings. However, he was a devoted reader of Yeats, who had gained a profound knowledge of alchemy from the Hermetic Order of the Golden Dawn. As well as Yeats, several writers who influenced Beckett – including Dante, Bruno, Descartes, Jung, and Joyce – were, to some extent, attracted by the occult. So how, then, could Beckett remain unconcerned with occultism? A careful examination of his works in fact reveals within them a large number of such allusions. They are recondite, but, like anamorphic paintings,[1] once we see his works from a certain point of view, they magically emerge. In particular, *Quad* presents an idea of alchemy in that it looks like a moving iconography of a revolving square wheel. Its visual image interestingly connects Yeats and Joyce, as we shall see.

I. Turning a Square Wheel, or the Quadrature of the Circle:

Quad is a simple, funny but enigmatic short piece for television. Four players repeat geometrical movements on a square divided into four triangles by two diagonals. The players emerge one by one in sequence to pace regularly counter-clockwise along the sides and diagonals, avoiding the centre.[2] When all players avoid it at the same time, they seem to form a circle around something invisible at the centre. The rhythmical, geometrical, and precisely regular movements of the four players seem like a machine, and the players look like cyborgs. The text somehow resembles a short piece of computer programming.

Yet, the similarity of the leftward movements to a form of ancient Greek ritual dance called the Crane Dance reveals another dimension of *Quad*. The dance is one of the so-called 'labyrinthine dances' in which a line of dancers spirals counterclockwise.[3] Its convolutions are an 'imitation of the labyrinth',[4] and the spiral is usually stylized in angular form. In ancient Greece, labyrinthine dances were performed in the mystery rites of Eleusis to celebrate the Goddess Demeter and her daughter, Persephone.

The resemblance of *Quad* to the labyrinthine dances does not necessarily demonstrate that Beckett had knowledge of the mystery rites of Eleusis, but Yeats was evidently familiar with them. In his short prose piece 'Rosa Alchemica', the first-person protagonist at first resists the efforts of his friend Michael Robartes to draw him into a secret society called the Order of the Alchemical Rose by asking, 'Even if I grant that I need a spiritual belief and some form of worship, why should I go to Eleusis and not to Calvary?'[5] By the phrase 'go[ing] to Eleusis', the protagonist here refers to initiation into the society, for initiations were closely connected with such mystery rites.

After agreeing to join the society, the protagonist is required to learn a magical dance which resembles 'certain antique Greek dances', tracing upon the floor the shapes of rose petals. It is natural that the initiation dance for the Order of the Alchemical Rose takes the form of a rose; notably, a rose is one of the principal symbols of alchemy. Yet also, the dance articulates a repetitive, stylized, and in some senses spiral pattern akin to that of the labyrinthine dance. Insofar as 'the dance wound in and out',[6] it can be understood to describe a line that spirals to contract inwards and expand outwards like the outline of the petals in a rose. In view of the centrality of the theme of 'life in death' and 'death in life' in Yeats, the 'certain antique Greek dance' resonates deeply with the labyrinthine dances of ancient Greece. The relationship between *Quad* and the initiation dance in 'Rosa Alchemica' emerges from this similarity.

It is also noteworthy that according to *A Dictionary of Symbols*, 'when the rose is round in shape it corresponds in significance to the mandala'.[7] It bears further consideration in this regard that the dance-like movements in *Quad* closely resemble what C.G. Jung called the 'mandala dreams' of a certain patient whom he introduced in *Psychology and Alchemy*, dreams which he interprets in terms of alchemy. In the dream, the patient saw people walking 'to the left around a square'.[8] Jung views the square in this dream as having arisen from a circle that the patient had seen in a former dream, interpreting the square in terms of the Quadrature, or squaring, of the circle, and thus as denoting an alchemical mandala. That is, the Quadrature of the circle symbolizes alchemy; it affords a way from chaos to unity, a method by which the four elements – earth, air, fire and water – represented by the square, can be brought into unity in the shape of the circle.

Eliphas Lévi, who greatly influenced the occult thought of Yeats and Joyce, defines the Quadrature of the circle in similar terms:

> So unity, complete in the fruitfulness of the triad, forms therewith the square and produces a circle equal to itself, and this is the Quadrature of the circle, the circular movement of four equal angles around the same point.[9]

In light of this understanding, the patterns of the four players in *Quad* moving along the sides of the square and their division of it into four triangles along its diagonals – symbolizing the circulation of the four elements – can also be understood to represent the Quadrature of the circle. This alchemical notion is key to understanding the connection between Beckett, Joyce and Yeats.

For an insight into the alchemical significance of this symbolism, consider that in *A Dictionary of Alchemical Imagery*, the Quadrature of the circle is related to the image of a great wheel:

> During the opus the matter for the Stone must be dissolved and returned to its primal state before it can be recreated or coagulated into the new pure form of the philosopher's stone. This cycle of separation and union has to be reiterated many times throughout the opus. During this circulation, the elements earth, air, fire and water are separated by distillation and converted into each other to form the perfect unity, the fifth element. ... In another alchemical metaphor, this process is described as the transformation of the square into the circle. This process of transformation, of successively converting the elements into each other, is often compared to *the turning of a great wheel*.[10] (My emphasis).

This image of 'the turning of a great wheel' brings Yeats to mind. The Great Wheel is the central idea of his work of occult philosophy, *A Vision,* in which appears a figure captioned 'The Great Wheel' that consists of triangles, squares, and circles; that is, the Great Wheel is interestingly portrayed as a mandala. Similarly, Clive Hart finds the mandala symbol in the circular structure of Joyce's *Finnegans Wake*:[11]

> The symbol of the circular universe with its timeless centre is also found in the figure of the Buddhist *mandala* which is of such importance to Jung. This is the symbol $\oplus$ which, in the MSS, Joyce gave the highly important ninth question in I.6. His use of it to designate a passage dealing with the structure of *Finnegans Wake* suggests that in one structural sense the whole of the book forms a *mandala,* ... , in which the four four-part cycles make the Wheel of Fortune, while Book IV lies at the 'hub'.[12]

The two masters' interest in the mandala-like wheels was not a coincidence. Eyal Amiran observes that Joyce had the Yeatsian wheel in mind when he wrote *Finnegans Wake*, as he introduces a diagram with an allusion to W.B. Yeats; 'in the lazily eye of his lapis' (*FW* 293).[13] Joyce regarded *Finnegans Wake* as 'an engine with one wheel', which is 'a perfect square', as he once wrote to Harriet Shaw Weaver.[14]

In *Finnegans Wake*, Joyce actually refers to the Quadrature of the circle as 'circling the square': 'So Perhaps, agglaggagglomeratively asaspenking, after all and arklast fore arklyst on his last public misappearance, *circling the square*, for the deathfête of Saint Ignaceous Poisonivy, of the Fickle Crowd ... ' (*FW* 186, my emphasis). The 'circling the square' is mentioned obviously in an alchemical context, because in the same chapter, Shem, who is called an 'alshemist', transmutes his own excrement into ink.[15]

Finnegans Wake is indeed filled with images of the turning wheel. The so-called 'memory wheel' well exemplifies them: 'Now by memory inspired, turn wheel again to the whole of the wall'.[16] (*FW* 69)

Beckett's *Texts for Nothing* apparently reflects this, as its narrator compares his/her memory to a turning wheel: 'What thronging memories, that's to make me think I'm dead, I've said it a million times. But the same return, like the spokes of *a turning wheel*, always the same, and all alike, like spokes'.[17] It is noteworthy that the narrator dreams of infirmities moving '*round* and *round* this grandiose *square*' (my emphasis).[18] This phrase conceives the idea of the squaring of the circle. Beckett's way of embedding the geometrical images in a sentence echoes the geometrical description in the 'Ithaca' episode of Joyce's *Ulysses*: 'Approaching, disparate, at relaxed walking pace they *crossed* both the *circus* before George's church diametrically, the chord in any circle being less than the arc which it subtends'[19] (my emphasis). In the same episode, Joyce again referred to the Quadrature of the circle.

> Because some years previously in 1886 when occupied with the problem of *the* Quadrature *of the circle* he had learned of the existence of a number computed to a relative degree of accuracy to be of such magnitude and of so many places, ... (*U* 820, my emphasis).

Thus, Yeats, Joyce, and Beckett turn and turn wheels in their works. The wheels, which are sometimes squares, represent the idea of the Quadrature of the circle, one of the fundamental notions of alchemy.[20] Let us examine Yeats's and Joyce's works respectively in relation to *Quad*.

II. *A Vision* and *Quad*:

Yeats presents the idea of the Great Wheel in the form of dance in *A Vision*. Book One of the first edition of *A Vision* (1925),[21] which was issued in a private circulation of 600 copies under the pseudonym Owen Aherne, includes a short prose piece entitled 'The Dance of the Four Royal Persons'. According to the narrator, it is an 'account of the diagram called 'The Great Wheel'.[22] In the story, a Caliph decided to offer a large sum of money to any person who could fully explain human nature. Four splendidly dressed persons, who introduced themselves as the King, the Queen, the Prince and the Princess of a most distant country, came to reveal all wisdom by a dance on the edge of the desert. Yet the Caliph found their dance dull and them unintelligible. While awaiting execution, each dancer said to the executioner, 'In the Name of Allah, smooth out the mark of my footfall on the sand.' (*V* 10) When the Caliph heard what the dancers had said, he thought that there must surely be some great secret in the marks made by their feet.

There is no direct reference to alchemy here, but the idea which the eponymous 'royal persons' reveal by dance may be understood as alchemical, for the wheel, as mentioned above, is an important symbol in alchemy. Yeats also regarded the King and Queen as alchemical symbols, as William Gorski observes in his study *Yeats and Alchemy*: 'another medieval motif that Yeats employed was the alchemical idea of the mystical marriage ... symbolized as the conjunction of sun and moon, the embrace of king and queen'.[23] Although this brief story does not describe the dance of the royal persons in detail, it notes that 'some great secret of human nature' is hidden in the 'mark of their footfalls' (*V* 10).[24] This brings to mind Beckett's deep attachment to footsteps: the stage directions of *Quad* specify that 'each player has his particular sound' (*CDW* 452), and Beckett is the author of a play called *Footfalls*.

In 'The Dance of the Four Royal Persons', the 'great secret of human nature' in the marks of the footfalls of the dancers is not revealed. But, in Book Two, Yeats presents a diagram explaining the Great Wheel that consists of two whirling, interlocking cones called 'the gyres'. Notably, the double cones oppose each other, one expanding as the other contracts. The conjunction of opposites is an essential idea in alchemical thought. The diagram of the double gyres illustrates the marks drawn by the footfalls of the four royal persons, revealing their dance to be the movement of the four elements in opposing gyres, or spirals, which engender the fifth element.

These points also support the interpretation of the dance of the four royal persons, like that of the four players in *Quad*, as representing the alchemical conception of the spiral movement of the four elements. However, the dance-like movements of the four players in Beckett's *Quad*, never reaching the centre, do not give rise to the fifth element.

As the four royal persons represent 'some great secret of human nature' in the form of the 'mark of their footfalls', the alchemical thought was passed on from generation to generation in iconographies, because it was hidden wisdom and could not be explained logically by words or mathematical figures. The framing picture of the four players revolving in the square looks like a moving iconography.

What aspect of alchemy attracted Yeats so particularly? One possible answer is its key concept of the unity of opposites, the conjunction of the dead and the living, in particular, as Yeats describes gyres as 'each dying the other's life living the other's death' (*V* 130). In fact, Yeats's poem 'The Tower' represents this alchemical idea of the unity of opposites. Yeats himself refers to the symbolic meaning of a tower, saying 'I have used towers, and one tower in particular, as symbols and have compared their winding stairs to the philosophical gyres'.[25] According to *A Dictionary of Alchemical Imagery*, a tower is 'a synonym for the athanor or philosophical furnace'.[26] In the process of alchemical transmutation that occurs in the tower, 'such opposite states and qualities as sulphur and mercury, hot and cold, dry and moist, fixed and volatile, spirit and body, form and matter, active and receptive, and male and female are reconciled of their differences and united'.[27] This union of the substances, or the reconciliation of opposites called a 'chemical wedding' is the goal of alchemy.

Therefore, the tower can be a magical place for the Yeats poem in which the discord between old age and imagination, and the boundary between the dead and the living can vanish. Beckett presumably knew this symbolic meaning of the tower. In 1961, he wrote a play for radio, *Words and Music*.[28] In the play, a master called Croak tries to reconcile the personified characters, Words and Music, to each other, but in vain. That is because words and music are inconsistent with each other, being verbal and non-verbal, logical and illogical, or rational and irrational. The only way Words and Music collaborate with each other is to sing a song. In the song, a woman, who was supposedly loved by Croak but is now dead, appears. She is at first described rather grotesquely by Words in the image of a corpse: '[the lips] ... tight, a gleam of tooth biting on the under, no coral, no swell, ...' (*CDW* 292). Yet, her face and body come to be miraculously restored through alchemical transmutation. What deserves our attention is that the scene seems to be located in a tower, because, at the beginning, Croak requests forgiveness from Words and Music for his having been late, saying: 'Forgive. [*Pause.*] In the tower. [*Pause.*] The face' (*CDW* 288). The 'face' reminds us of the woman's face in *...but the clouds...*, written for television in 1976, where the woman actually quotes from 'The Tower'. *Words and Music* must have been developed into *... but the clouds ...* that was named after a part of the last stanza of 'The Tower'. In the play, a man begs a supposedly dead woman to appear, like the kind of séance with which Yeats was familiar. When the face of the woman appears, the boundary between the dead and the living disappears.[29]

III. *Finnegans Wake* as an Uroboros:

Beckett's interest in wheel-like imagery had already appeared in his first published writing 'Dante ... Bruno . Vico .. Joyce', in which he discussed the cyclic structure of James Joyce's *Work in Progress*, which was later entitled *Finnegans Wake*.[30] In this novel, Joyce adapted Giambattista Vico's theory of the cyclic evolution of history for his 'cyclewheeling history' (*FW* 186). Joycean wheels, however, cannot be attributed solely to Vico. It is well known that when Joyce wrote *Finnegans Wake*, he was inspired by the *Book of Kells*, a mediaeval Irish manuscript illuminated with motifs based on the combination of multiple circles and spirals. According to James Atherton, when Joyce described his own manuscript of *Finnegans Wake*, he frequently compared it to the *Book of Kells*.[31] Atherton points out that Joyce claims to have found signs of non-Christian influences in it despite its Christian provenance. It was not only some non-Christian elements that Joyce found in it. He interestingly connected its wheel-cross combination to the idea of alchemy.

The 'Tunc page' in the *Book of Kells*, specifically referred to in *Finnegans Wake*, contains double serpents, one of which forms a uroboros-like square, while the other spirals form a letter 'T', and an X-figure patterned after St Andrew's cross. Since the serpents are linked, they also look like a double-headed uroboros. It is believed that St Patrick, who brought Christianity to Ireland, expelled the snakes that used to be worshipped in Druidic Ireland.[32] Barbara Walker states that serpents were originally identified with the Great Goddess of birth and death, because in the ancient world they were believed not to die of old age but to shed their skins periodically and emerge renewed or reborn into another life.[33]

Given that Joyce suggested to Stuart Gilbert that he read Blavatsky's *Isis Unveiled*, a large part of his knowledge of occultism as well as theosophy could be attributed to Blavatsky.[34] In *Isis Unveiled*, she regards the annular shape of a serpent with its tail in its mouth as an 'emblem of eternity in its spiritual and of our world in its physical sense'.[35]

The Uroboros, a serpent biting its own tail, is also regarded as one of the significant symbols of alchemy, because the cycle of death and rebirth is crucial in alchemy, too. Abraham says: 'In biting its own tail the uroboros makes a complete circle, aptly symbolizing the circular nature of the transformative process, the rotation of the elements, the opus circulatorium'.[36] In the alchemical process, four elements circulate, just as the four-part structure of *Finnegans Wake* circulates as the last words 'a long the' run into the first word 'riverrun'.[37] In this sense, *Finnegans Wake* itself forms an uroboros, as in 'Dante ... Bruno . Vico .. Joyce' Beckett puts 'a series of stimulants to enable the kitten to catch its tail'.[38]

The symbol of the Order of the Rosy Cross, or the Rosicrucians, an occult group that linked aspects of Christianity with alchemy, also consisted of a cross and a rose which is equated with concentric circles or a spiral. It is worth mentioning that 'the crucian rose' is referred to in the same sentence as the *Book of Kells* in *Finnegans Wake:*

> ... then (coming over to the left aisle corner down) the cruciform postscript from which three *basia* or shorter and smaller *oscula* have been overcarefully scraped away, plainly inspiring the tenebrous *Tunc* page of the Book of Kells (and then it need not be lost sight of that there are exactly three squads of candidates for the crucian rose awaiting their turn in the marginal panels of Columkiller, chugged in their three ballotboxes, ...) ... (*FW* 122, original emphasis).[39]

Beckett, who had many opportunities to discuss *Finnegans Wake* with Joyce in Paris, is supposed to have recognized those Irish and alchemical aspects of Joycean 'cyclewheeling' cosmology. Although he never directly mentions alchemy in 'Dante ... Bruno . Vico .. Joyce', it does contain such allusions as 'the circular transmutation' and 'phoenix'[40] which he picked up from *Finnegans Wake*. In reference to Tunc page, it is worth mentioning that a Latin sentence written on the cross is a quotation from Matthew 27.38: 'TUNC CRUCIFIXERANT XPI CUM EO DUOS LATRONES'; i.e. 'Then were there two thieves crucified with him'. The two thieves are mentioned by Vladimir in *Waiting for Godot*: 'Our Saviour. Two thieves. One is supposed to have been saved and the other ... [*He searches for the contrary of saved.*] ... damned'. (*CDW* 13)

According to the authors of *Beckett in the Theater*, in the Schiller Theatre production of *Waiting for Godot* directed by Beckett himself in 1975, the actors moved geometrically to form circles and crosses on the stage.[41] Also, the tree on the stage could symbolize the cross of the Crucifixion. These facts do not necessarily demonstrate the direct influence of the *Book of Kells* on *Waiting for Godot*. Nevertheless, the possibility is undeniable that it was passed from Joyce to Beckett. *Waiting for Godot* has a wheel-like structure, as mentioned above. It also contains several minor but visible or audible wheels such as the circulation of the hats between the two tramps and the circular song about dogs which Vladimir sings at the beginning of the second act. This complex of the multiple spirals in *Waiting for Godot* evokes the combination of a variety of spirals in the Irish illuminated manuscripts.[42]

IV. Joyce's 'Geomater' and Beckett's 'Wombtomb':

The wheel-cross combination with spiral illumination, found in so-called Celtic crosses as well as the *Book of Kells*, is considered to symbolize the heretical Druidic doctrine of metempsychosis; the cycle of birth, death and rebirth.[43] Therefore, Celtic crosses bear a close relation to the mother goddess. The centre of the spiral is regarded as an ambivalent hole that gives birth and engulfs life at the same time.

In *Finnegans Wake*, 'mother' and 'geometry' are combined into the word 'geomater' (*FW* 296-7), which suggests 'mother Earth'.[44] In the 'Triv and Quad' chapter in Book II, the twins, Dolph (Shem) and Kev (Shaun), are solving a geometry problem. The diagram Dolph is drawing consists of double circles and double triangles within them. It not only demonstrates Euclid's first proposition, but also reveals 'the mother secrets of ALP'.[45] A, L and P in the diagram stand for Anna Livia Plurabelle, the mother. Dolph says:

> I'll make you to see figuratleavely *the whome of your eternal geomater*. And if you flung *her headdress* on her from under her highlows you'd wheeze whyse Salmonson set his seel on a hexengown. ... Outer *serpumstances* beiug ekewilled, we carefully, if she pleats, lift by her seam hem and jabote at the spidsiest of her trickkikant (like thousands done before since fillies calpered. Ocone! Ocone!) the maidsapron of our ALP., fearfully! ... (*FW* 296-7, my emphasis).

As he calls it 'the whome of your eternal geomater', the diagram represents the womb of the eternal mother Earth. Here ALP is universalized to the mother archetype; the Great Mother, as Kev says: 'Mother of us all!'. The two deltas may imply the mother Goddess Demeter, because, according to Walker, 'De' for Demeter means 'delta', which symbolizes the triangular door of 'birth, death, or the sexual paradise'.[46] Dolph and Kev, the names of the twins, might be a reminiscence of the dolphin and dove which Demeter carries. Walker regards the dolphin and the dove as symbols of the womb. Or, if 'her headdress' suggests the 'veil of Isis' as Ronald McHugh notes,[47] it may refer to Blavatsky's *Isis Unveiled*. In the same section, Dolph mentions 'serpumstances' which is a combination of the words 'serpent' and 'circumstances'. Isis, too, corresponds to the archetype of the Great Mother and the primordial archetype of the Feminine and of uroboros. At the same time, the coined word reminds us of the serpent biting its own tail in the *Book of Kells*. In fact Dolph states: 'I've read your tunc's dismissage', which is considered to refer to the Tunc page.[48] Thus, geometry related to the mother Goddess leads us back to the *Book of Kells*.

Furthermore, here too we can find some alchemical aspects. As mentioned above, Joyce introduces the diagram with the phrase 'in the lazily eye of his lapis' (*FW* 293). The word 'lapis' means a philosopher's stone which is the sought-after goal of the alchemical process. The authors of *A Skeleton Key to Finnegans Wake* claim that the 'lapis' is 'the philosopher's stone of Dublin', and that the boys are drawing 'the geometrical counterpart of the philosopher's stone'.[49] Here the diagram of the mother's womb is identified with the alchemical philosopher's stone.[50]

Mircea Eliade remarks that the alchemical reduction to the *prima materia* may be equated with a regression to the pre-natal state.[51] As Hart claims,[52] in Book IV Shaun retires via the vagina into the womb in his journey backward to annihilation. Since the diagram is located in the middle of the whole volume of *Finnegans Wake* which has a circular structure, it is considered to be a womb-like hole opening its mouth at the very centre of the wheel, and symbolizes the gate of birth, death and rebirth.

This reminds us of Beckett's combined word 'wombtomb' in *Dream of Fair to middling Women*. As Beckett puts it in *A Piece of Monologue*: 'Birth was the death of him' (*CDW* 425), birth is directly linked to death in his world. The following passage in *Texts for Nothing* clearly presents this:

> Yes, I'd have a mother, I'd have a tomb, I wouldn't have come out of here, one doesn't come out of here, here are my tomb and mother, it's all here this evening, I'm dead and getting born, without having ended, helpless to begin, that's my life.[53]

Mary A. Doll identifies some of Beckett's female protagonists with Demeter. She states that such Beckett plays as *Not I*, *Footfalls*, and *Rockaby* bear an astonishing similarity to the motifs of Demeter, and '[a]ll follow a rhythm of Demeter's sorrowful search as a cycle of finding and losing'.[54] In *Not I*, a mouth isolated from body and elevated in the dark onstage recites a story of an old woman who seems dead and suffers from the memory of her life. Although the mouth narrates in the third person, the narrative gradually comes to coincide with its own situation, as if the mouth of the woman were telling her own story. Therefore, the mouth open in the dark looks like the gate of hell. According to Walker, 'mouth' comes from the same root as 'mother', and in ancient belief, the mouth of hell was identified with female genitals. This ambivalence of 'mouth' has been expressed in the words 'toothed vagina'.[55] In this sense, the mouth in *Not I* seems to be the 'wombtomb'.

In the 'Ithaca' episode of *Ulysses*, when Bloom goes back home, he recognizes a sign of his wife's betrayal on her bed. Molly, the listener and Bloom, the narrator are described as follows:

> **Listener:** reclined semilaterally, left, left hand under head, right leg extended in a straight line and resting on left leg, flexed, in the attitude of *Gae-Tellus*, fulfilled, recumbent, big with seed. Narrator: reclined laterally, left, with right and left legs flexed, the indexfinger

98   Ireland on Stage: Beckett and After

> and thumb of the right hand resting on the bridge of the nose, in the attitude depicted in a snapshot photograph made by Percy Apjohn, the childman weary, *the manchild in the womb*. (*U* 870, my emphasis)

'Gae-Tellus' is the combined word of 'Gaea', the Goddess of earth, and a Latin word 'tellus' which means 'earth'. As A. Walton Litz states: ' ... we must believe that Molly has merged into her archetype, Gae-Tellus, while Leopold Bloom has become the archetype of all human possibility, "the manchild in the womb"',[56] Molly becomes the archetype of the Great Mother whose womb conceives 'the manchild'. Declan Kiberd's indication of the androgyny of Bloom and his wife in this part is quite suggestive:

> As they sleep head-to-toe in the bed in Eccles Street, Leopold and Molly unwittingly re-enact the experimental attempt at alchemical fusion by the saintly couples of early Christianity. St Francis and St Clare, St Theresa and St John of the Cross were simply the most famous exponents of a tradition that sought the wisdom of an androgynous godhead.[57]

This androgynous nature of their posture on the bed interestingly reflects the definition of uroboros by Erich Neumann.

> As symbol of the origin and of the opposites contained in it, the uroboros is the 'Great Round,' in which positive and negative, male and female, elements of consciousness, elements hostile to consciousness, and unconscious elements are intermingled.[58]

Here the two archetypes of mother Earth and 'the manchild' in her womb conjoin in an uroboros or the Great Round at 'alchemical fusion'. In this sense, it is remarkable that the mattress of their bed is described as 'the snakespiral springs of the mattress'.[59]

Thus, both in the Joycean and the Beckettian world, the alchemical Quadrature of the circle and the mother Goddess are combined to represent the cycle of death and rebirth. What strikes us is the astonishing concentration of these aspects in Beckett's *Quad*.

V. 'Triv and Quad' in *Finnegans Wake* and Beckett's *Quad*:

The 'Triv and Quad' chapter of *Finnegans Wake* contains the phrase 'his [Dolph's] sinister cyclopes' and the word 'spirals' in 'ownconsciously grafficking with his sinister cyclopes' (*FW* 300). Dolph, who is identified with Shem, unconsciously draws leftward spirals.[60] This also echoes Joyce's description of the Tunc page: 'utterly unexpected sinistrogyric return to one peculiar sore point in the past' (120). 'Synistrogyric' is the combined word of 'sinister' and 'gyre'. Four elements in the Jungian alchemical dream, Shem the 'alshemist' in the four-part structured *Wake*, and the four players in *Quad* all circulate leftward. Jung regards the centre of the square in the dream as the symbol of the unity which embraces both the conscious mind and the unconscious. Beckett's *Quad*, however, is decentred. Umberto Eco asserts that the *Book of Kells* is an acentric labyrinth:

> ... it is a structure whose every point can be connected to any other, in which – for all intents and purposes – there are no points or positions but only lines of connection, any one of which may be interrupted at any point whatsoever since it will begin immediately to follow the same line; it can be disconnected and overturned – It has no centre. The Book of Kells is a labyrinth, the Book of Kells is an open and unparalleled masterpiece.[61]

Joyce in fact describes the *Book of Kells* as a 'maze'; 'a word as cunningly hidden in its maze of confused drapery as a fieldmouse in a nest of coloured ribbons' (*FW* 120). As mentioned before, the leftward movement in *Quad* is similar to the so-called 'labyrinthine dances' of ancient Greece, which were performed in the mystery rites of Eleusis to celebrate Demeter, the mother Goddess.[62] When searching for her daughter abducted into the underworld, Demeter came to Eleusis and found her there. Neumann says that the rite of the mother Goddess as a way begins always as a 'walked' or danced archetype, as labyrinth or spiral, as image of a spiral, as image of a spirit, or as a way through a gate of death and rebirth.[63] The 'gate of death and rebirth' is ambivalent. Neumann relates the labyrinth to the Terrible Mother.

The labyrinthine way is always the first part of the night sea voyage, the descent of the male following the sun into the devouring underworld, into the deathly womb of the Terrible Mother. This labyrinthine way, which leads to *the centre of danger*, where at the midnight hour, in the land of dead, in the middle of the night sea voyage, the decision falls, occurs in the judgment of the dead in Egypt, in the mysteries both classical and primitive, and in the corresponding processes of psychic development in modern man[64] (my emphasis):

> The centre of *Quad*, which Beckett describes as 'a danger zone. Hence deviation', seems to reflect 'the centre of danger'. Similarly, at the mid-point of the circular universe in *Finnegans Wake*, there is 'no placelike no timelike absolent' (609).

When he wrote 'Dante ... Bruno . Vico .. Joyce' in 1929, he might have already conceived the idea of *Quad*. Referring to the four old men in *Finnegans Wake* in his essay, Beckett mentioned: 'The four 'lovedroyd curdinals' are presented on the same plane'.[65] Joyce's coined word 'lovedroyd' is considered to refer to the Druids. According to Walker, Irish druidic law insisted on 'the counterclockwise movement around the holy omphalos at Tara, shrine of Mother Earth'.[66] George Cinclair Gibson regards Tara as the model of Joyce's fourfold microcosm in that it was designed with the 'four provincial halls', representing the four provinces, cardinal directions, elements, and all other Quadratures in Irish mythology, arranged around the Central Hall called the temple Quadrata that symbolized the cosmos.[67] It would be interesting to know if Beckett was aware of this. Taking into consideration the monk-like costumes of the four players of *Quad*, Beckett might have imagined the four Druid monks were circulating leftward at the shrine of Mother Earth.

As we have seen, *Quad* reflects a number of Irish and alchemical aspects which can be found in *Finnegans Wake*. In this sense, I presume that this minimal piece could be regarded as Beckett's version of *Finnegans Wake*, as well as an homage to Yeats. Of course, between *Finnegans Wake* and *Quad* lies an enormous difference. Joyce oriented his immense verbal universe of *Finnegans Wake* to encyclopedic richness, while Beckett ascetically pointed to the minimalism of an infinite decimal with his non-verbal short piece. In this fashion, however, the distance between the two is dissolved; as in the *Book of Kells* the spirals distend outwards and contract inwards at the same time, and as in alchemy the opposites are conjoined just like Beckett's discussion about Bruno: 'The maxima and minima of particular contraries are one and indifferent.'[68] Hence, Joyce's centrifugal spiral and Beckett's centripetal one are linked to mirror the double-headed uroboros on the Tunc page of the *Book of Kells*.

Conclusion:

Amiran suggests Joyce's and Yeats's influence on Beckett regarding the cycle by saying, 'From Yeats, Beckett takes an impersonal, metaphysical construction of the cycle; from Joyce, he receives a lecture on the cycle's sexuality'.[69] As we have seen, it is not only the cycle that the three greatest Irish writers share but also the alchemical idea of the Quadrature of the circle which represents the unity of opposites, the conjunction of the dead and the living. Beckett's *Quad* seems magically to unite Yeats's gyres and Joyce's 'cyclewheeling' cosmology in this regard.

Declan Kiberd remarks that, although 'to many modern minds, the notion of history as a circular repetition is a matter for despair', Joyce was 'positively entranced by the cyclical, gyring pattern of history propounded by Yeats in *A Vision*, regretting only that it did not figure more prominently in the poetry'.[70] In a sense, Beckett figured it into his visual poetry of *Quad*. In the production of *Quad* directed by Beckett himself in Stuttgart, he added a black-and-white version of the dance-like performance after the colour one. In the additional version, the four figures continue to pace around the same square, but the speed of their pacing is much slower and the beating of percussion that accompanied the colour version ceases, rendering the wearily shuffling footfalls of the players audible. According to Martin Esslin, Beckett said that relative to the colour version, this black-and-white version takes place 'a hundred thousand years later'.[71] Although it seems to express a rather negative vision, it may be Beckett's modest representation of what Yeats described as '[the place] where the blessed [people] dance' in 'All Soul's Night', the epilogue to *A Vision*. It represents how Beckett accepted the 'cyclewheeling history' of Ireland, just as Yeats and Joyce did.

[1] In *Anamorphosis in Shakespeare* [*Shakespeare no Anamorufohzu* in Japanese] (Tokyo: Kenkyusha, 1999), Mitsuru Kamachi analyses an anamorphic painting and explores the hidden alchemical symbols in Shakespeare's works.

[2] The permutations and combinations of their movement are described as follows: '1 enters at A, completes his course and is joined by 3. Together they complete their courses and are joined by 4. Together all three complete their courses and are joined by 2. Together all four complete their courses. Exit 1. 2, 3 and 4 continue and complete their courses. Exit 3. 2 and 4 continue and complete their courses. Exit 4. End of 1st series. 2 continues, opening 2nd series, completes his course and is joined by 1. Etc. Unbroken movement.' Samuel Beckett, *The Complete Dramatic Works* (London: Faber and Faber, 1986): 451. Subsequent references to Beckett's plays are cited in the text as (*CDW* 451).

[3] See Minako Okamuro, '*Quad* and Jungian Mandala', *Samuel Beckett Today/ Aujourd'hui* 6 (1997): 125-34. In the paper, I pointed out the similarity of *Quad* to the labyrinthine dance, a mandala dream, and the alchemical process.

[4] C.G. Jung and C. Kerény, *Essays on a Science of Mythology: The Myth of the Divine Child and the Mysteries of Eleusis*, trans. R.F.C. Hull (Princeton: Princeton University Press, 1978): 134.

[5] William Butler Yeats, *The Secret Rose* (London: Lawrence & Bullen, 1897): 232.

[6] Yeats, *The Secret Rose*, 257-58.

[7] J.E. Cirlot, *A Dictionary of Symbols*, trans. Jack Sage (London: Routledge, 1971): 275.

[8] C.G. Jung, *Psychology and Alchemy*, trans. R.F.C. Hull (Princeton: Princeton University Press, 1968): 124.

[9] Eliphas Lévi, *Transcendental Magic: Its Doctrine and Ritual*, trans. A.E. Waite (York Beach: Samuel Weiser, 1999): 37.

[10] Lyndy Abraham, *A Dictionary of Alchemical Imagery* (Cambridge:

Cambridge University Press, 1998): 137-38.

[11]James Joyce, *Finnegans Wake* (London: Faber and Faber, 1975). Subsequent references to this edition are cited in the text as (*FW*186).

[12]Clive Hart, *Structure and Motif in Finnegans Wake* (London: Faber and Faber, 1962): 77.

[13]Eyal Amiran, *Wandering and Home: Beckett's Metaphysical Narrative* (Pennsylvania: The Pennsylvania State University Press, 1993): 202.

[14]James Joyce, *Letters of James Joyce*, ed. Stuart Gilbert (London: Faber and Faber, n.d.): 251.

[15]Barbara DiBernard asserts: 'Joyce used alchemy, especially in *Finnegans Wake*, as a metaphor for change and the artistic process; the alchemical transmutation of lead into gold parallels the artistic transmutation of life into art.' Barbara DiBernard, *Alchemy and Finnegans Wake* (Albany: State University of New York Press, 1980): 7.

[16]Lorraine Weir regards the 'geomater' diagram in *Finnegans Wake* as 'the visual image of a complex memory theater from which the discourse system of the whole may be generated in performance'. She remarks: 'That poetic geography in *Finnegans Wake* is epitomized in the geomater diagram's "Vieus Von DVbLIn", where the "doubling bicirculars" meet and *where the memory wheel is turned.*' Lorraine Weir, *Writing Joyce: A Semiotics of the Joyce System* (Bloomington: Indiana University Press, 1989): 74-75.

[17]Samuel Beckett, *Texts for Nothing, Collected Shorter Prose 1945-1980* (London: John Calder, 1986): 94.

[18]Beckett, *Texts for Nothing*, 99.

[19]James Joyce, *Ulysses: Annotated Students' Edition* (London: Penguin Books, 1992): 776. Subsequent references to this edition are cited in the text as (*U* 820).

[20]Dante refers to the squaring of the circle, too (Canto XXXIII, 11.133-37). Dante Alighieri, *The Divine Comedy*, trans. Charles S. Singleton (Princeton: Princeton University Press, 1975): 79.

[21]William Butler Yeats, *A Vision: An Explanation of Life Founded upon the Writings of Giraldus and upon Certain Doctrines Attributed to Kusta Ben Luka* (London: T. Werner Laurie, 1925). Subsequent references to this edition are cited in the text as (V 10).

[22]I fully discussed the influence of 'The Dance of the Four Royal Persons' on *Quad* in 'Alchemical Dances in Beckett and Yeats', *Samuel Beckett Today/Aujourd'hui* 14 (2004): 87-103.

[23]William Gorski, *Yeats and Alchemy* (New York: State University of New York Press, 1996): 11.

[24]The footprints made by holy figures are believed to have been preserved and worshipped in ancient Ireland.

[25]William Butler Yeats, *The Variorum Edition of the Poems of W.B. Yeats*, eds Peter Allt and Russell K. Alspach (New York: Macmillan, 1957): 831.

[26]Abraham, 203-04.

[27]Abraham, 35.

[28]Yeats's collection of poems entitled *The Winding Stair and Other Poems*

(1933) contains a series of poems entitled 'Words for Music Perhaps'. Katharine Worth points out the similarity of the titles, *Words for Music Perhaps* and *Words and Music* in *The Irish Drama of Europe from Yeats to Beckett* (London: Athlone, 1986): 259.

[29]For Yeats's influence on *Words and Music*, see Minako Okamuro, '*Words and Music, ...but the clouds...* and Yeats's "The Tower"', *Beckett at 100: Revolving I All*, eds Linda Ben-Zvi and Angela Moorjani (New York: Oxford University Press) to be published in 2007.

[30]My discussion about alchemical aspects of *Finnegans Wake* and *Quad* is based on the paper entitled 'Circles, Spirals, and Crosses in the Works of Beckett and Joyce: A Study of Their Celtic and Alchemical Aspects', which I read at 'Beckett in Berlin 2000' symposium held at Humboldt Universität zu Berlin in September 2000.

[31]James S. Atherton, *The Book at the Wake: A Study of Literary Allusions in James Joyce's Finnegans Wake* (London: Faber and Faber, 1959): 61.

[32]Sir Edward Sullivan mentioned this in his introduction to *The Book of Kells* (London: "The Studio", n.d.). Atherton points out that, although Joyce pokes fun at his introduction in *Finnegans Wake*, Joyce finds a connection between himself and Sullivan in that 'they both claim to have found signs of non-Christian influences.' See Atherton, 64.

[33]Barbara Walker, *The Woman's Encyclopedia of Myths and Secrets* (San Francisco: Harper Collins, 1983): 903.

[34]Hart regards the writings of H.P. Blavatsky as the source of the enormous theosophical allusions in *Ulysses* and *Finnegans Wake* in spite of their hopeless inaccuracy. See Hart, 49. Tindall also states: 'we know from Stanislaus Joyce that his brother, like many other Dubliners around the turn of the century, dabbled in Theosophy, attended meetings at the home of AE, and read occult literature.' William York Tindall, 'James Joyce and the Hermetic Tradition', *The Journal of the History of Ideas* 15. 1 (1954): 32. In *Ulysses*, Joyce mentions AE and Blavatsky: 'What do you think really of that hermetic crowd, the opal hush poets: AE the mastermystic? That Blavatsky woman started it. She was a nice old bag of tricks.' See Joyce, *Ulysses*, 178.

[35]H.P. Blavatsky, *Isis Unveiled: A Master-Key to the Mysteries of Ancient and Modern Science and Theology*, 2 vols (Pasadena: Theosophical University Press, 1976): Vol. 2, 489-90. The emblem of the Theosophical Society which Blavatsky founded in New York in 1875 consists of a combination of the western uroboros, the eastern Swastika, the Jewish Star of David and the ancient Egyptian Ankh. Alexander Roob asserts that Blavatsky appears in *Finnegans Wake* as a hen scratching a mysterious piece of writing from a dung-heap. Alexander Roob, *The Hermetic Museum: Alchemy & Mysticism*, trans. Shaun Whiteside (Köln: Taschen, 1997): 430.

[36]Abraham, 207.

[37]Hart indicates 'the implicit identification' of the four four-chapter cycles of *Finnegans Wake* with the four elements. See Hart, 62.

[38]Samuel Beckett, 'Dante ... Bruno . Vico .. Joyce', *Disjecta: Miscellaneous Writings and a Dramatic Fragment*, ed. Ruby Cohn (New York: Grove

Press, 1984): 33.

[39]The word 'columkiller' seems to refer to St Columba whose successors created the *Book of Kells*. Sir Edward Sullivan states that the *Book of Kells* is often called 'the Book of Colum Cille' in his introduction to the *Book of Kells* which Joyce read. Alternatively, it may refer to St Columbanus (Columban). Terence de Vere White describes the 1930s as the time when 'there were certain enthusiasts who never let the public forget that the Masons were conspiring against Ireland in general and the Church in particular; ... ; and there was a set-off in the criticism by many Catholics of the Knights of St Columbanus.' Terence de Vere White, 'The Freemasons', *Secret Societies in Ireland*, ed. T. Desmond Williams (Dublin: Gill and Macmillan, 1973): 46.

[40]In alchemy, the 'phoenix' is a symbol of resurrection signifying the philosopher's stone.

[41]See Dougald McMillan and Martha Fehsenfeld, *Beckett in the Theatre: The Author as Practical Playwright and Director* (London: John Calder, 1988): 99-115.

[42]Clive Hart points out that *Finnegans Wake* also contains a full variety of the cycles. 'Not only is the scheme of *Finnegans Wake* itself cyclic, but the inhabitants of this re-entrant world themselves spin in a crazy, tiring whirl around circular paths of endeavour, always with new hope, always frustrated, maintained by the wan satisfaction that, like Bruce's spider, they will always be able to try again. Their cycling is as much literal and physical as metaphorical and spiritual.' Hart, 112.

[43]Malcolm Chapman claims that Celtic crosses originated from early Christian Mediterranean styles in monumental religious stonework which came to Ireland, *The Celts: The Construction of a Myth* (New York: St. Martin's Press, 1992): 116. Since the seventh century, crosses have been braided with interlaced works in Ireland. Yet before Christianity was brought to Ireland, the Celts were already familiar with spiral illumination. Celtic spirals are considered to be related to the Druidic belief in immortality. Referring to John Irwin, Derek Bryce suggested that the origin of the wheel-cross symbol is the Assyrian rayed cross which dates from many centuries before the Christian era, and is considered to have been a solar symbol in *Symbolism of the Celtic Cross* (York Beach: Samuel Weiser, 1989): 38.

[44]See Ronald McHugh, *Annotations to Finnegans Wake* (Baltimore and London: The Johns Hopkins University Press, 1991): 297.

[45]Joseph Campbell and Henry Morton Robinson, *A Skeleton Key to Finnegans Wake* (New York: Harcourt, Brace, 1944): 25.

[46]Walker, 218.

[47]McHugh, 297.

[48]Campbell and Robinson point out: 'Joyce here seems to suggest that the Tunc-page illuminations of the *Book of Kells* carry the message revealed in the present chapter.' Cambell and Robinson, 156.

[49]Cambell and Robinson, 154.

[50]In *Dublin's Joyce* (London: Chatto and Windus, 1955): 327-28, Hugh

Kenner also finds the diagram alchemical. Quoting from Jung's *The Integration of the Personality*, he states: 'In the geometry lesson in *Finnegans Wake*, Dolph performs for the scandalized Kev a lewd grammatical exegesis of a diagram strikingly like the alchemical formula quoted by Jung: "Fac de masculo et foemina circulum rotundum, et de eo extrahe quadrangulum et ex quadrangulo trianglum; fac circulum rotundum (of the triangle) et habebis lapidum Philosophorum."'

[51] Mircea Eliade, *The Forge and the Crucible: The Origins and Structures of Alchemy*, trans. Stephen Corrin, 2nd ed. (Chicago: The University of Chicago Press, 1978): 154. In this sense it is important that ALP is identified with a hen in the chapter called 'The Manifesto of ALP' in Book I. In alchemy, hens and eggs are among the significant symbols, because the athanor, a vessel used in alchemy, is called an 'egg', which should be kept at the same temperature as hens hatch their eggs, and so it is also compared to the womb. In 'The Cartesian Egg: Alchemical Images in Beckett's Early Writings', *Journal of Beckett Studies* 9. 2 (2000): 63-80, I pointed out that the 'hens and eggs' motif appears in Beckett's works such as *Whoroscope*, 'For Future Reference', and *Dream of Fair to middling Women*, all of which were written under the strong influence of Joyce. In my view, the motif carries an alchemical implication in those of Beckett's works as in Joyce's.

[52] Hart, 68.

[53] Beckett, *Texts for Nothing*, 101.

[54] Mary A. Doll, *Beckett and Myth: An Archtypal Approach* (Syracuse: Syracuse University Press, 1988), 58.

[55] Walker, 1034.

[56] A. Walton Litz, 'Ithaca', *James Joyce's Ulysses: Critical Essays*, eds Clive Hart and David Hayman (Berkeley: University of Califirnia Press, 1974): 403.

[57] Declan Kiberd, Notes, *Ulysses: Annotated Students' Edition* (London: Penguin Books, 1992): 1182.

[58] Erich Neumann, *The Great Mother: An analysis of the Archetype*, trans. Ralph Manheim (Princeton: Princeton University Press, 1955): 18.

[59] Quoting Blavatsky's *The Secret Doctrine*, Roob claims that Joyce was familiar with her interpretation of the letter T (Greek 'Tau') as an androgynous symbol of the 'reciprocal containment of two opposite principles in one, just as the Saviour is mystically held to be male-female' (Roob, 635). This reminds us that in the Tunc page of the *Book of Kells*, one of the serpents forms a 'T' while the other forms an uroboros. Joyce might have referred to the Tunc page in particular because of the androgynous image accompanied with a uroboros in it.

[60] Regarding Shem and Shaun's circular movement, Hart claims: 'Of all the spatial cycles in the book, these are the two which are most clearly established' (Hart, 113), and 'the orbits of Shem and Shaun are more nearly circular, because in *Finnegans Wake* there is no centre on to which a true spiral might be made to converge.' (Hart, 114)

[61] Umberto Eco, Foreword, *The Book of Kells*, trans. Oscar Ratti (Zurich:

Faksimile Verlag Luzern, 1990): 16. Echo remarks that since 'the *Book of Kells* has revealed itself to be a model for every experimental language of the future', it was not by chance that it inspired Joyce when he wrote *Finnegans Wake* (Eco, 14).

[62]The convolutions of the Crane Dance imitated the windings of the Cretan labyrinth which is said to be built by Daedalus , after whom Joyce named his hero.

[63]Neumann, 177.

[64]Neumann, 177.

[65]Beckett, 'Dante ... Bruno . Vico .. Joyce', 23. MacArthur states that the four old men are associated with the four elements. See Ian MacArthur, 'Alchemical Elements of *FW*', *A Wake Newsletter* 12. 2 (1975): 22.

[66]Walker, 532. Roob states that the lapis which connects the four points of the compass symbolises the 'omphalos', the navel of the world (Roob, 342).

[67]George Cinclair Gibson, *Wake Rites: The Ancient Irish Rituals of Finnegans Wake* (Gainesville, Florida: University Press of Florida, 2005): 215.

[68]Beckett, 'Dante ... Bruno . Vico .. Joyce', 21.

[69]Amiran, 193.

[70]Declan Kiberd, Introduction, *Ulysses: Annotated Students' Edition* (London: Penguin Books, 1992): xxvii.

[71]Martin Esslin, 'Towards the Zero of Language', *Beckett's Later Fiction and Drama*, eds James Acheson and Kateryana Arthur (New York: St. Martin's Press, 1987): 44.

7 | Multiple Monologues as a Narrative: From Beckett to McPherson

Naoko Yagi

Unnamed and aptly referred to as 'Speaker'[1] in the script, the lone figure in Samuel Beckett's *A Piece of Monologue* is almost like a legacy of the kind of 'speaker' that we find in any Victorian dramatic monologue. As Elisabeth A. Howe reminds us, '[t]he dramatic monologue is spoken by a persona who is not the poet';[2] the reader of a dramatic monologue should be able to sense a clear 'distance between author and speaker'.[3] We might also remember that the 'speaker' in a dramatic monologue 'addresses a silent auditor';[4] the reader has to fathom the distance between 'silent auditor' and herself, too, which could be tricky since, as W. David Shaw points out, it is not uncommon in a dramatic monologue that more than one, or more than one kind of, 'silent auditor' are intended by the 'speaker'.[5] In what follows, we will examine monologues not in poetry but in plays. Our concern has little to do with the possible identity of 'Speaker' in *A Piece of Monologue* or who the implied 'silent auditor(s)' may be in this particular play; rather, *A Piece of Monologue* triggers our discussion in that the piece lays out a solid distance, or, as it were, a 'vertical' relationship, between author, speaker, silent auditor(s), and reader/audience. In the essay I shall use the term 'speaker' when referring to a monologue-uttering figure on stage whose 'vertical' connections I focus upon. The term 'character' in the discussion shall imply that we foreground the fictional framework in which a monologue-uttering figure finds herself. Last but not least, by the term 'actor' I will refer to a person who, as a monologue-uttering figure on stage, plays the role of a specific 'character' while functioning as a 'speaker'.[6]

I

Narrators in prose are not the same as speakers on stage. '[N]ovelistic space, being predicated on language', explains Daniel Katz, 'is necessarily dependent on the enunciating subject as the space of narrative'.[7] As for Beckett's narrators, it cannot escape our notice that they tend to 'choose' words and phrases with which the 'narrated' nature of a narrative will be abundantly clear to the reader. *Molloy* immediately springs to mind. On the other hand, and if we turn to Katz again, 'the "subject" of the prose is replaced not by the "character" but by the *stage* in the theater' [original emphasis].[8] The manner in which a play is written does not always highlight a solid distance, or a 'vertical' relationship, between author, speaker, silent auditor(s), and reader/audience; more likely, it is according to theatrical conventions that such a distance shall be detected by the reader/audience either subconsciously or consciously. Sentences like 'Yes, it was an orange pomeranian, the less I think of it the more certain I am'[9] and 'Shall I describe the room? No. I shall have occasion to do so later perhaps'[10] may work wonders if we stumble upon them as readers of prose fiction, but such sentences might run the risk of 'sounding' redundant or exaggeratedly comical if they are uttered by the lone speaker in a play unless, of course, redundancy or the comical effect is exactly what the speaker intends to convey to the silent auditor(s). *A Piece of Monologue* happens to be a relatively straightforward play in the sense that it neither disrupts nor overly emphasizes the author-speaker-auditor-audience relationship. Should a lone character in a Beckett play, or, for that matter, in any play written by anyone, be for some reason deprived of verbal language, she would still fulfil her role as a kind of 'speaker' so long as she remained, in one form or another, on stage.

Harold Pinter, whose lines for characters in multi-cast plays often hinge upon what seems to be the dividing mark between dialogue and soliloquy/monologue, is nonetheless more inclined to write a short piece of prose fiction which has a distinct narrator in it than to write a play with a single character on stage. A typical narrator, as far as Pinter's prose fiction is concerned, may be found in the piece called 'Tea Party'. *Monologue*, a play for a single actor by Pinter, proves to be less of an anomaly in the Pinter canon if we choose to read/see the play in the light of his prose fiction. Still, there obviously is a crucial difference between Pinter's *Monologue* and his narrator-oriented works of prose: *Monologue* prompts us to have a renewed and careful look at the relationship between speaker and silent auditor(s) in the

From Beckett to McPherson

works of some playwrights, especially Beckett, as well as in other plays by Pinter. The lone character in *Monologue*, who is seated and whom the script simply refers to as 'Man',[11] sounds as if he were addressing a rather close friend, who, we would imagine, should likewise be seated in what the stage directions briefly specify as 'another chair';[12] the non-presence of the 'silent auditor' will be intensely palpable to the reader/audience precisely for the fact that in the performance space there exists this other chair, which, as the stage directions tell us, is 'empty' (*M* 121). Unlike narrators in prose fiction, who forever reside in their 'novelistic space', and unlike 'Speaker' in Beckett's *A Piece of Monologue*, whose silent auditor(s) is/are never hinted at by any visual means on stage, the character 'Man' in Pinter's *Monologue* has what we might call a 'physical void' to talk to, the void which *occupies the chair* and which 'Man' keeps addressing with the pronoun 'you':

> [**Man:**] Now you're going to say you loved her soul and I loved her body. You're going to trot that old one out. I know you were much more beautiful than me, much more *aquiline*, I know *that*, that I'll give you, more *ethereal*, more thoughtful, *slyer*, while I had both feet firmly planted on the deck. But I'll tell you one thing you don't know. She loved my soul. It was my soul she loved.
>
> *Pause* [original emphases] (*M* 123)

What if the 'void' spoke? What if its speech were a monologue and not a response to the lines uttered by 'Man'? In other words, can it be that the 'void' is a potential 'speaker' as well as being the 'silent auditor'? The gap between Pinter's *Monologue* and some of his plays with two characters in performance space, most notably *Landscape*, may be much smaller than it seems.

II

The very singularity of the 'speaker' in a play like *A Piece of Monologue* keeps the author-speaker-auditor-audience relationship quite solid, or 'vertical' as we call it, whereas the existence of more than one 'speaker' in a play, as in Pinter's *Landscape*, implies that the author-speaker-auditor-audience relationship can also branch out in a 'horizontal' direction: a single 'speaker' splits into two or more 'speakers'; 'silent auditors' could be the same lot across the board, but it is more than likely that they will vary for each speaker. On the other hand, no matter how diverse their silent auditors may be, two or more speakers in a play do in fact share performance time as well as performance space, which makes it inevitable that lines uttered by each speaker either fall into place along the temporal axis of a play or, as in the 'chorus' sections in Beckett's *Play*,[13] overtly and intentionally clash with one another in defiance of theatrical convention. Focusing on the former, we can take up *Landscape* for a case in point; according to the stage directions, neither of the two characters in this particular play 'appear[s] to hear'[14] each other's 'voice' (*L* 8), and that, in effect, turns the characters' lines into a string of monologues. A portion of the string goes:

> **Beth:** He felt my shadow. He looked up at me standing above him.
> **Duff:** I should have had some bread with me. I could have fed the birds.
> **Beth:** Sand on his arms.
> **Duff:** They were hopping about. Making a racket.
> **Beth:** I lay down by him, not touching.
> **Duff:** There wasn't anyone else in the shelter. There was a man and woman, under the trees, on the other side of the pond. I didn't feel like getting wet. I stayed where I was.
>
> *Pause*
>
> Yes, I've forgotten something. The dog was with me.
>
> *Pause*
>
> **Beth:** Did those women know me? I didn't remember their faces (*L* 10-11).

Whether or not the reader/audience will refer to the entire length of string as the 'narrative' of a play is yet another question, especially when 'narrative depends on the addressee seeing it as narrative',[15] the 'addressee', in this case, being the reader/audience and not the silent auditor(s). Would the reader/audience find it difficult to 'compose' a 'narrative' of the whole string of monologues uttered by the two characters in *Landscape*? The answer depends, after Michael Toolan, on the reader/audience reconciling the setting in which the characters Beth and Duff find themselves with the manner in which the string of their monologues unreels itself. The monologues in *Landscape* habitually break into chunks, and even mere fragments, of words, phrases, and sentences with an overwhelming number of 'pauses' or 'silences' dotting them all,[16] which altogether seem to encourage the reader/audience to swim, as it were, in the uttered sounds and imposing non-sounds that fill the performance space and time; still, the fact remains that the two characters are in '[t]he kitchen of a country house' (*L* 8), a strong incentive for the reader/audience to at least try to interpret the entire string of monologues on a mock-realistic plane.

Seemingly in contrast to such a piece of work, Beckett's *Play* has its three characters not only utter their lines alternately in chorus and independently but in 'rapid tempo throughout' (*P* 307) as well, which again leaves the reader/audience with no choice but to swim, albeit this time possibly with their heads spinning, in the torrents of sounds; this at the same time has to be reconciled, as far as the reader/audience is concerned, with the fact that the three characters are presented in 'urns' on stage (*P* 307). Curiously enough, if the country-house setting in *Landscape* helps the reader/audience compose something that may pass for a narrative of the characters' monologues, the pointedly metatheatrical setting that is specified by the author of *Play* does in its own way also help the reader/audience delineate a kind of narrative along the characters' monologues; it is precisely because the setting in *Play* happens to be so individualistic and yet hardly informative that the reader/audience will be strongly encouraged to look for a narrative of this particular play. As Anna McMullan puts it, '[t]he minimalism of [Beckett's] dramatic material *forces* the audience to concentrate intently on the few perceptual elements offered' [emphasis added].[17]

Play is not a quintessential Beckett any more than *Landscape* is a typical Pinter. Nonetheless, the fundamental difference between Beckett and Pinter seems clear enough: as succinctly explained by Les Essif, for whom characters in Beckett's works are 'hypersubjective',[18] Pinter 'rouse[s] a story out of nothing'[19] while Beckett 'evoke[s] the emptiness underlying the human story'.[20] More importantly, the difference betrays what the works of the two playwrights have in common, namely, they are intrinsically narrative-dependent. Once on the lookout for a narrative, and once in tune with the unusually fast tempo adopted by the characters, the reader/audience does not have to make much effort to realize that the characters in *Play* are letting their version of ménage à trois unreel through the monologues they utter. A narrative that emerges out of their monologues could not be more classic in terms of what the reader/audience would expect from a play with two female figures and one male figure on stage; in other words, it is 'deliberate melodramatic cliché'.[21] If Beckett's *Play* on either a verbal or a visual basis leaves nothing 'crucial' to hide from the reader/audience, we might point out that any likely narrative which the reader/audience would compose of Pinter's *Landscape* should also involve a variation on the theme of ménage à trois but without the third person in the picture having, in this case, *his* say as a character on stage. In effect, by drawing on a cliché in a most lucid manner, a narrative of *Play* more than sufficiently 'compensates' a shockingly inexplicable appearance of the three characters and a bafflingly contrived speed of their monologues.

In neither *Landscape* nor *Play* do the characters acknowledge each other's presence on stage. This is to say that a character, whether it is Beth or Duff in the Pinter play or either of the two females or the male in the Beckett play, behaves and talks as if she or he shares the performance space and time with no one, when in reality all the characters take turns in uttering the lines assigned to them and, in Beckett's *Play*, the three characters say their fragments of lines in chorus on cue. The paradox brutally reminds us of the fact that each of the characters in *Landscape* and *Play* fulfils her or his duty as a 'speaker', that the vertical relationship between author, speaker, silent auditor(s), and reader/audience still sustains itself in the two plays even with the horizontal branching-out of the 'speaker'. Put another way, a play which consists of multiple monologues can truly be 'interesting' only when actors uttering their lines are convincing enough not merely as characters but as independent 'speakers' at the same time. Indeed, we might be inclined to regard the never-faltering balance between the 'character' element and the 'speaker' element in each figure on stage as nothing other than *the* lifeline of such a play.

Here, another question arises: what happens to the 'speaker' element when it comes to a play in which lines given to more than one character are predominantly but not entirely monologues? *Silence*, a three-character Pinter play that has '[t]hree areas' on stage with '[a] chair in each area'[22] may serve as a good example. Well into a fifth of this one-act piece, none of the characters Ellen, Bates, and Rumsey seems prepared to acknowledge the presence of the other characters on stage; while the lines they utter are reminiscent of those assigned to Beth and Duff in *Landscape*, the three chairs on a bare stage may be interpreted as a watered-down version of the setting for *Play*. In short, Ellen, Bates, and Rumsey are all 'speakers' as well as 'characters' until, quite abruptly, Bates 'moves to' (*S* 37) Ellen; this marks the beginning of the end, as it were, of the three characters' unbroken string of monologues. With Bates's line, 'Will we meet to-night?' (*S* 37), which is followed by Ellen's 'I don't know' (*S* 37), the play-in-progress seems to have discarded what we might call an invisible grid, that is, the author-speaker-auditor-audience relationship. Granted that the twenty-odd lines of a dialogue between Ellen and Bates duly dissolve into the three characters' second round of monologues, the grid in the sense mentioned above is never fully restored for the rest of the play. The verbal exchange, in effect, has 'tainted' what otherwise would have been a pristine world of the female and the two males; each of the

From Beckett to McPherson 113

three figures would have been a character-cum-speaker through and through.

III

In some plays with a single character on stage, lines are written in such a way that it seems to the reader/audience as if the character splits, whenever required, into multiple sub-characters. There are moments, for example, when the sole character in Frank McGuinness's one-act piece *Baglady* detaches her body from the lines she utters; the character impersonates her father just as freely as she impersonates herself as a younger person.[23] Nevertheless, instead of addressing silent auditors, the 'father' and the 'baglady-when-she-was-younger' either address each other directly or address the character indirectly, in which sense neither of the impersonated figures is what I have in this essay referred to as a 'speaker'. Sub-characters within a character would not have a chance to become 'speakers', which is to say that multiple speakers in a play will always presuppose *multiple characters*, not multiple sub-characters. A play which consists solely of multiple monologues uttered by multiple characters, then, may take yet another course in manipulating performance time as well as performance space and helping the reader/audience compose a narrative that would somehow explain the very nature of those monologues. This we will discuss in what follows, and for that we shall turn to plays by Brian Friel and Conor McPherson.

Divided into 'parts', which for the sake of the argument we will interpret as scene-equivalents, Friel's *Faith Healer* has each of its three characters harangue a lengthy as well as intense monologue that covers the entire scene assigned to her or him. Each monologue makes up an episode, or what the reader/audience is likely to regard as a narrative, and to that extent we might even call this particular play a precursor of *Talking Heads*, a series of episodic monologues by Alan Bennett.[24] If the very term 'talking heads' implies more than one character uttering monologues, the Bennett play has leeway for a production to select a few 'heads' from the entire pool of 'heads', whose monologues, after all, are not directly related to one another; only two characters and their monologues were chosen for the Comedy Theatre production of the play in 1997, to cite one example. In the same vein, the order of episodes in *Talking Heads* may differ from production to production, with each reshuffling bringing about a new effect. The crux of *Faith Healer*, on the other hand, is that each of its four episodes turns out to be *in*conclusive enough to require the other three episodes; just as importantly, the four episodes must always come in the order as shown in the play-text. One of the three characters in *Faith Healer* appears twice: this not only accounts for the play's fourth scene but also proves to be an indispensable part of the 'trick' with which the play manipulates performance space, performance time, and what the reader/audience would regard as a narrative of the play. The reader/audience is expected to delineate a 'grand narrative' for *Faith Healer* as a whole, be it a far cry from the kind of grand narrative we find in a nineteenth-century novel, indeed to perceive in the play something which should be more than a mere sequence of four episodic narratives.

If indeed '[t]he narrative structure of [*Faith Healer*] teaches a budding playwright so much about storytelling',[25] it only seems natural, as Eamonn Jordan among others points out, that *Faith Healer* 'has had a huge impact on McPherson's work'.[26] We sense the 'impact' most acutely in *This Lime Tree Bower* and *Port Authority*; each of these two McPherson plays consists of episodic monologues that are to be uttered in turn by three characters. Still, somewhat reminiscent of Pinter's *Silence*, two of the characters in *This Lime Tree Bower* have a very brief break from their monologues and address each other, which never happens between any two of the characters in *Port Authority*. We can also see more clearly in *Port Authority* than in *This Lime Tree Bower* that the playwright does not simply make good use of the nuts and bolts of Frielian 'storytelling', which, as Ulf Dantanus among others reminds us, has the 'tradition' of 'seanachie' [sic][27] for at least part of its 'vehicle'.[28] The reader/audience will certainly be led to compose a 'grand narrative' of the chain of smaller episodes in *Port Authority*, but that in fact shall be done according to the plan which McPherson explicitly lays out for the play.

By saying that Frank, Grace, and Teddy in *Faith Healer* 'are present'[29] we simply mean the three figures are physically 'there' on stage; the audience will scrutinize Frank or Grace or Teddy as they would, for example, either Beth or Duff in *Landscape*. If each of the three figures in the Friel play is in the position of asserting her or his status as a 'speaker' on stage, whether or not she or he is also 'present' as a 'character' on stage remains less certain: the monologue uttered by Grace confirms the 'fact' that Frank is dead, while it is Grace's death that Teddy describes vividly in his monologue; Frank, on the other hand, seemingly defies both Grace's and Teddy's monologues by appearing on stage for the second time to sum up the entire play. The three 'characters', as Christopher Morash puts succinctly, are evidently and unabashedly 'part of the past',[30] which we might rephrase in broader terms: the temporal axis for *Faith Healer* is warped. N.J. Lowe defines three kinds of 'time'. 'Story time', according to Lowe, 'is

From Beckett to McPherson

the absolute chronology of the story universe, ... [which] obeys the rules of real-world temporality'.[31] What Lowe calls 'text time' is just as 'absolute'[32] but strictly in the sense that 'it is measured by the yardage of physical signs from which the text is constructed'.[33] To Lowe, and more importantly to us in the discussion of *Faith Healer*, 'narrative time'[34] should never be confused with either 'story time' or 'text time':

> [Narrative time] can start, stop, run faster or slower, suspend movement, or reset to an earlier or later date. In some cases, it can even run backwards.[35]

Put plainly, 'narrative time' is not 'absolute' but 'fluid'.[36] A far cry from a narratives' narrative like *Odyssey* or *Iliad*, from which Lowe in explaining the three kinds of 'time' takes examples quite extensively,[37] what the reader/audience may eventually regard as a 'grand narrative' of *Faith Healer* can only be conceivable with the reader/audience being deprived of a reliable 'story time'. The play's 'narrative time' exerts an overwhelming power: no explicable 'rule' seems to apply as far as the temporal axis of the play is concerned, and the reader/audience would freely bask, as it were, in the 'time' which has been custom-made for this particular play.

Morash claims that *Faith Healer* is one of a few Irish plays from the latter half of the 1970s which 'attempt to reconfigure Christian (and, more specifically, Catholic) faith outside the limits of institutionalized religion';[38] it is by way of 'theatrical forms'[39] having gone through 'breaks with stage realism'[40] that the 'reconfigur[ation]' is made visible as well as audible to us. A quasi-religious connotation in *Faith Healer*, I would argue, has much to do with the predominance of 'narrative time' which we cannot fail to detect in the play. Could we, then, venture to assert that each of the three figures in *Faith Healer* shows a sign of being what Ken Frieden in *Genius and Monologue* calls a 'monologist [who] steers a course between divinity and madness',[41] whereas, and to quote from Frieden again, '[i]n the beginning only God is capable of monologue, but sin and *satan* [sic] generate new possibilities for monological speech at a distance from God'?[42] We might at least say this much: if Frank, Grace, and Teddy all look and sound more 'speakers' than 'characters', it is because the three figures embody both mentally and physically the custom-made narrative time, the 'fluidity' of which is divine and/or *maddish* enough to betray the piercingly potent author, if not God with a capital 'G'. It must be added that, as far as the Friel canon is concerned, mad/divine 'monologists' are not necessarily confined to an indicatively entitled play like *Faith Healer*. The mid-1990s saw the premiere of *Molly Sweeney*, another play by Friel that is entirely made up of a series of episodic monologues; the piece highlights 'narrative time', albeit not nearly as drastically as in *Faith Healer*, and the three figures, Molly, Frank, and Mr Rice, reminisce in their respective monologues about a shared once-in-a-lifetime experience, which has apparently 'healed' them in different ways.[43] In short, a quasi-religious connotation is hinted at gently in *Molly Sweeney*: with a touch of mad-/divineness, the three figures look and sound more 'speakers' than 'characters'.

At first glance being firmly embedded in Frielian 'storytelling' tradition, McPherson's *Port Authority* does call for a trio of actors who, respectively and together, will be prepared to show a perfect speaker-character double exposure to theatre audience. *Port Authority* is a play in which 'story time', 'text time', and 'narrative time' neither interfere with nor melt into one another. Whereas in *Faith Healer* it is only the character Frank who appears twice, which, as briefly mentioned above, works as the final and most 'devastating' key for the reader/audience to perceive the 'past-ness' of the three characters in the play, Kevin, Dermot, and Joe in *Port Authority* utter their episodic monologues in perfect rotation, each being automatically given five turns; in other words, the 'text time' moves on of its own accord in *Port Authority*, seemingly irrespective of either the 'story time' or the 'narrative time' of the play. Meanwhile, in contrast to the contradictory characters in *Faith Healer*, none of the three figures in *Port Authority* utters anything that would prompt the reader/audience to question the reliability of the 'story time' of the play. With the steady 'text time' along with the highly dependable 'story time', the power of 'narrative time' in *Port Authority* will never be as dominant as it is in *Faith Healer*.

The published play-text of *Port Authority* has a simple 'note' in lieu of formal stage directions: '[t]he play is set in the theatre'.[44] Interpreted literally, this particular instruction invites the reader of *Port Authority* to imagine a setting which displays an extreme version of a theatre-within-a-theatre. The 'silent auditors' in the play turn out to be the entire theatre audience, who, in terms of the author-speaker-auditor-audience relationship that we have discussed in this essay, are *not* the actual audience in an actual theatre, seeing and listening to three actors playing the roles of Kevin, Dermot, and Joe. While reminding us of Brechtian metatheatre, *Port Authority* nonetheless unreels episodic monologues which are all 'deeply private tales',[45] and that may suggest the following: the play draws on a metatheatrical framework as a means to an end. Thrown into the 'theatre', Kevin, Dermot, and Joe find themselves going through a 'public performance of theatrical confession'.[46] This we can see, for example, in Kevin's admission that, 'if [curly haired Patricia] was going to fight for' him

(*PA* 55), he himself 'was going to go with the flow' (*PA* 55), or in Dermot's account of his wife's reaction when he told her that 'the job was gone' (*PA* 56), namely, she 'laughed at' him (*PA* 56) and made an observation that he 'was someone to whom things happened' (*PA* 56), or in Joe's remembering that, after having a drink with Marion and Tommy, the couple who lived 'next door' (*PA* 49), he came home and 'curled up on the sofa, half expecting a soft knocking at the front door or the window' (*PA* 50), by which he means he was imagining Marion following him home. Each of the three figures in *Port Authority* is 'redeemed'[47] by his uttering the lines of monologues, and that coincides with his securing a speaker-cum-character status.

If the narrated 'lives' of Kevin, Dermot, and Joe brush against one another in *Port Authority*, no two 'lives' actually meet head on in the play; uttering their lines, the three figures hardly dwell for long on the preciously few topics which seem to connect their 'lives' together. Whatever we as the reader/audience compose of the series of monologues in *Port Authority*, it is not destined to either look or sound as *grand* as what a play like *Faith Healer*, with its mad/divine 'monologists', shall unravel for the sake of us; a 'grand narrative' of *Port Authority* will never be *grander* than, and if we borrow David Ian Rabey's expression, 'the moat of isolation and failed communication which the characters sense around themselves'.[48] Following Rabey, we might regard the setting of *Port Authority*, the 'theatre', as a huge confessional, to the extent of which it seems that a quasi-religious connotation shall not be totally wiped off in the play. On the other hand, neither the would-be 'confessors', namely, Kevin, Dermot, and Joe, nor the would-be 'priest', namely, the entire 'theatre' audience, come equipped with anything that could match the quaint mad/divineness which we find in Frank, Grace, and Teddy of *Faith Healer*. Instead, what we discern in the lines uttered by Kevin, Dermot, and Joe is a trace of the kind of multiple monologues which Beckett's *Play* and Pinter's *Landscape* make manifest through their speakers-cum-characters.

This piece is an expanded version of a paper which I read at the annual conference of the International Association for the Study of Irish Literatures (IASIL) at Charles University, Prague, in July 2005.

---

[1]Samuel Beckett, *A Piece of Monologue, The Complete Dramatic Works* (London: Faber and Faber, 1990): 425.
[2]Elisabeth A. Howe, *Stages of Self: The Dramatic Monologues of Laforgue,*

Valéry and Mallarmé (Athens: Ohio University Press, 1990): 2.

[3]Howe, 2.

[4]W. David Shaw, *Origins of the Monologue: The Hidden God* (Toronto: University of Toronto Press, 1999): 12.

[5]Shaw, 12. Scholars do not always agree on what qualifies a poem as a dramatic monologue. In the words of Linda K. Hughes, '[t]he dramatic monologue is, inherently, a loose and baggy form, like the Victorian novel'. Linda K. Hughes, *The Manyfacèd Glass: Tennyson's Dramatic Monologues* (Athens: Ohio University Press, 1987): 12.

[6]As Minako Okamuro points out, we do not even kick-start a close reading of *A Piece of Monologue* until we realize that the 'character' in the play is the inevitable outcome of the lone 'actor' functioning as what Okamuro calls a 'highly-charged speaker'. Minako Okamuro, e-mail communication, 17 May 2005.

[7]Daniel Katz, *Saying I No More: Subjectivity and Consciousness in the Prose of Samuel Beckett* (Evanston: Northwestern University Press, 1999): 182.

[8]Katz, 182.

[9]Samuel Beckett, *Molloy: A Novel*, trans. Patrick Bowles in collaboration with the author (New York: Grove, 1970): 14.

[10]*Molloy*, 24.

[11]Harold Pinter, *Monologue*, *Harold Pinter: Plays Four*, expanded ed. (London: Faber and Faber, 1998): 121. Subsequent references to the play are cited in the text as (*M* 121).

[12]Here, we shall not draw our attention to the fact that *Monologue* was a production for television.

[13]Samuel Beckett, *Play*, *The Complete Dramatic Works* (London: Faber and Faber, 1990): 319. Subsequent references to the play are cited in the text as (*P* 319).

[14]Harold Pinter, *Landscape*, Landscape *and* Silence (London: Methuen, 1969): 8. Subsequent references to the play are cited in the text as (*L* 8).

[15]Michael Toolan, *Narrative: A Critical Linguistic Introduction*, 2nd ed. (London: Routledge, 2001): 7.

[16]For us to find the stage directions 'pause' and 'silence' in Pinter's dialogues is one thing; our seeing the same directions in Pinter's monologue-only plays is quite another since, in the latter, a Pinteresque tension between characters simply does not apply.

[17]Anna McMullan, 'Samuel Beckett as Director: The Art of Mastering Failure', *The Cambridge Companion to Beckett*, ed. John Pilling (Cambridge: Cambridge University Press, 1994): 199.

[18]Les Essif, *Empty Figure on an Empty Stage: The Theatre of Samuel Beckett and His Generation* (Bloomington: Indiana University Press, 2001): 152.

[19]Essif, 153.

[20]Essif, 153.

[21]Paul Lawley, 'Stages of Identity: From *Krapp's Last Tape* to *Play*', *The Cambridge Companion to Beckett*, ed. John Pilling (Cambridge: Cambridge University Press, 1994): 100.

[22]Harold Pinter, *Silence*, Landscape *and* Silence (London: Methuen, 1969): 32.

Subsequent references to the play are cited in the text as (*S* 32).

[23]Frank McGuinness, *Baglady, Frank McGuinness: Plays One* (London: Faber and Faber, 1996): 396-97.

[24]*Talking Heads* was initially aired on television.

[25]Eamonn Jordan, 'Introduction', *Theatre Stuff: Critical Essays on Contemporary Irish Theatre*, ed. Eamonn Jordan (Dublin: Carysfort, 2000): xxxiv.

[26]Jordan, xxxiv.

[27]Ulf Dantanus, *Brian Friel: The Growth of an Irish Dramatist* (Göteborg: Acta Universitatis Gothoburgensis, 1985): 202.

[28]Dantanus, 203.

[29]Christopher Morash, *A History of Irish Theatre: 1601-2000* (Cambridge: Cambridge University Press, 2002): 264.

[30]Morash, 264.

[31]N.J. Lowe, *The Classical Plot and the Invention of Western Narrative* (Cambridge: Cambridge University Press, 2000): 36.

[32]Lowe, 36.

[33]Lowe, 36.

[34]Lowe, 36.

[35]Lowe, 36-7.

[36]Lowe, 36.

[37]Lowe, 37-41.

[38]Morash, 249.

[39]Morash, 249.

[40]Morash, 249.

[41]Ken Frieden, *Genius and Monologue* (Ithaca: Cornell University Press, 1985): 18.

[42]Frieden, 18.

[43]One of the play's two epigraphs is a poem by Emily Dickinson, which starts with the line 'Tell all the Truth but tell it *slant—*' [emphasis added]. Brian Friel, *Molly Sweeney, Brian Friel: Plays Two* (London: Faber and Faber, 1999): 452.

[44]Conor McPherson, *Port Authority* (London: Nick Hern, 2001): 7. Subsequent references to the play are cited in the text as (*PA* 7).

[45]Morash, 267.

[46]David Ian Rabey, *English Drama Since 1940* (London: Longman, 2003): 162.

[47]Rabey, 162.

[48]Rabey, 162.

8 | Frank McGuinness:
Plays of Survival and Identity

Joseph Long

In Frank McGuinness's *Observe the Sons of Ulster Marching Towards the Somme*, premiered in 1985, and *Carthaginians*, premiered in 1988, memory, identity and a sense of place engage to negotiate the painful passage from past to future and to articulate a possible strategy for survival, for the individual and the group. Both plays center primarily on a group of characters rather than on individuals: they focus on what constitutes the group, what process brings them together in the first place and what sustains the fragile identity that the group represents. The group has endured an historic and destructive experience: in the earlier play, the annihilation suffered by the Ulster volunteers at the Battle of the Somme (July 1916); in the later play, the events of Bloody Sunday when, on 30th January 1972, thirteen young protestors taking part in a Civil Rights march were shot dead in the streets of Derry by the forces of the British Army. In both plays, there is a particular tension between personal experience, historic moment and the possibility of healing. The outcome for the group becomes a pointer for ourselves.

In *Carthaginians*, a group of people from the city of Derry — three women, three men — is squatting in the cemetery outside the city walls. Each of them in different ways, directly or indirectly, has been shattered by the events of Bloody Sunday, although not all the pain was inflicted by the toll of political events. Maela, in particular, has suffered the loss of her daughter who died of cancer on the infamous Sunday but, as she walks home from the hospital, at every street corner the tally of the dead is spiraling upwards and the city itself is becoming a living mausoleum of the slain:

122   Ireland on Stage: Beckett and After

> I'm walking home through my own city. ... Two dead, I hear that in
> William Street. I'm walking through Derry and they're saying in
> Shipquay Street there's five dead. I am walking to my home in my
> house in the street I was born in and I've forgotten where I live. I am
> in Ferryquay Street and I hear there's nine dead outside the Rossville
> flats ... (352).[1]

To reach this point of recognition and tell her story, Maela has an
inner journey to make. The central scene of the play is a fantastical
and farcical acting-out of the traumatic events of the infamous Bloody
Sunday, scripted and stage-managed by Dido, forming a play-within-
the-play derisively entitled *The Burning Balaclava*, which takes on the
healing function of a psychodrama. Dido distributes the *dramatis
personae* on a principle of cross gendering and the reversal of roles.
Thus the one-time republican activist Paul is given a blond wig and
must play the part of the Protestant girl friend, Mercy Dogherty. 'How
am I a Protestant with a name like Docherty?' he objects. 'You spell
Dogherty with a "g"', retorts Dido, the relevance of the proposed
emendation being far from clear. Most of the characters discover they
are to be named as variants on Doherty/O'Doherty. 'Everybody in
Derry's called Doherty', comments Hark, 'it's a known fact.' Dido
himself is left to play two parts simultaneously, the pram-pushing
Doreen — 'one of life's martyrs who never complains' — and the
British Soldier, 'in deep torment because he is a working class boy sent
here to oppress the working class.' *The Burning Balaclava* is the
catalyst which allows the characters in the play to release themselves
from the grip of the past, to realize that they are themselves the very
Dead whose resurrection they have been waiting for. This play-within-
the-play has been compellingly analysed in terms of group
psychotherapeutic practice and, in particular, the techniques of
psychodrama developed by J. L. Moreno after the First World War.[2]
The present study will examine other strands within the texture and
complexity of Frank McGuinness's dramatic writing and his
exploration of history and identity.

Dido is an openly gay character and when in Scene 5 he enters
brandishing the script of his newly written playlet, he is outrageously
dressed in drag. As gay playwright, he has assumed the identity of
Fionnuala McGonigle. By mischievously playing on his initials, Frank
McGuinness has projected a figure of the author into his own text, but
this playwright, we learn to our surprise, is French. With a name like
Fionnuala? *Sans problème* ... it is to be pronounced Fionn — oooh! —
aaah! — là! Dido-in-Drag reveals his character's mission:

> Oui. I have come to your city and seen your suffering. Your city has changed its name from Londonderry to Derry, and so I changed my name to Fionnuala in sympathy. What I see moves me so much I have written a small piece as part of your resistance (331).

The target of this lampooning might well be seen in general terms, not so much with reference to the events of January 1972 but rather to a more recent period, nine years later, when the death of Bobby Sands and the ordeal of the Republican hunger-strikers created unprecedented interest and sympathy throughout continental Europe, and brought, specifically, droves of French journalists and intellectuals to Derry. The focused attention of foreign media was generally received with sharp suspicion by the nationalist community of Derry, who had learned by experience to mistrust the appropriation of their situation and their objectives by left-wing ideologues of every hue. One French playwright and filmmaker had, however, won the trust of the Derry Youth and Community Workshop, and that was Armand Gatti. Through my own mediation, he put in place a community-based film project and, after a lengthy period of preparation, the first week of the shooting schedule in May 1981 coincided, by a painful irony of circumstances, with the death of Bobby Sands and the turmoil that ensued. Gatti's experimental scripting of his film had involved gathering stories and experiences from the unemployed young people, both Catholic and Protestant, attending the Workshop, and also from those of the adult population of Derry who agreed to take part in the project. Having assembled these anecdotes into a formal script, he invited the young people and the adults to play, in the film, the fictionalized version of themselves, as appeared in the script. In most cases, this was agreed. Thus it came about that a real-life episode in the life of the Workshop was transposed into the film, namely an exercise in group dynamics, in which the young people were called upon to act out roles most opposed to their own beliefs and situations: Protestant young people were to re-invent themselves as IRA activists, Catholic youngsters were to project themselves into the role of members of the RUC or the British Army, pacifists were to be militants, hardliners were to be clergymen, and so forth. The Director of the Workshop at the time, who had devised this experiment in self-questioning both in real-life and in the fictional world of the film, was a visionary community leader known widely by the nick-name of Paddy Bogside and whose name was Paddy Doherty. The issue which, in the film, challenges the assumptions of the young people is the death of a British soldier who falls victim to a shooting incident and who is revealed to be an unemployed young man from the north of England whose social circumstances have brought him to that end.

Dido's lampooning of stereotypes in *The Burning Balaclava* has therefore some more specific targets than might at first appear. The targets, all in all, are many and varied. They include some of the most sacred icons of nationalist sentiment. The pathos of Sean O'Casey's evocations of nationalist motherhood in *Juno and the Paycock* is derisively parodied at several points with lines such as: 'Son, son, where were you when my Sacred Heart was riddled with bullets?' The consecrated media icon of a nationalist Catholic priest waving a white handkerchief under gunfire is subverted by the character Seph, playing a Fr Docherty and waving two great white sheets. The socialist construction of the British soldier as alienated working-class youth is ironized by the reference to his 'deep torment'. The wider target of all this is, clearly enough, the inadequacy of any ideology or any form of representation to account comprehensively for the contradictions of experience, and the way discourse appropriates and distorts the reality it claims to express, an issue which McGuinness's play has in common with Brian Friel's *The Freedom of the City*. Fionnuala/FrankMcG's ironic deconstruction of Gatti's script and indeed of his very presence in Derry is therefore part of a larger scheme, and clearly not a specific score to settle with the French writer. None-the-less, it has to be admitted that Frank's personal encounter with Armand Gatti had been somewhat fraught. Gatti's own ideological position is complex enough. He has never been a member of any political party. His driving philosophy is a form of utopian anarchism, which he traces back, in part through his own father's experiences, to the Anarcho-Syndicalist movement of the 1920s. It has as its references, among others, Antonio Gramsci in Italy and, in Russia, Bakunin and Makhno. Frank McGuinness's engagement with politics, notwithstanding the Republican tradition of his family, is based on personal witness and an acute awareness of the ambiguities on every side. He felt, as he has expressed to me more than once, that there were enough complexities in the Northern situation without Gatti adding further complexities of his own. On the other hand, his encounter with Gatti's dramatic writing, some years earlier, had been a shock and a revelation, and he acknowledges to this day the extent to which Gatti's work first opened up for him the full potential of theatre and the 'utopian space' of the stage.

The encounter with the French playwright dates back to 1977, when Gatti came to University College Dublin for the English-language premiere of his play *The Stork*[3] which I had translated and staged with a talented group of student performers. Frank was cast as Engineer

Plays of Survival and Identity

Kawaguchi. As often in Gatti's formal drama, the character is based on documented, real-life experience. On 6th August 1944, the fictitious Kawaguchi, like his real-life counterpart, was working on a construction site in Hiroshima, at the moment the first atomic bomb was dropped. Being a strong swimmer, he escapes by the river from the inferno on either bank. By evening, he makes his way to the shore. He clambers onto a freight train, not knowing where he is or where he is going. Three days later, the train has brought him to Nagasaki, in time to witness the second bomb. In order to dramatize experience of such a scale, both personal and historic, Gatti moves away from the conventions of realism and its contrived plausibility. Thus, Frank McGuinness as performer is not asked to make himself up and move and speak as if he were a survivor who had received two massive doses of radiation within three days. There might seem to be something presumptuous, even obscene, about such a mode of representation on the stage. Instead, at the start of the play, the performers present themselves as a group of volunteer workers clearing the ruined streets of Nagasaki. They have decided not to take part in the celebrations to mark the Commemoration of the Dead: instead, they present a play and each performer has chosen an atomized object from the rubble of the city. Thus Frank McGuinness's character has chosen a burnt-out watch, and that object will conjure up the Engineer Kawaguchi to whom the watch once belonged. The performer may therefore speak *as the watch*, that is, as a carbonized relic, or as the one-time Kawaguchi, or indeed as the volunteer worker in the here-and-now. The play will thus move seamlessly between the 'that time' before the bomb and the here-and-now. A central issue of the play is how can those from before the trauma find a language to speak to us in the present day — how can a carbonized watch speak to us and what can it say? — and indeed how can we, in the here-and-now, as volunteer workers or as members of their audience, find words to cope with what is an undeniable part of our past and part of what we have now become.

The group of volunteers, in *The Stork*, has come together around a dying child, Oyanagi, a victim of atomic radiation, with the project of making a thousand paper storks to save her life. She dies, and the thousandth stork, which was never made, becomes the central symbol of the play. Here Gatti has transposed the Japanese legend of the crane as giver of health, and the practice of hanging paper cranes, in the origami tradition of paper folding, around the bed of a sick person. His use of the legend echoes the real-life experience of Sasaki Sadako, a Japanese child victim of the effects of radiation, whose vain attempt to construct a thousand paper cranes before she died became the emblem of the Peace Movement in the fifties. In Gatti's play, Tomiko, one-time Hostess of the Tea Ceremony, pieces together a garment for the Day of the Dead: 'Do you know why I took to sewing this kimono today? Because I thought that Oyanagi must have grown. And that she would be happy to see that we think of her as a living person, already of an age to wear a woman's kimono.' Her gesture reaches out to that of Maela, in *Carthaginians*, as Maela lays out her child's garments on a grave and, in her state of denial, makes ready for her dead daughter's birthday:

> **Greta**: What age would she have been?
> **Maela**: You mean what age she is?
>
> *Silence*
>
> I'm saving for her birthday. (*Whispers*) A leather jacket (300).

The hope of a positive future is invested, in both plays, in the character that challenges the enclosed existence of the group, their self-imposed incarceration and their refusal of a world that is moving on without them. In McGuinness's play, it is Dido who suggests, in the final scene, the possibility of reconciling past and future, or rather of carrying the past into the future, without denial or capitulation, as he takes leave of the others in a movement of transcendence:

> While I walk the earth, I walk through you, the streets of Derry. If I meet one who knows you and they ask, how's Dido? Surviving. How's Derry? Surviving. Carthage has not been destroyed. Watch yourself (379).

In Gatti's play, it is the demobilized soldier Enemon who leaves, who sets out to challenge the world, and it is Tomiko, in the final scene, who evokes, like Dido, the possibility of the past speaking to the future, and enters a plea for recognition and acceptance:

> Forgive us if our district is different from yours. Ours faces the sea — Yours faces the sky — Between the two the ruins of Nagasaki circle the earth. — If one day they come to rest among us, who will be able to recognize them, and who will know how to speak to them? We are clumsy in what we call life (162).

In March 1979, McGuinness had travelled to Belfast to see an earlier play by Armand Gatti, produced by The Lyric Theatre, *The Second Life of Tatenberg Camp*. The play is rooted in a different historical context, that of the Holocaust, but engages with similar themes of past and present, of memory and identity, and the need to find a language capable of uttering the unspeakable. Tatenberg Camp is a fictitious name, standing in a sense for all of the camps, but its location identifies it with the notorious camp at Mauthausen, in Austria, close to the banks of the river Danube. Gatti does not bring us directly into the violence of the Camps: instead he locates the action some ten years later, when survivors are still squatting in the railway station that served the camp, for the post-war world has left them no homeland to go to: a Spanish deportee, a Ukranian, Jews from Cracow or from the Baltic states. The reality of this situation is historical, and corresponds to what Gatti himself found when, as a young journalist, he visited Austria in the mid-fifties, ten years after the liberation. However, the play has nothing of a documentary drama. The characters are caught in a world where no fact is verifiable: who was traitor? who was victim? Did the Jewish Kapo play a double game, feigning collaboration, while secretly saving lives? Did Moïssevitch kill him in the end? In Gatti's dramaturgy, there is no healing psychodrama to release the stranglehold of the past: in its place, a surreal carnival on an imagined Prater in Vienna, where the characters are caught in nightmarish sideshows, and the figures from his past return to engulf Moïssevitch in the unrelenting self-questioning of the survivor:

> Do you know the reproach that Mordochy threw in my face? (Mordochy Auerbach!) and Sabbatay Zaks? That I was in luck the day they asked: who do you want to save, your wife or your mother? I was alone. And they both sent their mothers off to die. Not you? You sent your wife ...[4]

The long monologue scene which closes *Tatenberg* and in which Moïssevitch is inexorably drawn in by the figures from his past — 'What do you want of me now? I can give you nothing ...' — might be seen to point to the lengthy monologue of the Elder Piper which opens *Observe the Sons of Ulster Marching Towards the Somme*, and during which his dead comrades, the figures from his past, surround the lone survivor. The real affinities, however, between the two playwrights are not on the surface, in the coincidence of situations or characters, but in fundamental dramaturgical choices, a flexibility, for example, in the representation of time and space, and a concept of character which is based more on the function of witness within the structure of a group than it is on any psychological model. When Frank McGuiness comes to represent the reality of trench warfare and the soldier William Moore cracking up under the trauma of gunfire, he consciously avoids 'the trap of realism, of people running and going *bang, bang*'.[5] Instead, he imagines the scene of the rope bridge at the cliff face of Carrick-a-Reede, on the north Antrim coast, where Moore is brought by his comrade Millen and forced to cross over, in an attempt to regain his nerve. As he moves across the rope bridge, Moore — a dyer by trade — enters into a time beyond death, in which

128   Ireland on Stage: Beckett and After

he sees his comrades waiting for him beyond the grave, and in which his own life is encapsulated in a intuition of selfhood and integrity:

> This bridge is a piece of cloth. It needs coloring. I'm a dyer. When I step across, my two feet are my eyes. They put a shape on it. They give it colour. And the colour is my life and all I've done with it. Not much, but it's mine. So I'll keep going to the end (160).

The undermining of the realist parameters of time, space and character was not of course new to Irish dramatists in the early eighties. Frank McGuinness has frequently paid homage to Brian Friel, both for his daring in the issues that he introduced to the Irish stage and for his innovations in dramatic form. These innovations were perhaps rarely fore-fronted, as they tend to be with the French dramatist, but they were no less radical. *Faith Healer*, premiered in Dublin at the Abbey Theatre in 1980, after a less successful New York premiere directed by José Quintero with James Mason in the title role, is constructed as four monologues, delivered in turn by each of the three characters, who never encounter each other on stage. When Frank Hardy, the faith healer of the title, returns for the final act, we realize before long that he is recounting the process and the circumstances of his own death. Frank McGuinness has several times in interview[6] cited this production as the catalyst which clarified in his own mind his ambition to become a writer and in particular to write for the stage.

Nonetheless, Frank McGuinness positions himself as an Irish dramatist very explicitly in a European tradition of drama. This is most obvious in his commitment to developing new versions or adaptations of major playwrights of the European canon, from Ibsen and Chekhov to Lorca and Brecht, and more recently, Sophocles and Euripides. He feels the need to re-appropriate these authors from an established British theatre practice and interpretation:

> Irish literature has always been far too much defined in terms of its relationship with English literature. It's been part of the taming of the Irish by the British to do that. But in fact, if you look at our major authors of this [20th] century, O'Casey has more in common with Brecht than he would have with any other playwright, particularly in English. Joyce and Beckett looked to the continent. Joyce was deeply in touch with Dante and the Greeks, and Beckett with both French and Italian literature. I remain at home and try to make the great European playwrights part of our vocabulary.[7]

This concern to reclaim their place in an autonomous European tradition, independent of the cultural hierarchies of the former colonial power, was shared, especially in the eighties, by several leading Irish playwrights and notably by Thomas Kilroy and Brian Friel. It might indeed seem to forge a link with the aspirations and practice of the Field Day Theatre Company, founded in Derry in 1980 by Brian Friel and the actor Stephen Rea, and inaugurated by a ground-breaking premiere of Friel's own play *Translations* in the Derry Guild Hall. That initiative had a number of objectives. The first was a populist objective, a policy of bringing their work to new audiences, especially in provincial venues North and South where theatre was little known. Far more ambitious was their aspiration to create 'a space between unionism and nationalism, and proving by example the possibility of a shared culture in the North of Ireland.'[8] That perhaps foolhardy aspiration towards a cultural vision capable of transcending politics was embodied in a series of pamphlets authored by poets Seamus Heaney and Tom Paulin and academics Seamus Deane, Declan Kiberd and Richard Kearney.[9] Seamus Deane, who was the most active pamphleteer, was no doubt unaware at the time how resolutely nationalist his own idealistic agenda would appear, while the attempt to introduce an alternative, postcolonial cultural discourse — drawing on Franz Fanon and Edward Said — into the debate on national identity was greeted with magisterial disdain and incomprehension by reactionary academic voices.[10] Brian Friel's version of Chekhov's *The Three Sisters* was produced by Field Day in 1981, but it was not until 1995 that any of Frank McGuinness' writing was produced by them, namely his version of Chekhov's *Uncle Vanya*, and that was to be the final production before the demise of the company. *Carthaginians* was in fact originally written for Field Day, but was withdrawn by the author in 1987. Whatever the particular reasons for that withdrawal, by the late eighties Field Day appeared caught up in its own orthodoxies, in debates on what did or did not constitute a 'Field Day play': in 1990, Brian Friel decided to give his play *Dancing at Lughnasa* to the Abbey Theatre and not to the Derry-based company and, although he remained on the Board of Directors for another four years, this appeared to many as a fatal rupture.

With hindsight, both *Observe the Sons of Ulster Marching Towards the Somme* and *Carthaginians* would appear to respond, in some large degree, to the original aspirations of the Field Day enterprise. *Sons of Ulster* engages with Ulster Protestant experience and sensibilities in a manner unique in drama emanating from the South, and this was reflected in the reception of the touring production which the Abbey brought to Coleraine and to Belfast. This engagement springs from Frank McGuinness's personal encounter, in the early eighties — when a newly appointed lecturer at the New University of Ulster at Coleraine[11] — with the day-to-day realities of

Northern Ireland. There he discovered an entirely different way of being Irish, and a different relationship to oneself and to history. In almost every town, every small village, he found a central monument of a kind rarely seen in towns in the republican south: a monument to the dead of the First World War. Down the four sides of the grey stone, the seemingly endless list of family names attested to the decimation of the entire male population of these isolated communities. By this human sacrifice, he was to say later,[12] the Ulster protestant community had sealed a pact in blood with the British Empire and could no longer detach itself from it. That allegiance is celebrated every year by pilgrimages to Flanders, by flags and marches and by the wearing of the poppy on Remembrance Day. The participation of Catholics and southerners in the Great War, a lesser but significant participation, is passed over in silence by their respective communities and ignored in the traditional teaching of history in the schools. The poppy is never worn by the Southern Irish. On both sides of the sectarian divide, the state, both North and South, sought to maintain their youth in total ignorance of the culture and traditions of the other side. Frank McGuinness's portrayal moved away from the established perception of Northern Protestantism, rooted in the hegemony of the great property owners, the leaders of the Belfast shipyards and the textile industries. His group of protestant volunteers springs from the small-town people and is gathered from the four corners of the province. David Craig is the son of a blacksmith from the north-western lake region of Enniskillen, Moore and Millen are respectively a dyer and a baker from country Antrim, Roulston is a one-time preacher from County Tyrone, Martin Crawford is a football player from Derry, Anderson and McIlwaine are shipyard workers from Belfast. Only the misfit Pyper is from the officer class of the Big Houses, and he has renounced his class, his education, his artistry and his faith.

Observe the Sons of Ulster Marching Towards the Somme is the first of a series of plays which deal with the shifting relationship, through history, of the island of Ireland and the island of Great Britain, and which include *Mary and Lizzie* (1989), *Someone Who'll Watch Over Me* (1992) and *Mutabilitie* (1997). This was not a conscious project worked out in advance, but a recurring thematic which Frank McGuinness recognizes in retrospect. For his own part, he is much more inclined to recognize, in the development of his own work over the years, a conscious design to extend his range as a dramatist, to experiment in dramatic form and to accommodate that form to the nature of the material he is dealing with. Thus *Someone Who'll Watch Over Me* is conceived of as a chamber piece, a stark enclosed prison drama focused on the exploration of the self, on

Plays of Survival and Identity

identities and origins and particularly on 'a very close examination of the three main dialects of the English language, as I understand them to be, the Irish, the English and the American.'[13] *Mary and Lizzie* embodies the desire to write a great folk play, influenced by his experience of working on a version of Ibsen's *Peer Gynt*[14] and drawing, through Ibsen, on the Norwegian folk tradition. *Mutabilitie* adopts the form of an Elizabethan play in five acts, in which the form and in particular the use of language is stretched beyond its traditional limits.

Historically, the play is set in Ireland in 1598, amidst the violence of the Munster Wars, at a critical, defining moment of Irish history. After the failure of the Reformation in Ireland, a new order is being imposed. The English crown will no longer accommodate itself to the loose, fragmented control of mediaeval feudalism. The imperialism of Queen Elizabeth I is no longer content to seize lands: souls must now be seized, for their own betterment and salvation. The struggle is interiorized: it will no longer be a matter of territorial conquest, it has become ideological and religious, a struggle for identity. Lord Grey is appointed Lord Deputy of Ireland, to be the agent of the new imperialism. Before he sets out in 1580, he recruits as his secretary a young intellectual by the name of Edmund Spenser (1552-1599), destined to become the greatest poet of his generation, who will serve the Crown in Ireland for seven years and receive as his reward the Castle of Kilcolman, set among the wild forests of west Cork, where the disinherited Irish are plotting their resistance. In this perilous and implausible situation, more an enforced exile than a sinecure, Spenser writes his famous allegorical poem, *The Faerie Queene*. In 1598, the castle is destroyed by fire. Spenser and his family escape and return to London, where he dies the following year.

Into this historical framework, Frank McGuinness introduces, with a characteristically provocative humour, the fantasy that the young William Shakespeare might well have travelled across Ireland with a group of players and be rescued from destitution and drowning by the dutiful hospitality of Edmund Spenser. In the confrontation of these characters, two differing and conflicting types of the English imagination are dramatized. Spenser is, on the surface, the untroubled, official creative artist and chronicler, totally committed to the service of the imperial power. Beneath the regulated exterior, are raging terrors and disturbances, a man who had a desperate struggle with his own psyche, with his own soul:

> He had to keep a firm grip, he had to regulate his conscience in order to carry out the policies of the Crown he served. ... Then with Shakespeare, you get a much more diverse, a much more liberated

consciousness, a much more challenging, invigorating imagination, because he was in the process of inventing the theatre.[15]

The third party in this dramatic structure is the group of the native Irish, living in the woods. Here, McGuinness's experimental dramaturgy moves the play into myth and legend: King Sweney, whose name suggests King Sweeney of Dal Arie, the seventh-century hero defeated at the Battle of Moira, who goes mad and is changed into a bird; Queen Maeve, the better known figure from the *Táin Bó Cuailgne*, the warrior queen of Connaught; whereas their two sons Hugh and Niall evoke Hugh O'Neill, the foremost historical Irish leader of the time. The strangest moment, perhaps, in this remarkable play occurs in the fourth act, when William conjures spirits and the Irish appear and chant the Homeric story of Hecuba and Cassandra and the fall of Troy. The play within the play has a political message, fore-fronting the title theme of inevitable change:

> Chaos of change that none can flee
> This earth is Mutabilitie.[16]

The text becomes prophetic: the British Empire will fall, as Troy fell in the past. For Frank McGuinness, the embedded play also dramatizes a moment of what others than he might term postcolonial re-appropriation:

> Here you have a reduction of the whole basis of Western civilization, the story of Troy, told by the Irish, who are taking control of it and presenting it in their own particular voice.[17]

The dense and complex texture of Frank McGuinness's writing for the theatre brings together many influences and experiences. It is embedded in the mainstream of Irish writing, bringing the creative imagination to bear upon the central issues of conflict, identity and survival which have deeply marked his own generation. At the same time, it has remained open to the forces of renewal which characterize dramatic writing in continental Europe, in Great Britain and elsewhere over the past quarter of a century. It has the nature of a conscious project, consciously pursued. Frank McGuinness has extended the accepted boundaries of what can be represented on the Irish stage, and he has explored a full gamut of different modes of representation, contributing to widening the horizon of expectations which an audience brings to the experience of theatre. His theatre is, in a sense, a theatre of extremes. In *Someone Who'll Watch Over Me*, an intimate chamber piece with three characters, he brings us close to a form of realist document drama, based as it is on accounts by Brian Keenan of his hostage experience. In *Mary and Lizzie*, premiered by the Royal Shakespeare Company at the London Barbican in 1989, he sketches out an epic canvas, closest perhaps of all his plays to Armand Gatti's 'utopian space', where imagination has only the limits which it invents for itself. In that play, the historic journey of Mary and Elizabeth Burns brings the audience from a time-out-of-time where women chant in Gaelic in the tree-tops, to Manchester in the mid-nineteenth century and a dinner party with Karl and Jenny Marx; and from a descent into the underworld to meet a dead father to somewhere closer to present times, to the Stalinist work-camps and the long queues of women in deportation. The scope of the issues which McGuinness opens up in his theatre and the energy of his explorations in dramatic form have asserted the place of contemporary Irish theatre within the context of a European consciousness and imagination.

> *Some of the material presented in this paper has been examined in an earlier study: Joseph Long, 'Frank McGuinness', in Anthony Roche, ed.,* The UCD Aesthetic. 150 Years of UCD Writers *(Dublin: New Island, 2005): 209-17.*

---

[1]Frank McGuinness, *Carthaginians*, in *Plays One* (London: Faber and Faber, 1996): All further references will be to that edition.

[2]Hiroko Mikami, *Frank McGuinness and his Theatre of Paradox* (Gerrards Cross: Colin Smythe, 2002): 42-46.

[3]See Joseph Long, ed., *Armand Gatti, Three Plays* (Sheffield: Sheffield Academic Press, 2000).

[4]Long, ed., *Armand Gatti*, 82.

[5]From a discussion with international students, Abbey Theatre Dublin, July 1995, on the occasion of the revival of the play, directed by Patrick Mason.

[6]I have gathered, over a number of years, a body of interview material with Frank McGuinness, much of which has been published. Marianne McDonald and J. Michael Walton, *Amid Our Troubles: Irish Versions of Greek Tragedy* (London: Methuen, 2001): 263-282; *Etudes Irlandaises* CCXLIV, Spring 1999, 9-19.

[7]In Lilian Chambers et al., ed., *Theatre Talk: Voices of Irish Theatre Practitioners* (Dublin: Carysfort Press, 2001): 305.

[8]Marilynn J. Richtarik, *Acting Between the Lines. The Field Day Theatre Company and Irish Cultural Politics 1980-1984* (Oxford: Clarendon Press, 1994): 7.

[9]The first six pamphlets were republished as *Ireland's Field Day: Field Day Theatre Company* (London: Hutchinson, 1985).

[10]See Denis Donoghue, 'Afterword' in *Ireland's Field Day*, 107-120.

[11]The New University of Ulster at Coleraine was founded in 1968 as the second university in Northern Ireland, and it became the University of Ulster, in a merger with the Ulster Polytechnic at Jordanstown, in 1984.

[12]In discussion with international students, Abbey Theatre Dublin, July 1995.

[13]*Theatre Talk*, 301.
[14]Premiered at the Gate Theatre Dublin in 1988.
[15]*Theatre Talk*, 299.
[16]Frank McGuinness, *Mutabilitie* (London: Faber and Faber, 1997): 78.
[17]*Theatre Talk*, 302.

9 | 'The saga will go on':[1] Story as History in *Bailegangaire*

Hiroko Mikami

Introduction:

During the Christmas season of 1985, two companion pieces by Tom Murphy premiered in two cities of Ireland: the Druid production of *Bailegangaire* in Galway, and the Abbey production of *A Thief of a Christmas* in Dublin. Murphy's attempt to put two complementary plays on stage at one time by two different theatre companies was a rare and innovative enterprise for a playwright, though there are many cases of playwrights who write a series of plays one after another, of course.[2] *Bailegangaire,* subtitled as 'the story of Bailegangaire and how it came by its appellation', is set in 1984 and Mommo, a senile old woman who used to be 'known as a skilled storyteller', recollects what happened thirty some years ago[3] and tells her two granddaughters, Mary and Dolly, how she and her husband fought through the laughing competition in a village called Bochtán. In *A Thief of a Christmas,* as its subtitle, 'the Actuality of how Bailegangaire came by its appellation' shows, the play's present is set at the time when the laughing competition actually took place in a local pub and the competition is acted out and shown on the stage.

In this essay, I will mainly deal with *Bailegangaire* and analyse Mommo's story about the laughing contest and what happened after as a narrative of family trauma. Shaun Richards has examined *Bailegangaire* in a context of the trauma of Irish society in his article written in 1989, which provides a wider perspective of Modern Irish history to help understand the play.[4] Here, I would rather concentrate on the limited context of family trauma and underline the mechanism of memory and storytelling. In order to make a close examination of the play, its companion piece, *A Thief of a Christmas*, is read in tandem and the two texts are to be compared and contrasted: the text of *A Thief of a Christmas* presents hints to analyse Mommo's storytelling, especially the mechanism of her unconscious distortion of reality. In *Bailegangaire,* Mommo's retelling of the past first appears in fragments, gradually takes a shape as a story, and is finally recognized in the context of what I refer to as family history. This is the process in which this story/history assists in family regeneration and brings about healing.

I would also like to make note of the intensity of emotion that arises from the rich text of *Bailegangaire*. The play is tightly woven and has its own rhythm gained through repeated phrases as if it is a piece of music. Murphy has a recognition that '[a]ll art aspires to the condition of music'.[5] In an interview with Michael Billington, he expresses his envy and admiration of composers: 'Words, literature, writing drama is such a linear thing, whereas when I listen to music, I hear emotion, I hear mood; when I listen to the sound that people are making, I hear emotion and character.'[6] This is what the audience/reader of *Bailegangaire* is required to do: we have to listen to the sound the three women are making, and we have to hear their emotions. We then witness the process of how the 'unfinished symphony' of Mommo's is transformed into an accomplished symphony of healing. When Mommo wishes for the possibility of reliving her life again, which is almost everyone's wish, — 'Isn't life a strange thing too? 'Tis. An' if we could live it again? ... Would we? (*live it differently?*) In harmony?' (119)— , she unconsciously mentions that whenever relived, it would bring harmony.

I. How the Story Begins:

Murphy recollects an encounter with a woman at the opening night of *A Whistle in the Dark* in London in 1962. She pointed out that he knew nothing about women and *Bailegangaire* was written as a kind of response to this incident. Murphy says: 'I have generally observed the Aristotelian unities of time, action, place, and I thought I would introduce a fourth, gender.'[7] Among the three women Murphy created, Mommo, who is over eighty years of age, is regarded as a contemporary variation of 'Sean Bhean Bhocht', or Poor Old Woman, in Irish literary tradition.[8] In addition to this archetypal representation of Ireland, Murphy seems to have introduced two different archetypes of Irish women, Mommo's two granddaughters: Mary is serious and hard-working, while Dolly is bawdy and easygoing. The two sisters as a pair are analogous to Edna O'Brien's two heroines, Kate and Baba, in *The Country Girls* (1960). In 1986, O'Brien wrote an essay, 'Why Irish Heroines Don't Have to Be Good Anymore', in which she explained the characteristics and relationship of her two heroines: Kate, 'timid, yearning, and elegiac', a type regarded as 'what an Irish woman should be', and Baba, the very opposite type, being frowned upon by social and religious mores. These two heroines are tied firmly by bonds of comradeship and, according to O'Brien, 'their rather meager lives would be made bearable by the company of each other.'[9] Mary and Dolly in *Bailegangaire* are also supporting each other, while opposing each other at the same time. Nicholas Grene sees 'fraught sibling hostility' in Mary and Dolly, and thus summarizes their relationship: 'They have been defined in the crudest polarities, Mary has the brains, Dolly the looks, and they each resent the other one's attributes.'[10]

Mommo used to be Dolly's responsibility when Mary was working as a nurse in London. Since her return home, Mary has taken over Dolly's role and been living with and taking care of Mommo in a traditional thatched cottage. Dolly left home and now lives nearby with her children, while her husband, Stephen, works away in London. At the opening of *Bailegangaire*, we see the three women are at a deadlock: Mommo, like a broken gramophone, repeats a story that happened some thirty years before the play's present; Mary, having given up her professional career, seems to regard herself as a loser without husband or children; Dolly is pregnant out of wedlock and does not know what to do. Each has her own story of failure and is locked in her predicament. Emotional dysfunction among family members is very clearly apparent.

Mommo's story, which has never been told to the end, is about 'the stranger' and 'the stranger's wife' who are actually Mommo's husband and herself. They went to a big fair for the preparation of Christmas and after unsuccessful, disappointed trade there they set off for home where three grandchildren, Mary, Dolly and their young brother Tom, awaited them. On their way back, the couple were forced to involve themselves in a laughing competition in a village called Bochtán, which came to be known, since the competition, by its new appellation, Bailegangaire, 'town without laughter'. *Bailegangaire* is a play about Mommo's homecoming at two levels, as Fintan O'Toole points out, one at the level of the archetypal folk tale of Mommo and another at the level of the present existence of Mary and Dolly.[11] Their homecoming is to be completed when Mommo's story eventually comes to an end. When Mommo makes her symbolic homecoming, both Mary and Dolly also find their true home with Mommo and thus the family reunion is completed. The journey has taken some thirty years, but at the very beginning of Mommo's story, when the couple came to the crossroads, she clearly states that 'the road to Bochtán, though of circularity, was another means home' (98).

When the play opens, Mary is busy reading or doing housekeeping jobs and tries to attract Mommo's attention to anything but her storytelling. She knows its already-told sections by heart and has no interest in it. Mommo occasionally strays from the straight plotline of her story and interjects questions to Mary, whom Mommo does not recognize as her granddaughter:

> **Mommo:** And how many children had <u>she</u> bore herself?
> **Mary:** Eight?
> **Mommo:** And what happened to them?
> **Mary:** Nine? Ten?
> **Mommo:** Hah?
> **Mary:** What happened <u>us</u> all?
> **Mommo:** Them (*that*) weren't drowned or died they said <u>she</u> drove away.
> **Mary:** Mommo?
> **Mommo:** Let them say what they like.
> **Mary:** <u>I'm very happy here.</u>
> **Mommo:** Hmmph!
> **Mary:** I'm Mary.
> **Mommo:** Oh but <u>she</u> looked after <u>her</u> grandchildren.
> **Mary:** Mommo?
> **Mommo:** And Tom is in Galway. He's afraid of the gander.
> **Mary:** But I'm so ... (*She leaves it unfinished, she can't find the word*)
> **Mommo:** To continue.
> **Mary:** Please stop. (*She rises slowly.*)
> **Mommo:** Now man and horse, though God knows they tried, could see the icy hill was not for yielding.
> **Mary:** Because <u>I'm so lonely</u> (97-8, underlined emphasis mine).

Mommo is talking about herself but uses 'she/herself', the third person singular. She thus tries to distance herself from the painful, unbearable incidents in her own life.[12] Mary, on the other hand, uses 'us' in order to make the two of them feel closer, hoping that this use of 'us' triggers Mommo's recognition of Mary as her granddaughter. Mary also implies that she is part of Mommo's story, by saying 'what happened us all.' When Mommo is about to go back to and continue her autistic story, Mary tries to stop her. What Mary really wants is Mommo's attention to her and a conversation, an exchange of dialogue between family members. It must be painful to listen to a story repeated over again and again, especially a story which never moves further than a certain point. Being ignored by Mommo, the only thing left to Mary is to mumble to herself that she is happy or she is lonely. There is little prospect of a breakthrough in this stifling situation. Mary is too straightforward and serious to bring about effective change as she wishes.

When Dolly makes her occasional visit to Mommo and takes the role of listener, her reaction to her grandmother is more flexible and easygoing: she casually reacts to Mommo's sexual innuendo and joyously joins her story with refrains such as 'Good man Josie!' as if chanting in unison. Contrary to her appearance of enjoying Mommo's story, however, she is actually fed up with it and wants her to stop it. Dolly says:

> And that old story is only upsetting her, Mary. ... Harping on misery. And only wearing herself out. And you. Amn't I right, Mary? And she never finishes it – Why doesn't she finish it? And have done with it. For God's sake (102).

Dolly's remark of this is not a well-thought, constructive suggestion but an utterance that comes out of frustration: she is tired of her life and stuck with an unwanted pregnancy. When she uses the phrases, 'to finish it' and 'to have done with it', Dolly just wants Mommo to stop the story: what she simply wants is Mommo's silence. There is a big difference between completing the story ('finish it') and stopping telling it in the middle and keeping silence. Dolly's careless choice of words, however, introduces here the notion of telling the story to the end for the first time in the play. Her casual, somewhat ironical remark acts as a catalyst for change in Mary, or at least gives a hint for change. Even for a moment, Mary is captured by the moving force in Dolly's remark. The stage direction that follows is suggestive: 'Mary considers this (*Finish it? And have done with it*), then forgets it for the moment.' (102) This implies that Mary will come back soon again to consider what Dolly said, but it requires some time for Mary to be actively involved in the process for completing the story.

After Dolly leaves, Mary still tries to make conversation with Mommo: what she wants is a warm touch of family. If that is not acquired, she just hopes 'Mommo will stop, will sleep' (118). When Mommo does fall asleep, Mary mumbles a few words, according to the stage direction, 'to herself' (120), but, in her heart, to Mommo:

> Give me my freedom, Mommo ... What freedom? ... No freedom without structure. ... Where can I go? ... How can I go (*looking up and around at the rafters*) with all this? (*She has tired of her idle game of lighting the candles*) ... And it didn't work before me, did it? ... I came back (120).

She is unable to go on because Mary as a speaker initially needs a listener: she could only go further if she receives responses from Mommo, who could approve or disapprove of what Mary said. In a situation in which nobody is listening, Mary repeats Mommo's half-told story which is already so familiar to her '[t]o herself, and idly at first'(120):

> Now as all do know ... Now as all do know ... Now as all do know the world over the custom when entering the house of another – be the house public, private with credentials or no – (120).

Every single word is remembered but here she is just parroting Mommo's words. She has not yet become a true teller of the story, because she lacks the impetus as a storyteller to move on the story. Still she continues and in the meantime acquires a style of storytelling with 'a touch of mimicry of Mommo' (121), and 'a piece of sardonic humour' (120) is added.

Hamm, in Beckett's *Endgame,* explains, in a way, the transformation that happens in Mary. He says: 'You weep, and weep, for nothing, so as not to laugh, and little by little ... you begin to grieve.'[13] Hamm tells the very truth that if one makes a pretence of grieving, he/she will soon be possessed by the true distress. The process Mary undergoes is a variation on Hamm's theme: Mary 'tells', and 'tells', for nothing, so as not to 'fall silent', and little by little ... she begins to 'be possessed by a story.' While she imitates Mommo's whimpering, 'I wanta go home, I wanta go home', Mary's inner quest for home responds to it. Here, Mary is not just telling Mommo's story: she comes to realize that her own trauma is emotionally tied up with that of Mommo. It is at this moment when Mary is actively involved in Mommo's story.

II. Mommo's Narrative of Trauma:

Mommo's story of trauma originates in the incident that happened thirty-four years before. This family tragedy has been tormenting Mommo all through the years. In order to analyse the play in this perspective, recent studies on trauma provide a framework to the interpretation of the play. Cathy Caruth, one of the leading trauma theorists, for example, suggests that literature has a great role to play in helping us work through trauma and argues in *Unclaimed Experience: Trauma, Narrative, and History* that a story of trauma is 'a kind of double telling, the oscillation between a *crisis of death* and the correlative *crisis of life*: between the story of the unbearable nature of an event and the story of the unbearable nature of its survival'.[14]

Mommo in *Bailegangaire*, as the survivor of a traumatic incident, is unable to tell the story, because this oscillation tears her into two. Remembering the incident in Bochtán and the traumatic deaths of family members that follow is unbearable, and at the same time she has been tormented by her own survival of the incident for all the years since.

Dolly unconsciously notices the guilt that has been felt by Mommo, but is unable to pinpoint exactly what the guilt is about (142), when Mary asks for its explanation. Dolly is not the type to analyse what is seen and felt. Instead, she accuses Mommo for not having shed even a single teardrop at the time of Tom's death, and also of her husband's that followed: 'She stood there over that hole in the ground like a rock – like a duck, like a duck, her chest stickin' out. Not a tear ... Not a tear ... Tom buried in that same hole in the ground a couple of days before. Not a tear, then or since' (143). This is a typical case of 'latency', a Freudian term for a period during which effects of traumatic experience are not apparent. Freud gives an example of a victim of a train accident:

> It may happen that someone gets away, apparently unharmed, from the spot where he has suffered a shocking accident, for instance a train collision. In the course of the following weeks, however, he develops a series of grave psychical and motor symptoms, which can be ascribed only to his shock or whatever else happened at the time of the accident'.[15]

Mommo, who looked 'apparently unharmed', as Dolly points out, at the time of the funerals of Tom and her husband, was certainly in a period of latency. Mommo, as the survivor of the family tragedy, has to go through the nightmares, 'a series of grave psychical and motor symptoms', again and again.

In order to get Mommo out of her nightmares, involvement of Mary and Dolly, Mommo's granddaughters, in the process is crucial. As Caruth aptly comments on the intergenerational structure of trauma in her note to the chapter on Freud's *Moses and Monotheism*:

> That is, described in terms of a possession by the past that is not entirely one's own, trauma already describes the individual experience as something that exceeds itself, that brings within individual experience as its most intense sense of isolation the very breaking of individual knowledge and mastery of events. This notion of trauma also acknowledges that perhaps it is not possible for the witnessing of the trauma to occur within the individual at all, that it may only be in future generations that 'cure' or at least witnessing can take place.[16]

142 Ireland on Stage: Beckett and After

Through generations, memories of both crisis and survival are passed on, and healing can only be possessed within a history larger than any single individual or any single generation. This very process happens to Mommo, Mary, and Dolly, who have their own stories of failure and predicament: each is involved in the family tragedy in one way or another and has her own role in this process of transformation from tragedy to healing: Mommo as a teller, Mary as a listener and co-teller, and Dolly as a catalyst. And the three women cooperate with each other in order to spin a continuing family saga.

Mary, as a patient listener and co-teller, encourages Mommo to reveal the untold part of the story. Telling her story is the only way for Mommo to make sense of the past in the present:

> They could have gone home. (*Brooding, growls; then*) Costello could decree. All others could decree. (*Quiet anger.*) But what about the things had been vexin' *her* for years. No, a woman isn't stick or stone. The forty years an' more in the one bed together an' he to rise in the mornin' (*and*) not to give a glance. An' so long it had been he had called her by first name, she'd near forgot it herself ... <u>Brigit</u> ... Hah? ... <u>An' so she thought he hated her ... An' maybe he did, like everything else</u> ... An' (*Her head comes up, eyes fierce.*) Yis, yis-yis, he's challe'gin' ye, he is!' She gave it to the Bochtán. And to her husband returning? – maybe he would recant, but she'd renege matters no longer. 'Och hona ho gus hah-haa' – <u>she hated him too</u> (140, underlined emphasis mine).

Here, Mommo recalls one of the most memorable moments in which her husband called her by her first name, Brigit. This moment, as we see, is remembered in a context of hatred: Mommo thought that her husband hated her and that she herself hated him.

It is revealing to compare and contrast this scene with the seemingly identical moment in *A Thief of a Christmas*, which is depicted through all-seeing eyes. When Costello, the opponent of the laughing competition, asks how they would decide its winner, Mommo, the stranger's wife, replies that 'he who laughs last' (226) will win. The stranger, Mommo's husband, does not like the way a woman steps in the domain of men, and is 'about to reprimand her – "Stop" or "Whist" – but she is smiling at him very softly and without knowing why, he smiles back at her' (226). Then the crucial moment arrives:

> *The Stranger's Wife is smiling: he goes to her.*
> **Stranger:** Ar, whist. Heh-heh- heh- heh! What's come over us?
> <u>*She starts to laugh with him, quietly. They stop. Tears brim to her eyes. The misfortunes of a lifetime.*</u>
> Ar, Bridget[17]...

Story as History in *Bailegangaire*   143

She titters again. He laughs with her.
Stranger's Wife: I see the animals in the field look more fondly on each other than we do.
Stranger: It's rainin'. The thaw is set in. Shouldn't se be goin'?
Stranger's Wife: (*Shakes her head, no*) ... How long since we laughed or looked upon each other before?
Stranger: *(Nods. Laughs quietly. His laugh, like hers, near tears)* ... But shouldn't we go?
Stranger's Wife: No. ... An' you have him bet.
She embraces him. They start to sway, as in a dance. It is like as if they have forgotten everyone around them in this moment.
Stranger: But 'twas only the comicalest notion that comes into a person's head. Heh-heh-heh.
Stranger's Wife: Whatever it was, you have them bet. We've been defeated in all else but this one thing we'll win.
They separate. The Stranger chuckles, perhaps a little embarrassed.
You'll get him with misfortunes (227-28, underlined emphasis mine).

This is the scene when the couple come to understanding after long, cold, barren years. Remembering the past misfortunes happened among the family members, they are smiling at the same time in tears. This is the context in which Mommo's name, Brigit, was actually used.

As long as Mommo places this moment of understanding in the context of hatred in her memory, as is told in *Bailegangaire*, enmity possesses her and controls her retelling. Being asked by Mary what happened next, Mommo, according to the stage direction, 'growls' and replies that 'there-was-none-would-assuage-her' (141). In the midst of her confusion with anger and hatred, Mommo's story still moves on a little towards the end and she declares the beginning of the final stage of the competition, 'the arena was ready' (141), the phrase repeated from then on several times until the final scene is told. Mommo's telling, however, comes to a halt at this point and she cannot move on further. The only thing left to her is to go between the fragmented utterance and sleep.

It is again Dolly who acts as a catalyst and brings about change in this stagnant situation. Being unable to handle the situation and having failed to convince Mary to help her, Dolly bursts into anger and shouts out that she hates everybody around her: she hates her husband Stephen, Mommo, and Mary. Mommo's cottage and the house of her own are added to the list of hatred. Dolly goes on that Mommo also hates Mary (149-50). Dolly is unconscious, but her hatred echoes that of Mommo's: what lies behind their hatred is cold, barren feelings that come from their own married relationships. Dolly's refusal of empathy, however, paradoxically has an impact on

144 Ireland on Stage: Beckett and After

Mary and evokes the true and certain reception of her address to Mary, who then returns her address not to Dolly but to Mommo.

Mary nurses a notion that the night is the last chance for both Mommo and herself to complete the story: if only they can finish it and relive it through, change will be brought about for them. It is symbolic that the whole action of *Bailegangaire* takes place within the space of three or four hours starting at around seven o'clock on Mary's birthday evening, observing the Aristotelian unity of time. Mary decides to celebrate the day also as Mommo's birthday, which Mary never knew for certain. To 'share the same birthday together in future' (93) could mean, for Mary, to share a new start in life between them and they could symbolically be reborn again together on the day. That is the reason she is so determined to complete Mommo's story within their birthday. Mary declares: 'I don't want to wait till midnight, or one or two or three o'clock in the morning, for more of your – unfinished symphony' (122). Near the end of the play, Mary summarizes her own life and makes her last plea to Mommo:

> No, you don't know me. But I was here once, and I ran away to try and blot out here, I didn't have it easy. Then I tried bad things, for a time, with someone. So I came back, thinking I'd find – something – here, or, if I didn't, I'd put everything right, Mommo? And tonight I thought I'd make a last try. Live out the – story – finish it, move on to a place where, perhaps, we could make some kind of new start. I want to help you (153).

Mommo, however, does not reply to this and asks for a cup of milk for the night, instead. Mary agrees to get it, something which she has been refusing during the evening, half-admitting that the evening might end without completing the story. Mommo's drinking the milk symbolizes for both Mommo and Mary the end of night. Mary then addresses herself 'gently to Dolly' (153), replying to her remark on hatred:

> She may hate me, you may hate me. But I don't hate her. I love her for what she's been through, and she's all that I have. So she has to be my only consideration. She doesn't understand. Do you understand, Dolly? (153)

Mary confesses that her love is not affected even though Mommo hates or ignores her. No matter how provoked she is, Mary is gentle and calm to Dolly. It is symbolic that Mommo begins to tell her story again, saying that 'the full style *was* returning' (154, original emphasis), just after Mary's remark about love, as if admission of unconditional love is necessary for Mommo to escape from the memory of hatred.

Mommo reproduces the laughing contest, enacting the exchanges between Costello and the stranger. Since Mommo is a skilled storyteller, both Mary and Dolly cannot help 'laughing at Mommo's dramatisation' (155) of the newly told section: it induces them to laugh a hearty laugh, to which Mommo herself joins. Telling/listening to the story of laughing competition, the three women are laughing together. After such joyous laughter being shared between Mommo and her two granddaughters, Mommo is almost close to recognising Mary, but she goes back to sleep again. When asked about her intention by Dolly, Mary admits that it is over:

> **Dolly:** What were you trying to do with her?
> **Mary:** 'Twas only a notion ... She's asleep.
> **Dolly:** ... Maybe she'd wake up again?
> **Mary:** (*Slight shake of her head*, 'No'). Sit down (159, underlined emphasis mine).

Mary's use of the past tense well explains her acceptance of failure. This failure, however, is not a bitter, hopeless one for Mary, because she knows that she did her best; at least the three of them laughed together; and Mommo was even on the verge of recognition of Mary. In this condition, Mary states her resolution to take Dolly's newborn baby away from home.

At the very moment when Mary accepts everything, Dolly, looking at her belly as if in self-mockery, utters the word, 'misfortunes'[18](161), to which Mommo unexpectedly reacts. 'Misfortunes' is the topic that kept 'them laughing near forever' (162) in the laughing competition in Bochtán. Mary's admission of love and Dolly's utterance of the keyword act as a trigger for the resetting of the volatile memory of Mommo. She begins to retell that crucial moment and replaces it in a more favourable context:

> An' didn't he ferret out her eyes to see how she was farin' an' wasn't she titherin' with the best of them an' weltin' her thighs. No heed on her now to be gettin' on home. No. But offerin' to herself her own congratulations at hearin' herself laughin'. An' then, like a girl, smiled at her husband, an' his smile back so shy, like the boy he was in youth. An' the moment was for them alone. Unawares of all cares, unawares of all the others. An' how long before since their eyes had met, mar gheal dhá gréine, glistenin' for each other, Not since long and long ago.
>
> And now Costello's big hand was up for to call a recession. 'But how,' says he, 'is it to be indisputably decided who is the winner?' And a great silence followed. None was forgettin' this was a contest. An' the eyes that wor dancin', now pending the answer, glazed an' grave in

dilation: 'Twas a difficult question. (*Quietly.*) Och-caw. Tired of waiting male intelligence. 'He who laughs last' says she.

An' 'cause 'twas a woman that spoke it, I think Costello was frikened, darts class of a glance at her an' – (*She gulps.*) 'That's what I thought,' says he (161-62).

Like a young courting couple, Mommo and her husband are smiling at each other. Here, the mystery of memory is at work. Mommo unintentionally distorts what happened at Bochtán and says that it was Costello who was annoyed with Mommo's intervention as to make a crucial comment on the laughing competition, that is, the man's field. In *A Thief of a Christmas,* the scene is depicted as follows:

> **Costello:** ... Now, the question is, *how*, is it to be indisputably decided who is the winner?
> **John:** Oh, sh-sh-sh-sure – Hah?
> **Costello:** Indisputably the winner. (*And he nods solemnly.*)
> *Silence.*
> **Stephen:** (*To the fire*) 'Tis a difficult question.'
> **Stranger's Wife:** ... He who laughs last.
> **Stranger:** Ar ...
> *About to reprimand her – 'Stop' or 'Whist' – but she is smiling at him very softly and without knowing why, he smiles back at her.*
> **Costello:** That's – that's what I thought (225-26, original emphasis).

It was the stranger, Mommo's husband, who was about to cast a reprimanding glance at her. In Mommo's retelling, however, Costello is falsely accused of his darting hostile glance at the stranger's wife. In order to put her husband in a context of understanding between the couple, Mommo has to distort the fact that actually happened. Cathy Caruth regards this kind of distortion as a mechanism of history: 'historical memory ... is always a matter of distortion, a filtering of the original event through the fictions of traumatic repression, which makes the event available at best indirectly.'[19] Mommo goes through this process and is thus able to continue her story.

In the laughing competition at Bochtán, the crucial topic was unhappiness. The list of Mommo's misfortunes ranges from a bad crop to premature deaths among the family members. The relation between laughter and misfortune is one of the favourite themes of Beckett's. Nell in *Endgame* says: 'Nothing is funnier than unhappiness, I grant you that. But— ... Yes, yes, it's the most comical thing in the world. And we laugh, we laugh, with a will.'[20] Mommo is reproducing what happened in Bochtán: she begins to talk about her sons, who died premature deaths, and takes a roll call of them. Mommo makes an all-out effort not to sob, as the stage direction states: 'the "hih-hih-hih" which punctuate her story sounds more like tears trying to get out rather than a giggle.' (164) Mommo's heart is aching behind the notion that nothing is funnier than her own personal misfortunes. This act of telling has the power to appease the souls of the deceased and at the same time Mommo's soul. And the sons in the photograph on the wall have always been watching over Mommo and her granddaughters.

When Mommo has revealed the episodes about her dead sons, she can at last tell that the stranger and his wife set out for home: 'home without hinder' (168). Ironically enough, the villagers of Bochtán would not let them go 'home without hinder'. When the stranger and his wife were about to leave, Jogie, one of the villagers, became hysterical and attacked the stranger, and soon after, all whole villagers followed suit: 'They pulled him down off the cart an' gave him the kickin'.' (168) Mommo's story then comes to a halt at the point when the stranger and his wife got home, telling that 'the three small childre, like ye, their care, wor safe an' sound fast asleep on the settle' (168). Here again Mommo has to distort the reality: the three small children were not safe at all. It seems to still be painful for Mommo to admit the tragic death of Tom, one of the grandchildren, and the death of her husband that followed.

Here Mary receives the baton from Mommo and takes over the role as storyteller, starting with the opening phrase of Mommo's story, 'It was a bad year for the crops, a good one for mushrooms' (168). Mary knows the part she is going to tell, because she was there and witnessed what happened: Mary was part of the tragedy. Contrary to her insistence on using the first person plurals, 'we/us', in Act One, she uses the third person pronoun when she tells her story. As Grene writes, 'when its tragic consequences in the early childhood lives of Mary and Dolly are brought to light, connections are made allowing the lost generations of the dead and the trauma of their loss to be acknowledged'.[21]

Mary and Mommo are finally able to relive the tragedy they experienced some thirty years before: telling it is reliving it. Mommo is then able to address her dead husband by his first name, Séamus (169). It is her belated response to her husband's use of her first name Brigid in Bochtán. And she can finally recognize Mary as her granddaughter, saying: 'And sure a tear isn't a bad thing, Mary, and haven't we everything we need here, the two of us.' (169) The phrase, 'the two of us' is a repetition of what Mary said to Mommo at the very start of the play: 'We'll have a party, the two of us.' (93) As in the case of 'misfortunes', repeated several times in the play, the repetition of the phrase has an effect similar to that of a theme and variation in a piece of music. When the phrase, 'the two of us' is repeated here in the

148 Ireland on Stage: Beckett and After

play's final scene by Mommo, it evokes a synergistic effect, like 'basso continuo', which leads the (ideal) audience/readers to an enhanced feeling of denouement. Mary thus concludes both the story and the play:

> To conclude. It is a strange old place alright, in whatever wisdom He has to have made it this way. But in whatever wisdom there is, in the year 1984, it was decided to give that – fambly ... of strangers another chance, and a brand new baby to gladden their home (170).

Mary regards her family as 'fambly of strangers', implying that herself, Dolly, and her newborn baby are the direct descendants of the stranger and the stranger's wife in Mommo's story, which is also Mary's. The baby is to be called Tom after its uncle. As Richards aptly points out, 'the monosyllabic simplicity of the name ... encapsulates the alliance which projects a unified past and present into a potential future'.[22] The intergenerational structure of trauma is clear and insightful here: certainly the sense of survival is handed down through generations, and healing can only be possessed within a history larger than any single individual or any single generation.

III. Mary, Dolly and Stephen; the Eternal Triangle:

Mary had an affair with Stephen, Dolly's husband, while she was working in London. According to Mary, Stephen called her 'dearest' and 'wined and dined and bedded' her and wanted to have a girl by her who'd look like her (113). Their affair ended when Mary 'told him to keep away from (her), to stop following (her)' (115). When Mary mentions there were '*other* offers of marriage' (115, emphasis added), she implies there was one from Stephen, which she turned down. Stephen, according to Dolly, appeared in front of her all of a sudden and courted her. Dolly accepted his proposal of marriage, because she believed that he was her 'hero, (her) rescuer' (149). But she also says she 'never once felt any – real – warmth from him' (149). Dolly wonders to herself: 'why the fuck did he marry me' (154). In order to annoy Mary who had rejected himself, Stephen might have married her younger sister, Dolly, whom he did not really love.[23]

In Act One, when Dolly left, Mary shouts at the door and says: 'you'll never know a thing about it.' (113) Dolly, however, seems to notice the affair between her husband and her own sister:

> **Dolly:** An' you owe me a debt.[24]
> **Mary:** What do I owe you?
> **Dolly:** *And* she *had* to get married (143, original emphasis).

Mary replies to this just by one word, 'impossible', pretending that Dolly is talking nonsense. She still knows what Dolly means. The main concern of *Bailegangaire* is how Mommo's story is completed with the aid of Mary, but there is always some sort of undercurrent of strain and tension between Mary and Dolly. The sisters have an ongoing, bitter rivalry: Mary envies Dolly's easy way of life, even her liberty that leads to her promiscuity, admitting her silliness at the same time; Dolly envies Mary's intellectual and social success, saying that she had it easy. From the moment when they cry together at the end of Act One, however, their relation begins to change gradually: Dolly puts her arms around Mary and 'the two of them (are) crying through to the end' (131) of Act One. As Mommo says, 'a tear is not such a bad thing' (169). Their tears, along with the laughter they share with Mommo later on, has power to cleanse, to bring about catharsis. In the address Mary makes to Mommo, she implies an indirect message to Dolly: 'Then I tried bad things, for a time, with someone. So I came back.' (153) The identity of this 'someone' is obvious to Dolly and Mary adds her apology to her sister:

> **Mary:** ... And I'm sorry.
> **Dolly:** (*Drunkenly*) For What?
> **Mary:** (*Turn away tearfully*) I'm not the saint you think I am.
> **Dolly:** The what? Saint? That'd be an awful thing to be. 'Wo ho ho, ho ho ho!'
> *Mary puts the milk by the bed* (153-54).

Dolly, like Mary, also pretends not to understand what her sister means. Instead, she mimics Mommo's laughter at the competition: the very theatricality of this laughter serves to disguise the tension between the sisters. Dolly, in this way, accepts Mary's apology. She knows that it is sometimes better to keep things unsaid, because their fragile 'home' will fall apart, if they bring what they know into the open. The story of the triangle of Mary, Dolly, and Stephen has not yet become part of the family history: it is too early to be told. Later generations may spin it into a story and tell it, if they feel it necessary. This sense of imperfection paradoxically suggest a strong continuation and possibility: their lives go on, as their family saga will go on.

---

[1]Tom Murphy, *Plays Two* (London: Methuen, 1993), 147. All quotes from Murphy's plays, *Bailegangaire* and *A Thief of a Christmas*, are from this edition and are indicated parenthetically in the text.

[2]Before the two plays about Bailegangaire/Bochtán were written, Murphy had written *Brigit*, a TV play for RTE made in 1987 and broadcast in 1988, as a part of the trilogy of this family. See Fintan O'Toole, *Tom Murphy: The*

Politics of Magic (Dublin: New Island Books, 1994), and Nicholas Grene, *The Politics of Irish Drama: Plays in Context from Boucicault to Friel* (Cambridge: Cambridge University Press, 1999), 219-241 and also note 5 in 287.

[3]About the date of the laughing competition, there seems to be a disparity in description between *Bailegangaire* and *A Thief of a Christmas*. *Bailegangaire* is set in 1984 and at the time of the play's present, Mary is forty-one, while when the laughing competition took place, Mary was seven years old (169). Therefore, the competition took place thirty-four years ago in 1950, according to the time scheme of *Bailegangaire*. The time of *A Thief of a Christmas*, however, is set 'about 50 years ago' (172) from 1985, meaning sometime in 1930s. See Grene, *The Politics of Irish Drama*, 237, O'Toole, *Tom Murphy*, 231.

[4]Shaun Richards, 'Refiguring Lost Narratives – Prefiguring New Ones: The Theatre of Tom Murphy' in *The Canadian Journal of Irish Studies*, XV, 1, 1989, 80-100.

[5]Tom Murphy, 'Tom Murphy: In Conversation with Michael Billington' in *Talking About Tom Murphy*, edited by Nicholas Grene (Dublin: Carysfort Press, 2002), 108.

[6]Murphy, 'In Conversation with Michael Billington', 108.

[7]*Talking About Tom Murphy*, 109.

[8]See Richards, 'Refiguring Lost Narratives – Prefiguring New Ones: The Theatre of Tom Murphy', 95-96, and Anthony Roche, *Contemporary Irish Drama: from Beckett to McGuinness* (Dublin: Gill & Macmillan, 1994), 147. Nicholas Grene compares Mommo with Maurya in Synge's *Riders to the Sea* and also with the title role of Yeats' *Kathleen ni Houlihan*. See *The Politics of Irish Drama: Plays in Context from Boucicault to Friel* (Cambridge: Cambridge University Press, 1999), 227-30.

[9]Edna O'Brien, 'Why Irish Heroines Don't Have to Be Good Anymore', *New York Times Book Review*, 11 May 1986, 13.

[10]Nicholas Grene, 'Talking it through: *The Gigli Concert* and *Bailegangaire*' in *Talking About Tom Murphy*, 77.

[11]Fintan O'Toole, *The Politics of Magic* (Dublin: New Island Books, 1987, 1994), 242.

[12]See Roche, *Contemporary Irish Drama*, 151-54, and Grene, *The Politics of Irish Drama*, for their arguments in Mommo's use of the third person in relation with storytelling..

[13]Samuel Beckett, *The Complete Dramatic Works* (London: Faber and Faber, 1986, 1990), 125.

[14]Cathy Caruth, *Unclaimed Experience: Trauma, Narrative, and History* (Baltimore, Maryland: the John Hopkins University Press, 1996), 7.

[15]Quoted in Caruth, 16.

[16]Caruth, 136.

[17]The spelling of Mommo's first name varies in the trilogy. The title of the TV play is spelled as *Brigit* as in *Bailegangaire*, while 'Bridget' is used in *A Thief of a Christmas*. Obviously, they are variations of the same name.

[18]In a scene in Act One, how the word 'misfortunes' acts as a trigger for

Mommo to come to herself is introduced. When Dolly unconsciously utters the word, Mommo is brought back to life from 'her own thoughts' (108) and recognises Dolly.

[19]Caruth, 16.

[20]Beckett, *The Complete Dramatic Works*, 101.

[21]Nicholas Grene, 'Talking it Through: *The Gigli Concert* and *Bailegangaire*' in *Talking About Tom Murphy*, 80.

[22]Richards, 96.

[23]It is not clearly stated in the play when their affair started and ended. It possibly started before Stephen's marriage with Dolly and continued for a while after it, since Mary seems to be carrying the sense of guilt.

[24]In an earlier scene in Act One, Dolly once brings up the topic of Mary's debt to her, saying: 'You are away awful long time. I was left holdin' the can. Like, when you think of it, you owe me a very big debt.' (103) Dolly's emphasis on the burden she felt is intended to arise Mary's feeling of guilt, so that she will take Dolly's baby away. The context is slightly altered here in Act Two when Dolly insinuates about Mary's affair with Stephen. And the repetition of the word 'debt' has certainly an effect on Mary like that of 'basso continuo'.

10 | *Dancing at Lughnasa*:
Between First and Third World

Declan Kiberd

Set in Donegal during the late summer of 1936, Brian Friel's *Dancing at Lughnasa* asks a question: who is to inherit Ireland? That question is implicit rather than explicit, however, in a work which is thoroughly addressed to the integrity of the local moment. The long decline of rural Ireland over the previous century has almost come to an end, and the five Mundy sisters are just about clinging onto a way of life that cannot last. The oldest, Kate, is a local primary schoolteacher and her income holds the home together. She played a part in the War of Independence, but neither that nor its outcome is ever discussed. Two of the sisters, Agnes and Rose, earn pin-money by knitting gloves at home. Another, Maggie, keeps house. They are in their thirties. The youngest, Chris, is twenty-six and mother of a seven-year-old boy named Michael. He is the offspring of an affair with a travelling salesman, Gerry, who returns twice during the action. Michael appears both as a boy and as the young man who narrates the events over a quarter of a century later.

Apart from a passing line urging people to vote for de Valera, there is no reference to the politics of the new Ireland. In fact, there is more interest in the wars in Abyssinia and Spain. Yet the very lack of a visible political structure in a Donegal well remote from the affaires of Dublin opens the way for a deeper set of questions as to whether, in that condition of vulnerability, the received culture of these sisters might sustain them. There is something strangely exhilarating, as well as terrifying, about their raw exposure to the resources of culture as they face into the future. Like Edward Said's Palestinians, they live at those frontiers 'where the existence and disappearance of peoples fade into each other, where resistance is a necessity, but where there is sometimes a growing realization of the need for an unusual, and to some degree, an unprecedented knowledge'.[1]

These people's access to the traditional interior of the ancestral culture – the fire-festival of Lughnasa celebrated in the back hills of Donegal – has been blocked by the codes of a prim Catholicism, epitomized by the censorious but not bad-hearted Kate. So they attempt to find a margin of hope and of culture, by which to locate themselves. There is little reference to the past by the sisters, other than a brief recollection of a local dance and of the moment when their mother waved an unsmiling farewell to their older brother Jack as he left for the African missions. It is as if all their energies must be invested in holding onto the present moment, prolonging it just a little, before it disappears. For the war-clouds gathering over Spain are paralleled by the hairline cracks appearing in the little world of Ballybeg. 'Uncle' Jack has now returned, an apparently sick and dying man, in such disrepute with his church as to threaten Kate's continuing viability as a teacher employed by the parish priest in charge of the local school.

'I had a sense of unease', says the narrator, 'some awareness of a widening breach between what seemed to be and what was, of things changing too quickly before my eyes, of becoming what they ought not to be.' (2) Even a child, confronted by a fatherless landscape, could sense something amiss. The transfer of power at the start of the previous decade had been no more than a transfer of the crisis facing rural communities. The flight from the land was a global phenomenon in the 1930s, but in most other countries, whether the United States or Uganda, it meant simply a shift of poor people from the countryside to the nearest big city. Even in East Africa by 1936, one in every six of the people was living outside the rural areas in which they had been born.[2] In Ireland that shift meant, more often than not, a flight out of the country itself; and this migration masked to some extent the huge transformation that was taking place, as rural ways yielded to urban living. What seemed like a crisis of overpopulation in the 'congested districts' of the west was really a failure to produce goods and distribute food more efficiently. The manager of the crisis invariably referred to it as a painful but challenging period of transition. What it led to, in fact, was a growing sense of conflict between country and city. Power – cultural as well as economic – was wielded in the cities and it was there that the leaders of the emerging societies ran the business.

Friel's narrator has a clear memory of the ways in which these factors worked: 'Irish dance music beamed to us all the way from Dublin', by means of the new wireless set (2). Thus did the new rulers

Between First and Third World 155

create a sort of retro-nationalism by means of electronic technology. As in Africa, the new state might appear to be the product of a vibrant national movement, whereas in fact the reverse was often the case. Political nationalism was a product, not always well-fitting, of the pre-existing state.[3] In any tussle between them, the forces of the state could be guaranteed to win. Poor people, such as the young Kate Mundy, were exploited to advance the nationalist cause, and then cast to one side. The entire country of Donegal was a blatant example of the wider pathology; hence Kate's silence on the independence struggle. The thought was just too painful to contemplate.

Michael recalls how his mother and his aunts took to the radio. Sets had been sold widely in Ireland just four years earlier, so that loyal Catholics could tune into the Eucharistic Congress celebrations broadcast from Dublin. It was in the course of one of these programmes that Count John McCormack's rendition of 'Panis Angelicus' became the most famous challenge to male tenor voices across the land. Whether the leaders of the Catholic church were making wily use of the new technology or the manufacturers of radio sets were cashing in on a people's devotion to religion has never been fully clear, but the technologists got the better deal. The sets remained in houses long after the praying had ceased, with the consequence that a boy like Michael can watch 'Marconi's voodoo change those kind, sensible women and transform them into shrieking strangers' (2). The modern, far from putting an end to mythology, turns out to be the most potent myth of all and may help to explain the sisters' forgetfulness of their parents and of past events. 'The electronic whirlpool', it would soon be observed, 'far surpasses any possible influence father and mother can now bring to bear.'[4] Radio technology encouraged the involvement of the listener: by it youth could learn once again how to live mythically as part of the global village.

The radio is brand-named Minerva, but the sisters christen it 'Marconi'. The other classical deity which presides over their lives is the gold Lugh, in whose honour the August festival is held. In mythology Lugh was believed to have been father of Cuchulain, but that paternity was never fully clear-cut, for other names were canvassed too as likely fathers for the Celtic hero; and, indeed, other offspring were attributed to Lugh. Michael has his own reasons for recalling the summer of 1936, because it brought the revelation of his father ('and for the first time in my life I had the chance to observe him' (2)) who would also turn out to have other children in another family. Gerry is himself at once a down-at-heel Romeo, unable to hold even the most tenuous of jobs, and a presence filled with mythic possibilities. Apart from the pagan Lugh analogy, he may also evoke the Christian St Patrick, the poor boy from Wales transported to rural Ireland and there put to his shifts. Kate seems vaguely troubled by that distant echo. Accused by the emotional Chris of not calling him by his familiar name, she retorts: 'Don't I know his name is Gerry? What am I calling him? St Patrick?' (34)

The search for expressive freedom on the part of the sisters has been frustrated even before it begins. The drab overalls and aprons of the period lie like strait-jackets on their bodies, degrading clothes to the level of seedy costume: and father Jack's resplendent uniform of a British army chaplain simply confirms, by way of contrast, that here are people who will never wear their own clothes. His uniform and hat are pure comic opera, in recognition of the fact that, wherever the British upper-class went they gave the impression of a people at play, impersonating those higher home types they could never hope to be. In Jack's case the impersonation continues even after his return home.

The youngest sister Chris opens the play with a telling query: 'When are we going to get a decent mirror to see ourselves in?' (2). This evokes many previous moments in Irish writing, from Maria Edgeworth's fear that the people would only smash any glass which offered an honest reflection of their condition to Synge's Christy Mahon who rails against the devilish mirror in his father's home, which 'would twist a squint across an angel's brow'.5 In *Ulysses* Stephen Dedalus had suggested that the cracked looking-glass of a servant was a fitting symbol of Irish art. Synge's use was perhaps the most radical of all, for he had seen in the image the limits of a literary realism which could render only social surfaces but give no deeper account of the psychic condition of country people. In his eyes all mirrors were problematic, since they afforded only a distorted image of the self, the distorting factor being an image of the power of public opinion. For him, a true freedom would be possible only when the mirror was thrown away and people began to construct themselves out of their own desires. The Mundy sisters are still far from that insouciance, being greatly exercised by what the neighbours think of them and of Jack. 'The only way to avoid seven years' bad luck is to keep on using it', says Maggie (3). Yet what the cracked looking-glass will reveal is the multiple, fractured state of the family which peers into it.6

The impression is soon conveyed that postcolonial Ireland has not been transformed by political independence: it is rather a place filled with emigration and arguments about votes. De Valera seems almost as remote as Gandhi: but the sisters know that they are expected to vote for him:

Will you vote for de Valera, will you vote? If you don't, we'll be like Gandhi with his goat ... (4).

The parliamentary system is nothing more than a race for the spoils of office: what is actually done with the power is never discussed. Ownership of the system rather than its transformation turns out to have been the issue all along. Or, as Kwame Anthony Appiah would put it: 'When the postcolonial rulers inherited the apparatus of the colonial state, they inherited the reins of power; few noticed, at first, that they were not attached to a bit.'[7] The world of the Mundy sisters is filled with absences brought on by emigration – Danny Bradley's wife and children have gone, enslaving him as the only sexual opportunity for the 'simple' Rose. All the men with get-up-and-go have got up and gone. As in Synge's *Playboy*, there is a sense of bristling sexuality just below the surface of the women's demeanour, along with a curious tendency to impersonate the absent men. 'I'm your man' is one of Maggie's turns of phrase when Chris suggests that they go to a dance (3) but the same Chris has just tried on Father Jack's surplice. Her own childhood friend, Bernie O'Donnell, has been in London for eighteen years, and has just come home on a visit 'the figure of a girl of eighteen', making her look like the sister of her own daughter (18).

This is another feature of the play: its dissolution of the borders which ordinarily separate adult from child. As a narrator, the actor who plays the adult Michael also uses the same voice to represent the seven-year-old child he once was; but the effect is to suggest a premature ageing process, brought on in the boy by excessive early exposure to the cares of the grown-up world. Conversely, some of the adults behave in a fashion more common among children: Maggie with her riddles and Father Jack playing with the kites. The man-child and child-woman meet in Ballybeg, as if to suggest the impossibility of real childhood under such conditions: but whether the blame lies with modernity or tradition remains radically unclear. When Maggie hears of Bernie O'Donnell's ravishing good looks and beautiful daughters, she silently confronts those thoughts already voiced to the boy: 'Just one quick glimpse – that's all you ever get. And if you miss that ...' (14). But she looks out the window so that the others cannot see her face: only at the every end of the play will she and they face the audience with that knowledge fully decipherable in their bodies.

Meanwhile, optimism and pessimism are held in a fragile balance. Maggie wagers that Michael's kites will never leave the ground, but Kate still hopes to fix up the old bicycle for future use. (It may have fallen into disrepair because of priestly injunctions in the Congress year against provocative young women who rode bicycles.) Agnes decides also to accentuate the positive, resolving to attend the local harvest dance: 'I'm only thirty-five. I want to dance.' (13) But Kate will have none of it: the spectacle of mature women dancing might leave the whole countryside mocking them. Still, there is a seasonal madness in the air. Up in the back hills, the old fire-rituals of Lughnasa are still observed by wild people who light fires by spring wells and drive cattle through flames as a way of casting out devils. Some of the young people, crazed with drink, dance around those flames in a reprise of the old rituals of St John's Eve, recorded by Synge in his travels through the west.

Perhaps it is some distant intimation of this holy frenzy which grips Maggie at this moment. As a céilí band beats out 'The Mason's Apron' on the radio, she rises with her face daubed in white flour and animated 'by a look of defiance, of aggression' (21); 'a crude mask of happiness' she launches into the dance of 'a white-faced dervish'. Taking up her mood of carnivalesque masking, Chris dons the priest's white surplice and joins in. 'But the movements seem caricatured,' insist the stage directions, 'and the sound is too loud; and the beat is too fast.' White may be the colour of innocence: but there is something not quite right about the scene. Eventually, even Kate joins the other sisters, but like a more modern dancer improvising in her own space, she dances alone. The impression is of women 'consciously and crudely caricaturing themselves' (22). There may be a feeling of release and defiance in their gestures of energy and physical self-expression, but it comes with a bitter anger at their condition. For the dancing is furtive, enclosed in the kitchen rather than performed as ritual in a public space; and, worse still, it is over all too soon, as the radio peters out and fails to prolong the promised orgasm. Even the modern myth fails them: 'It's away again, that aul thing' (22). Far from being a male fantasy of sexually voracious dervishes, the scene depicts a world in which the radio, overheated, wilts like a man who cannot satisfy the sisters. Their search must be for a further surrogate, which will be no more satisfactory: 'Wonderful Wild Woodbine. Next best thing to a wonderful wild man.' (23)[8]

This great climactic scene in Friel's oeuvre comes in the middle of the first act. All that follows is a slow, dying fall – a long slide into nothingness. This is a huge technical risk on the part of the playwright, but the sense of anticlimax created is wholly effective. The suggestion is that all the educational and cultural training of these women has been a preparation for something that will never quite happen. The emotional graph already traced by Joyce in *Ulysses* or by Yeats in his *Autobiographies* – a rising curve of expectation followed by frustration and disappointment – is shown here to apply to women as much as to men. For the rest of the action, the sisters will be seen holding onto a way of life which, although it should not be despised, just has to go. The fact that so much is distorted even in their dance suggests that already they feel a degree of removal from their own experience: and since most of them are no longer young, they feel that sense of distance all the more deeply. Their dance is a defiance of the ageing process and of a society which offers them so little emotional scope – a swan-song before its final break-up.

What should be a harvesting of the fruits of independence by a 'risen people' is revealed as anything but. At that very moment in distant Dublin, the Taoiseach Éamon de Valera is preparing a new constitution for ratification in the following year: this will give the rural Irish family its destined recognition as the foundation of Irish society, but at that very moment when thousands of such families are being broken by emigration.[9] Previously, the young had gone rather than defer to a hated British law; now they were leaving because (in the words of Frank O'Connor) the life held out to them by an independent Ireland seemed boring and mediocre. Yet *Dancing at Lughnasa* manages also to suggest that something good is being lost, and even more tantalizingly, that the society depicted had within its reach the sources of its own renewal.[10]

Apart from teaching or manual labour, rural Ireland has no work to offer the Mundy sisters commensurate with their talents: yet by focusing on five unmarried but sensuous sisters, Friel brilliantly avoids the usual stereotypes – mother, martyr, virgin. The dance expresses a longing for a world that passed them by. It might even be seen as a validation of Chris's brief rebellion against the mores of Ballybeg, which left her with Gerry Evan's love-child. Yet the céilí music to which they move is scarcely more venerable than the Cole Porter hits which also issue from the radio set: for Irish dance music is another 'invented tradition', dating back no further than the 1890s. Against the fire ritualists of Lughnasa, it may seem to offer a paltry, private experience. Even if Chris manages to subvert the clerical order by donning the robes of a priest, her gesture has no meaning for the wider community. In earlier decades country kitchens were places where a community gathered to sing and dance, but this is a purely private rebellion – a compensation for the fact that the sisters will not be taking part in any public festivity.[11]

Chris is normally a mild person, not likely to be fooled by the empty promises of her lover: but under the influence of the dance, she assumes a different identity. Which is her true self? The submerged buried one might seem so, but, like her sisters, she appears to be sheepish and embarrassed when the music stops. The fade-out of the

160   Ireland on Stage: Beckett and After

music before its proper conclusion seems indicative of much else in the Mundys' world – the kites that will not fly, the bike that never goes, those sentences of Uncle Jack which peter out, even the memories of Michael-the-narrator which never quite come to a clarifying point. It is as if everyone has difficulty in telling or living a story from start to finish, as if all impulses are arrested before they can fructify, as if the very festival of Lughnasa becomes a mockery of their unharvested desires. The old integrity of experience has been replaced by a search for mere sensation: and this is why the very idea of a past seems all but untransmittable. Jack wishes to tell the sort of story which might feed the collective illusion, but he fails repeatedly to shape one. Michael struggles to disentangle the real from the illusory and succeeds, but only to a limited extent, coming in and fading out like a distant radio signal.

The outside world appears to hold all the aces. Already, it has erased Jack's Irish and Gerry's Welsh accents. The new technology has left the members of the family all focused on distant sources of authority which their own local culture seems unable to provide. They are more than willing to participate in its schemes: songs like 'The Isle of Capri' and 'Anything Goes' resonate as freely through the kitchen as jingles for Wonderful Wild Woodbine Cigarettes. There is no central myth or coherent theory to hold the traditional Ballybeg society together anymore, and no way of telling what belongs to it and what doesn't. 'Anything Goes' may be a myth of the modern, but could equally well have been said of the Festival of Lughnasa. The sisters, because theirs is a world of shreds and patches, have mastered the art of speaking through the available materials ('the most exciting turf we have ever burned'), but in such angular ways as to leave them sometimes a mystery even to themselves.[12] The songs which provoke their curiosity also serve to leave them feeling restless: and the technology of radio and gramophone, coming at the primitive phase of a wholly new civilization, appear to be at once pagan and modernist, but in either guise quite at odds with approved local codes. The new gadgets are helping to abolish the very idea of 'home', since their traces can be left anywhere in the world. Joyce had made this mythical potential of radio one of the major elements in *Finnegans Wake*, recognizing that it was a new sort of tribal drum. Field Day, under Friel's guidance, had been derided for its old-fashioned naturalism as a pre-electric movement,[13] but the playwright here shows that if anything, the reversion to mythical experience is now a frankly post-electric phenomenon. The spread of jazz rhythms across the western world in the 1930s, often by performers who were themselves happily illiterate, was a further illustration of that truth. Many decades later,

Between First and Third World 161

in the 1980s, what was still left of local communities would learn how to use radio for such people's own expressive purposes.[14]

In the 1930s this was not yet possible. What was broadcast from national transmitters in the great capital cities was what a people's lords and masters wished it to hear. The signals emitted from Dublin exemplified the cultural confusion of an elite uncertain as to whether to promote a distinctively Irish music or to submit to the forces of the international market. So céilí faded into Cole Porter. The Mundy sisters are just old enough to have been educated into a world of print technology in classrooms as rigid and stratified as a factory conveyor-belt (for which they were the logical preparation). Print itself was, after all, the first of millions of 'assembly-lines' and a mastery of its processes was an essential precondition for work in the new knitting factory near Ballybeg. The hand-knitting crafts of Agnes and Rose are by 1936 as obsolete as the old weaving of a text by oral tellers in the form of a rhapsody: and their flight from the fate of factory life is a final protest against the new dispensation. But before they go, they connect via radio with an even more advanced technology which carries within itself a promise of a return to the mythical. This they love, as much as they hate the other mode.

The vibrant response of the sisters to the music of 'The Mason's Apron' indicates the ways in which electronic media serve as extensions not only of the body but of the central nervous system, involving the person as a whole rather than this or that organ.[15] Something of that ecstatic power is unleashed in the dance ... and the theatre audience, which was first struck through the eye by the spectacle of a golden field of August corn, now submits to the aural experience of the music, as the democratic ear takes from the hierarchical, surveying eye. Yet so persistent are the old print modes that, once the moment of excitement has passed they reassert themselves: and so Maggie can suggest that they put roses on Jack's window-sill 'with a wee card – ROSES – so that the poor man's head won't be demented looking for the word' (27).

And *that* is the nature of cultural transmission: one new form doesn't necessarily kill off another. Gerry, now selling Minerva gramophones, attests to the fact: 'People thought gramophones would be a thing of the past when radios came in. But they were wrong' (29). Even cows with single horns have survived the onset of modernity; and a form as ancient as spoken drama can contain both the radio and the gramophone, as well as the short story. But the hand-over is always difficult and the strain is likely to show in a world where the climax comes always too soon. 'Suddenly', says Kate, 'you realise that hair cracks are appearing everywhere that control is slipping.' (35) To her this loss of control is manifest in exactly those zones where her ancestors might have thought themselves to exercise it: in the ritual sacrifice at the Lughnasa fire, the sacrifice of a goat. The Sweeney boy was 'doing some devilish thing' with the animal when he fell into the flames. Now, some hope of peace is to be derived from the knowledge that he has been 'anointed' by the parish priest (35).

That same priest, however, makes no appearance on stage, as if to suggest that he is not a force in the spiritual lives of a people. This may be a homage to Synge, who tended to keep his priests offstage in order to show that the instincts of rural people were of more ancient lineage than the Christian scheme of things. The only priest allowed to appear is more in the tradition of Shaw's Peter Keegan, a holy fool defrocked by superiors too obtuse to appreciate his deeper vision. Father Jack Mundy has just returned after more than two decades on the East African missions. If Gerry Evans is a sort of latter-day St Patrick on a mission to convert the Irish to Minerva gramophones, Jack embodies the more traditional notion of the Irish missionary seeking to found a spiritual empire for his people beyond the seas. Such young men and women went out, perhaps, with a somewhat patronizing idea of converting the heathen (including the 'buying' of 'black babies'), but they were in the main animated by a desire to help poorer peoples. The Irish missionary campaign had no ulterior political imperial motive, such as disfigured other European efforts; and this meant that its exponents were more willing to identify with the struggles of native peoples for self-development. Both sides were involved, after all, in the attempt at decolonization.

Even those who went as missionaries with the British forces were more likely than imperial administrators to find themselves exposed to local cultural rays. A soldier or governor needed only to know how to issue orders, but a missionary needed to understand the natives' souls (if they were to be transformed). E.M. Forster had noted how in India, as a consequence, administrators travelled first-class in rail carriages, while missionaries went third, among the ordinary people. His novel *A Passage to India*, investigated the confrontation between a European and non-European mind-set: would the result be a happy confluence or sickening conflict? Would each group take the best from the other, or would the discrepant codes cancel one another out, removing all self-restraint and opening a cultural chasm into which the credulous might fall? Forster, like Joseph Conrad, tended to be pessimistic.

Father Jack's return should, in theory, have been a moment of triumph for the Mundy family, for local newspapers had long celebrated his work and local parishes had saved pennies to support it.

Between First and Third World 163

At first the sisters were worried that his mind might have been unhinged by prolonged exposure to African ways, but soon they decided that his problem was linguistic: after twenty-five years of speaking Swahili, he had forgotten most of his English. Their task was simply to teach it to him again. Kate, however, broods on the question after the doctor assures her that Jack's mind is far from confused and 'his superiors probably had no choice but send him home' (35). The implication is that he has gone native. He frets about his mother's impassive face on his departure in 1911. Kate says that it simply indicated her knowledge that she would never see her son again:

> **Jack:** I know that. But in the other life. Do you think perhaps Mother didn't believe in the ancestral spirits?
> **Kate:** Ancestral – What are you blathering about, Jack? Mother was a saintly woman who knew she was going straight to heaven ... (38-9).

Jack tells the story of a fellow-priest addicted to quinine who had been given up for dead, but was cured by a medicine-man and lived to eighty-eight. He fully approved of ritual sacrifices of animals to appease ancestral spirits. The English District Commissioner in Uganda befriended Jack and rebuked him for going native. In accordance with imperial policy, this DC offered Jack money for schools and hospitals in return for co-operation, but Jack refused. Although beguiled by the British uniform, Jack keeps faith with the ideals of those Irish missionaries who refused to implicate their programme of spiritual renewal in the colonial agenda. The DC must have been fond of Jack, however, for on departure he made him a present of the last governor's ceremonial hat.

In Ryanga, where he worked, Jack tells Chris that women are eager to have love-children: and seems mock-surprised at her confession to having just one. The harvest rituals of Donegal and Ryanga appear to have become hopelessly entangled in his head, leaving him a cross between Joseph Campbell and Edward Casaubon, armed with the key to all mythologies. He seems to be using his knowledge of Africa to parody the ancestral Irish culture which sent him out here. The overlaps between the sacrifice of animals and the birth of love-children are too exact to be mere accident. By the early decades of the twentieth century, German scholars had established that ancient Irish society (with only rare exceptions) regarded all children as legitimate and that its women were keen to bear children to admired men in the knowledge that such offspring would be seen as a blessing.[16]

If Jack is being mischievous, it is possible that his mischief is of long duration. Friel's use of a comparative ethnography goes clean against the trend of cultural nationalism, which had always seen

Ireland as a unique and privileged place, like no other on earth. The myth of Irish exceptionalism, much reinforced by its island status, was augmented in later years by the reluctance of scholars to engage in comparative literature or comparative politics, such matters being the preserve of creative rather than scholarly minds. By implying an extended set of comparisons between Ireland and Africa, Friel is enabled to pen a large question: whether the exodus of young missionaries in the first half of the century was brought about not only by idealism but also by boredom? Perhaps that was why Jack's mother looked so stern and unforgiving as her son flew the nest? In like manner, it could be argued, against the orthodox Marxian explanations, that much colonial activity by Europeans was motivated less by economic imperatives – the search for new materials and markets – than by an intolerance of *ennui* and emptiness at home.

The search for a meaning to life might be conducted with greater intensity in some faraway place. At all events, this would tally with the illuminating remark of Chinua Achebe concerning the disinclination of West African tribes to proselytize: 'I can't imagine the Igbos travelling four thousand miles to tell anybody their worship was wrong.'[17] A cultural motivation would always leave missionaries open to the counter-claim by those natives too serene for self-assertion.

Michael's next narrative is a sudden flash-forward which works to almost brutal effect: it warns that Rose and Agnes will leave and Kate will lose her job in the school. The audience by now shares with the characters the desire to hold onto each moment a little longer, to slow down the march of time so that the present might be made real. As if to confirm such unreasoning optimism and to prove that not all predictions are necessarily correct, Gerry falsifies Kate's prophecy by returning within days. He and Chris dance silently together on the boreen, while their son watches from behind a bush; what he sees is, in effect, their wedding ceremony. The vows there exchanged are felt with sufficient depth for Chris to experience no depression, no urge to sob, on this occasion after Gerry goes.

The second act opens with further revelations about Ryangan life. Its people have blended old and new in a living tradition. They have blended the sacrifice of the mass with offerings to Obi, the earth goddess, so that their crops may flourish and so that departed ancestors may be contactable for their counsel. The Ryangans have not been relegated to the back hills, like the devotees of Lughnasa (no better than savages, according to Kate), but have been true to their beliefs, singing local songs and making no false distinction between the religious and the secular. Maggie is less than convinced by all this propaganda for an effortless hybridity in what is, after all, a sick-bay:

'A clatter of lepers trying to do the Military Two-Step' (49). But the alternative is outright surrender to a life on the conveyor-belt and endless commuting by bus to a factory in Donegal town.

Already the daily life of the Mundys is on fast-forward: their neighbour Vera McLaughlin is too old to work in the factory at forty-one. On his return visit, Gerry climbs the sycamore tree and seems to see ahead into a distant future, but Aggie, already sensing her doom, calls up: 'The tree isn't safe, Gerry. Please come down' (53). She sees that it can be dangerous to know too much of the future, for such knowledge can unfit people for life in the present. The fear of that future is, of course, wholly linked to the sisters' nervousness about the past, for to plant co-ordinates in either zone is to remind themselves of just how sickeningly fast their history is now moving them.

As if to embody that felt pressure, the older Michael's narrative breaks in ever more insistently, as one urgency overrides another with a grim, inexorable violence. 'The Industrial Revolution had finally caught up with Ballybeg.' (59) It is at this moment, more than any other, that the formal arrangements of the play become most effective. Throughout the action, even during the kitchen dance, there had been a problem of synchronization. The beat was stronger than the melody, or the music itself went too fast for the dancers. Four sisters sang and shouted, while Kate remained utterly silent. Gerry and Chris danced when there was no music at all. Gerry smiled when feeling terrible. But, above all, everything seemed somewhat distorted (like the expressions on the boy's masks), as if some elements of life were more developed than others. Such effects may have owed something to the expressionist depiction of war-scenes in Sean O'Casey's *The Silver Tassie*: but in this case they are also the signs of that uneven development which afflicted many postcolonial societies. In the years before Friel completed his play, many books had been written exploring the problem: one even bore the title *Uneven Development*.[18] Put simply, the thesis was that Ireland contained elements of both a First World and Third World economy, the former manifest in middle-class urban enclaves and larger farms, the latter among unemployment black-spots of the urban and rural proletariat.[19] Their problem of internal synchronization reflected a wider global issue: the fact that the modernizing countries of the Third World were being asked to undergo in a single century a catastrophic set of adjustments to modernity which in most 'developed' countries of the northern hemisphere had taken three or four centuries to achieve.[20]

The structuring devices of *Dancing at Lughnasa* have a beautiful, even an astonishing, formal appropriateness in this context. The clinging of the sisters to the present moment is their response to being hurtled into the future at breakneck speed and the uneven pace of the narrator and dramatization perfectly render the reality of lives lived at different speeds. It is as if the older Michael is impatient to give history a forward shove, while the actual *dramatis personae* do their utmost to retard it. While Friel worked on the play, a famous advertisement for Industrial Development Authority at Dublin Airport proclaimed: 'Missing out on the Industrial Revolution was the best thing that ever happened to Ireland' (this by way of celebrating its accession to the age of clean industry). But the lesson of *Dancing at Lughnasa* is that if you miss out on some historical phase, you have to catch up on it at a horrific speed which leaves little room for intelligent choices. The problem of synchrony is the tragedy of uneven development.

The Sweeney boy is reported by Rose as having made a full recovery from burns: but whether it is due to the Catholic anointing or the ancestral Lugh will never be known. Rose looks radiant and young, following her ramble through the back hills in the company of the dreaded Danny Bradley. It is as if, freed of the family designation of being 'simple', she can become her true, destined self: but when next we hear of her, in Michael's narrative, she is dead, a quarter century later, in a Southwark hospital for the destitute. Michael only pieced small details of her life together with the greatest difficulty: the sisters worked as toilet-cleaners, until Rose's health broke and they ended up sleeping rough on the Thames Embankment. As they quit the farm, Agnes wrote: 'We are gone for good. This is best for all. Do not try to find us.' Those lines are a bleak epitaph on whole generations of emigrants who by leaving solved two sets of problems. In the first instance, they gave themselves a chance of material improvement in a new world; and, in the second, by removing themselves from the scene, they ensured that those who stayed had greater comfort. Put at its most brutal, the three eggs laid by the Mundys' pullet would have been divided more neatly among the three sisters who remained. Had those who emigrated stayed on, they would have been a drain on Kate's domestic purse – and Ballybeg would have looked even more like Uganda.

After such knowledge, what forgiveness? Against all odds, Jack's health rallies, but he never says mass again. Gerry Evans falls off his motorbike during the Spanish Civil War but survives with a leg injury. Years later, he dies in Wales, assisted by the wife and children whom Chris never knew he had. It is a strange revelation, adding to his mythical dimension, a little like the disclosure that there may have been two St Patricks. It also confirms Father Jack's contention that polygamy may be for some a more natural way of life than such

Between First and Third World 167

furtive, deceptive liaisons. As if to bear him out, Gerry is already making eyes at Agnes before he leaves for Spain.

The flash-forward technique puts immense pressure on the actors in these final scenes. The audience now knows all that can ever be known of their fates, such as the fact that Chris worked in the Donegal factory to her death, hating every day of it – but the characters don't know such things. The effect is identical to that achieved by Yeats in 'Long-Legged Fly': the future which still lies before these people is already a long retrospect to the audience. It sees the characters in a moment of vulnerability, of jeopardized solitude, of sheer insouciance. Somehow, the acting must restore to these late moments the openness they truly had, before hindsight: yet it cannot escape the available foreknowledge. Roland Barthes observed that once you have been shown a photograph of a man who died at thirty years of age, that fate seems to proclaim itself to the viewer in every line of his face, even as the picture is snapped.

This adds immeasurably to the bittersweet poignancy of those closing scenes, much as a similar technique conferred a retrospective aura on the actions of Stephen Dedalus in *Ulysses*. He is depicted in its pages as fully aware that all future reconstructions of his past life will be made at the mercy of their immediate moments: and so in the National Library he muses:

> So in the future, the sister of the past, I may see myself as I sit here now but by reflection from that which then I shall be.[21]

Like the Mundy sisters, he feels himself at a remove from his own gestures, already storing them up for these future savourings. The whole thrust of *Ulysses* is to restore to a moment many years earlier a sense of its multiple potentialities before life gave to subsequent developments the look of inevitability:

> Had Pyrrhus not fallen by a beldam's hand in Argos or Julius Caesar not been knifed to death? They are not to be thought away. Time has branded them and fettered they are lodged in the room of the infinite possibilities they have ousted. But can those have been possible seeing that they never were? Or was that only possible which came to pass? Weave, weaver of the wind.[22]

Although Friel's characters do not know their fate as they walk like somnambulists through the closing scenes, perhaps there is a sense that this is the moment when each embraced a destiny, even though it would not be revealed as the time of choice until much later. The ability to step back from experience even as one submits to it is recommended by Jack as a way of being at ease with the world. He involves Gerry in a ritual exchange of hats, swapping his imperial headgear for his friend's tricorne: and he suggests that they both place them on the ground and take three steps back, as 'a symbolic distancing of yourself from what you once possessed' (69). The moment is both sublime and absurd, having analogies in Beckett and the Marx Brothers, and also in customs of marginal tribesmen exchanging precious objects (or nowadays jeans). Jack's equanimity may be more apparent than real, however, for it transpires that he is most likely the one who slaughtered Rose's pet rooster in a private ritual of sacrifice. Maggie remains as unimpressed by the two weak men in their borrowed costumes as any O'Casey woman was with her strutting male peacocks (69).[23]

That so much of Jack's gesturing and his sisters' language is parodic suggests that they have already achieved a measure of distance from their past. The final movement is a gentle farewell to the lost world, with all characters assembled onstage swaying ever so slightly side to side, as in a wistful wave. The nostalgic beauty of this hazy tableau is undercut somewhat by the young boy's kites, turned at last to the audience, which sees the working of his imagination all through the play: and on each is a cruelly grinning face, primitively drawn.[24] Any illusions of a gentle childhood among doting adults are violently dispelled: and in so far as the kites fly, they do so only to add a tinge of tart mockery to the closing tableau. The note of bitterness amidst such sweetness helps the older Michael to express the essential criticism of the nostalgia to which even he finally submits.

Feminist readings have seen in Michael a Frielian device of control – that of the male narrator who frames a female experience. But if there had been no male presence, the action would have been not only incredible but also monotonous. Moreover, there is a strong implication that the anarchic, subversive energies of these five women will be more than a match for the framer: by making his narrator male, Friel may be simply recognizing his own authorship.[25] The very fact that Michael is split into two characters – child and man – is hardly an assertion of unproblematic male power: and the tendency of producers and actresses to play up the positive implications of the kitchen dance (ignoring darker aspects) is a sign of just how easy it is for such figures to elude all attempts at an honest valuation.

Michael-as-narrator admits at the end that his recollections are likely to be false. Through the preceding action, he was the weakest of all the figures framed, a seven-year-old child, observed by others who didn't understand him, even as now he, as grown man, observes and does not wholly comprehend that experience. The others exist in his remembering more at the level of atmosphere than of incident, as in a photograph where everything is at once actualized and illusory:

> ... everybody seems to be floating on those sweet sounds, moving rhythmically, languorously, in complete isolation; responding more to the mood of the music than to its beat. When I remember it, I think of it as dancing. Dancing with eyes half closed because to open them would break the spell ... (71).

He admits that the characters may be projections of his imagination, yet he also honours his characters, according to each an autonomy, a free space. Through the play, his memories had seemed at times to race against the pressure of actual experience, but he was also content at certain moments to see them exceed his own designs for them.

The pattern is like that enacted in earlier masterpieces by Irishmen who adopted a female voice in projecting an *anima*: and it asserted itself at a rather similar moment in Friel's career. He was in his fifties as he worked on the play, which is in many ways a response to those critics who accused him of privileging male voices in his work. By then he had enjoyed success with *Translations* and *Faith Healer*. It was almost as if the censors which had kept his *anima* firmly under control were finally relaxed and the voices and repressed energies of women came pouring out. Yeats had an analogous experience with his Crazy Jane persona: another female voice unleashed by an artist in his fifties. And Beckett's Winnie in *Happy Days* could be seen as coming in that tradition, much like Mommo in Tom Murphy's *Bailegangaire*. Having been kept under wraps for so long, it is hardly surprising that their voices should be powerful, menacing, even sometimes (in Yeats's word) 'unendurable'.[26] And, since the feeling of manliness is less assured in men than the sense of womanliness in women, it would not amaze should a male author seek to retain some illusion of control in the face of the onslaught. Clearly, some male anxieties are revealed in those nervous references to surplices worn by women and to the garnish sweaters donned by Father Jack. But this is no more than to recognize that the holy man, like the artist, is an androgynous shaman. After all, to become a writer in a macho culture was to expose oneself to certain ridicule for being effeminate: and the use of male narrators is an attempt to assert a virility which the very act of writing may have thrown into question.

If Michael is honest enough to raise doubts about the veracity of his narration, similar questions need to be raised about Father Jack's. Perhaps in his version of Ryangan culture there is more dreamy atmosphere than hard incident. After all, his devotees were lepers and presumably their people were also being modernized by radios and factories. Like the Irish they would have wished to know the benefits of modernity as much as the liquidation of its costs, and to have held on to what was valuable in the past even as they moved confidently into a better future. But they also had been colonized. This meant that they should cease to uphold their native traditions, without ever becoming fully English: in the words of Basil Davidson, 'the British were the most systematic in imposing this sentence to nowhere'[27] on Africans for whom there was not even the empty promise of assimilation.

This condition of nowhereness is, however, also endured by the sisters in the early decades of an independent Irish state; the late assimilation of two of them to London will merely be the *coup-de-grâce*, of a battle lost way up the line. They, rather than Jack, are the ones living in something like a cultural vacuum after discrepant codes have cancelled one another out: and so they cannot enjoy the elementary liberty of taking the surviving shreds of their culture for granted, but must instead practise the dance in secret, as if they were functioning like an underground movement in their own country. The play is in some sense a prehistory of the new marginals who will crowd from colonial peripheries into the great cities of the First World, there to live 'at once within, between and after culture'.[28] It is perhaps symptomatic that neither the Ryangan nor the Lughnasa festivals can be directly presented: instead they are merely reported, like the denouement of a classic tragedy, as something which happens always elsewhere.

Even though there are no overtly political themes in the play, it is a reminder of the ways in which public events such as the Spanish Civil War or great economic forces like multinational capital leak into personal lives, becoming also distinctly personal experiences. One implicit irony of the action may be found in the fact that the 1930s were the years when even relatively strong European nation-states were brought under the control of the emerging neocolonial order. De Valera was leading an Economic War against the rulers of Westminster at the very time that people like the Mundy sisters were being ever more closely assimilated to the world of the Thames Embankment. The nation-state had been turned to by Cosgrave and de Valera as one possible means of controlling, or at least softening, the catastrophic onset of modernity. Its failure to do that left the Mundys even more pathetically exposed to economic forces and with fewer cultural resources to contest them. Yet the one comparison which Friel steadfastly refuses in his own artistic anthropology is that between Ireland and England: in earlier work, the comparisons are with the United States, in later with Africa, but never with England, perhaps because its stresses are those of a colonizing force rather than of a colonized people.

Between First and Third World

In portraying the sisters as caught in a no-man's-land between cultures, Friel seems once again to be doing what he did so effectively in *Translations* and *Making History*: writing out the last gestures of a Gaelic Ireland. The displacement of the sisters from their ancestral culture may be less intolerable in London than in Donegal, where the estrangement is all the more glaring. Yet most audiences will feel at the close that Rose and Agnes would have been better off to stay in Ballybeg. There is clearly nothing for them in London but an even more extreme loss of all ideas of ritual and ceremony. Such rituals may be deeply distrusted by those who call themselves modern, yet they are indispensable to humanity: even the feasting on crumbs in hungry Donegal could generate the improvised menu 'eggs Ballybeg' and a planned meal is the start of a return to real ritual. Without such ritual, life declines to mere routine and people are compelled to construct themselves only by props, possessions and settings. What Friel seems to be hinting at is a superior survival of such ritual in an Africa that was less than fully penetrated by the colonials and the hope that similar zones may persist in Ireland, such as the 'back hills'. This was the implication also of postcolonial critics such as Basil Davidson, who wrote in the 1990s:

> Now, with disaster having followed on colonial dispossession, it must be useful to look at what was seldom or never discussed before: at the possibly permanent and surviving value of the experience that came before dispossession. Not as colourful folklore, nor as banal assertion of Africa's possessing a history of its own, but as a value that may be relevant to the concerns and crises of today.[29]

The spiritual values which underwrote the Irish Revival at the start of the last century contained within their codes ideas of sovereignty which had little enough to do with political structures as such. A study of the Celtic past, in particular, animated most of the great leaders of that movement, whether they were politicians or intellectuals, from Eoin Mac Néill to W.B. Yeats, from De Valera to Hannah Sheehy Skeffington. They staked their claims in the spiritual and sociocultural sphere, regarding political nationalism merely as a means to achieving them (and not as an end in itself). Long before the 1916 Rising, they had defines the cultural values of the risen people, much as the Sinn Féin courts were to set up a virtual republic within the British scheme of things, which they broke like the exterior casing of a shell. What happened after that is too well known: the maintenance of one of the means for implementing that cultural freedom became an end in itself, and those Celtic practices which were to provide a set of principles remoulding the new polity were soon expelled to the margins, as subjects of arcane study by learned professors. It is a mark of the

172   Ireland on Stage: Beckett and After

depth of that defeat that most audiences of Friel's play had never even heard of Máire Mac Néill's classic book, *The Festival of Lughnasa*, when first it was staged.

In the play, Kate recognizes that what is at issue is Jack's search for a world whose rituals and symbols answer real human needs. In that he is no different from his sisters, whose desire is less for a self than for a viable culture. Friel conspires in that search, by presenting as the focus of his drama not any particular individual but an entire social group. What is depicted is the fate of a community – and of one boy communally mothered. In some ways this might be seen as a return to the techniques of Sean O'Casey, whose mockery of male heroism was reinforced by his refusal to supply in his Dublin plays the sort of central character with whom audiences could easily identify. In a testy response to Yeats's criticisms, O'Casey said: 'God forgive me, but it does sound as if you peeked and pined for a hero in the play. Now, is a dominating character more important than a play, or a play more important than a dominating character?'[30]

Friel's reasons for adopting the same approach go well beyond the political and into the domain of culture. The qualities of the individual sisters are subordinated, as in Synge's *Riders to the Sea*, and for similar reasons: to permit a deeper anthropological search for some sign of the persistence of a viable common culture. Traditional forms – whether African or Celtic – are no longer fully available to the sisters, and the new state scarcely connects with any of their needs, the need (above all) for ceremony. Nor can the Catholic church fill that vacuum, since its priest seems implicated more in systems of power than in a search for true authority. Stripped of ritual, denied ceremony, the sisters have to improvise these things in snatched moments – in the posing of riddles, the telling of stories, the sudden dancing in the kitchen. These are the utopian instants when ritual might be reborn and the culture might heal itself.

The African analogy is important solely because of the encouragement it affords in such moments. This is not just a matter of ticking off useful comparisons between the loose familial structures in Ryangan Africa or Celtic Ireland. More fundamentally, it concerns the openness of peoples to the numinous: what impressed all missionaries in Africa was the readiness of even its radical political thinkers to embrace a spiritual dimension. As Kwame Anthony Appiah reported their saying in Ghana: 'There are no atheists or agnostics in Africa.'[31] The rediscovery of pagan or Celtic spirituality in the 1990s and the attempts to link it with more recent Christian forms suggest that Friel's own 'search' resonated with many. Beneath the flux and desolation of modern living, a more real life was continuing to go on, a

Between First and Third World 173

life which might even in its moments of blessedness see the ancestral spirits subtly intervene in the daily surfaces of things.

Friel wrote his play at the close of a decade, which had witnessed intense debate as to whether Ireland itself might be a Third World country. Economic stagnation and rampant unemployment reopened the question of whether the 'experiment' of political independence had been a success,[32] or even a good idea. During every year up to 1988, over 40,000 people – most of them young –left Ireland for work overseas, as factories closed. If the cottage industries of Donegal had been dying a full seven years before De Valera's speech on cosy homesteads, the postmodern equivalent was the shut-downs of the local factories which had replaced them.

The horrific carnage in Northern Ireland also raised the common postcolonial issue of how wisely the old departing elites had redrawn the political borders. In the republic the new managerial class, intent on further Europeanization, proved resistant to these suggestions, but artists were more responsive. A young novelist like Roddy Doyle constructed *The Commitments* (a successful movie as well as novel) around the thesis that the Irish were the blacks of Europe: and the leading part taken by Irish musicians such as Bob Geldof in African relief led many young people to commit themselves to 'development' work on that continent. At the same time, many missionaries who had spent lives of hardship and dedication out there returned in a more purposeful frame of mind than Father Jack's, imbued with the principles of liberation theology and intent on reforming the ecclesiocracy and on introducing more democratic procedures to parish structures. Meanwhile, postcolonial theory was on the rise in the world's universities: and some of its leading exponents, like Edward Said and Fredric Jameson, wrote pamphlets exploring the cultural analogies between Ireland and the Third World. Among the young there was – especially after the collapse of the Soviet Empire in 1989 – a turning way from political to cultural nationalism, epitomized above all in a renewal of interest in Irish dancing, and a rediscovery of radio as a medium for higher culture.

All these elements formed a complex weave in the tapestry of *Dancing at Lughnasa*, a play which uses the 1930s to explore the 1980s. Some productions have been unashamedly pastoral and have neglected the bleaker emphases in the text. By 1971 more Irish people lived in cities and towns than in the countryside, giving a new lease of life to nostalgic depictions of country living: but the undeniably affectionate celebration of that life by Friel was finely balanced against an honest depiction of poverty and cultural losss.[33] The play's astonishing success with audiences across the world suggests that it not only captured the meaning of its cultural moment in 1990, but answered many felt needs. It provided many emigrant communities overseas with a myth of self-explanation at just the time when the presidency of Mary Robinson began to reconnect them to the greater Irish nation, for 1990 was also the year of her election. That president found a healing way in which to combine the Europeanization of the managerial elite with the postcolonial analysis favoured by some of the intelligentsia. Mrs Robinson's presidency began with a campaign video containing grainy footage of men and women dancing at a country crossroads: it evoked a nostalgia for a lost Ireland, while launching a youthful female president purposefully into the new one.

Friel's play worked in similar ways. It confronted very honestly the pain and the defeats of the past, the hairline fractures and the sad removals, but its experimental form was buoyant, vibrant and beautiful. The sheer bleakness of the content was somehow contained and defeated by the astounding energy with which a contemporary artist framed it: and a reinvented Ireland at last found a way to cope with both its colonial past and European present. The method of that coping was very familiar. The play which most fully embodied the themes and projects of Field Day was presented at the Abbey Theatre in Dublin. Field Day did not die, but its agendas were broadened until they filled a national canvas: and this also was prophetic of the ways in which the problem of Northern Ireland would once again be seriously reimagined by all the peoples in Ireland, north and south, at home and overseas.

Dancing at Lughnasa *by Brian Friel is published by Faber. The 1990 edition is used in this article.*

This paper was originally published in The Irish Review *27, 2001, 18-39.*

---

[1]Edward W. Said, *After the Last Sky* (New York: Pantheon Books, 1986): 159.

[2]Basil Davidson, *The Black Man's Burden: Africa and the Curse of the Nation-State* (London: James Currey, 1992): 191.

[3]Ibid., 138.

[4]See Marshall McLuhan and Quentin Fiore, *The Medium is the Message* (London: Allen Lane,1968).

[5]J.M. Synge, *Collected Works: Plays Book 2*, ed. Ann Saddlemyer (Gerrards Cross: Colin Smythe, 1982): 95.

[6]For further readings of the mirror, see Declan Kiberd, *Inventing Ireland* (London: Jonathan Cape, 1995): 166-88.

[7]Kwame Anthony Appiah, *In My Father's House* (London: Methuen, 1994): 2.

8On these debates see Claudia W. Harris, 'The Engendered Space: Performing Friel's Women from Cass Maguire to Molly Sweeney', *Brian Friel: A Casebook*, ed. William Kerwin (New York: Garland, 1997): 43-76.

9See J.J. Lee and Gearóid Ó Tuathaigh, *The Age of de Valera* (Dublin: Ward Riter in association with Radio Telefis Eireann, 1982).

10Terence Brown, 'Have We a Content? Tradition, Self and Society in the Theatre of Brian Friel', *The Achievement of Brian Friel*, ed. Elmer Andrews (Gerrards Cross: Colin Smythe, 1992): 201.

11See Helen Brennan, *The Story of Irish Dance* (Dingle: Brandon, 1999).

12See Said, 53-5. He reports a similar pathology in Palestinians.

13The phrase was used of Field Day by Colm Tóibin.

14The process began in Algeria during the late 1950s, when the resistance movement set up Radio Fighting Algeria: see Frantz Fanon, *A Dying Colonialism* (Harmondsworth, Middlesex: Penguin Books, 1968); by the 1970s a Gaeltacht radio station had been established in the west of Ireland, but only in the 1980s was local radio widely broadcast in most European countries.

15See McLuhan and Fiore; also McLuhan's *War and Peace in the Global Village* (New York: McGraw-Hill, 1968).

16Donnchadh Ó Corráin 'Women in Early Irish Society', in *Women in Irish Society: The Historical Dimension*, eds. D. Ó Corráin and M. MacCurtain (Dublin: Arlen House, 1978): 11.

17Cited by Appiah, 184.

18Brian Rothery, published by Institute of Public Administration (Dublin, 1987).

19Brian Girvin, *Between Two Worlds: Politics and Economy in Independent Ireland* (Dublin: Gill and MacMillan, 1989).

20See Peadar Kirby, *Has Ireland a Future?* (Cork: Mercier, 1988): and *Ireland and Latin America* (Dublin: Trócaire and Gill and MacMillan, 1992). See also Therese Caherty ed., *Is Ireland a Third World Country?* (Belfast: Beyond the Pale Publications, 1992).

21James Joyce, *Ulysses* (Harmondsworth, Middlesex: Penguin Books, 2000): 249.

22Ibid., 30.

23If Friel found Steiner's *After Babel* of service in the writing of *Translations*, or O'Faolain's *The Great O'Neill* an aid to *Making History*, then the book which lies behind *Dancing at Lughnasa* could be Victor Turner's *The Ritual Process*. There the beheading of a cock at the close of a ritual represents the suffering of the women, and the slaughterer is the witch-doctor (or African priest). Equally, the boy's use of masks enacts his progression from the female-dominated family to the men's house, his removal from the domestic sphere.

24The monstrous faces on the masks would be explicable as identifications with a terrifying object (a fearful authority figure), a way for the vulnerable child to increase his own power by assimilating himself to that very power which subjugates him.

25See Claudia Harris, 44-9.

[26]This is from a letter by Yeats to Olivia Shakespeare.

[27]Basil Davidson, 47.

[28]James T. Clifford, *The Predicament of Culture* (Cambridge, Massachusetts: Harvard University Press, 1988): introduction.

[29]Davidson, 76-7.

[30]For the full exchange, see 'The Silver Tassie: Letters' in *Sean O'Casey: A Collection of Critical Essays*, ed., Thomas Kilroy (New Jersey: Princeton-Hall, 1975): 113-17.

[31]Quoted by Appiah, 36.

[32]See J.J. Leed, *Ireland 1912-1985: Politics and Society* (Cambridge: Cambridge University Press, 1989); and Declan Kiberd, 'Fasten Your Seat-Belts for the Third World' and 'Hall-Marks of the Third World', in *The Irish Times*, February and August 1987.

[33]See Patrick Burke, 'As If Language No Longer Existed: Non-Verbal Theatricality in the Plays of Brian Friel', *Brian Friel: Casebook*: 19.

Contributors

Noreen Doody is Lecturer of English literature at St Patrick's College, Dublin City University. Her areas of research are 19th and 20th century drama and contemporary Irish literature. She has a specialist interest in W.B. Yeats and Oscar Wilde and is co-writer of the TV film script 'Happy Birthday, Oscar Wilde' with Frank McGuinness. Publications include 'Oscar Wilde: Nation and Empire' in *Palgrave Advances in Oscar Wilde Studies* (New York, 2004), and 'Dancing to Diagrams: patterns and symbols in Yeats's Dance Plays' in *Yeats Studies* (Osaka, 2004). She is currently working on a book on the influence of Oscar Wilde on W. B. Yeats.

Declan Kiberd is Professor of Anglo-Irish Literature and Drama in the School of English and Drama, University College Dublin. He is the author of *The Irish Writer and the World* (Cambridge University Press, 2005), *Irish Classics* (Granta Books, 2000), which won the Truman Capote Award for the best literary criticism published in 2002, and *Inventing Ireland* (Jonathan Cape, 1995), which won the *Irish Times* Literature Prize for 1997. He was Parnell Visiting Fellow at Magdalene College, Cambridge, for 2003 and Visiting Professor of Irish Studies at Duke University in 2004.

Cathy Leeney is Lecturer at Drama Studies Centre in the School of English and Drama, University College Dublin. She is especially interested in links between live art and feminist theory and is the co-editor with Anna McMullan of *The Theatre of Marina Carr: 'before rules was made'* (Carysfort Press, 2003), and the author of 'The New Woman in a New Ireland: Grania After Naturalism' (*Irish University Review*, Special Issue on Lady Gregory, 34(1), Spring/Summer 2004) and 'Ireland's Exiled Women Playwrights: Teresa Deevy and Marina Carr' (*The Cambridge Companion to Twentieth-Century Irish Drama*, edited by Shaun Richards, Cambridge UP, 2004).

Joseph Long is former Director of the Drama Studies Centre at University College Dublin and Senior Lecturer in the Department of French, *Officier de l'Ordre des Palmes Académiques* and *Chevalier de l'Ordre des Arts et des Lettres*. He is active in the promotion of Irish theatre in France and in the translation of French dramatists into English, and has collaborated on a number of theatre and film projects with Armand Gatti. He has also written on different aspects of Irish theatre, from Frank McGuinness to Samuel Beckett.

Hiroko Mikami is Professor of Irish Studies in the School of International Liberal Studies, Waseda University. She obtained her PhD on Frank McGuinness from University of Ulster, and compiled a list for the Tilling Archive of Frank McGuinness there. She is the author of *Frank McGuinness and His Theatre of Paradox* (Colin Smythe, 2002), 'Kilroy's Vision of Doubleness: the Question of National Identity and Theatricality in Double Cross' (*Irish University Review*, Special Issue on Thomas Kilroy, 32(1), Spring/Summer 2002), and has translated many contemporary Irish plays, including Murphy's *Bailegangaire* and *A Thief of a Christmas*, Kilroy's *Double Cross*, McGuinness's *Innocence* and *Mutabilities* into Japanese.

Christopher Murray is former Professor of Drama and Theatre History in the School of English, University College Dublin. He is the author of *Seán O'Casey: Writer at Work* (Gill & Macmillan, 2004), *Twentieth-Century Irish Drama: Mirror Up to Nation* (Manchester University Press, 1997; Syracuse University Press, 2000), and *Faber Critical Guide: Seán O'Casey/Three Dublin Plays: The Shadow of a Gunman, Juno and the Paycock, The Plough and the Stars* (Faber & Faber, 2000). He is former chairperson of IASIL (The International Association for the Study of Irish Literatures).

Minako Okamuro is Professor of Theatre and Film Arts in the School of Letters, Arts, and Sciences, Waseda University. She is coeditor/author of *Beckett Taizen* (*All about Beckett*, Hakusuisha, 1999). Her publications include '*Words and Music, ... but the clouds ...* and Yeats's "The Tower", *Beckett at 100: Revolving It All* (Oxford University Press, 2007), 'Alchemical Dances in Beckett and Yeats' (*Samuel Beckett Today/Aujourd'hui* 14, 2005), 'The Cartesian Egg: Alcehmical Images in Beckett's Early Writings' (*Journal of Beckett Studies* 9.2, 2000), and '*Quad* and the Jungian Mandala' (*Samuel Beckett Today/Aujourd'hui* 6, 1997).

Anthony Roche is Associate Professor in the School of English and Drama, University College Dublin. His books include *Contemporary Irish Drama: From Beckett to McGuinness* (New York: St. Martin's

Irish Drama: From Beckett to McGuinness (New York: St. Martin's Press, 1995), and *The Cambridge Companion to Brian Friel* (Cambridge University Press, 2006). He was editor of the *Irish University Review* from 1997 until 2002 and is currently director of the Synge Summer School.

Futoshi Sakauchi is Lecturer in the School of Letters, Arts, and Sciences, at Waseda University. He received a BA and an MA from Waseda University and has just completed his PhD on Irish male playwrights' and writers' representation of women's experience of sexual trauma and deviancy, at University College Dublin. Among his published papers are 'Child Murder and Abortion in Contemporary Anglo-Irish Drama' (*The Institute for Theatre Research: Bulletin I*, 2003), 'The Metaphorical Function of Theatre Productions in Contemporary Irish Society', '*The Hen House* and 'Bye-Child': Redressing the Idea of Mother/Womanhood' (*Bulletin IV*, 2005), and 'W.B. Yeats's *At the Hawk's Well* and the Easter Rising' (*Bulletin VI*, 2006).

Naoko Yagi is Associate Professor of English in the School of Political Science and Economics, Waseda University. After obtaining an MA in Linguistics from Sophia University, she completed an MA and a PhD, both in Theatre Studies, at the University of Warwick. Essays include 'Paratexts of Non-Dramatic Pinter: A Derridean Approach' (*English Literature* 89, 2005) and 'Putting Irish "Space" on the Stage' (*The Institute for Theatre Research: Bulletin VI*, 2006).

Index

—A—

Abbey Theatre, the, 6-8, 55, 60, 128, 129, 133n., 134n., 174

Ahern, Bertie, 48

Alchemy, 87-106

Aldrich, Robert, *Whatever Happened to Baby Jane?*, 26

Antoine, André, 30

—B—

Babylone, Théâtre de, 56

Bakunin, Mikhail Aleksandrovich, 124

Barry, Sebastian, 5, 7-11, 15, 17-19, 26n., 27n.
Boss Grady's Boys, 7, 18, 26
Only True History of Lizzie Finn, The, 7, 19, 26n., 27n.
Our Lady of Sligo, 19, 26n.
Prayers of Sherkin, 7, 19, 26n.
Steward of Christendom, The, 7-10, 15, 26n., 27n.

Barthes, Roland, 167

Battle of Moira, the, 132

Battle of the Somme, the, 7, 121

BBC (British Broadcasting Corporation), 52n., 55

Beckett, Samuel, 1-2, 5, 7, 12, 16-18, 20, 24, 25, 26, 29, 37n., 55-68, 87-106, 107-112, 117, 118n, 128, 140, 146, 150n., 168, 169
All That Fall, 55
... but the clouds ..., 93, 103n.
Come and Go, 55, 60
Company, 57
'Dante ... Bruno . Vico .. Joyce', 93-5, 99, 103n., 106n.
Dream of Fair to middling Women, 56, 61, 63, 68n., 97, 105n.
Eleutheria, 2, 55-67
Endgame, 18, 140, 146
Footfalls, 92, 97
Happy Days, 169
Krapp's Last Tape, 63, 118n.
Malone Dies, 58
Molloy, 58, 108, 118n.
More Pricks Than Kicks, 56-7, 68n.
Not I, 97
Ohio Impromptu, 29, 37n.

Piece of Monologue, A, 97, 107-109, 117n., 118n.
Play, 87, 110-12, 117
Proust, 64, 68n.
Quad, 2, 87-103
Rockaby, 97
Texts for Nothing, 91, 97, 102n., 105n.
Unnamable, The, 58
Waiting for Godot, 1, 12, 17, 55, 56, 64-6, 87, 95
'Wet Night, A', 63-4
What Where, 12
Words and Music, 93, 103n.

Belfast, 126, 129, 130

Bennett, Alan, 113
Talking Heads, 113, 119n.

Blavatsky, H.P., 94, 96, 103n., 105n.

Bloody Sunday in Derry, 121-22

Book of Kells, the, 94-96, 99-100, 103n., 104n., 105n., 106n.
Tunc page, 94-96, 98, 100, 104n., 105n.

Boston, 61, 66

Brecht, Bertolt, 116, 128

British Army, the, 121, 123

Bruno, Giordano, 88, 100

Burns, Mary and Elizabeth, 133

—C—

Carr, Marina, 1, 2, 5, 11-19, 27n., 55
Low in the Dark, 12, 27n.
Mai, The, 12-14, 18, 27
Portia Coughlan, 12, 14-16, 18, 27n.
Ullaloo, 12

Caruth, Cathy, 140-41, 146, 150n.

Castle of Kilcolman, the, 131

Chekhov, Anton, 128-29
Three Sisters, The, 129
Uncle Vanya, 129

Civil War (Irish), 8

Clarke, Larry, 33, 38n.
Kids, 33-5, 38n.
Tulsa, 33

Collins, Michael, 9, 11

Conrad, Joseph, 162

Coward, Noël, 59, 67n.

—D—

Dante Alighieri, 58, 88, 102n., 128
Divine Comedy, 102n.

De Valera, Éamon, 8, 11, 153, 156-57, 159, 170-73, 175n.

Deane, Seamus, 129

Derry, 6, 121-24, 126, 129, 130

Descartes, René, 88

desperate optimists, 2, 29-32, 37
Play-boy, 30-33, 37
Time-bomb, 30-37

Doyle, Roddy, 45-7, 52n., 53n., 173
Commitments, The, 45, 52n., 173
Family, 46, 52n.
Woman Who Walked Into Doors, The, 46, 52n., 53n.

Druid Theatre Company, the 135

Dublin Youth Theatre 30, 33, 38n.

—E—

Easter Rising, 1916, 8

Edgeworth, Maria, 156

Eliade, Mircea 97, 105n.

Esslin, Martin, 101, 106n.

Euripides, 128

—F—

Fanon, Franz, 129, 175
Farquhar, George, 24
Fianna Fáil, 8
Field Day Theatre Company, the,
6, 129, 133n., 160, 174, 175n.
Fly by Night Theatre Company, 20
Forster, E.M., 162
Passage to India, A, 162
Friel, Brian, 1, 2, 5-6, 12, 17, 20,
23, 26, 55, 113-15, 119n., 124,
128-29, 150n., 158-75
Dancing at Lughnasa, 2, 5-6,
13, 20, 129, 153-75
Faith Healer, 6, 20, 55, 113-17,
128, 169
Freedom of the City, The, 124
Give Me Your Answer, Do, 6
Making History, 171, 175n.
Molly Sweeney, 6, 115-16, 119n.
Philadelphia, Here I Come!, 5,
17
Translations, 5, 26, 129, 169,
171, 175n.
Wonderful Tennessee, 6

—G—

Gandhi, Mahatma, 156
Gate Theatre, the, 15, 20, 59, 61,
67n., 134n.
Gatti, Armand, 2, 123-27, 133n.
*Second Life of Tatenberg
Camp*, 126
Stork, The, 125
Geldof, Bob, 173
General Post Office (GPO), 8

Gramsci, Antonio, 124
Gregory, Lady Augusta, 5, 21
Grene, Nicholas, 137, 147, 150n.,
151n.

—H—

Heaney, Seamus, 129
Hughes, Ted, 58, 64, 67n.

—I—

Ibsen, Henrik, 128, 131
Peer Gynt, 131
Incres, Fernand, 30
Les Bouchers, 30
Irish Independent, the, 61

—J—

Jameson, Fredric, 173
Johnston, Denis, 62, 68n.
Moon in the Yellow River, The,
62
Joyce, James, 1, 2, 35, 57-8, 64,
87-106, 128, 158, 160, 175n.
'Ithaca', 91, 97, 105n.
Finnegans Wake, 87, 90,
93-106, 160
Ulysses, 35, 91, 97, 102n.,
103n., 104n., 105n., 106n.
Jung, Carl Gustav, 88-90, 99,
101n., 105n., 108n.

—K—

Keane, John B., 6, 26
Field, The, 6
Sive, 6
Kearney, Richard, 129

Keats, John, 62

Keenan, Brian, 132

Kiberd, Declan, 51, 53n., 98, 100, 105n., 129, 153

Kilroy, Thomas, 6-7, 18, 24-6, 129
Double Cross, 18
Secret Fall of Constance Wilde, The, 7

King Sweeney, 132

Kubrick, Stanley, 40-42, 52n.

—L—

Leonard, Hugh, 6, 17
Chamber Music, 6
Da, 17

Lorca, Federico Garcia, 128

Lyric Theatre, the, 126

—M—

Mac Néill, Eoin, 171

Mac Néill, Máire, 172
Festival of Lughnasa, The, 172

Makhno, Nestor, 124

Manning, Mary, 55-67
Outlook Unsettled, 60, 67n., 68n.
Youth's the Season . . .?, 56, 59-66, 67n., 68n.

Marx Brothers, 168

Mason, Patrick, 7, 133n.

Mathews, Aidan, 39, 45, 52n.
Communion, 39-40, 45, 48-9, 51n., 52n.

McCann, Donal, 8

McDonagh, Martin, 2, 5, 19-20, 23-6, 27n.
Beauty Queen of Leenane, The, 23-6, 27n.
Lonesome West, The, 24
Skull in Connemara, A, 24-5

McGowan, Shane, 24

McGuinness, Frank, 1-2, 5-8, 12, 16-17, 26n., 27n., 52, 55, 67n., 69-85, 113, 119n., 121-34
Baglady, 55, 85n., 113, 119n.
Bird Sanctuary, The, 71, 75, 77, 80-81, 85n.
Carthaginians, 2, 7, 81, 85n., 121, 126, 129, 133n.
Dolly West's Kitchen, 70-72, 75, 79-84, 85n.
Factory Girls, The, 71, 81, 83, 85n.
Mary and Lizzie, 85n., 130-32
Mutabilitie, 70, 77, 85n., 130-31, 134n.
Observe the Sons of Ulster Marching Towards the Somme, 2, 7, 18, 72-3, 78, 82-4, 85n., 121, 127, 129
Someone Who'll Watch Over Me, 7, 74, 82-3, 85n., 130, 132

McPherson, Conor, 1, 2, 5, 6, 19-21, 27n., 55, 107, 113-14, 116, 119n.
Port Authority, 114, 116-17, 119n.
St. Nicholas, 21
This Lime Tree Bower, 19-20, 27n, 114
Weir, The, 20-21, 27n.,

Mikami, Hiroko, 70, 85n., 133n.

Molière, 65

Moreno, J. L., 122

Motley, 61, 68n.

Mullan, Peter, 47, 53n.

Magdalene Sisters, The, 47, 53n.

Murphy, Tom, 2, 6, 12, 17, 18, 37, 39-40, 51, 55, 135-51, 169
Bailegangaire, 2, 39-40, 49, 51n., 55, 135-51, 169
Gigli Concert, The, 17-18, 150n., 151n.
Seduction of Morality, The, 6
Thief of a Christmas, A, 135-36, 142, 146, 149n., 150n.
Wake, The, 6
Whistle in the Dark, A, 136

—N—

Nabokov, Vladimir, 2, 39-43, 50, 52n.
Lolita, 2, 49-53

Neumann, Erich, 98, 99, 105n., 106n.

New University of Ulster at Coleraine, 129, 133n.

Northern Ireland, 7, 130, 134n., 173-74

—O—

O'Brien, Edna, 68n., 136-37, 150n.
Country Girls, The, 137

O'Casey, Sean, 1, 8, 16, 124, 128, 165, 168, 172
Juno and the Paycock, 124
Silver Tassie, The, 8, 165

O'Connor, Frank, 159

O'Neill, Hugh, 132

O'Rowe, Mark, 55

O'Toole, Fintan, 10, 26n., 27n., 40, 42, 137, 149n., 150n.

—P—

Paddy Bogside, 123

Paris, 56-7, 73, 95

Parker, Alan, 45, 52n.

Paulin, Tom, 129

Peacock Theatre, the, 7, 15, 39, 42, 45, 49, 51n., 53n., 55

Pike Theatre, the, 55

Pinter, Harold, 3, 20, 22, 108-17, 118n.
Homecoming, The, 22
Landscape, 109-12, 114, 117, 118n., 128n.
Monologue, 108-9, 118n.
Silence, 112, 114, 118n.

poppy, 130

Postcolonialism, 129, 132, 156-57, 165, 171, 173-74

Proust, Marcel, 57-8, 64, 68n.

psychodrama, 122, 127

—Q—

Queen Elizabeth I, 131

Queen Maeve, 132

Quintero, José, 128

—R—

Racine, Jean Baptiste, 65

Rea, Stephen, 129

Remembrance Day, 130

Richards, Shaun, 135, 148, 150n., 151n.

Robinson, Mary, 174

Roche, Anthony, 26, 26n., 52n., 67n., 133, 150n.

Royal Court Theatre, the, 20

—S—

Said, Edward, 129, 153, 173
Sands, Bobby, 123
Sean Bhean Bhocht (Poor Old
 Woman), 136
Shakespeare, William, 9, 58, 67n.,
 101n., 131
Shaw, George Bernard, 1, 17, 162
Sinn Féin, 171
Skeffington, Hannah Sheehy, 171
Sophocles, 128
Spenser, Edmund, 131
 Faerie Queene, The, 131
Synge, John Millington,1, 2, 5, 15,
 16, 17, 19, 21, 23, 24, 32, 78,
 150n., 156-58, 162, 172, 174n.
 Aran Islands, The, 21
 *Playboy of the Western World,
 The*, 2, 21, 32, 78, 157
 Riders to the Sea, 21, 150n., 172

—T—

Táin Bó Cuailgne, 132
Théâtre Libre, 30
Tony Award, the, 6, 23
trauma, 1, 22, 39, 48, 56, 58, 122,
 125, 127, 135, 140-41, 146-48
Trinity College, Dublin, 57, 65

—U—

Ulster, 7, 78, 84, 121, 129-30,
 133n., 134, 134n.

University College, Dublin (UCD),
 2, 3, 12, 19, 53n., 124, 133

—V—

Vico, Giambattista, 93-5, 99,
 103n., 106n.

—W—

West, Michael, 2, 39-53
 Lolita, 39-53
Wilde, Oscar, 1, 2, 65, 69-85
 'Critic as Artist, The', 70
 'Decay of Lying, The', 76
 De Profundis, 69, 83-5
 Ideal Husband, An, 74
 *Importance of Being Earnest,
 The*, 70-72, 74, 76, 80-81
 Lady Windermere's Fan, 73
World War I, 7, 10, 11, 122, 130
World War II, 56, 66

—Y—

Yeats, William Butler, 1, 2, 5, 16,
 21, 76, 87-103, 150n., 158, 167,
 169, 171, 172
 'All Soul's Night', 101
 Autobiographies, 158
 'Dance of the Four Royal
 Persons, The', 91-2, 102n.
 'Long-Legged Fly', 167
 'Rosa Alchemica', 88-9
 'Tower, The', 92-3, 103n.
 Vision, A, 87, 90-91, 100-101,
 102n.

CARYSFORT PRESS

Carysfort Press was formed in the summer of 1998. It receives annual funding from the Arts Council.

The directors believe that drama is playing an ever-increasing role in today's society and that enjoyment of the theatre, both professional and amateur, currently plays a central part in Irish culture.

The Press aims to produce high quality publications which, though written and/or edited by academics, will be made accessible to a general readership. The organisation would also like to provide a forum for critical thinking in the Arts in Ireland, again keeping the needs and interests of the general public in view.

The company publishes contemporary Irish writing for and about the theatre.

Editorial and publishing inquiries to:
CARYSFORT PRESS Ltd
58 Woodfield, Scholarstown Road,
Rathfarnham, Dublin 16,
Republic of Ireland

T (353 1) 493 7383 F (353 1) 406 9815
e: info@carysfortpress.com
www.carysfortpress.com

NEW TITLES

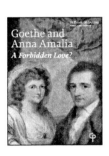

GOETHE AND ANNA AMALIA: A FORBIDDEN LOVE?
BY ETTORE GHIBELLINO, TRANS. DAN FARRELLY

In this study Ghibellino sets out to show that the platonic relationship between Goethe and Charlotte von Stein – lady-in-waiting to Anna Amalia, the Dowager Duchess of Weimar – was used as part of a cover-up for Goethe's intense and prolonged love relationship with the Duchess Anna Amalia herself. The book attempts to uncover a hitherto closely-kept state secret. Readers convinced by the evidence supporting Ghibellino's hypothesis will see in it one of the very great love stories in European history – to rank with that of Dante and Beatrice, and Petrarch and Laura.

ISBN-13   978-1-904505-24-2
EAN   9781904505242
€25

MUSICS OF BELONGING: THE POETRY OF MICHEAL O'SIADHAIL
EDITED BY MARC CABALL AND DAVID F. FORD

An overall account is given of O'Siadhail's life, his work and the reception of his poetry so far. There are close readings of some poems, analyses of his artistry in matching diverse content with both classical and innovative forms, and studies of recurrent themes such as love, death, language, music, and the shifts of modern life.

Paperback €25
ISBN 978-1-904505-22-8

Casebound €50
ISBN: 978-1-904505-21-1

NEW TITLES

EDNA O'BRIEN
'NEW CRITICAL PERSPECTIVES'
EDITED BY KATHRYN LAING
SINÉAD MOONEY AND MAUREEN O'CONNOR

The essays collected here illustrate some of the range, complexity, and interest of Edna O'Brien as a fiction writer and dramatist…They will contribute to a broader appreciation of her work and to an evolution of new critical approaches, as well as igniting more interest in the many unexplored areas of her considerable oeuvre.

ISBN 1-904505-20-1
€20

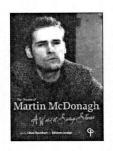

THE THEATRE OF MARTIN MCDONAGH
'A WORLD OF SAVAGE STORIES'
EDITED BY LILIAN CHAMBERS AND
EAMONN JORDAN

The book is a vital response to the many challenges set by McDonagh for those involved in the production and reception of his work. Critics and commentators from around the world offer a diverse range of often provocative approaches. What is not surprising is the focus and commitment of the engagement, given the controversial and stimulating nature of the work.

ISBN 1-904505-19-8
€30

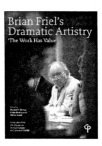

BRIAN FRIEL'S DRAMATIC ARTISTRY
'THE WORK HAS VALUE'
EDITED BY DONALD E. MORSE, CSILLA
BERTHA, AND MÁRIA KURDI

Brian Friel's Dramatic Artistry presents a refreshingly broad range of voices: new work from some of the leading English-speaking authorities on Friel, and fascinating essays from scholars in Germany, Italy, Portugal, and Hungary. This book will deepen our knowledge and enjoyment of Friel's work.

ISBN 1-904505-17-1
€25

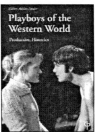

PLAYBOYS OF THE WESTERN WORLD
PRODUCTION HISTORIES
EDITED BY ADRIAN FRAZIER

'Playboys of the Western World is a model of contemporary performance studies.'

'The book is remarkably well-focused: half is a series of production histories of Playboy performances through the twentieth century in the UK, Northern Ireland, the USA, and Ireland. The remainder focuses on one contemporary performance, that of Druid Theatre, as directed by Garry Hynes. The various contemporary social issues that are addressed in relation to Synge's play and this performance of it give the volume an additional interest: it shows how the arts matter.' *Kevin Barry*

ISBN 1-904505-06-6
€20

NEW TITLES

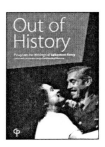

OUT OF HISTORY
'ESSAYS ON THE WRITINGS OF SEBASTIAN BARRY'

EDITED WITH AN INTRODUCTION BY CHRISTINA HUNT MAHONY

The essays address Barry's engagement with the contemporary cultural debate in Ireland and also with issues that inform postcolonial criticial theory. The range and selection of contributors has ensured a high level of critical expression and an insightful assessment of Barry and his works.

ISBN 1-904505-18-X
€20

IRISH THEATRE ON TOUR

EDITED BY NICHOLAS GRENE AND CHRIS MORASH

'Touring has been at the strategic heart of Druid's artistic policy since the early eighties. Everyone has the right to see professional theatre in their own communities. Irish theatre on tour is a crucial part of Irish theatre as a whole'. *Garry Hynes*

ISBN 1-904505-13-9
€20

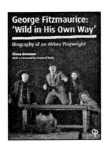

GEORGE FITZMAURICE:
'WILD IN HIS OWN WAY'

BIOGRAPHY OF AN ABBEY PLAYWRIGHT
BY FIONA BRENNAN
WITH A FOREWORD BY FINTAN O'TOOLE

Fiona Brennan's...introduction to his considerable output allows us a much greater appreciation and understanding of Fitzmaurice, the one remaining under-celebrated genius of twentieth-century Irish drama.
Conall Morrison

ISBN 1-904505-16-3
€20

THE POWER OF LAUGHTER

EDITED BY ERIC WEITZ

The collection draws on a wide range of perspectives and voices including critics, playwrights, directors and performers. The result is a series of fascinating and provocative debates about the myriad functions of comedy in contemporary Irish theatre. *Anna McMullan*

As Stan Laurel said, it takes only an onion to cry. Peel it and weep. Comedy is harder. These essays listen to the power of laughter. They hear the tough heart of Irish theatre – hard and wicked and funny. *Frank McGuinness*

ISBN 1-904505-05-8
€20

NEW TITLES

EAST OF EDEN
NEW ROMANIAN PLAYS
EDITED BY ANDREI MARINESCU

Four of the most promising Romanian playwrights, young and very young, are in this collection, each one with a specific way of seeing the Romanian reality, each one with a style of communicating an articulated artistic vision of the society we are living in.
Ion Caramitru, General Director Romanian National Theatre Bucharest

ISBN 1-904505-15-5
€10

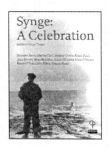

SYNGE: A CELEBRATION
EDITED BY COLM TÓIBÍN

Sebastian Barry, Marina Carr, Anthony Cronin, Roddy Doyle, Anne Enright, Hugo Hamilton, Joseph O'Connor, Mary O'Malley, Fintan O'Toole, Colm Toibin, Vincent Woods.

ISBN 1-904505-14-7
€15 Paperback

POEMS 2000–2005
BY HUGH MAXTON

Poems 2000-2005 is a transitional collection written while the author – also known to be W. J. Mc Cormack, literary historian – was in the process of moving back from London to settle in rural Ireland.

ISBN 1-904505-12-0
€10

HAMLET
THE SHAKESPEAREAN DIRECTOR
BY MIKE WILCOCK

"This study of the Shakespearean director as viewed through various interpretations of HAMLET is a welcome addition to our understanding of how essential it is for a director to have a clear vision of a great play. It is an important study from which all of us who love Shakespeare and who understand the importance of continuing contemporary exploration may gain new insights."

From the Foreword, by Joe Dowling, Artistic Director, The Guthrie Theater, Minneapolis, MN

ISBN 1-904505-00-7
€20

NEW TITLES

GEORG BÜCHNER: WOYZECK
A NEW TRANSLATION BY DAN FARRELLY

The most up-to-date German scholarship of Thomas Michael Mayer and Burghard Dedner has finally made it possible to establish an authentic sequence of scenes. The widespread view that this play is a prime example of loose, open theatre is no longer sustainable. Directors and teachers are challenged to "read it again".

ISBN 1-904505-02-3
€10

THE THEATRE OF FRANK MCGUINNESS
STAGES OF MUTABILITY
EDITED BY HELEN LOJEK

The first edited collection of essays about internationally renowned Irish playwright Frank McGuinness focuses on both performance and text. Interpreters come to diverse conclusions, creating a vigorous dialogue that enriches understanding and reflects a strong consensus about the value of McGuinness's complex work.

ISBN 1-904505-01-5
€20

CRITICAL MOMENTS
FINTAN O'TOOLE ON MODERN IRISH THEATRE
EDITED BY JULIA FURAY & REDMOND O'HANLON

This new book on the work of Fintan O'Toole, the internationally acclaimed theatre critic and cultural commentator, offers percussive analyses and assessments of the major plays and playwrights in the canon of modern Irish theatre. Fearless and provocative in his judgements, O'Toole is essential reading for anyone interested in criticism or in the current state of Irish theatre.

ISBN 1-904505-03-1
€20

THE THEATRE OF MARINA CARR
"BEFORE RULES WAS MADE" - EDITED BY ANNA MCMULLAN & CATHY LEENEY

As the first published collection of articles on the theatre of Marina Carr, this volume explores the world of Carr's theatrical imagination, the place of her plays in contemporary theatre in Ireland and abroad and the significance of her highly individual voice.

ISBN 0-9534-2577-0
€20

NEW TITLES

THEATRE TALK
VOICES OF IRISH THEATRE PRACTITIONERS
EDITED BY LILIAN CHAMBERS & GER FITZGIBBON

"This book is the right approach - asking practitioners what they feel."
Sebastian Barry, Playwright

"... an invaluable and informative collection of interviews with those who make and shape the landscape of Irish Theatre."
Ben Barnes, Artistic Director of the Abbey Theatre

ISBN 0-9534-2576-2
€20

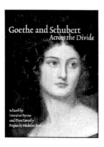

GOETHE AND SCHUBERT
ACROSS THE DIVIDE
EDITED BY LORRAINE BYRNE & DAN FARRELLY

Proceedings of the International Conference, 'Goethe and Schubert in Perspective and Performance', Trinity College Dublin, 2003. This volume includes essays by leading scholars – Barkhoff, Boyle, Byrne, Canisius, Dürr, Fischer, Hill, Kramer, Lamport, Lund, Meikle, Newbould, Norman McKay, White, Whitton, Wright, Youens – on Goethe's musicality and his relationship to Schubert; Schubert's contribution to sacred music and the Lied and his setting of Goethe's Singspiel, Claudine. A companion volume of this Singspiel (with piano reduction and English translation) is also available.

ISBN 1-904505-04-X
Goethe and Schubert: Across the Divide. €25

ISBN 0-9544290-0-1
Goethe and Schubert: 'Claudine von Villa Bella'. €14

SACRED PLAY
SOUL JOURNEYS IN CONTEMPORARY IRISH THEATRE BY ANNE F. O'REILLY

'Theatre as a space or container for sacred play allows audiences to glimpse mystery and to experience transformation. This book charts how Irish playwrights negotiate the labyrinth of the Irish soul and shows how their plays contribute to a poetics of Irish culture that enables a new imagining. Playwrights discussed are: McGuinness, Murphy, Friel, Le Marquand Hartigan, Burke Brogan, Harding, Meehan, Carr, Parker, Devlin, and Barry.'

ISBN 1-904505-07-4
€25

GOETHE: MUSICAL POET, MUSICAL CATALYST
EDITED BY LORRAINE BYRNE

'Goethe was interested in, and acutely aware of, the place of music in human experience generally - and of its particular role in modern culture. Moreover, his own literary work - especially the poetry and Faust - inspired some of the major composers of the European tradition to produce some of their finest works.' *Martin Swales*

ISBN 1-904505-10-4
€30

NEW TITLES

THEATRE OF SOUND
RADIO AND THE DRAMATIC IMAGINATION
BY DERMOT RATTIGAN

An innovative study of the challenges that radio drama poses to the creative imagination of the writer, the production team, and the listener.

"A remarkably fine study of radio drama – everywhere informed by the writer's professional experience of such drama in the making…A new theoretical and analytical approach – informative, illuminating and at all times readable." *Richard Allen Cave*

ISBN 0-9534-2575-4
€20

THE IRISH HARP BOOK
BY SHEILA LARCHET CUTHBERT

This is a facsimile of the edition originally published by Mercier Press in 1993. There is a new preface by Sheila Larchet Cuthbert, and the biographical material has been updated. It is a collection of studies and exercises for the use of teachers and pupils of the Irish harp.

ISBN 1-904505-08-2
€35

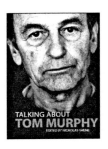

TALKING ABOUT TOM MURPHY
EDITED BY NICHOLAS GRENE

Talking About Tom Murphy is shaped around the six plays in the landmark Abbey Theatre Murphy Season of 2001, assembling some of the best-known commentators on his work: Fintan O'Toole, Chris Morash, Lionel Pilkington, Alexandra Poulain, Shaun Richards, Nicholas Grene and Declan Kiberd.

ISBN 0-9534-2579-7
€15

THE DRUNKARD
TOM MURPHY

'The Drunkard is a wonderfully eloquent play. Murphy's ear is finely attuned to the glories and absurdities of melodramatic exclamation, and even while he is wringing out its ludicrous overstatement, he is also making it sing.'
The Irish Times

ISBN 1-904505-09-0
€10

NEW TITLES

THREE CONGREGATIONAL MASSES
BY SEÓIRSE BODLEY,
EDITED BY LORRAINE BYRNE

'From the simpler congregational settings in the Mass of Peace and the Mass of Joy to the richer textures of the Mass of Glory, they are immediately attractive and accessible, and with a distinctively Irish melodic quality.' *Barra Boydell*

ISBN 1-904505-11-2
€15

BACK LIST

SEEN AND HEARD (REPRINT)
SIX NEW PLAYS BY IRISH WOMEN
EDITED WITH AN INTRODUCTION
BY CATHY LEENEY

A rich and funny, moving and theatrically exciting collection of plays by Mary Elizabeth Burke-Kennedy, Síofra Campbell, Emma Donoghue, Anne Le Marquand Hartigan, Michelle Read and Dolores Walshe.

ISBN 0-9534-2573-8
€20

UNDER THE CURSE
GOETHE'S "IPHIGENIE AUF TAURIS",
IN A NEW VERSION BY DAN FARRELLY

The Greek myth of Iphigenie grappling with the curse on the house of Atreus is brought vividly to life. This version is currently being used in Johannesburg to explore problems of ancestry, religion, and Black African women's spirituality.

ISBN 0-9534-2572-X
€10

BACK LIST

THEATRE STUFF (REPRINT)
CRITICAL ESSAYS ON
CONTEMPORARY IRISH THEATRE
EDITED BY EAMONN JORDAN

Best selling essays on the successes and debates of contemporary Irish theatre at home and abroad.

Contributors include: Thomas Kilroy, Declan Hughes, Anna McMullan, Declan Kiberd, Deirdre Mulrooney, Fintan O'Toole, Christopher Murray, Caoimhe McAvinchey and Terry Eagleton.

ISBN 0-9534-2571-1
€20

URFAUST
A NEW VERSION OF GOETHE'S
EARLY "FAUST" IN BRECHTIAN MODE
BY DAN FARRELLY

This version is based on Brecht's irreverent and daring re-interpretation of the German classic.

"Urfaust is a kind of well-spring for German theatre… The love-story is the most daring and the most profound in German dramatic literature." *Brecht*

ISBN 0-9534257-0-3
€10

IN SEARCH OF THE
SOUTH AFRICAN IPHIGENIE
BY ERIKA VON WIETERSHEIM
AND DAN FARRELLY

Discussions of Goethe's "Iphigenie auf Tauris" (Under the Curse) as relevant to women's issues in modern South Africa: women in family and public life; the force of women's spirituality; experience of personal relationships; attitudes to parents and ancestors; involvement with religion.

ISBN 0-9534-2578-9
€10

THE STARVING
AND OCTOBER SONG
TWO CONTEMPORARY IRISH PLAYS
BY ANDREW HINDS

The Starving, set during and after the siege of Derry in 1689, is a moving and engrossing drama of the emotional journey of two men.

October Song, a superbly written family drama set in real time in pre-ceasefire Derry.

ISBN 0-9534-2574-6
€10

HOW TO ORDER
TRADE ORDERS DIRECTLY TO

CMD
Columba Mercier Distribution,
55A Spruce Avenue,
Stillorgan Industrial Park,
Blackrock,
Co. Dublin

T: (353 1) 294 2560
F: (353 1) 294 2564
E: cmd@columba.ie

or contact
SALES@BROOKSIDE.IE

FOR SALES IN NORTH AMERICA
AND CANADA

Dufour Editions Inc.,
124 Byers Road,
PO Box 7,
Chester Springs, PA 19425,
USA

T: 1-610-458-5005
F: 1-610-458-7103